The Forgotten Life of Sarah Grady

Enjoy

Mary Lynn

Second Edition

3 Millikin Place Decatur, Illinois
Built by Mr. and Mrs. W.J. Grady in 1910

The Forgotten Life of Sarah Grady

Mary Lynn

Edited by Danielle Patricio

ISBN: 1535302194
ISBN 13: 9781535302197

Dedication

I dedicate this book to my husband, Duane, who has patiently listened to the story of Sarah every day for the last two years. And to the rest of my family who have waited over forty years for me to write this story. A special dedication goes to my granddaughter, Danielle Patricio, who became my editor.

Acknowledgements

I would like to thank my friends and family for their patience and encouragement as they listened to my story for two years before my novel became a reality. A special thanks to my writer's group who gave me an educated, honest critique of the book's chapters that I presented to them. I am grateful to my grandchildren who had to "save" me when I couldn't communicate with my computer. My gratitude also goes to my Tri Delta sorority sisters who at our monthly meetings were always encouraging and supportive.

A very special thank you goes to my granddaughter, Danielle Patricio, who has the ability to see beyond the pages and knows when to delete entire paragraphs and replace them with something both charming and concise. Her enthusiastic support and editorial talent have made my novel much more readable.

Finally, I can never thank my husband enough for not only being my sounding board but also for giving me the time to write. His opinions and support made my dream of writing a novel possible and his hours of research led to major discoveries into each of the characters' pasts.

Full responsibility for the faults of this book go to me alone.

Note from the Author

THE LETTERS INCLUDED in the text, written between 1915 and 1920 by Ed Rockafellow and Charles O. Elwood, are printed verbatim, including mistakes in spelling and punctuation. However, I translated the part of the letters composed in Morse Code, for ease of understanding. In their correspondence, Sarah and Ed also utilized an elaborate system of symbols for people and for numbers. I was able to break the code for most of their secret language and translated such details for the reader. Additionally, included in the novel is an image of the first page of one of Ed's 450 letters to Sarah Grady.

After living for many years in the home that William and Sarah Grady built, having the letters tell of their day to day activities, and conducting extensive research into their lives, I developed a great affinity for Sarah. As I sat in the sitting room where she retreated with her problems, I felt I knew what her decisions would have been. As I ate in the dining room where she entertained William's business associates so often, I could feel her personality dominating the room. Eating breakfast in the room where she and William had their foremost conversations, I believed I knew her. So I chose to write mainly from Sarah Grady's point of view. I tried to tell the story she would have told.

I was as truthful as possible while composing this novel. The people are real, as are the places. I followed the narrative of the letters as far as I could, but since I only had one side of the couple's correspondence, it was necessary for me to create situations and conversations to form the storyline.

Therefore, *The Forgotten Life of Sarah Grady* is historical fiction inspired by true events.

❧

The Treasure of 3 Millikin Place

Decatur, Illinois 1970

I LOVE OLD houses. I am comfortable living in a dwelling where you have to kick the radiator in the hallway or it will not heat, where you must turn a faucet on and off three times to shut it down. My whole family was fond of the nine older houses we had lived in as each had its own fantastic character, architecture, and tales of all those who dwelled there at one time or another. But none of these nine aged homes held the treasure that awaited us in the attic of number 3 Millikin Place.

When I first saw the overgrown landscape, the peeling paint on the shingles, and the dirty undraped windows (some with broken glass) I knew this was the house for us. You see, our family adopts unwanted run-down houses. There are seven people in our group; my husband Duane who acts as the lead carpenter and general manager of our team; myself as an historian, woodworking specialist, and band aid keeper; and our five children ranging in age from nine to sixteen, each of whom has a specialty in renovation. Having totally rejuvenated three houses, we were an experienced crew.

Our family rented a house when we moved to Decatur, Illinois and began to search for one to call our own. Both Duane and I stopped cold in our tracks when we spotted the Millikin Place house.

"It's spooky," I said.

But already we were hooked. The area was an historian's dream. Three houses and the street itself had been commissioned to Frank Lloyd

Wright's office. The structure was big enough to hold our family; the building was sound, and there was something about it... spooky or not, it was meant to be ours.

Prior to our purchase, this house had been built and enjoyed for forty-eight years by Mr. William J. Grady, a prominent industrialist and community activist. It seems he was active in almost every civic and social organization in the city beyond his duties as president of a large manufacturing facility and owner of several smaller companies. After his death, Mr. Grady's will disclosed that the house would be given to the local university as he and his deceased wife had no children or close family. When we bought the house from the university, it was still basically as Mr. Grady had left it. The rumor around the neighborhood was that after the death of his second wife, he had not let any of the servants repair or clean the house, not even to dust. He still would have the occasional party and when he did, the servants would meet people at the door and apologize for the condition of the house.

While our family refurbished the mansion, I scoured every nook and cranny trying to find the fortune that surely was hidden in my large old house. After all, Mr. Grady was a wealthy, eccentric man so he was bound to have tucked away something of value in a house he built and remained in for so many years. Our kids uncovered a massive pile of empty whiskey bottles in a closet on the second floor of the garage, but to my disappointment nothing else was found.

After spending our first winter in the 5400 square foot house and struggling with huge utility bills, Duane decided we needed to have some insulation blown into the closed-in attic spaces on the sides of the third floor party room. When the contractors finished the job, Duane went upstairs to check on their work. Trying to make sure everything inside the area was covered evenly with the insulation, he opened one of the little side doors and shined a flashlight into every corner. From a distance he detected a bump protruding from behind the chimney. Something seemed amiss to him so he got down on his knees and crawled across the floor to check it out. He blew the insulation to the side and discovered a non-descript cardboard container two feet square, unmarked and bound by heavy twine. Until the insulation was blown into the space, the box had remained undetected.

Feeling this could be the treasure for which we had been searching, he dragged the box out into the room. He was beginning to get excited and hurriedly pulled the twine aside and opened the package. What he found was a large bundle wrapped up tightly in newspapers dated 1919. Seeing the date, he was certain now that he had found a long hidden fortune. Wanting to be alone to savor his good luck, he carried the box downstairs to our bedroom and locked the door. He had known that something of value would be found in this house and now he had it.

Carefully unwrapping the 1919 newspaper, he saw a sachet of folded papers bound with a blue silk ribbon. Could this be stock certificates? Then he spotted a key. He pictured an antique lock box filled with gold coins. After that came another packet of papers also tied in blue silk ribbon. Diving into the box again, he found dried flowers and some old train tickets. Another package of papers greeted him as he dug deeper into the box. Going through the contents with a little less caution, he determined that the whole box was full of letters and mementos. Truly disappointed that he had not found his fortune but had only come across the Grady's old forgotten keepsake box, he shoved the cardboard container and its contents aside.

Coming downstairs, Duane told me the story of how he had found a cardboard container full of the Grady's mementos behind the chimney in the attic. He took me up to our bedroom and showed me the box which I instantly opened. Pawing through the bundles of papers, I removed one of the neatly bound packets of letters and started reading one of them. It didn't take long to determine that these were love letters to Sarah Grady, Mr. Grady's socialite wife. My interest was aroused, so I quickly scanned the letters that had been perfectly preserved in the tightly wrapped newspaper and to my surprise found they were not from Mr. Grady.

"These letters are none of our business," I resolved.

Duane had come to the same conclusion. Being proper people, we immediately replaced the letters we had read and closed the container. We both agreed that the box should be destroyed.

Curiosity is a very compelling human force. As I completed my chores in the kitchen, my mind kept wandering back to the box. Finally, I sneaked back up to our bedroom to take another peek at those letters. Upon entering the room, I found Duane sitting on the floor surrounded by piles of papers. It was rather humorous to see my sedate husband sitting on the floor reading old correspondence tied up in blue ribbon, until I saw his face. Duane's whole countenance was very sad.

He said, "Mrs. Grady had a son that was killed in World War I. Here is a letter from his birth father entreating him to stay in college at Princeton and not join the Navy. I guess the son didn't heed his father's advice."

I picked up a pile of letters and began reading, wanting to know more about who had written them. After reading several, I determined that the author was esteemed in both social and political society in New York City. This man had President Wilson's ear and was friends with many other influential people. I became fascinated with his account of events happening in 1915 and 1916 right before the United States became engaged in World War I. His references to the opinions of Mrs. Grady from provincial Decatur, Illinois versus his attitudes from New York City and Washington, D.C. were intriguing.

I had no idea who this man was, but he had made it difficult to read his letters. Because of the intrigue of the affair, he had tried to hide his identity. There were no envelopes to tell us the address of the writer and many parts of each letter were written in Morse code with which I was not familiar. The signature on each letter read: **. -..** (Ed in Morse code), but that was the only clue as to the identity of the author.

As someone who has a vivid imagination, I could feel Mrs. Grady in my sitting room curled up on my window seat thinking of her lover. As a history major in college, I was somewhat versed in the techniques of research, so I began my journey to uncover the true story behind these fifty-five year-old documents.

Over the next few weeks I devised a cheat sheet to interpret the Morse code and painstakingly went through many of the letters. Each one took an astounding amount of time to decipher. As I read Ed's letters to Sarah Grady, their story began to unfold and I realized that I had in my hands the remnants of a four-year love affair that took place amidst World War I. The first letters began in 1915 and the last ones were at the beginning of 1920. The love story, fascinating as it was, soon took second place in my interest to the description of the events happening in the East and in the Mid-West, and to the life style of the wealthy. Since Ed was close enough to Woodrow Wilson to reflect the president's views, Ed's thoughts on the war provided an extraordinary view of the times. He also described his day-to-day activities which gave me a look into his everyday life.

I estimated that the box contained about four-hundred and fifty letters. This correspondence was written from all over the country on stationary from the most upscale clubs. The more I read, the more interesting I found the story, but I needed to find out some of the facts. As I started my research, I found that no one could tell me what happened to Sarah Grady. Mr. Grady's neighbors and even his business associates recognized that Sarah had had an affair, but no one knew who the man was. In fact the whole thing seemed to be a mystery. Sensing that this fascinating story was worthy of being told, I decided to write it down. So I delved into my research, letting the contents of the letters guide me. Finally, I have been able to determine nearly all of what occurred and to whom it happened.

This is an account of how members of the upper echelons of society lived during the period of 1915 – 1921, and a story of two people and their four-year love affair. The treasure discovered within our 3 Millikin Place home.

Sarah Grady's Sitting Room
3 Millikin Place

CHAPTER 1

Our Love Remembered

3 Millikin Place January 1920

Sarah could take no more. She wondered were her hands trembling from grief or anger as she held in her palms the letters containing the last words she would ever hear from Ed?

Sitting in the small old chair she had placed on the third floor to make a comfortable spot where she could commune with him, she gingerly wrapped the four letters in a single sheet of newspaper, opened the little door to the attic space, dropped to her knees, tearfully crawled over to the chimney, and brought into the room the special box that contained four years of correspondence and mementos of her time with Ed. She placed the letters with the others, tightly wrapped the whole container in more newspaper, and secured it with twine. Crawling back into the small area, she stuffed it behind the chimney that protruded through the attic. Reaching deep into her soul, she heard a voice telling her to burn everything, but she quieted the sound knowing she was incapable of destroying all that was left of her life with Ed. Maybe someday, she reasoned, someone would find these letters and bear witness to their love and to the wonderful years they shared together -- but she would never touch the box again.

Wiping her eyes, Sarah determined she had shed her last tear for Ed Rockafellow. Holding her head high, she descended the stairs stopping on the second floor to stare into the sitting room. Slowly approaching the built-in window seat that was constructed just for the purpose of looking out the window and ruminating over all the important parts of life, she realized, at this time, that was exactly what was needed. A place to think, to ponder. Where had she gone wrong? Or had she? William wouldn't be home for hours from the office, so she had time to sit and contemplate what she had done and what the next step in her life would be.

Sarah snuggled into the cushioned seat, looked out of the window and remembered that it was only four years ago that she had curled up in this exact spot on the same puffy pillows. She closed her eyes as 1915 bloomed within her mind's eye.

February 1915

On that glistening February morning as she gazed out the windows at the bright sun on the light snow that appeared to have spread a white fluffy cover over the entire world, Sarah thought everyone should feel peaceful and calm. She did. Snow always brought back contented recollections of the farm where she grew up, tramping through the new fallen snow to get to the big red barn and milk the cows. Even now, she could feel the cool fresh air on her face, the warmth of the animals' large bodies and her father's presence always close by.

There was no sound inside or outside of the house. Sarah allowed herself to lean back on the pillows bunched up on the built-in seat and look around the room. This was her nook. In the entire large Grady house, this was the only place she could call solely her own. Even though she had some input into the plans during the construction of the building, William had made most of the decisions about the décor and furnishings, except for those in this room. He had allowed her to decorate and keep it as she saw fit. At times she was resentful of William's dictates, but she adored him for giving her this space as a safe haven. Being the smallest area in the house, it was still big enough for a desk, a chair and a table. There were built-in bookcases and this glorious window seat where she could look out at the pastoral landscaping and dream.

On this morning she was doing exactly that –dreaming. All the things in life she wanted to do paraded themselves before her eyes; she was standing under Big Ben in London as she traveled extensively abroad, then flying down a steep mountain with the fresh snow flying around her as she learned to ski. She visualized riding her horse on a narrow path up a tall mountain and looking down over a spectacular sunset in the Grand Canyon. Maybe starting her own business would be rewarding and, certainly, she had to get a patent for her invention. After all, she was thirty-seven years old now and it was time to do the things she dreamed of instead of just being the prominent socialite, Mrs. William J. Grady. Where was SARAH Grady? Trying to determine a path to realize her dreams, she began to feel anxious. The negative thoughts destroyed her peaceful interlude and she looked at her watch, 8:00 a.m. already.

William decreed that she be up to start her morning at precisely 5:45 a.m. He insisted that she dress and join him for breakfast before he left for his daily activities. To Sarah that would not seem an unreasonable request except she usually had to work until at least midnight or later to wind up his dinner parties. When they attended other social events it was 1:00 or 2:00 a.m. before they retired. She envied her unmarried friend June who did not have to arise in the morning until she wished and did not have to stay up all hours of the night to entertain.

Every single day seemed to bring numerous activities without any relief, so Sarah was exhausted and sleep was something she craved. Often when the day was done, she was so stressed that sleep would not come. Many a night she would crawl out of bed, go to the barn, and saddle her horse for a ride. Oh how she enjoyed those night time rides on Midnight, galloping through the silent acres of park land that were close to her house. She allowed her long hair to blow freely in the wind, often not changing out of her nightgown. This was relaxation and freedom.

Midnight – not a very original name for a black horse, but she reasoned it seemed to fit him well. He was a beautiful coal black stallion with only one spot on his nose in the form of a white triangle. Five years ago on her birthday William had given him to her as a gift. Sarah recognized that

Midnight was one of only two beings in her life that received her uncon-ditional love, the other being her son Sam. The horse received her pure devotion, but there was always a twinge of guilt when she thought of Sam.

Her dreaming done, she uncurled herself from the window seat and moved over to her desk, urgently beginning the day's work. First, the ser-vants needed their duties for the day. James took most of his orders from William, but Sarah often required him to do chores for her as she pre-pared for the Grady's parties, like the one tonight. Seeming to have a sixth sense, her maid Sadie always knew what Sarah wanted. How could she sur-vive without Sadie? Too flippant at times, she was more to Sarah than just someone to do the cleaning and some of the cooking for the household. For some unexplainable reason, Sarah wanted Sadie's approval for her ac-tions. Sadie was always the voice of reason and without her emotional en-couragement Sarah would be unable to keep her strenuous schedule.

Today the schedule required Sarah to attend a 10:00 a.m. meeting at First Methodist Church to plan the spring fundraising activities for the poor farm. She exhaled in frustration as she contemplated how far off course the ladies would take the discussion, but this was one of the organizations that William picked for her to join. He insisted that she do a great deal of charity work.

"After all," he said, "a man of my position should have a wife that ex-cels in this type of work."

So, she would go "excel" at ten as expected. She thought some char-ity work of her own choosing would be more satisfying than only doing those things William picked for her, but his choices came first and she simply had no time left to implement her own desires. Besides William did not approve of the organizations she wanted to join such as the Women's Suffrage Movement.

She remembered being upset at the last meeting at the church because of the way the women were treating one of the group. As she listened to the ladies discussing how to raise money for the poor farm, she noticed one dedicated matron kept trying to say something, but the others would ignore her. Looking critically at the group she realized that the figure they were disregarding was dressed very poorly and stood out as an indi-vidual of a lower class than most of the women.

"They are treating her badly," thought Sarah, "only because she does not have as much money as they do."

Always ready to right the injustices of the world, Sarah came to her rescue. When Sarah Grady spoke everyone listened.

"Mrs. Moore has a great idea she was telling me about and I think it would work to make money. Why don't you tell the women about it, Mrs. Moore?"

The appreciation that showed in the grateful woman's eyes was Sarah's reward for her efforts, and when the group praised Mrs. Moore for her idea, Sarah knew she had done a good deed. But she still wanted to be a part of the groups she, not William, valued.

Her good friend June Ewing had invited her to a luncheon at the Decatur Club with seven of Sarah's closest acquaintances. Lunch would be tolerable, she reasoned, because three of the women attending were really friends. Sarah was intelligent enough to realize that many of her so-called "friends" only attached themselves to her for their own social advancement. Seeing them trying to gain her favor for their own purposes made Sarah angry. She loved attention and wanted to be highly thought of for her own qualities, not for some faux friend's selfish reasons. Knowing Sarah's position in the community as number one on the social register and president of several of the prominent charitable groups, the country club ladies were often jealous and envious; she longed for friends, like June, that were honest and fun.

After lunch her afternoon was free, but she needed that time to prepare for the dinner party William was hosting in the evening. Luckily, he had scheduled this party to be held at the country club, not at their home. However, there was much to do to make it the perfect evening for William's New York guests. This was a business affair for, of course, an all-male contingency, so Sarah would have to make sure the club dining room looked striking yet masculine.

One could not trust the country club staff to arrange the seating, set the table correctly, or be imaginative in folding the napkins. Men disliked their napkins looking like flowers, so she would have to teach a quick folding lesson to the waiters so the napkins would look more geometric. The club employees also had not been trained to set the table in the European fashion to which the New Yorkers were accustomed. Even the wine glasses would not be placed properly unless she put them on the table herself, white wine glasses to the left of the water glasses and red wine to the right. Sarah knew she had to take care of every detail, remembering to order flowers and creating an atmosphere to make the room look both stunning and professional. Even ordering flowers would take much thought; William's guests would not be fond of heavy scents like gardenias produced. In fact, the table should have no scent on or around it besides the food itself. Why was the staff not trained to know this? At least the food was almost always up to her standards.

Planning for the dinner would take the afternoon. Of course, in the evening she would be expected to be properly dressed at the door to greet the entourage and then stay behind the scenes to make sure the dinner was perfect. When the dinner was over and the men adjourned to the Oak Room to enjoy their drinks and cigars, she would arrange for James to get the sleigh to bring her home. A sleigh would be better than the automobile in the snow and she would be done and home for the day about 10:30 p.m. Good, that would give her a couple of hours to work on tomorrow's schedule which was going to be much busier than today's.

Sarah understood William realized what a treasure he had in his wife and knew she was helping further his rise in the business world. He was now General Sales Manager of Faries Manufacturing Company, but he intended to be President as soon as possible. She wanted to help him accomplish his goal, but wished that the schedule were a little lighter. Sarah was tired, really tired. When she had a moment to consider her life, she realized that part of her happiness came from knowing she was doing a superior job for William. Her role as promoter made her confident and proud, but lately she began to wonder if there was not more to life.

Having put the day's schedule in order, she arose from her desk and giving a big sigh, dived into her activities wondering again when time would be available to do the things of which she dreamed. When would be a good time for Sam to come visit? He was now fourteen years old and still lived with her ex-husband's mother on a farm outside of Colo, Iowa. He wrote occasionally and visited Sarah whenever his teenage schedule could coincide with the Grady's busy activities, so his trips to Decatur, Illinois were infrequent. Both she and William looked forward to the times he would come and stay for a week or so. Not having any children of his own, William doted on Sam and Sarah was grateful for every minute she could spend with him.

Sarah's day went as expected and she returned home exhausted from hosting a successful dinner for William, but still had to finish planning for the next day. Finally at 1:30 a.m., not being able to drag one foot after the other, she fell into bed, going to sleep easily for a change. Tomorrow would be better she had told herself before the blackness of sleep enveloped her.

Four hours later she awoke as usual and dressed quickly, anxious to get downstairs and join William in the breakfast room. She said a silent thank you to the woman who invented the brazier and in doing so had released her from the time- consuming corset. Her morning dressing ritual was now a much easier and swifter affair. Sarah hurried to be on time for breakfast. William expected her to be prompt and as a businessman was accustomed to having people obey his directives. She knew that he had no idea of the grief he caused her by issuing his orders and not paying attention to the things she wanted.

As she walked into the room and saw him bright-eyed and well groomed, she thought to herself, "How does he do it? He came in later than 1:30 a.m. and was up before I was this morning."

His appearance belied the fact that he was thirty-nine years old. He was six foot two inches tall with a strong muscular build. His sandy hair was thick and wavy saying to all that he was an Irish man with a countenance not to be trifled with.

William could hardly wait for Sarah to sit down to breakfast. He had a surprise for her and was sure she would love it.

Eagerly, he said, "How would you like to go on a little vacation?"

Sarah looked at him expectantly. That would be about the nicest thing she could think of right now. It would give her a chance to relax, even play some golf if the weather would permit; she would not have to plan parties and meetings, and she could talk to new people.

She smiled at William, "Of course, that would be nice. Where shall we go?"

"I have a business meeting in New York and am planning to meet some contacts at Hot Springs for a few days of enjoyment before my meetings in the city. I would like you to go with me. I need your conversational skills, as several couples will be joining us: Mr. and Mrs. James Prentice, and my good friend Ed Rockafellow and his wife Florence. Do you remember them? I believe you met both couples briefly when we were in San Diego." He paused and looked up at Sarah, before continuing, "You have been looking a little pale and tired lately, so I think this would be good for you. We'll leave in three days; I already have our train tickets."

"Perfect," thought Sarah. "Hot Springs, Virginia is one of the finest resorts in the country and I'll have some time to myself."

She nodded in response as she recalled the new golf course at Hot Springs designed by Donald Ross, the foremost golf course designer in the world. Previously when Sarah had been to the resort, the course was not very enjoyable. It was only nine holes and there were still many stones on the fairways. In 1904, she and William had met J. P. Morgan who had purchased the resort and he had assured them the appearance of the hotel and golf course was going to change for the better. After fire destroyed much of the resort in 1901, he had vowed to rebuild it and make it the best vacation spot in the country. When Sarah had been there in 1912, most of the hotel building was new, but the golf course had not been done. Being such an avid golfer, she was excited about the new eighteen-hole course. Also, she had heard from some of the ladies in her bridge club that the new main lobby of the hotel was beautiful and terribly extravagant. This vacation would preserve her number one social standing with her country club friends, especially if they could talk to Mr. Morgan again.

It would take a superhuman effort to get organized in three days, but she could do it. Luckily, after today their social schedule was light for the rest of the week requiring that only two events be cancelled because of their vacation. As for clothes, the advance of machine-made dresses in the last couple of years had made wardrobes so much easier to acquire. Sarah's "special event" outfits were still custom made from a shop in Chicago, but she reasoned she could go to Linn and Scruggs Department Store right here in Decatur and buy the garments she needed for their trip. A new evening dress was a must and a fresh golf skirt would be nice. Since there was no time to go to Chicago, her only option was shopping in Decatur.

For the next seventy-two hours Sarah tore around like a whirlwind, packing her trunk, canceling events on her social calendar, shopping for new clothes, and outlining what James and Sadie should do while they were gone. Finally, she and William boarded the train as scheduled. The plan was for both of them to spend two days in Hot Springs, and then Sarah would be left there while William went to New York to conduct his business.

Although the décor on the train was elegant, their compartment was dusty, cold and jerky, but Sarah was content to lie down in her berth, snuggle under the blankets and contemplate sleep. It was so good to leave Decatur for a while and get a feeling of the rest of the country. 1915 was predicted to be a tumultuous year for the countries of Europe and their troubles seemed to be spreading to more countries. Already Germany was at war with Britain. Sarah wanted to know all she could about the war situation. She brought a copy of the *New York Times* and the *Decatur Herald* with her to read on the train, knowing that William would not discuss the war or politics with her. Sarah found each question regarding the war posed to her female counterparts easily dismissed and to her great frustration, she soon realized no woman in Decatur was supposed to talk about the world situation. It would be exhilarating to meet Easterners at Hot Springs with whom she could finally discuss current events.

CHAPTER 2

Mr. Morgan's Hotel

Hot Springs, Virginia Spring 1915

WHEN THEY ARRIVED at the hotel, the bellhop immediately ushered the Gradys to their room. Without delay, William prepared to go downstairs to meet his business friends and Sarah began to unpack.

As he was leaving the room, he called back to her. "You have an hour to dress for dinner. Why not dazzle these people with your new dress? The red one."

Sarah swallowed her displeasure at that remark. William's suggestions always sounded more like orders. He, as usual, wanted to use her as a business asset and she was happy to be of help, but she had anticipated these few days at Hot Springs were to be a vacation for her and William. It was already obvious that the expectations for the evening would be that she impress William's clients.

"Oh well, dinner would be enjoyable anyway," she determined, unable to stop herself from thinking: "but how nice it would be if I could choose what dress to wear when we went out?"

When Sarah was Mrs. W.J. Grady, she had impeccable social graces and charm. As she entered a room, men would stare and then turn to their wives with a guilty look. She had a commanding presence with her five foot seven inches in height and slender body. Her movements were smooth and flowing making her tall figure that much more alluring. Her voice floated on the air like a soft melody and being well read, she could discuss almost any topic, current or otherwise, with astuteness. Sarah unfailingly charmed William's business friends with her style, wit, and elegance. By dinnertime this evening she would be playing her part.

Looking around her hotel room, Sarah appreciated what she saw. The large space was more of a suite, with a cozy sitting area on one side and on the other a lavishly appointed bed dripping in both silk and satin. Mr. Morgan had not exaggerated when he said he would build the finest resort in the country.

The lobby had been spectacular with all its sparkling crystal chandeliers; tall, gold palace vases; plush carpets; and furniture that would entirely consume anyone who would dare to sit. Brightly colored oriental statutes rested upon every ornately carved table. It made Sarah pleased that she and William had gone with a Chinese decorating scheme in their home; they were truly avant-garde, especially for Decatur, Illinois.

Dinner that night was enjoyable. The impressive dining room seemed as though it was trying to outshine the lobby. The huge room had beautiful dark walnut chairs pulled up to tables amply covered with the whitest linen Sarah had ever seen, and she was accustomed to seeing fine linen. There were four couples at their table, husbands and wives. Besides Sarah and William, the other couples were from New York and came often to Hot Springs to relax for a few days. All the men had important sales positions in their respective companies. One couple Sarah remembered meeting briefly before, Mr. and Mrs. Ed Rockafellow. Mr. Rockafellow sold goods from his company, Western Electric, to Faries Manufacturing Company so he and William had been business partners and friends for a long time.

The food was decadent with the star of the meal being prime rib so tender it was not necessary to cut it.

Looking at the printed menu on the table Sarah joked with Mr. Rockafellow who was seated beside her, "We are going to be served the hotel's famous Oysters Rockefeller. It seems the chef does not know how to properly spell Rockafellow."

Ed smiled and replied, "My distant cousins the Rockefellers are much more famous than the Edward Rockafellows even though they do not spell their name correctly."

Sarah had seen Ed's name printed out on some of William's business documents and had wondered if he were related to the famous Rockefellers. She was pleased that he was sitting next to her as he turned out to be a brilliant conversationalist and William on her other side was discussing business with Mr. Prentice seated across from him.

The dinner service was outstanding with not one, but two waiters, standing stiffly by the table, a white towel folded on their arm ready to assist in any manner. Lively conversation continued throughout the evening and, as the group dispersed, the men made plans for all the couples to play golf the next day.

That night in their room William complimented Sarah, "You were the 'belle' of the dinner party and were able to keep the festive atmosphere throughout the evening. You outshine all the other wives at that, Sarah."

"Thank you. I am adept at being your ambassador because I have had so much practice, but maybe tomorrow we can just enjoy ourselves playing golf? No business for a change," said a hopeful Sarah.

Sarah felt excited to have been in good company for dinner and anticipated she would enjoy the next event. Next to riding Midnight, golf was her favorite sport. Tomorrow, as social custom dictated, she would play with one of the other men instead of her husband, and he hopefully would be better than William at the game. Being paired with William was difficult because he was not the best golfer and, feeling the need to let him win, she declined to hit the ball as well as she was able.

Morning came and with it the sunshine and perfect temperature for golfing. As the couples gathered for their outing, Mr. Rockafellow took charge of pairing up the couples. Sarah was to play with him.

"Great," Sarah thought, "he can't be any worse than William and he seems like a pleasant, intelligent man -- and very handsome. I'm going to enjoy this." She smiled to herself, thinking: "Perhaps he chose me deliberately."

As Mr. Rockafellow was addressing his ball, Sarah was addressing his appearance. He wasn't much taller than she – about 5'9", but he stood so straight that Sarah expected him to salute and bark orders to his ball, "Forward March!" Obviously, he had been in the military. But his fluid golf swing belied his military presence as his ball soared 205 yards down the fairway. It did, however, settle in the rough.

"Oh no," thought Sarah, "he's going to beat me if I don't pay attention."

With eyes narrowed she teed up the ball and took an extra thirty seconds to compose herself as she stared at her target. Her competitive spirit had manifested itself.

"Beautiful shot," yelled Mr. Rockafellow as her ball flew about 185 yards and landed in the middle of the fairway.

"I believe I can give you a decent game, Mr. Rockafellow," said Sarah provocatively as they strolled down the fairway toward their balls.

Ed smiled, flashing an almost boyish grin, "Please call me Ed, especially if you are going to humiliate me by displacing me as the best golfer in our group."

Sarah's eyes twinkled as she stared at him, "Ed, you will probably beat me but, you should know, it won't be easy." Her next shot put her ball right by the pin on the green.

"I see that," said Ed.

Besides enjoying the course that J.P. Morgan had promised her years ago would be one of the best in the country, Sarah was getting much pleasure from engaging Ed in conversation by asking questions about the war in Europe.

"Do you believe America should be aiding the countries overseas that Germany seems to be tearing apart? Your bearing suggests you have been in the military."

Ed answered as he sank a twenty foot putt, "I was part of Teddy's Rough Riders, but I am not a supporter of his right now. Woodrow has it correct I believe – we, as a nation, need to stay away and not take sides."

"You address President Wilson as Woodrow?" inquired Sarah in jest.

Ed grinned. "Woodrow and I have been friends for a long time – ever since his days at Princeton. He calls on me to come to Washington once in a while to give him a business view on world affairs, but you are right, out of respect I should always refer to him as President Wilson."

Sarah became so interested in the conversation that she missed her putt. As they played their game, Sarah realized she was having a wonderful time. This man who told her to call him Ed had amazing charisma and wonderfully expressive eyes. There was something about him. Even more exciting, he was a good golfer, two strokes ahead of her, and she was playing her finest game. But best of all, they were discussing world affairs and he was paying attention to what she was saying. In fact, he seemed to be genuinely enjoying their conversation. He said he liked hearing the Mid-Western (he called it the "Western") prospective on the war abroad.

Since they had teed off first and were such good players, the couple finished their round quite a bit earlier than any of the others. They sat in the lounge, ordered a drink, and continued their discussion. Finally, the others joined them leaving Sarah disappointed because she wanted to continue her private conversation with this interesting man with whom she shared so many interests.

The group decided to play bridge after lunch. Again Sarah was paired with Mr. Rockafellow, or Ed as she was now calling him, and they won all their matches. Sarah liked winning and realized she was having a fantastic time with this friend of William's. It seemed like it had been a long time since she really had had any fun. Ed's wife, Florence, was keeping William occupied, so Sarah did not have to worry about him.

Next on the agenda was dinner and dancing. William was a passable dancer. He knew the steps to all the old dances, but was not familiar with new ones, nor could he follow the rhythm of any dance besides the waltz or fox trot. When there were others to dance with, Sarah usually took advantage of any offers.

This evening Ed asked Sarah to dance after she had done her obligatory two dances with William. He took her out on the dance floor and the magic began. What a wonderful dancer he was. She was literally floating to her favorite Strauss waltz, "The Merry Widow."

Sarah caught herself thinking, "I could be a merry widow with a dance partner like Ed. I would make a good widow –" Realizing what she had just wished for, Sarah cancelled her previous proclamation. "Oh please, God, I don't mean I want William dead. Lord, forgive my thoughts."

Next, stomping to a foxtrot, both she and Ed realized they had an exceptional dance partner, but they were not aware they had emptied the dance floor; all eyes were on them. Ed was not concerned about anyone besides this attractive woman with whom he was dancing. Throwing caution to the wind, he then led her through what was considered in many circles the somewhat improper "Grizzly Bear." Sarah had never done this dance herself, but had seen the professionals do it many times. As they went through the steps with all four of their hands flapping in the wind, Sarah's flawless performance went sour as her foot got caught in Ed's at the exact moment her head was supposed to rest on his shoulder with her arms flying in the air to replicate a bear hug. She felt her heart skip a beat as Ed saved her by putting his strong arms around her waist to right her fall. The diners all clapped and the couple became conscious of the fact they had been entertaining the entire room. Never before had dancing been so much fun, but after the three dances, Sarah glanced over at their table and saw William staring at her with a disapproving look on his face. Knowing he was getting anxious for her to return to the group, she reluctantly asked Ed to take her back to their table.

William was ready to go to their room. In front of the group, he apologized to Sarah telling her he would be leaving for New York in the morning instead of spending more time at Hot Springs. He explained the rest of his associates would be heading for the city tomorrow and he needed to go as well. Since he had a big business day ahead of him, he wanted to get a good night's sleep. Grudgingly, Sarah told everyone good night and went upstairs with her husband.

William's only comment as they went into their room was, "You need to be careful of the dances you choose to do. 'The Grizzly Bear' is too risqué. Don't do that in Decatur."

Lying in bed she couldn't begin to close her eyes, while William immediately went into a sound sleep. After resting there for an hour or so, she determined that sleep would not come. If she were at home, she would be out riding Midnight, but here there was little for her to do except to get up and go for a walk.

Outside she breathed in the clean, fresh air. A full moon was out, spreading light all over the gardens. The breeze was gentle and the temperature was cool but not cold. This is heavenly she thought as she walked through the gardens and sat down on a bench to enjoy the whole of her surroundings. Seemingly out of nowhere, a figure appeared before her. It was Ed.

Noticing her befuddled expression, he spoke immediately, "I didn't mean to startle you. Why are you out here by yourself at two o'clock in the morning?"

She replied, "I couldn't sleep and besides, it is gorgeous out here in the gardens, so peaceful and quiet. I guess you couldn't sleep either. Please join me, Ed."

He sat down on the bench beside her and effortlessly they fell into a conversation unmatched in Sarah's lifetime. They chatted about everything; the theater, books, the world situation, sports, and even shared several personal thoughts. At some point Sarah realized they had been outside for several hours and had lost track of time. She glanced at him trying to tell him that they needed to go inside, but something happened. He met her gaze. They were both silent as the kiss unfolded. Pulling away after a moment, Sarah ran inside and up to her room.

William was still sleeping soundly. Sarah quietly climbed into bed and lay still with her eyes wide open.

"What just happened?" she wondered.

Knowing the pain betrayal could inflict on a marriage, Sarah had never been unfaithful to her husband, nor did she want to be, but she could not deny the feelings she was experiencing for this man whom she had just started calling by his first name. This connection they had was not intended, but it seemed real. Ed was a man she did not believe existed, as driven and meticulous as William, yet passionate and caring. Sarah had been the recipient of many flirtatious kisses from men at her country club, but those meant nothing. At the moment she felt a strange fluttering in the pit of her stomach, almost like the nervousness she felt before she gave a speech to a crowd of people.

Thankfully William would be going to New York in the morning, leaving her at the resort to enjoy herself while he conducted his business. Ed would also be gone and things would return to normal giving her a few days to get her emotions under control.

With this thought, she fell into a deep, dream-filled sleep.

EDWARD W. ROCKAFELLOW
1924

CHAPTER 3

❧

Ed Rockafellow

Hot Springs, Virginia Spring 1915

THE FOUR COUPLES gathered for breakfast the next morning before they were to go their separate ways. Still reeling from the previous night's unexpected kiss, Sarah was not herself. Like a teenager she felt giddy, but at the same time experienced moral twinges weighing down her happy mood. As she entered the dining room with William, she didn't know what to do with her eyes. Involuntarily they stared straight at Ed who was already at the table, then quickly shifted to William as he seated her. Taking a safe path, she looked down intently at the silverware by her plate. Being polite Ed had risen from his chair as Sarah claimed her place at the table.

He mumbled "Good Morning, Sarah," and sat back down. Sarah slightly nodded her head not trusting herself to speak. If she could just get through breakfast, she would then be alone at this beautiful resort and have time to regain her composure while the other couples, including Ed and William, would be in New York.

Breakfast was an outwardly pleasant event with Sarah and Ed both trying to display their normal demeanor. No one seemed to notice that Sarah was only picking at her food and Ed's voice was about two decibels louder than normal. There was a lull in the conversation at the table so Sarah, who usually led the dialogue, felt she should break the silence or people would perceive something was amiss.

Searching her mind for a topic of conversation and coming up empty, in an uncharacteristically harsh voice, Sarah blurted out, "It's sunny outside."

People were taken aback by the intensity with which she spoke; it was as though she dared anyone to contradict her. Everyone at the table stopped eating and looked fixedly at her.

It was turning into a very awkward moment, but Ed interjected quickly, "I believe Sarah always worries about the weather because she is so dedicated to golf." He turned to her with a smile, "I'm happy for you that the weather is cooperating today."

All the couples went back to eating and the conversation dwelled on the weather for a while. Ed had saved the day. No one was thinking any more about Sarah's outburst. A thankful Sarah who still seemed to have no control over her eyes kept glancing at Florence and saw her give Ed a puzzled look when he bestowed a high pitched laugh on Mr. Prentice's joke. As breakfast concluded, Ed announced, "Florence isn't going shopping with you ladies because she is leaving for a trip to France in a couple of days so she wants time at home to pack. I've decided to stay at Hot Springs and enjoy some more relaxing time. The rest of you men can handle all the business in New York."

Sarah swallowed hard. Despite her misgivings, she was excited to hear that Ed was staying. Her thoughts flashed back to the kiss. Why had it happened?

She shook away her thoughts, "Ed and I were both exhausted from the lateness of the hour and the fast pace of our schedule during the day. That must have been the reason for our actions… but why did I react with such feeling? Several men at our country club have kissed me, but then I felt no excitement and certainly no guilt. I think the vacation atmosphere at the resort promotes different outlooks – more freedom to do things one wouldn't do at home. This is silly. Why in the world do I even feel guilty?" Sternly she told herself, "The kiss was just an accident. Don't give it another thought."

William left to catch the train for New York and Sarah sat down in her room to read the book she had brought from home. No sooner had she settled into her chair, than there was a knock on her door. The bellhop handed her a note written on hotel stationary.

Dear Mrs. Grady,
Mr. Ed W. Rockafellow requests the pleasure of your
company for a round of golf at 10:30 a.m. this morning.

She asked the bellhop to remain while she penned a reply. "Mrs. W. J. Grady would be delighted."

Dressing for the golf match, she felt dizzy. Telling herself it was a combination of the excitement of doing something different and not eating much breakfast; she ignored her physical reactions to this exciting invitation. Was it a wise idea to see him alone again? But this was just golf. After all, she rationalized, she had really enjoyed their game yesterday.

The lush green of the fresh, spring grass, the stature of the mature trees and the melancholy echo of the distant hills as their golf balls cut through the air, promoted silence on the course with only their caddie's chatter interrupting the beauty surrounding them. Both Sarah and Ed played a serious game and delighted in every successful stroke. Wholly present, but unspoken, their evening in the garden accompanied them as they golfed. At lunch they both displayed a ravenous appetite and afterwards went outside to walk on the grounds.

The gardens were breathtaking as the daffodils, violets, and pansies were popping up in rows, in circles, and randomly. In this ethereal setting Sarah felt safe and comfortable with her companion. Her feelings of guilt and the necessity of self-inflicted moral punishment were buried under the blooms of the flowers and she wanted to hear more from Ed about his life.

"Tell me about the things you enjoy doing the most," Sarah queried.

"I love to read and am not too particular about the subject I am digesting. I'm now reading *The Birth of a Nation* and finding I do not agree with many things being said in the book. You should read it and then we can chat about the author's premises. Politics I could discuss every day all day. You already know my fondness for President Wilson."

Sarah interrupted, "Yes, but I was ecstatic to hear that you were a Rough Rider with Teddy Roosevelt. As much as you love Wilson, I love Roosevelt. What do you think of him?"

"I felt I was doing good things for my country when I joined the Riders. Teddy was a good leader, but I find myself disagreeing with most of his policies right now. He would have us involved in the war abroad in no time."

"I'm sorry. I got you off of the subject -- tell me more about the things that you are involved in."

"I am a first-nighter at the theater. There are very few plays and musicals that I don't see."

"Oh, I love the theater also. You have the advantage of being in New York. I go to Chicago to see many of the shows, but not on the scale you do," said Sarah.

"I know both of us love the game of golf and you are an outstanding player. Also, I fancy myself as a sort of historian. Remembering what I read and traveling all over the place, including overseas, gives me a better understanding of history," Ed proclaimed.

"I believe we are interested in all of the same things. The only thing I love and have not heard you mention is horseback riding."

After hearing Sarah lament Midnight's beauty and speed, Ed expressed an interest in learning to ride.

Sarah found it unbelievable that in two days she knew more about this man than she did her husband of twelve years. She was drawn to Ed as she never had been to another man, and not just physically. Never had she been around such an intelligent person. He could expound on any subject and, best of all, he gave credence to her views.

The pair dined together in the evening and then found themselves dancing to every song the band played. Suddenly realizing that she must remember her behavior before the dozens of couples they danced amidst, Sarah timidly suggested they sit out for a song.

"Better make it two, Darling." Ed replied with a gentle cadence, wiping his brow with a wink. Sarah's breath caught, locked in her chest by his address.

Patiently they sat together for two songs, never once looking away from the other. "How we must look," Sarah mused and then threw the thought away as she did all the others that attempted to pull her from these moments.

At the end of the second song, they were once again on the ballroom floor in each other's arms. They danced until the band stopped playing, then strolled in the garden and sat outside on the bench they felt belonged to them until Sarah was astounded to see the sun coming up.

As they parted for the night, or really for the morning, there was another kiss. Just a sweet kiss Sarah noted, but she knew. This was love.

Although he had had only a couple of hours sleep, Ed again sent an invitation to Sarah to play golf at 10:30 a.m. Ed addressed the unmade bed in his hotel room, perusing the scene of his tossing and turning during the early morning hours as he tried without success to fall asleep.

Finally, he stood declaring to the empty room, "I have to see her!"

He paced. "How can this be? This beautiful, intelligent and energetic woman..." He turned to the mirror. "You are a married man with a family and a high position in my company, as well as in New York and Washington society; and even worse, you have been a business associate and friend to William for many years!"

He turned away from his reflection, "I have everything. And I've worked so hard for it all." Ed thought of his wife Florence and their endless rows, yet his moral fortitude had never allowed him to consider breaking his marriage vows, even when given the opportunity.

Edward Rockafellow was a man of driving ambition, setting out to prove that anyone who labored diligently could realize the American dream of rising to the top in his profession. He saw the accomplishments of his ancestors who had come to this country before the American Revolution and had forged successful lives here. His distant cousins, one of the wealthiest dynasties in America, changed the spelling of their name when they arrived in this country, but were still part of his family of which he was very proud. Ed's immediate family did not participate in the wealth of his cousins, but he observed how men could elevate themselves in business with hard work and make a fortune in so doing.

When he had come to New York from New Jersey, he was about nine years old. Ed's father drank to excess nightly and only returned home each night to fight with his wife. The tumultuousness of his home life often left Ed in the care of his widowed aunt and her son throughout the majority of his childhood.

Ed remembered asking, "Aunt Debbie, why can't I go live with my mother?"

And she would reply, "Because I love you too much. You must stay with me, Child."

As a teenager, he left his aunt's house to go to work in New York as an office boy for Western Electric, a relatively new company that would eventually sell electric supplies and appliances to utility companies and retailers. He had little formal schooling, only a burning desire to learn and a great imagination. Fascinated with electricity, he invented several items that made big improvements in his industry. As his superiors saw his dedication and intelligence, they rewarded him first with the position of company salesman and then of General Sales Manager. In the latter capacity he traveled all over the United States, Canada, and abroad.

Ed had married well. Though he was not proud of the fact, he had to admit that he married as much for money as for love or respect. Florence Gould came from an established family and was able to bring some resources to the marriage. They found common ground in their two children. Perrine was in school and doing well, and Gwen, who was eight, was "his little princess" and obviously his favorite.

Ed did not spend much time at home, traveling extensively on business and staying many nights in Manhattan at one or the other of his clubs. Belonging to the most prestigious groups in the city, he thoroughly enjoyed engaging in lively conversation with the influential men in the East. Politics, books, history and the theater were his favorite topics and he stood out in any discussion on these subjects. These esteemed club members sought Ed's opinion on a variety of current affairs.

Years of extensive business travel had only lengthened the distance between the Rockafellows. At home he and Florence had endless rows, so his solution was to simply limit his time with her. Luckily, she enjoyed traveling abroad in the spring and fall and spent her summers in Maine to escape the heat of the city. Florence did not like to play golf, did not read books, was not interested in history, did not swim, and only enjoyed the theater because of the people she could see at intermission. Still Ed had remained a dutiful husband and they did things together for the good of the children. Ed had not considered himself to be unhappy and had always been faithful to Florence.

However, thoughts of his wife were at present far from his mind. Sarah was different he told himself. Saturated in conflicting emotions; frustration, guilt, anger, euphoria, happiness, and delight, he blamed himself for having feelings for her, but he could not deny them. He became resentful of his seemingly ceaseless thoughts of her. Here he was, forty-five years old and had just met the perfect person. He could not believe a woman like Sarah Grady existed. He would drag his consciousness away from her and then the next second, he would imagine a glimpse of her smile and see the twinkle in her eyes. Then he would think of something he wanted to tell her or ask her. His mind was full of Sarah and he wanted to be with her. He stopped his pacing and settled his feet in the middle of the room.

"Yes," he told himself, "this is what love feels like – I have met my soul mate."

CHAPTER 4

⚜

Sarah Unveiled

Hot Springs, Virginia Spring 1915

Sarah was also up early again and returned Ed's second invitation for golf with an excited "yes."

Being only slightly warm but very sunny, it was another beautiful day to be outside. Since it was a weekday as opposed to a weekend the resort and consequently the course were not crowded whatsoever. In fact, Sarah and Ed found themselves alone, not that they noticed because they were entirely absorbed in their golf shots and their conversation. Sarah was not playing her best game. She was losing by five strokes, not purposefully, but because her attention was mainly focused on the topic they were discussing – politics. Although Ed was an acquaintance and admirer of President Wilson, he still professed to be an Independent rather than a Democrat or Republican. Sarah, on the other hand, held a Republican view of the world situation and was an admirer of Teddy Roosevelt. Instead of causing dissension between them, the discussion seemed to draw them closer together. Ed was simply amazed that a woman could debate a political issue with such intelligence, far more in depth than most of his male friends.

Lunch in the dining room after golf was an intriguing affair. Both Sarah and Ed revealed their personal histories and some of their most guarded private thoughts.

"How can I tell him things I can't even begin to talk about with my own husband, some things I haven't brought up in my own mind for years?" wondered Sarah.

Entranced with each word that she uttered as though he had never heard the language before, Ed encouraged her to reveal facts about her background.

"Tell me about your family and where you were born. Do you have brothers and sisters? Tell me all," whispered Ed.

Made a little self-conscious by the intimacy of the question, Sarah's voice modulated to just below her normal conversational tone and she straightened a bit in her chair. "Well, I guess one starts with 'I was born', not that I remember that, but it happened in 1878, I think" said Sarah softly in half-hearted jest.

"You think?" asked Ed.

"Yes, the year of my birth seemed to change from time to time when my parents were asked to disclose that detail. Sometimes they said 1874, sometimes 1877 and occasionally 1878. It didn't seem like an important fact to them so I guess it is not that important to me," replied Sarah sticking out her lower lip a tad as she contemplated the facts.

"Anyway, around that time I was born on a small wheat farm near Grimstad, Norway where my father Hans and my mother Trine lived and that was the whole of our Petersen group until our family grew by adding my three sisters, Petrina, Nina, and Anna.

"My father told me that Norway was not a very forward looking country and the people were embroiled in many disputes, especially violent labor conflicts. He determined that America had much more potential for success in life than Norway, so, even though Norway was his native land, he decided to leave and try to make a home in the United States. Many of his friends had left for what they felt to be greener pastures in America in a state called Minnesota where there was an abundance of farmland to be had for a very inexpensive price.

"When Father told us to prepare for the journey, I recall being totally devastated because I had to leave my church, my grandparents, my friends and virtually everything I knew and held dear, and, even at my age, I knew we were never coming back. We were allowed to take our clothes and two small objects with us. I chose my doll and a small box with rose mauling on it that my grandmother had given me."

Ed leaned toward her and asked, "Do you still have those precious things?" His interjection was full of such heart-felt emotion that Sarah was taken aback.

"Well yes, and, as you seemed to have guessed, those objects are dearer to me than any of my other possessions."

Sarah continued, "I was only five or seven years old but I remember every detail of the journey across the ocean. We first got on a small ship that took us to Liverpool, England. Leaving Norway put us on very choppy seas and all my sisters and I were sick. To this day, if I close my eyes, I can still feel the motion of that ship, rising and falling, up and down, side to side, and get nauseous whenever I think how we were thrashed about for three miserable days and two miserable nights.

"Arriving at Liverpool, we had to spend a week there on land before our big ship was ready to leave for America. I really wanted to go back home and I asked my father if I could go back to Norway and live with my grandmother. Father was not impatient with me for asking, but in one of the tenderest moments I can remember having with him, he put me on his lap and explained that we were a family and had to stick together so we could all have a good life. What he was saying didn't impress me, but the gentleness with which he spoke has stayed with me forever."

Since they had both finished their lunch, Ed suggested a walk in the garden. He felt it was best to interrupt Sarah as he could see she was a little uncomfortable with her memories of the past. Still, as they strolled, he encouraged her to continue with her tale.

"Please go on. By learning your history I can know the real you better and I am so intrigued by your stories. You fascinate me, Sarah."

Sarah's voice became stronger and she continued. "The trip to America was unforgettable for everyone aboard our ship. I honestly don't know how our family survived it. As we boarded the big ship, I caught a glimpse of the inside of one of the cabins. The cabin looked really nice and my spirits were lifted. However, we were shuffled with many others down some stairs through a narrow hall and into a big room that was rather dark, damp, and smelly. My father explained to me that it was very expensive to cross the ocean and these accommodations were what we could afford."

"You were in steerage?" Ed asked, swallowing the image of Sarah's young face within a disheveled crowd.

"Yes," she replied entranced in her memories. "I can still remember the panic I felt upon entering that huge room. The enormous room got smaller and smaller as more and more people poured into it; soon it was literally packed with people and their luggage. I can remember in my innocence asking where we were going to sleep and where would we take a bath. Again my patient father explained what was happening and how lucky we were to have three single cots, one for my youngest sister and me, one for Petrina and Nina, and one for my parents. I remember wondering how both of my parents were going to fit on one little cot.

"I hardly had time to adjust my thinking to these conditions before the ship started moving and I knew I had more to worry about than our accommodations. My seasickness returned almost immediately and was compounded by the horrible food my mother gave me. My poor mother was sick herself and Petrina and Nina as well. If my father was sick, he managed to hide it so he could take care of the rest of us. Each evening I asked, 'How long will it take us to reach America?' His answer was vague, 'I can't tell you because it depends on the weather and whether or not the ship has any problems. With good weather and a little luck we might make it in ten or twelve days.'

"Most of the trip is shadowy. We did get to go up on deck in the fresh air for a little while on most days, but one day the weather was very stormy and the ship's crew locked us all into our big room. As those doors closed the light was drained from the room and, because of the storm, the ship was rolling violently from side to side. I remember trying to stay in my bed, but the jerking motion kept throwing me on the floor. My father couldn't help us because he was trying to keep our trunks from sliding across the room while he was dodging other trunks that were flying across the floor. The storm lasted for two days. The stench in our quarters from unemptied chamber pots, vomit, and who knows what else became unbearable. I couldn't eat, I was vomiting, I couldn't sleep, I couldn't breathe, and I was sure I was going to die.

"Then suddenly the ship became quiet. The stillness was ghostly. The crew unlocked the door and light flooded in. Everyone who could still move struggled to get upstairs to the fresh air. My whole family stayed on the deck for a long time just breathing in the cool fresh air. Suddenly my father said we all had to go below again, but before we left the deck, I saw the sailors throwing bodies into the ocean. I knew that those people had not survived being in steerage during the storm."

Sarah raised her face and met his compassionate gaze. "Ed, I shouldn't tell you any more. I have never talked about that trip, even though it has not been far from my consciousness. It's unsettling because my memories of the whole horrible voyage are so vivid. Let's go inside."

The color had drained from Sarah's face and her eyes reflected panic. Ed was concerned, but thought maybe encouragement to relate the whole story might be best. Taking her hands gently and pulling the two of them down on a bench, Ed apologized.

"I'm sorry. I'm upset as well. I didn't realize urging you to talk about your background would be so upsetting. Accept my apologies." He whispered.

However, convinced that it was best for her to relate the tale out loud, Ed continued with his support of Sarah's narrative.

"But please do go on, Sarah. Today, when people are coming into this country the first thing they see is Ellis Island and the Statue of Liberty. I guess your greeting was Castle Gardens. Not a great way to start out, but soon your life changed for the better I assume."

Ed had a wonderful calming effect on Sarah. She reflected, thinking to herself, "He really seems interested in my life. I have never before had anyone truly engrossed in my experiences."

Aloud she said, "I will continue, if you wish. -- I did survive, although I was never again the sweet and innocent young girl I had been in Norway. One grows up quickly when exposed to those kinds of circumstances.

"Well, it took twenty days for us to reach our destination. And you are correct, when I arrived on the shores of America, what I experienced was Castle Gardens. To give you an idea of conditions in that structure, I found out later that the United States government voted to close the facility right after my immigration because conditions there were so ap- palling. All I can remember from that place was that a doctor poked me several times and put a steel rod under my eyelid and then my family was put into pens with what seemed like hundreds of other people and herded down a narrow chute just like I had seen farmers herd their cows in Norway.

"We eventually did get to Minnesota and my life there was no different than any other farm girl, except as the oldest child, I had to do the work of a boy on the farm. I did have two brothers but they were born after we got to Minnesota."

She rested her hand on his for a moment unable to refrain from the gesture of gratitude.

"Enough of Sarah Petersen, Ed." Sarah swiftly rose and began to pull Ed towards the lobby. "I saw Mr. and Mrs. Swope check in this morning. Let's find them and get a bridge game going."

That night in her room, Sarah reproduced the day. Still a little upset after revealing so much of her personal story to Ed, she also felt strangely relieved to be able to tell someone about the memories that were very much a part of her past. She had had many things go wrong in her thirty-seven years, and most of them were things that she was not able to talk about, until now. To Ed she felt wholly transparent, vulnerable, yet un-burdened, by her past choices. He seemed to know already all she hid from others.

Sarah was in a dream world for the next day and a half; Ed was her Prince Charming. They played golf, they played bridge, they dined, they danced, they strolled through the beautiful gardens, and they discussed everything in the universe. For Sarah the world seemed surreal. Simultaneously elated and awe-struck, she found herself doubtlessly in the presence of her soul mate.

On the evening before William was to return to the resort, Ed and Sarah sat on the same bench where they had had their first kiss. After several still moments, Sarah spoke, "This is our last evening together. I don't know what to do. I feel more connected to you than I ever have to anyone else, Ed." Sarah choked, "The thought of never seeing you again is more than I can bear."

Ed grabbed her hands as the words tumbled from his mouth, "Oh, Sarah, I was unsure of your feelings, but you are the perfect woman for me and, Sarah – I love you." He reached over and kissed her again. This time there was intense passion in their kiss. No doubt, they were in love.

Speaking no more after this, they were content in the unending moment before them. Finally, when they could stave off sleep no longer, they followed their opposing and respective paths to their own rooms.

Back in her room Sarah got ready for bed trying to squash the feelings that kept rearing their head. The bliss she had been searching for all her life seemed to be hers for the taking now, but thoughts of William kept intruding on her giddy mood. At home she had been feeling dead and unappreciated. Now she felt alive and desired. However, even though William was dictatorial and sometimes (she admitted shamefully) abusive, he was still her husband and he had been kind to Sam.

"But I deserve to be happy?" she thought as she hopped into bed.

For several hours in her bed Sarah thrashed around as she tussled with her conscience and waged a battle between what she considered right and what she considered wrong, loyalty to William or devotion to Ed. She turned on her left side and shut her eyes. Immediately a vision of William appeared. Her inner voice screamed at her, "William has been your husband for twelve years and he fits the definition of a good husband. He has been a stand-in father to Sam, he gave me Midnight whom I cherish, and he has helped me become the most prominent woman in Decatur society. She could feel guilt soaking into her consciousness as Ed's image poked through her thoughts. Trying to get rid of both images, she flipped over to her right side.

"I need to get some sleep."

Eyes shut and breathing deeply she admonished herself to be quiet and push all thoughts out of her head.

"Maybe count sheep. One, two, three ... The sheep aren't moving. Oh, wait... I need to build a fence for them to jump over. There they go. Four, five --"

Ed's image popped up on the face of sheep number five.

"Darn! Why can't I sleep?" Sarah tossed over to her left side pulling the top sheet with her. Uninvited her thoughts came flooding back. Ed was the most intriguing man she had ever met. He was wonderful to be with. She felt happy just looking at him. He was so intelligent and also, he gave her credit for being intelligent. They had so many things in common. And her final moments with Ed were slipping from her. In the morning he would be gone from her forever. Bereft and exhausted, sleep finally came.

About 2:00 a.m. there was a soft knock on her door. Sarah put on her robe and went to answer it.

"Yes, who is it?" she asked, already knowing the answer.

"It's me," said Ed softly.

She opened the door and they just stared at each other. Without a word he entered her room and they fell into each other's arms.

Blissfully lying in Sarah's bed after making love, Ed broke the silence. "How are we going to keep in contact with each other once we go home? Do you have long distance telephone service at your house?" Ed inquired; "If so, I could call when I suspect William would be at work. The service is not very reliable though; we need to plan to meet again."

Sarah was excited about the idea of keeping in contact with him and quickly put her sharp mind to work on an idea, "I have a thought. There's a hotel not too far from my house where I could rent a postal box under a friend's name, then no one would know it was my box. Do you have an address where you could discreetly receive mail? If so, I'll write you when I get things settled at the hotel. You're right that phone service is not reliable, but we do have long distance at home and my maid would answer, so we could get by with that sometimes."

Finally Ed arose from the bed and prepared to leave. Sarah grabbed her handbag and started rummaging through the contents. Triumphantly she produced a letter from one of her friends. Tearing off the flap of the envelope so she could write on it, she took the address of two of Ed's clubs at which he said he could receive mail any time.

After Ed carefully returned to his room, they both slept soundly for the rest of the night.

The next morning Sarah arose and packed for home. William would be returning to the resort in a couple hours, and then they would have lunch and catch the train for home. She couldn't help singing and even laughing to herself at some of the things Ed had said. He had a delightful sense of humor. She would put their plan to communicate into operation as soon as she got home.

Now it was time to be extra nice to William. Dressing in the most flattering clothes she had brought with her, she wanted to look fetching for her husband. She speculated he would be happy just having her around to entertain his business and social friends. Assuaging her guilt with that thought, she picked up the book that there had been no time to read during her stay. When she tried to read, it became obvious her thoughts couldn't be corralled into any meaningful pattern. Confusion, guilt, glee – all these feelings were running around in her head.

"Get hold of yourself, Sarah," she said out loud. "William will be here shortly and you have to act normally. No matter how you feel about Ed, William is your husband and you love him."

William strode into their hotel room saying, "I saw Ed down in the lobby as he was hurrying to catch his train back to New York. I wish he had been at our trade meeting; we could have used his input several times. I guess he felt he needed a little more relaxation. Western Electric works him pretty hard. You look radiant. This vacation certainly has done you good."

William went down to the lobby to check out leaving Sarah to her pondering. Flip-flopping her thoughts again, she made her decision. She would not take her relationship with Ed forward, but would keep this vacation in her bank of happy memories and nothing more. She resolved never to see Ed again. Reaching into her purse, she removed the scrap of paper on which she had written the addresses of two of Ed's clubs. Violently crumbling the small piece of paper, she threw it into the wastebasket.

She said to herself, "That is the end of it."

When William returned, Sarah gave him a big kiss, feeling happy with the decision she had just made.

"I am so glad to see you" she said, hands still resting on either of his shoulders.

William smiled in response, pleased his suggestion for her rest had restored her so well.

After a pleasant lunch, the two left for the train station.

CHAPTER 5

The 20th Century Limited

New York Central Railroad Spring 1915

SARAH WAS GRATEFUL for the train ride. She thought the New York Central notable when they put down a red carpet from the station to the cars so passengers would not get their feet muddy. Yes, the train was dusty and sometimes jerky, but the Gradys had the best accommodations the railroad could provide, a private drawing room with comfortable seats by the double window, a bed, and an acceptable bathroom. She expected the daytime ride would be quiet and peaceful, just what she needed. The train lurched forward as she settled in. Always loving to travel, Sarah contentedly sat on the cushioned built-in bench watching the view change from the city to a mesmerizing pattern of green leaves and black soil under a blue, blue sky. William had already pulled out his briefcase and started to take care of business tasks signaling that he was occupied and did not wish to talk. The train's gentle motion and clickity-clack reverberation lulled Sarah into a state of calm and thoughtfulness.

She started thinking about all the men in her life. There were five of them, the first being her father whom she adored. He was always there for her when she was young, but he died while she was in college, just when she needed his guidance the most to help her plan the rest of her life, choose a mate, and maybe even a career.

Her father, Hans Petersen, was a big, handsome man with a bearing that told Sarah that nothing bad would ever happen to her as long as he was around. As she closed her eyes she could see him plainly, about six foot two inches tall, big boned, blondish hair just like hers, and kind blue eyes. She remembered how he stood beside her in the fields and could still see the sweat pouring off his body as they drove the animals up and down the rows to sow the wheat. He taught Sarah how to plant and harvest the crops and how to take care of the livestock. More importantly, she realized she learned her life's lessons from him, especially how to be a strong, moral person.

Thoughts of Hot Springs and Ed jutted through her mind, but she quickly returned to her reminiscing about her father.

She knew that as a farmer, he really wished for a boy or two rather than four girls, but, as the oldest, Sarah was strong, able, and did the work willingly because she enjoyed being outside and doing physical activity; and best of all, he allowed her to go to school in the winter and she loved learning new things.

By the time Sarah was ready to go to high school, her father had purchased land in several states and had three operating farms with hired workers. He no longer needed Sarah as a farm hand, so for her last two years of high school Sarah insisted that her father allow her to go away to a prestigious girl's academy in St. Paul. Hans Petersen complied willingly because he realized what a superior mind Sarah possessed.

The land that he owned gave the family status in their small community of Verdi, Minnesota where the Petersens were considered very rich. Moreover, Verdi was full of Norwegian immigrants so the stigma of being foreign-born and not having a perfect command of the English language was not an obstacle for the family to overcome. Her father took the time to teach Sarah about the business part of running a farm as well as the physical work. He was very patient and Sarah was a good pupil. Realizing Sarah's intellectual capabilities, her father allowed her to stay in St. Paul and go to college, and she did extremely well in a business course designed primarily for men. Sarah recognized she owed Hans Petersen an enormous debt of gratitude for shaping her into the woman she had become and she missed him terribly. Strangely she realized she had no fond memories of her mother. While her mother did not neglect any of her children she was busy keeping the family of eight functioning.

She was nineteen when her father passed away and he had his affairs so well arranged that it was unnecessary for Sarah to come home to run the business. She stayed in St. Paul, finished school and met the second man in her life, Charles Elwood.

Sarah stared out the window of the train and the view seemed to become more bare and cloudy as she began to think about her first husband. This was not a happy chapter in her life, but there were some good things that came from her marriage to Charles.

Charles Elwood was eight years older than Sarah and seemed to be her ideal man. Good looking and intelligent, he had a very promising career ahead of him in land sales. Land in South Dakota and Minnesota was selling quickly and easily; it was hard to keep up with the volume of business. Charles worked for a company whose headquarters was in St. Paul and he was one of their best salesmen. Sarah saw her future husband in him and when she finished school, she was ready for the marriage proposal that came right after graduation. Charles earned a promotion from his company and was transferred to Elkton, South Dakota as sales manager for land that was being sold in North and South Dakota, Iowa, and Minnesota and he wanted to take his gorgeous fiancée with him as his wife. Since Sarah's father was deceased and her mother had her hands full with her five other children, Sarah and Charles decided to go to the county courthouse in St. Paul and be married by a Justice of the Peace.

Sarah smiled a little remembering now happy they had been and what a glorious future they were determined to create. Just then the clickity-clack on the train tracks seemed to grow a little louder and motion of the train a little more jerky. Appropriate she thought, as she forced herself to forge ahead with her recollections of her marriage to Charles.

They married in 1897 and moved to Elkton, South Dakota. Charles did very well with his land sales and she helped him with his bookwork. They made friends in the town, which was just nine miles away from her family farm in Verdi.

Soon Sarah was expecting and everyone was looking forward to a baby. The third man in her life Samuel Webster Elwood was born in March of 1898. His first name Sarah picked, but Charles insisted that his middle name be Webster in deference to Daniel Webster whose speeches Charles used to recite as a boy while sitting on a fence watching the cows in the pasture on his family farm in Iowa. Charles imagined as a child that someday he himself would be an orator just like Daniel Webster and vowed to name his first son after him.

Sam was a good baby, Sarah remembered, and she loved being a mother. He was healthy and quiet, as babies go, and the Charles Elwoods appeared to have everything they needed for a happy life. When Sam was two years old, Charles was transferred back to St. Paul. His company had given him a big promotion. He went back to the city thinking he would find a place to live and send for Sarah and Sam right away after he got settled. However, his ambition burst forward and he decided to open his own land investment company. He felt he knew the business and could do very well on his own. As he started trying to get his company started, he realized, with her business skills, Sarah could be invaluable to him, but not if she had to spend all her time with Sam. He came back to Elkton for a few days to talk to Sarah and presented her with a brilliant idea. Sam could go stay with his mother and brother who were on his family farm in near Colo, Iowa. The farm he rationalized would be good for Sam in his growing years and besides it would just be until they got the business off the ground.

Sarah disliked the idea of being separated from Sam, but was lonesome in Elkton without Charles and found it a little hard to handle everything by herself. Besides that, the idea of being part of Charles's business was very intriguing since she loved working on office matters. She knew she could do a better job for him than anyone else he could hire.

"Why not," she thought. "It would just be temporary, Grandmother Elwood was really good with youngsters, and the fresh air on the farm would be a better atmosphere for Sam than the big city."

Charles and Sarah took Sam to Grandmother Elwood who was delighted to have a baby around. Her husband was deceased and the only son who was still at home was twenty-two and ready to move out.

Even all these years later, Sarah could feel the pain she experienced in her stomach as she turned around in the carriage to wave goodbye to Sam, and, now as she stared out the train window, the tears weld up in her eyes as she remembered the sad train ride back to Elkton without her little boy, and her hope that she had made the right decision.

However, Sam seemed settled, so Sarah and Charles packed their belongings and headed for the city to make a success of their business. Sarah worked hard, beginning her day at seven o'clock so she could get a good handle on the daily operations before the office opened, and staying most days until at least six o'clock to conclude affairs. Charles joined her on Saturdays so they could wrap up the week together. The long hours were paying off with the success of the business, which helped Sarah forget how much she was missing Sam. Soon she thought they could buy a house and bring Sam to live with them once again. Charles always admonished her to be patient. As the face of the company and the salesman, Charles spent most of his time making outside contacts with people, one of whom was named Clara Donaldson, the daughter of one of his biggest clients.

The noise of the train fell louder on Sarah's ears and the sky was no longer blue as she looked out the window. Dark clouds seemed to be gathering. She let her thoughts go back to that time in 1901, with all its painful memories, thinking maybe if she went through the whole agonizing experience again it would become a little less important in her life.

Charles was playing the big business man and no longer appeared to have the values of a country boy raised on an Iowa farm. Sarah didn't get suspicious when Charles asked her to work more hours. She didn't get suspicious when he said they didn't have time to go see Sam. She didn't get suspicious when he declined to buy a house though they could have well afforded it. She only knew that she never saw him because he was "working" so hard.

Sarah blamed herself that she didn't see it coming. After all she thought, "I am intelligent and more aware of my husband and his needs than most women are. How could I have been so stupid?"

Sarah remembered every detail of the scene. One night she was supposed to be working late at the office on some important matters that Charles said had to be done that evening. However, she felt really sick and determined she needed to go home and tell Charles he would have to handle the books this time. As she let herself into their apartment, she heard someone scurrying around in the bedroom. Opening the bedroom door, she found Charles and Clara in a state of disarray.

Sarah had found out Charles's secret and was devastated. She loved him dearly and simply couldn't wrap her mind around the idea that he betrayed her, at the same time realizing that this had probably been the cause of him working her so hard. Reacting at the moment, she told him to get out of the apartment and she never wanted to see him again. He complied and left without even gathering some of his clothes.

That night, Sarah tried to sleep on the sofa in the living room as she could not bring herself to go into the bedroom. In the wee hours of the morning she finally did fall asleep, but still awakened with the sunrise. She propped the pillows up behind her and sat there staring at the wall with a pile of handkerchiefs beside her. She spent the entire morning crying.

At about one o'clock the doorbell rang and a courier called out "telegram". Getting out of bed, she signed for the telegram and ignored the stares of the deliveryman. She knew she looked horrible with her bright red nose and face swollen from the profusion of tears that had been shed so far that day. The telegram read, "Sarah Dear Stop I really love you dearly Stop I know I lost my way and I'm so sorry Stop Please forgive Stop Take me back and let me make it up to you Stop Much love Charles."

Sarah was having none of his apologies. She was too hurt to even consider his plea. In her experience husbands didn't do this to their wives and she knew she could never trust him again. The telegram only served to make her irate. She stopped crying as her anger took over, fueling her plans. She would leave Charles to handle the business and that would be part of her revenge. He would have a difficult time without her in the office. Putting some ice on her face to take care of the swelling, she sat at the kitchen table and ate a sandwich. Thinking she felt much better angry than hurt, she finished planning her strategy. She decided to divorce Charles and move to Dixon, Illinois where she had inherited some land from her father. After getting settled, she would go get Sam and they would live their lives alone and never would she allow another man to hurt her. Solemnly she vowed this to herself.

Moving to Dixon was relatively easy but getting Sam was challenging. Before bringing him into the picture, she had to work out how they would survive and had to go through the divorce to determine where things stood with custody and a settlement from Charles; after all, this whole thing was his fault and thanks to her he was doing very well financially, so she should be entitled to a big portion of his present estate. She hired a competent lawyer in Chicago and Charles contested nothing that she asked for. Sarah was well-off when the divorce was granted in February of 1902. Three months later in May of 1902, Charles married Clara, adding another insult to Sarah. Sarah felt he could have waited a decent amount of time before he took his mistress as his wife.

While Sarah was in Chicago on business, she met some professional people her own age who helped her forget the late trauma with her former husband; she found herself enjoying the city and the upper class life style. There were big department stores, theaters, nightclubs, and lectures. Being financially secure, she had no reason to stay in Dixon so she moved to Chicago to be with her new friends.

She went to visit Sam to discuss his coming to live with her, not knowing how Grandmother Elwood would take her visit. Charles Elwood's mother was a wise woman and told Sarah she was not taking sides and the only important thing was Sam's welfare. Grandmother felt Sam would be better off with her until Sarah could get herself permanently settled and, as much as Sarah wanted to take him with her, she agreed. Sam was happy so all was well. The revengeful side of Sarah hated the fact Charles would be allowed to see Sam whenever he wanted, but she didn't want to take Sam's father away from him.

Sarah released the breath she had been unconsciously holding and relaxed a bit. That phase of her life was over and she noticed that the train had returned to its gentle clickity-clack with only blue sky being visible out of the window. William was still deep in his bookwork so Sarah settled back in her chair again and watched the world go by. Finally, her gaze turned to the man sitting across from her still deep in his business papers. "So now to the fourth man in my life… William," she mused.

In Chicago one of her new friends was instrumental in helping her recover from her divorce. His name was William Grady. He was exceptionally handsome and approximately her age. In fact, Sarah picked from her multiple birth dates the one that was most recent so she would appear to be a couple of years younger than William whose birth date was 1876. He was born in Springfield, Illinois, the fourth child of an Irish immigrant. The family was stable but being Irish in Springfield in the late 1800's did not impart any social standing or even much respect from the general population who were German, English or French with the town leaders mostly being German. The Irish were looked upon as hard workers (for the physical and menial jobs) and hard drinkers. William's father drove a wagon for a lumberyard carrying supplies to various builders throughout the city. He worked hard to realize his main ambition which was to see that all of his male children attained at least a high school education.

William did his part to fulfill his father's dream and then left home. Armed with an aggressive but pleasant personality, he got a job as a salesman for the Faries Manufacturing Company in Decatur, Illinois and began working on his dream of becoming an important industrialist. He determined to someday become President of Faries Manufacturing and have the social standing he thought he deserved.

When Sarah met William in 1902, he was wooing clients for his firm. She was still recovering from her divorce and Charles's quick marriage to his mistress. As Sarah had done with Charles, she immediately saw William's potential to become a successful businessman and believed she could help him. Sarah knew she excelled at facilitating business affairs, even though as a woman she did not get the credit that was due her. It was obvious to her that William was totally in love with her, so when he proposed she said "yes". She felt he was a man of his word who would not stray, and anticipated that a life with him would live up to all the expectations she had had for her life with Charles.

"I need a husband who will prosper," she told herself, "and William promises a secure and even glamorous life."

Sarah peered hard at the landscape visible out of the window on the train. They were in the mountains where she could see the jagged mountaintops as well as the green valley below.

She thought, "Just like my life with William – peaks and valleys. Sometimes things are great and then sometimes things are unbearable."

Did she really love William? She answered her own question, "Of course I do."

But William had not made it easy. Although William was on track to becoming president of his company; they had a gorgeous home, belonged to the country club and many other groups, and were listed in the social register of Decatur. Sarah knew much of his success was due to her efforts. Sarah missed the attention he used to give her when they were first married, attention that now seemed to be bestowed only on his work or prominent women amongst Decatur society. His shameless flirtation with whatever woman he spoke with whenever Sarah was otherwise engaged did not go unnoticed by others; Sarah had often overheard whispers of such at the club or on the course. She resolved to ignore them however, because the fact that William was no longer aware of her as a wife and a woman and a partner was much more painful that any of the dowdy womens' gossip.

But Ed Rockafellow considered her an intelligent individual not a business asset… Ed. She could not keep him from her thoughts.

"Yes, Ed is the fifth man that has had influence in my life, but," she told herself firmly, "he is only a nice memory." Gazing at William she thought, "I will think of Ed Rockafellow no longer."

Feeling she needed a distraction, she turned her thoughts to William and asked, "Can I help with some of your paperwork?"

"That would be wonderful. My success in New York means a great deal of paper work. Here, you can total this whole stack of orders," said William while pushing a large pile of order sheets towards her.

Sarah was happy to have a task to do. The rest of the train ride was uneventful as the two of them accomplished all of William's work.

"New York was kind to me. It worked out well with my business and you were able to get a little vacation out of the trip. We'll have to do this again soon."

"We'll see," thought Sarah to herself, nodding slightly.

CHAPTER 6

⚜

The Finest Residence in Decatur, Illinois

3 Millikin Place Spring 1915

JAMES PICKED THEM up at the train station in William's new Reo. William swelled with pride as he noticed a small group of people standing close to the parked car all admiring his recent purchase. He stepped onto the running board, then settled into the leather seat of the sleek, black, rather ostentatious touring car. Unlike Sarah, he had no idea how to drive it, but that was why he had a chauffeur, or really James, who was required to do many different jobs for William.

"Did you take good care of Midnight and allow him to get some exercise?" Sarah asked James.

"All is well at home, including Midnight, but he missed you," he replied.

Sarah and James shared a mutual respect for each other. Going out of her way much of the time to see that he was fairly treated, Sarah considered him part of her family. Also, James understood her concern about Midnight. When William and Sarah built their home, they erected a carriage house for their two horses and carriage. Not long after the construction of the house was finished, William traded his horse for an automobile. Sarah knew it was the way of the world, but the new vehicle crowded Midnight who now had to share his domicile. Sarah respected that the car was a business and social must for William who needed to show the world that he was able to afford this status symbol – no matter that his horse was more reliable and less expensive. Consoling herself with the fact that William had allowed her to keep her horse, she thanked James and told him she would go for a ride as soon as she got home. Although William threw her a condemning glance, Sarah pretended not to notice.

The Reo lurched into the driveway and Sarah admired her house. It truly was one of the nicest in Decatur and she loved the fact that it was different. The Frank Lloyd Wright prairie style creations on the rest of the lane were wonderful architectural achievements, but her shingle-style California bred structure was a beautiful comfortable home. All of the interior woodwork was a warm, light quarter-sawn oak; the light fixtures resembled lanterns; the wallpaper and the hand-stenciled dragons on the walls reflected the Chinese décor that had trickled eastward from California. Because she loved being outside, her favorite feature of the house was the veranda that ambled around three sides of the house. It could be accessed from the front door, two sets of French doors in the living room, or from a set of French doors in the library. Whenever weather permitted, Sarah entertained on this special place, and since there was an outside fireplace that backed up to the one in the living room, the entertaining season could be lengthened to include many spring and fall evenings.

After Sarah and William were married, his business took him to California every two months for a while and Sarah, who loved to travel, usually went with him. At that time in their lives they were happier and closer together than they had been since. Sarah reminisced about quiet days they spent sitting on the beach with the enormity of the ocean captivating them for hours at a time, and how they enjoyed the bustle of the ethnic areas of San Francisco. They were a team then and life was so simple.

Since both of them loved California and the architectural style that was so popular there, they consequently determined to hire a prominent California architect to build their dream home in Decatur. Maybe central Illinois was unprepared for the firm of Hunt, Eager, and Burns, but California shingle style is what the Gradys wanted and in 1908 they had the firm draw up the plans. There were ideas for the house that Sarah proposed to William, but the majority of her requests were not incorporated. His authoritarian dictates only slightly bothered Sarah because the final product did turn out to be close to her dream and, to Sarah's delight, different than any other home in Decatur.

With plans in hand, they had to find a parcel of land on which to build the Grady Mansion. Decatur of 1910 was a very progressive fast-growing city. Housing a population of more than 25,000 people, the enterprising prairie town had much to offer both its natives and its newcomers. Decatur it seemed was home to more inventors than any other city in the Midwest. Inventions such as the fly swatter, a ring to put through a hog's nose to control the animal, plumbing valves, a way to measure electric usage – all these things and more were being developed by Decatur people. Distribution and travel facilities were enhanced because Decatur was an important railroad hub. The city had a new prestigious university, Millikin, which was a tribute to the generosity of several successful citizens. The wealthy people in the town built large impressive residences with each owner seemingly trying to outdo his neighbors.

Picking a building lot was not an easy task for the Gradys. Someday there was to be a man-made lake which would make a beautiful building site, but it was only a dream on paper in 1908. Eldorado Street was probably the most handsome one in town, but the houses there had been built from the 1860's to the 1880's and were beginning to look a little old-fashioned, which would not allow the Grady's California style masterpiece to show off as it should.

Finally after a year of searching, William and Sarah agreed on a lot in a new development. William decided to kill two birds with one stone. Feeling he would benefit in a professional way from his friendship with E. P. Irving, he joined Mr. Irving, who was an officer in Faries Manufacturing and son-in-law to the founder of the company, and Robert and Adolph Mueller in buying about sixteen acres of land that had belonged to a Mr. Hill. All four of the partners were to build their houses on this land, but the Grady's house was the first one finished in the area. Donor of the bulk of the funds to establish Millikin University, Mr. Millikin had built his home in 1878 on four acres adjoining the land bought by this partnership. The Grady's lot of approximately a quarter of an acre had a wonderful view of the Millikin's homestead.

Built in 1910 at the cost of $16,000, the Grady's home was considered to be one of the most impressive in the city, thought by some to outshine the Frank Lloyd Wright homes that were later built on the lane. Both William and Sarah were extremely proud of their house.

The Reo came to a stop in front of the garage/stable. Sarah could see William tense as he looked intently at his beautiful house. The stress was visible on his face as he was reminded that he was back at 3 Millikin Place in Decatur, Illinois and home to resume the role of Mr. W. J. Grady. Eager to escape William's mounting stress, she jumped out of the car, ran to give Midnight a hug, and then hurried into the house to change into her riding clothes.

William confronted her at the bottom of the stairs.

"Forget that silly horse and concentrate on what you should be doing around the house. You have been on vacation and now you need to tend to your duties. I have some business friends from Chicago coming tomorrow night for dinner so you need to start planning for company," said William to an astounded Sarah.

Although accustomed to his rages, she remained baffled by the level of his anger. This was overly aggressive even for William.

She stared at him as he continued in a harsher tone, "I've given you a live-in maid in addition to a cleaning lady two days a week. You have Dorothy who comes to do most of the cooking. Too often you also borrow James who should be taking care of the duties I give him. I work long hours to be able to afford to give you these luxuries. The Muellers and even the Irvings don't have the help that you do. And haven't you just come back from a pleasurable trip?"

William was glaring at her. His behavior was not only extreme, but totally uncalled for Sarah thought, and, furthermore, it ruined her return from a lovely vacation. He often shouted at her when he was strained, but this was an inordinately aggressive demeanor he was displaying.

Ed's image popped into her head. She couldn't help but remember how much she enjoyed his company, how much they had in common, and how respectfully he treated her.

"Oh, is it possible to keep my resolution to never see him again?" she thought, but anger blurred Ed's image.

Determined not to take William's abuse, Sarah spit back at him, "You don't think I work hard to keep your house perfect for the company you're always inviting here? You don't realize that people are not drawn to you? Your social standing would be nonexistent if it were not for me!"

There she had said it. She had wanted to verbalize that sentiment for a long time, but usually her better judgment and emotional control ruled.

Sarah raced up the stairs giving William no time to react to her diatribe. Shaking from anger, yet already regretting her outburst, she perched on her window seat in her sitting room and cried as she always did when she was frustrated or angry.

William did not know how to give her space, and he refused to recognize that women were coming into their own and developing lives that did not include being a slave to their husband's will. He made her feel small and rejected. Sarah wanted to be part of the Suffrage Movement, but William forbade her to join any group that would promote "such idiocy" as he put it. William had to be in control of his wife and every other aspect of his life. Finally ceasing her crying, she arose from her seat and went over to her desk.

Not daring to fuel William's anger by going for a horseback ride, she started shuffling through the mail that had come while they were gone. Sadie always put all the mail that came to the house on Sarah's desk for her to deal with. Flipping through the envelopes, she suddenly froze and her heart skipped a beat or two. Holding up a small card-sized white parchment envelope posted from New York and addressed to Mr. and Mrs. William Grady, she trembled as she opened the letter that she knew was from Ed. It was nothing to get excited about she told herself sternly. After all, Ed was a friend and business associate of William's and they had both been with him in Virginia.

The note was short and sweet simply stating how nice it was to have spent some time with them at Hot Springs. What Sarah noticed however, was the stationary. It bore the emblem of the Union Club, one of the addresses he had given her. She quickly determined that if, and there still was an "if", she wanted to write to him without anyone else knowing, she could send a letter there.

Sarah was full of emotions. Still terribly angry with William, yet thrilled to get a note from Ed, she decided to skip supper and retire early. William came upstairs just as Sarah was climbing into bed and sat on the mattress beside her.

"I'm sorry that I get so upset with you. I know that you are trying to help me – but you have to realize that my business events are for your benefit as well as mine and they must take priority over all else. Don't you want to be married to the President of Faries Manufacturing Company? Sarah, I want everything for us because you are my wife."

Although Sarah recognized he was sincere, she also knew that his behavior toward her wouldn't change. She reasoned that he just couldn't help himself. No apology came from Sarah; she merely turned over in bed away from his gaze. She had spoken the truth and was still upset. William left the room.

As the next few weeks passed, nothing was said about their tiff. Sarah and William settled into their regular routine, Sarah handling all of William's social affairs and business parties, and William tending to Faries Manufacturing business. William was working harder than usual because he was expecting to soon become secretary of the company, a very prestigious position. Perfection was a state that had to be achieved in their social, business, and private lives in order to rise in the industrial world.

As busy as she was, Sarah was bored and lonely. Even though she saw many people during the course of a day, they were not necessarily the people she wanted to see. The women and even some of the men she associated with did not care for world affairs, did not read the latest books, had no idea what was playing in the theaters in Chicago or New York, and were not interested in politics. In public Sarah found herself saying what she should and doing what she should, but feeling frustration and resentment when the things she cared about were not topics of conversation at the country club or in her charity meetings. She tried to ignore the members of the club who were only concentrating on drinking, smoking, and having a "good time". Flirting with another man's wife and making money seemed to be the men's greatest interests. The ladies were only concerned about fashion. These were not Sarah's prime concerns. She only felt emptiness, and the emptiness she filled with dreams of Ed.

Golf at the club was the only activity that satisfied both her needs and William's. She was boosting his social standing by being active and socializing with the club members and she did love playing golf, a game at which she won championships for the club every year in Bloomington, Chicago, Springfield, and Peoria. As she accepted her trophies, she imagined Ed was standing beside her with pride glowing in his eyes. In spite of the jealousy she had to own, her personality made her well-liked by everyone, but she only had one real friend in this circle of acquaintances, June Ewing. She often played golf with June, which made her time at the club much more enjoyable.

June Ewing was part of the old Decatur establishment. Her family had settled in the county in its beginning years and subsequently achieved financial success. At thirty-five she was unmarried and called a spinster by some in the community. This tag did not bother June as she had turned down several proposals of marriage and was enjoying her role as a single woman. Someday, she declared, I will settle down and find the right man to marry. In the meantime, she and Sarah truly enjoyed each other's company.

Following one such afternoon with June, Sarah returned home to find a letter from Charles on her desk. Sam's father wrote to Sarah stating, "I think it is time for Sam to leave the farm. He needs more exposure to the world and, besides, my mother is getting older and less capable of handling a teen-age boy. Would you and William consider taking him into your home?"

Sarah knew William was agreeable to having Sam come live with them permanently and immediately penned a response: "Of course I would be ecstatic to have him with me full time. I have always wanted just that, and William would also be delighted to have Sam around."

Even though Sam spent most of his holidays with the Gradys, his visits were never long enough for Sarah. Grandmother Elwood was not so sure Sam should be uprooted and Sam himself didn't know how he would like living in Decatur. Elated by the news, Sarah immediately set to work arranging Sam's move to Decatur. Sarah proposed he come in June after the close of his school semester and at least spend the entire summer. It was looking like that might happen.

But even as she busied herself with these tasks, Sarah's visions of Ed grew more frequent and detailed; her resolve to be true to William and not write to Ed wavered. William's desire for exerting control over her seemed to be growing by leaps and bounds, as he barked orders at her daily. And with each order directed at her, she drew closer to her pen.

The Breakfast Room
3 Millikin Place

CHAPTER 7

The Lusitania

Decatur, Illinois May 1915

SARAH AROSE EARLY on this beautiful, sunny morning in May. Picking up the newspaper on the breakfast room table as she waited for William to join her, she uttered a muffled groan as she read the headlines. Quickly she read the front-page article. What was going on in the world? What was the matter with Germany? First they used poison gas on the Allied troops and even women and children in the cities they wanted to destroy; now they had sunk *the Lusitania*, a passenger ship, with innocent vacationers and businessmen on board. Only five of the eleven hundred and twenty-four people aboard survived and the death total included one hundred and fourteen Americans.

"Well," she thought, "at least now President Wilson cannot ignore the situation any longer. He will surely declare war on Germany and send troops overseas to help the Allies."

Sarah carefully reread the newspaper article, hardly able to believe what she had just absorbed from the paper. Her face got redder and redder as the rage inside her increased.

Just then William walked into the room and taking one look at Sarah's scarlet face and narrowed eyes, gasped, "Sarah, what in the world is the matter with you?"

Sarah shoved the newspaper at him.

"Look what happened! I knew we would be drawn into this war. Didn't I tell you? One hundred and fourteen American passengers were killed. They were just passengers going to England. They weren't hurting Germany." Sarah became conscious that she had been shouting.

After glancing at the article, William looked at Sarah with a patronizing glance.

"Calm down, Sarah, for heaven's sake. For a woman, you get awfully worked up about the strangest things. I am upset as well, but let me explain to you what happened. The Lusitania was a passenger ship, but the Germans thought the ship was carrying war materials ..."

Sarah could hear William's voice droning on and on about the incident, but she wasn't paying any attention. William's knowledge of the situation was very limited and he was not really aware of the repercussions that would arise from the sinking of the ship. Sarah was certain that this event was not a total surprise to United States government or to the company that owned the Lusitania. The threat of a submarine attack was real enough that the ship's passengers amounted to only half of her capacity. However, the British had been certain the Lusitania could out run any German sub. Sarah now believed America had no choice except to declare war on Germany to save not only this country but other countries as well. She exuded patriotism and didn't want anyone taking advantage of her country and her freedoms. Her judgment of the war situation was more extreme than most Midwesterners, but she believed the U.S. needed to fight so that the world would be safe from countries like Germany who were committing atrocities, and the United States had to step up to help Britain and France.

"Innocent Americans have been killed and President Wilson needs to take us into the war," Sarah screamed internally, blinking away the tears.

Sarah knew that it would serve no purpose to discuss her opinions with William who, as an Irish-American, had more sympathy for Germany than for Britain and France. He resented the British for keeping his mother country from being free.

Feeling her anger rising from William's remark that her interest in the war was strange "for a woman" and also from the sinking of the Lusitania, she excused herself from the table and went upstairs to put on her riding clothes. A ride on Midnight was the only thing that would allow her to think rationally. She would miss a meeting of the program committee at the country club that was set to plan the activities for the year, but time to herself was more important this morning.

Eager to ride, she saddled Midnight herself as she reflected on the beauty of this animal that William had given her five years ago as a birthday present. What a handsome horse! Sarah enjoyed grooming him. His sleek black coat was eternally shiny and she loved kissing the white triangle on his nose. He could run with lightning speed and Sarah occasionally thought she should enter him in a race just to show him off, but really she did not want to share him. Midnight was hers and always showed her affection no matter her mood. When she felt no one else loved her, Midnight was there, and she called upon his kindred soul often following William's dismissive words or one of her fruitless committee meetings.

Away from the city streets, she quickly calmed down as she galloped through the unsettled wooded area not far from her house. Quietly speeding through the trees as she rocked back and forth on Midnight, she admitted to herself her biggest problem. She wanted Ed. When she read about the Lusitania, her first thoughts turned to how Ed would be reacting to the news. They would have sat down together and discussed the issue, each expressing his or her informed views of the situation. Never would Ed have said that a woman should not be paying attention to the war. He valued her opinion and enjoyed hearing it. She had to talk to Ed. Tightening her grip on Midnight's reins, she allowed herself the realization she had battled for weeks.

They were soul mates and should not be kept apart.

She turned Midnight towards home and determined to correspond with Ed and try to arrange to see him again.

A strange peace came over her as she rubbed Midnight down and put him in the stable/garage. She knew what she was going to do and wasted no time in doing it. Bounding up the stairs to her desk, she told Sadie not to disturb her and immediately started writing to Ed.

She carefully penned a short note that said, "I miss you and need to hear from you. I'll be sending you an address so you can write to me personally without interference from William."

She put postage on the note and walked to the post office to mail it.

While downtown, she stopped at the Wiltshire Hotel to inquire about renting a post office box in their lobby. She explained to the hotel clerk that a friend needed one because she didn't have a permanent address as yet. Sarah made up the name June York to be registered on the hotel mailbox and paid cash for a month's rental on the box. Now she had a private address, P.O. Box 22, Hotel Wiltshire, Decatur, Illinois. She would write to Ed and he could respond without William being any the wiser. Sitting in the hotel lobby, she quickly wrote another note to Ed giving him the name of June York and the address of the hotel post office box.

Sarah went back home that afternoon feeling in high spirits. Having no doubt that Ed would write to her as soon as he received the information about the post office box, she went home to plan how she could get away again to see Ed.

"I will fulfill my obligations to my husband as I have always done, but I cannot ignore the man who is truly my soul mate," she affirmed aloud.

Intrigued by the affair she was planning, Sarah felt she had a new lease on life and for the first time in a long time was looking forward to the future. How many days would it take for Ed to answer her letters? Maybe she could expect something in a week depending on his work schedule. That night she fell into bed early, worn out from the events of the day. As she slept, she had a strange dream. The Lusitania was sinking and William was aboard. She tried to swim to the ship and save him, but President Wilson kept throwing her back to the water's edge. Ed rushed past her, his steps skipping atop the waves and returned with William to the shore.

Four days went by and William noticed how chipper and happy Sarah seemed. She had given two dinner parties in the last week and did not look any the worse for wear. They had also been to the club for a dance on the night between her dinner parties and Sarah was even more charming than usual. Several people commented on it. Except for the disconcerting upset she had about the Lusitania, which she seemed to put behind her the next day, Sarah had been shining. This was more like the Sarah he knew William mused, and what a great boost she had given him with the officers of his company who were in attendance at all these functions.

He expected his promotion within the next few days. How lucky he felt to have a wife like Sarah who loved him and was such a business asset as well. Recognizing that he was very stern with her once in a while, he rationalized that the way he treated her reflected the fact that he loved her so dearly and wanted her to share in his rewards.

CHAPTER 8

June Ewing

Decatur Carnegie Library Summer 1915

TODAY SARAH WAS filled with doubt. Ed Rockafellow had likely forgotten all about her because of his prominence in both New York society and in Western Electric which he had propelled into an international company with his inventions and propensity for business.

He was close to President Wilson; he had influential cousins like J.D. Rockefeller and friends like J.P. Morgan who were responsible for Ed's invitations to all the important social and business functions in New York City and Washington D.C. Sarah questioned what a man like Ed would see in a married, Midwestern, Norwegian immigrant like Sarah Grady.

Catching a glimpse of herself in a wall mirror as she was passing by, she noted with pleasure her rather tall, slender figure, smooth skin and fine features.

"You are remarkable," Ed had whispered in the resort garden. But now his voice seemed to fade from her memory.

Vacillating all morning between the positive and the negative, Sarah informed Sadie that she would be gone for an hour or so. Not wanting to wait for the trolley to come by, she walked briskly down to the Wiltshire Hotel to check the mailbox following the same routine of the last two days. It was too early for a reply but checking couldn't hurt anything.

Stepping out of the bright sun into the dark and slightly dingy lobby of the hotel, she strode confidently over to June York's mailbox. Trembling slightly and holding her breath, she inserted the key and turned it.

There it was! A letter addressed to June York with a return address in New York. Sarah squealed. As the hotel clerk turned to look at her, she grabbed the letter, slammed shut the mailbox and darted out of the lobby.

"You will have to be calmer and act normally if you expect to get away with this subterfuge," she lectured herself.

Where would it be safe to go to read this exciting letter she had now in her possession? She started heading toward a bench in the town square. No, that wouldn't do. One of her acquaintances would come over to say hello and she would have to try and conceal the letter. Maybe go into a restaurant, sit down and order some tea. No, same problem. Someone would want to say hello to her. The solution --- go home and find a totally private place in the house to read it.

Fairly flying down the road, she arrived home in record time. Clutching her pocket book with the precious letter in it, she decided to go up to the third floor which the Gradys had never turned into a ballroom and really only used for storage and utility purposes. She shut the door tightly behind her.

Sitting on the floor, she opened her handbag and removed the letter as though it were made of spun glass. Carefully opening the envelope and unfolding the contents, which numbered three pages, she started reading:

> *My Dearest Darling,*
>
> *How long has it been since I've held you in my arms. I miss you so much. There is no one I can talk to or walk with or dance with that gives me any pleasure. I must see you...I cannot help the lumps and heart tugs, which constantly remind me how empty life is without you. My mind is made up. I can wait no longer. I must see you. I am coming to you unless you positively forbid it, unless you have plans for coming east.*
>
> *My heart and mind are in yours all the time and cannot be put anywhere else in this life...*
>
> *Your one and only lover, Ed*

The letter went on to encourage her to come to New York or let him know where and when she could get away for a trip so they could meet. Sarah read and reread the letter, first laughing then crying, so excited that she wanted to scream to quiet her emotions.

When Sarah finally composed herself and came down from the third floor, the grandfather clock chimed three. William had invited several friends over for dinner, which meant it was time for Sarah to put the finishing touches on the evening's activity. Checking the table and noticing that Sadie had again set the silverware incorrectly beside the plates, she began placing the silver pieces in their correct position. The phone rang and Sadie was nowhere to be seen so Sarah answered, "Hello."

As usual the connection was not clear, but she distinctly heard Ed say, "Hello, Sarah."

Sarah couldn't find her voice.

"Can you hear me, Sarah?"

She managed a soft, "Yes."

"Can you speak freely for a moment?"

Another soft, "Yes."

Ed's strong voice came distinctly through the static on the line, "I received your notes and you have made me the happiest man on earth. I have been terribly distraught thinking I would never see you again. I thought my longing to see you was a one-sided desire. Now I know you are anxious to see me as well. I wrote to you at the hotel but I wanted to take a chance on hearing your voice over the telephone."

Telling herself that Ed should never know how insecure she had been about their relationship, she tried to hide how happy he had made her, but her words had a mind of their own.

All modesty aside, she excitedly blurted out, "I want to see you, Ed. I will plan to go somewhere without William and maybe you can join me. I'll write you my plans."

Ed's voice began to cut in and out and then the line went dead, but Sarah knew now that he was as anxious to see her as she was to see him.

That evening dinner with the Grady's friends was torture for Sarah, although she was her usual charming self. Her one objective for the evening was to get through it and find time to be alone to plan how to get away and be with Ed. Happily the friends decided to make an early departure. Sarah told William she was going upstairs to read awhile before bed, which was not unusual for her. Giving her a quick kiss on cheek, he mumbled that she had been particularly fetching during the evening and had impressed their guests.

He watched her moving gracefully up the stairs, enjoying the thought that this beautiful creature was his wife. How happy she had been lately, how like her former self, this charming, engaging, passionate woman he had been determined to make his in Chicago.

As he stood in the reception hall, he took a rare moment to observe the room before him. He remembered what it had been like when they first finished building this magnificent house and how excited they had been to own it. They had searched long and hard for wall sconces that looked like lanterns and displayed the proper Chinese flavor, as well as the matching chandelier hanging down from the second floor ceiling. He noted the elegant, thick, Persian rug on the floor with the aqua marine and brown colors matching the wallpaper perfectly. When he remembered the dissension they had in picking out that canvas for the wall, he couldn't help smiling because Sarah later admitted that she loved it even though they decided upon his choice. Before they moved in, Sarah had parked herself in an unladylike fashion on the bare floor here in this hall and cried profusely. Thinking she was sad, he couldn't imagine how their beautiful new home could make her so unhappy. It was on this day that he realized Sarah cried on every occasion and, at this time, the tears she was shedding were tears of joy.

As he thought of her in this moment, longing overtook him. He was really terribly in love with Sarah and wished that he had more time to be with her. He mulled over the thought that they should get away again and he should not spend so much time on business, but because he loved her, he owed her his success.

Sarah could feel him watching her climb the stairs and sensed that he was pleased with her. She enjoyed his compliments and was happy to see him content with her for the first time in a long time, but she knew she could survive a life without Ed no longer. She took each step before her with ease.

After letting down her hair and putting on a nightgown, Sarah perched her lanky body on the window seat in the sitting room and grabbed a book so she would appear to be reading. Inside the pages she placed a train schedule, saved a while ago when she was planning an excursion to Chicago. The schedule listed trains all over the country, giving her what was needed to plan a trip with Ed. Concentrating on places to go, she did not notice William coming into the room. Seeing his wife curled up reading, looking so lovely, he sat down on the seat beside her and took the book away intending to kiss her. The train schedule fell on the floor. William bent over and picked it up.

"Are you planning a trip? I thought you were reading," he asked.

Detecting nothing but inquisitiveness on his part, Sarah decided to take advantage of the situation.

"I was reading but started thinking I really need to go shopping to get my fall wardrobe in shape. Instead of Chicago, I think I would like to go to New York this year. Since you are expecting a promotion, I need to upgrade my appearance to be more striking. I could take June with me and, besides buying some outfits that would make those gray, old country club ladies smile at me for a change, and we would have a gay time going to the theater."

That last reference to the envious country club ladies struck a note with William as he envisioned his wife being the hit of the social season. The Gradys had been listed in the 1914 social register of Decatur for the first time and William wanted to make certain their standing in the community remained at its peak. William could see the wisdom of a New York shopping trip for Sarah. Her new wardrobe would ensure social success.

"It would be nice if June could go with you, or if you want to wait until next month I think I could go with you," said William thoughtfully.

Sarah managed a rather subdued response, "I don't want to take up your time helping me decide on the green dress or the blue one. That job rather suits June than you. I'll finish checking the train schedule and to-morrow I'll check with June to see if she is free to go with me."

William went to bed thinking of his promotion instead of the kiss he had wanted to give his wife. Sarah remained perched on her window seat, elated and relieved to have her plans set so effortlessly. It had been so easy. She was too excited to feel guilty, and besides, there was no turning back now.

"I still can appease William. All he wants is to succeed in business, and I can help him with that as I always have."

Counting on June to help her, she dreamed that within a few days she would see Ed's face, watch his easy gait as he walked into the room, and hear his clear strong voice.

"Yes," she thought, "this is what I must do."

The next morning Sarah almost shoved William out the door on his way to work saying she had many chores to do that day. As soon as he was out of the driveway she called June.

Hardly noticing the connection was bad, she said, "June, meet me at the library. I have to talk to you."

Complying with her friend's wishes, June met Sarah in the large, serene, reading room at the Carnegie library. Sarah began telling her tale in a very low voice as they sat at one of the quiet tables.

"I have fallen in love with one of William's good friends," Sarah whispered.

"I can't hear you speak up a bit," June whispered back, eyebrows furrowing.

Several ladies at a nearby table turned and observed Sarah closely as if to say, "Did we hear you correctly?"

Not wanting to repeat her words, Sarah took a piece of paper and wrote, *I said I'm having an affair with a friend of William's.*

June leaned in closely to Sarah and said, "You are teasing me."

Sarah spilled the whole story to her friend. And at first June was reluctant to get embroiled in the scheme.

"You are playing at a very risky game, Sarah. Men get away with these things all the time, but--" June stopped, and looked at Sarah's wide eyes and hands that held tight her own in a desperate plea. Her friend needed her.

"Oh, alright," June continued, "if they can do as they please why should we play by their stipulations? Let us have an adventure then. I will help."

The ladies planned their trip. June, who was single, felt Sarah's excitement and soon found she was looking forward to something a little dangerous. It was decided that June actually would go to New York with her and they would get two adjoining hotel rooms, which would allow Sarah privacy. June also suggested she could buy some clothes for Sarah so William would never be the wiser and Sarah would be free to spend the whole time with Ed. Sarah sent a telegram to Ed at his club saying she would arrive in New York the following Thursday on the 2:30 p.m. train from Chicago and would be staying until the next Monday, and asking Ed what hotel they should book. Feeling the giddiness of youth, Sarah went over the details of their plan coming to the conclusion that it was fool proof. All she needed now was a telegram from Ed saying he would meet her and at what hotel; then her dream of being with her true love would be a reality.

Up early again the next morning, Sarah planned her busy day. There was a dinner dance at the club in the evening and she was chairing a lunch meeting of the club's women golfers to change some of the rules for women players, but the rest of the day was hers. She needed to check the mail box at the hotel for Ed's reply to her telegram and was so sure that Ed would be happy about her plans that she started packing her trunk.

Hopping on the streetcar later that day, she rode downtown to check the hotel box and found the expected telegram. Ed stated that he would call for her at the Biltmore.

One of the newest hotels in New York, the Biltmore was attached to Grand Central Station making the transition from the train absolutely painless. That thought pleased Sarah who had heard much discussion about this new hotel and the "Kissing Room," so called because the lobby was right in the same place where the train boarded and everyone kissed "hello" or "good bye" in this spot.

Also, she had heard different people talk about meeting in New York City "under the clock" at the Biltmore, as a popular landmark to reunite with their party. Going to the hotel was not as thrilling as seeing Ed, but she was excited to stay there.

In the postal box beneath the telegram she was thrilled to find a long letter from Ed. She raced home to be alone to read it. Snuggling into the old chair she had placed on the third floor of her house, she lovingly opened the long letter, smoothing out the pages as she began to read:

My Darling,

A beautiful day and a beautiful letter awaited me. Hadn't the inclination to play golf – so stole away to write to the light of my soul this P.M.

Tonight am going to see President Wilson again. I will be at the banquet at the Waldorf described in the enclosed. It will be interesting. I remember as a youngster the original dedication of the Statute of Liberty. President Cleveland was then the stellar luminary.

In the quiet of this beautiful club I have been reading over your last letter–. It will never be destroyed except by you or my executors. You, my darling, are my all as I have repeatedly said – there is nothing more for me but you. You are my Beacon light and without you to live for - well, for example, I pictured the happiness I might experience if I again visited a certain hallowed (for me) spot – but in the next thought – I realized that without sweetheart it would be torture – what you mean to me is beyond my power of expression and how happy I am to know that you in turn love me so...

I Do, I Do, Your, Ed

The next few days passed like a whirlwind. Sarah received a letter from Grandmother Elwood stating that Sam was going to arrive in Decatur on the train in a week and spend the summer with her and William.

William would be pleased. Having no children of his own, he enjoyed being a father to Sam. During each of Sam's previous visits, William had been very attentive to both Sam and his mother, and Sarah had already been planning Sam's summer activities. She determined that he would become a good golfer this season if he could be persuaded to spend time with her at the country club. Many of her acquaintances had children about Sam's age so he shouldn't lack for companions. All things considered, the summer should be wonderful. Sarah deliberately pushed Ed out of her mind for the moment and enjoyed the thought of Sam coming, and luckily he wasn't due in Decatur until after she got back from New York.

During the dinner party that night Sarah was the most perfect mate William could ever have hoped for. Her blonde-brown hair was fine and shiny, pulled back into a proper bun, but promising softness that the style contradicted. Her red dress was draped perfectly over her tall and slender figure and her eyes had a brightness and depth to them that was almost mesmerizing. Every male attendee at dinner reacted to Sarah's appearance and euphoric mood and William praised her over and over again.

After the meal, Sarah wandered alone out onto the veranda to get some fresh air and it was almost comical to see how many men followed her outside.

"This," thought William as he watched the parade, "is the downside of having such a beautiful wife."

But he knew Sarah was not impressed by any of their attentions; she took herself more seriously than that. Yet, he couldn't help but wonder what was causing the upswing in Sarah's disposition and attitude.

CHAPTER 9

The Biltmore Hotel

New York, New York Summer 1915

William kissed Sarah good-bye as he left for work and told her that James would take June and her to the train station. Wishing that Sarah were a little more money conscious, he told her to enjoy her stay at the Biltmore, but to pay attention to the bills she would be incurring since the Biltmore was a presidential hotel and very expensive. William said he did not want her spending money needlessly. His comments miffed Sarah because she seldom used his money on items for herself. In her opinion, the clothes she bought and money she spent on country club activities were not necessarily because she wanted them, but were usually things that he felt she should do or buy to enhance his social standing. Feeling a little guilty because of the purpose of her trip, she said, "I can use my own money if you would feel better about it."

William quickly replied, "Oh, no, Sarah. You deserve this trip. Go and have a great time."

"And that's what I hope to do," she thought.

June slept well on the train, but Sarah could hardly shut her eyes. It only took the better part of two days to get to New York but it seemed like a lifetime to Sarah. She read three books while traveling, knowing that Ed would be up on the latest offerings in the literary world and it was such fun discussing them with him.

Finally the train pulled into the station. Easily finding a porter to take their trunks, the ladies entered an elevator that took them to the magnificent lobby of the Biltmore. The wide marble stairs leading to the balcony and sparkling chandeliers hanging from the high dome, and the size of the building were more than they expected. Checking into the hotel was a quick procedure and then they were escorted to their rooms, which were large and luxurious. Sometimes the actual rooms in hotels were not up to the standards of their lobby, but the Biltmore didn't disappoint. June told Sarah to try and get a little nap while waiting for Ed's call and to not worry about her because she could entertain herself in New York. Sarah heeded her advice and slept until the room phone rang.

"Meet me under the clock in the lobby," said Ed, "right now if you can. We can have tea."

Sarah took about one minute to freshen up and dashed for the elevator that took her to Ed. Seeing him standing under the clock, she noted how strange it was that she didn't feel the least bit uncomfortable or awkward with him, reacting as though they had only been apart a few hours instead of several months. When they met, they simply held hands for a few minutes and stared at each other. Suggesting that they go into the courtyard and have tea, Ed finally led her out of the lobby. What they said at tea or what they did not say was totally irrelevant to both of them. Finally, Sarah suggested they go up to her room and plan their activities for the next few days. The lovers rushed to their haven.

Several hours later they decided to go down the street for dinner at a small family restaurant Ed knew. Here they talked and did plan their activities that included taking June to dinner and the theater the next night and touring the art museum. Ed said he was available for the following three days because Florence was already in Maine for the season with the children and his business in the summer months allowed him a bit of freedom.

Upon their return to the hotel Sarah insisted that Ed stay with her for the duration of the trip saying, "I don't want to spend one minute of my time without you."

Their evening was spent walking in the courtyard and talking. Sarah's desire to hear Ed's perspective on the war and the Lusitania issue left her asking him question after question. Ed related that he had had dinner with Wilson after the incident and the president was adamant about doing anything he could to remain out of the war, and even though he had sent strong rhetoric to Germany, he was intent on keeping peace for the United States. Sarah expressed her opinion that we needed to go overseas immediately and fight until Germany was defeated.

Ed listened to her and simply said, "You Republicans will get us into big trouble yet. I hope Woodrow sticks to his guns – no pun intended. Oh, and by the way, Sarah, let me tell you something our president has done that you will approve of. He just signed into law the Rocky Mountain National Park Act that has made it our tenth national park. You once told me one thing you desired to do was ride Midnight in the Rocky Mountains. Now it will be preserved until you can make your dream come true. Actually, I hope to make all your dreams come true."

Each of them had many questions on their minds, but the big one was where they stood as a couple. Being soul mates and so much in love, they wanted to be together. Should they leave their respective spouses to be permanently with each other? An answer did not come, so they decided to think about it.

But in the meantime, they pledged their love to each other and made up a prayer to guide their days. They invented symbols to keep the love they shared in the forefront of their lives and vowed to take care of their health so that they would be in good physical shape when they could be together always. For the sake of that vow they decided not to consume any alcohol. Ed said there might be a time when he would have to take a drink just to placate his business associates, but promised never to have over two drinks a week, and Sarah being a proponent of Prohibition, stated she would never imbibe.

Still enjoying the fresh air of the courtyard and both of them hearing the same music that existed only in their minds, they danced.

"Sarah, every time I go to a dance I will sit out two dances that will just be yours. As I sit on the sidelines, I will commune only with you and I will hear the same music that we are dancing to right now."

Sarah willingly promised the same. They danced and made promises to each other for hours. Again, as seemed to be their habit, they had completely lost track of time, but were able to get back to their room just before the dawn.

Next day was a dream for Sarah. Totally absorbed in Ed, she didn't know the rest of the world existed. She glided around the room and declared she knew at last what total happiness was.

By afternoon Ed sat her down in a chair and said, "Sarah we have to talk seriously for a bit. Yesterday we talked about being together forever. My dearest, I would like nothing better than to be with you every minute of every day and night, but I can't as yet. One must live in this world and that requires money. I am well off, but to stay that way, I have to continue working at my job, which is fairly demanding. And then there is my family. Florence and I are not in love the way you and I are, however, we do have two exceptional children together and I don't wish to make life difficult for them. Also, Florence did bring resources to our marriage and I have been the recipient of good things happening because of her family's influence.

"I believe for a while at least we will have to take our moments when we can and try to seize every opportunity to be with each other. We can work toward a permanent relationship though. I do quite a bit of trading in stocks on the curb market and I know you have some of your money invested. Since money is one thing keeping us apart, why don't we open an account and I'll buy stocks so we can start accumulating our profits and build towards our financial freedom. You can let me know what stocks you think we should own and I can navigate the market."

Sarah replied soberly, "I know you are right, and if we are working toward our goal, I guess I can stand it. I can contribute money to buy stocks. Actually I have a fair amount of land that I collect rent from and some land that I could sell if necessary. We must be practical. If I were to divorce William, money would be a problem in the long run and I have a child to think about as well. Sam should be with me right now; we've been separated for so long."

Sarah choked a moment on her guilt, and then regained her composure. "He and William do have a bond and I would not want to break it. After all, Sam has already been away from his birth father for most of his life.

"I can't bear to think of life without you, but I believe it to be very important that for now we keep our secret from William. How can we be sure to do that? --- At this time he must never know you are my lover; after all, you are also his friend."

Ed said in his most practical tone, "I think we have solved the problem of corresponding by implementing your ingenious idea of renting the postal box under a false name, but what if somebody accidentally found one of my letters? I think when you receive any correspondence from me, you must immediately destroy the envelope it comes in and-- oh, I know! I'll use Morse code to disguise some of the things I am saying and people's names. Most people don't know the code and, therefore, they couldn't understand the important parts of the letter."

Sarah joked, "Including me. I don't know Morse code."

"It isn't difficult to learn especially for a bright mind like yours. I'll make up a small sheet of paper with the letters and their corresponding dots and dashes on it so you will be able to translate them into English. It won't take you long to become familiar with the symbols so you don't have to take time translating."

To veil the details in their letters, they created new symbols to utilize in their correspondence. Ed picked up a piece of hotel stationary and drew a couple of symbols on it.

"We'll use this square box to denote William and let's use a zero to signify Florence. We must ensure that no one can tell what we are discussing even if our letters are found," he said.

Sarah considered for a moment then spoke, "And address me as Sallie in the letters, please, my love."

"Sallie?"

"Yes. Sallie is my given name. I felt Sarah more proper so when I attended college, I went by Sarah."

Ed smiled, "My Sallie it is then, my darling mate."

Sarah was fully engaged in the pact they had made.

"We must keep ourselves healthy so when we do get to be together forever, we will still feel young and will be able to enjoy life. Promise me you won't drink, Ed. Alcohol is really not good for anyone. I don't know about

New York, but my friends in Decatur just can't seem to have a good time until they have consumed at least four or five drinks and by that time they don't care about anything, so they have a couple of more drinks. I believe they are ruining their health. Is it that way with your friends?"

"I'm afraid so. A few states have already passed prohibition laws and it's inevitable that more will follow. The closer the government comes to taking liquor away from people, the more they want to consume. I love our pact to keep ourselves healthy for each other. I will swear not to have a drink when I go out. That will be a difficult resolution to keep because drinking is so social that my friends will keep insisting that I participate and will give me a very hard time if I don't join them in their drunken state. However, I will do it for you, my love. Don't you forget, we promised that every time we go out for the evening we will sit out two dances and dream that we are dancing with our special love."

"That's such a wonderful idea. When I am at dances I will be thinking of you all the time anyway, but that will draw us closer together if we do specific dances. Oh, Ed, can we do this? Can we be apart so much? Already I am planning how I can get away to see you again really soon."

Ed replied in a soothing voice, "A love as strong as ours can do anything. Let's get June and go to dinner. I'm so pleased you have such a friend in which you can confide. I can't wait to meet her."

Sarah introduced Ed to June and the two immediately liked each other. June thought if Sarah had to take a lover, she couldn't do any better than Ed. The three of them ate at the hotel because they thought it minimized the chance of them running into anyone they knew. But they were wrong.

No sooner had they sat down at their table than someone called, "Mrs. Grady and Miss Ewing? How lovely to see you both. Imagine running into you in New York."

It was Elizabeth Whitley the wife of Sarah's attorney in Decatur.

Sarah swallowed hard and determined that Elizabeth would not ruin her visit.

"We just came on a little shopping trip. The fall wardrobe must be in order, you know."

As Elizabeth looked inquiringly at Ed, Sarah volunteered, "Elizabeth, this is William's friend Mr. Rockafellow who lives in New York. We met him in Bergdorf's when we were shopping this afternoon and he kindly volunteered to take us to dinner this evening. His family is in Maine for the summer so he was dining alone also."

"How do you do, Mr. Rockafellow. I'm here with my husband. We are going to take in a couple of plays. Well, it was wonderful to see you and nice to meet you Mr. Rockafellow. Enjoy your evening. I'll see you two back in good old Decatur."

And she was gone, leaving Sarah to question if Elizabeth believed her.

June read her mind. "You were wonderfully normal with her, Sarah. Don't give it another thought. But, maybe you should tell the same story to William," June warned.

Thinking how disastrous the meeting with Mrs. Whitley could have been, all three of them were ready to call the evening finished and go back to their rooms, leaving part of their meal on the table. The rest of the long weekend went by without incident. Sarah and Ed were deliriously happy and, if possible, fell more in love as each moment passed. Ed promised to do his best to be available in the future at any time Sarah could get away from William. He also pledged to write several times a week and wanted her to do the same. After many assurances, kisses, and a few tears on Sarah's part, the ladies were on the train headed back to the reality of Decatur, Illinois.

Once home she found William was terribly glad to see her and in quite a good mood. Gathering her courage, she realized now was the time to tell him her story about Ed. Hoping she sounded very nonchalant, Sarah recounted how she had met his friend Ed while she and June were shopping and he had invited them to have dinner with him at the hotel.

William's mind was unquestionably elsewhere, "How nice for all of you since Ed's family was out of town. But, I have some news for you, Sarah. It's good news. While you were in New York, the company had a meeting and made it official, I am now Secretary of Faries Manufacturing Company. This is what you and I have been working towards for a long time."

Sarah responded with a kiss and an affectionate hug saying, "You certainly deserve it. No one in Decatur has worked harder than you."

She felt a little sense of pride in William, but at the same time resented that virtually none of the credit would go to her. Maybe now William would let her undertake more of her own activities and less of his entertaining.

William was very social. Sarah called him a social activist because he had been a charter member of all of the large clubs and organizations in Decatur. He facilitated the building of the fishing club, on which he worked later to turn into South Side Country Club; he helped grow the Country Club of Decatur and was a founder of the Sunnyside Golf Club. He was President of the Decatur Club, a director of the Chamber of Commerce, a member of the Elks Club and a Mason. These club activities, along with the time he spent taking care of his business, kept him from paying any attention to Sarah's needs and were the reason he needed her to do his entertaining and take care of all his home affairs. Every businessman in Decatur knew and liked "Bill" Grady. Sarah wondered why she called him "William" when the rest of the town called him "Bill".

Three days after Sarah arrived home from New York, she retrieved a letter from Ed in her postal box at the hotel. She adored his letters and he was so faithful about writing, but, so was she. On the train home from the big city, she had written him a long letter.

Still taking his correspondence to the third floor room in her house to read, she opened the envelope carefully.

> *My Darling,*
> *Have been out twice in the last week -- one to the ball, and two to a theatre and restaurant dance, the ball was the emptiest, flattest thing that I ever attended and right gladly did I keep my vow (to not drink and to dedicate two dances to my love)and do exactly as I said I would. It was voted a stupid affair anyway. So just imagine what it was to me. Last night a friend from Detroit arrived and hustled us to*

the theatre (Century) and then to Healey's new restaurant. I did just a quarter of a dance and no more, - hadn't the heart for it – it was just nothing plus torture. So you see it is the Soul Mate that my nature is calling for and all else is mere nothing.

Epons is my companion at the dinner tonight, so at least I will have intellectual male companionship and may enjoy myself.

Just read a very interesting passage from a book called "The Passing of a Great Race". The story was about America being the melting pot of the world – and the emigration of South and East Europeans is blotting out the Northern races. That the Northern or light complexioned races have always been the fighting or defensive races and proven it by showing in all our wars like the Civil War, Spanish, and more recent Texas troubles – when the call for troops would come and they would march away and observers would notice that in the ranks of the passing troops a preponderance of the light complexioned races would be noticed – while the silent speculation on the sidewalk would be the dark races such as Latins, Slavs, Maggars, Greeks – etc. never fighting always non combative so far as their adopted country was concerned.

It is a fascinating subject but I don't think I am ready to believe it all – because the chap writing it was really arguing for an Aristocracy against a democracy and frankly states that the former should rule the majority. He argues for a restricted education for the masses. He believes in the culture of Aristocracy and is against all short cuts to education for the people. A rather dubious program for our present day ills – don't you think? Am going up to Putnam's Book Store from here and mosey around a little. If I find an interesting book may send it to you.

Darling, send me some more letters and make me hap-
py by sending them.
I'll never tire of them and need them.
Have you started French – send me your first lesson.
The pouch is my great comfort.
With oceans of love and myriad of kisses – Am as ever
and more so,

Your devoted and loyal,
I Do, I Do

Sarah held the letter tightly in her hands and reread it. Ed's letters made her feel so close to him and she could imagine his life almost on a daily basis. It was exciting to her that he spent time with President Wilson and other men of prominence. Not only did he declare his undying love for her, but also he always discussed ideas he absorbed from books he read and shows he saw. He obviously enjoyed receiving her gift. It was just a tobacco pouch but it gave Sarah pleasure to know that he loved it and kept it near to him. Sarah loved receiving his letters, but now she was arranging to again see him in person.

CHAPTER 10

Samuel Webster Elwood

3 Millikin Place Summer 1915

ONCE BACK HOME Sarah put the memories of her wonderful trip aside and began preparing for Sam's arrival. She was a bit nervous because Sam was now sixteen, almost grown, and she hadn't seen him for almost a year. She knew he had changed, but how?

Both of the Gradys went to meet Sam's train. As they waited, William lightheartedly announced plans to take Sam to his fishing club saying he guessed most country boys liked to fish and be outside. Sarah nervously took her gloves off and on. It wasn't often that she was edgy, but she wanted to have an excellent relationship with Sam and she felt uninformed about sixteen year old boys. What foods would he like to eat now? Would he like to go fishing with William? Will I even recognize him?

The train chugged and puffed slowly to a noisy stop and the passengers began disembarking. Older women, businessmen and a young girl stepped down from the train, but no young boys. All of a sudden Sarah saw him. He seemed tall for a sixteen year old, slender, carried himself well and was very handsome, and easy for Sarah to spot because he looked just like her former husband. Tears immediately welled up in her eyes and the whole of her adult life flashed before her: her first husband's infidelity, leaving Sam when he was a baby, allowing Grandma Elwood to raise him after her divorce. She had missed most of this beautiful child's life.

Sarah reflected, "If only my father had been alive things would have been different. He would have made sure that the correct things were done, whatever that should have been, and he would have seen to it that Sam stayed with his mother." Sarah struggled desperately to control her emotions. By the time she reached Sam and gave him a big hug, she was her usual composed self.

All three of them were excited. Sarah soon forgot all her misgivings as Sam had a very friendly and natural personality. He really hadn't changed much since she had seen him, yet he was definitely more grown up. Sam showed enthusiasm about William's invitation to his fishing club.

"I love to fish. There's a pond on the farm and I go there a lot, but my catch is limited. I'll bet you have different kinds of fish here. City fish," Sam joked.

And to his mother's suggestion that she improve his golf game, he said, "The only chance I have to play golf is when I'm here. I play baseball with some fellas in Colo, but we don't have a golf course. Am I going to stay here after the summer is over? Grandma Elwood hinted at that."

Sarah replied, "I hope that will be the case, Sam. You know I've always wanted to have you with me."

"I wasn't sure," said Sam.

Sarah glanced quickly at Sam trying to ascertain what he had meant by that reply, but he had turned away and was happily gathering his luggage. She decided to ignore his response and concentrate on the summer ahead when both Gradys could reconnect with Sam.

Mondays and Saturdays William took time off to take Sam to his fishing club. They both loved to fish. Sitting on the soft green grass together in the warm sun with no one else around gave the two of them an opportunity to bond. They did nothing except listen to the sound of the water splashing against the bank and gaze at the clouds in the blue sky. Sometimes on Saturdays they even spent the night in the clubhouse.

On one such afternoon, both men silent in the peaceful breeze, Sam declared in an uncharacteristic burst of emotion, "William, I consider you my real father."

With that declaration William could hardly hide his joy. He considered Sam his son, as well. William clapped the young man on the back with pride, knowing that Sam was the legacy intended for him.

On Tuesdays, Thursdays, and Fridays, Sarah took Sam to the country club and they played golf and swam. Sarah was a good teacher and Sam a good pupil so he was soon an above average golfer. They enjoyed their time together but Sarah also began introducing him to other teenagers. He seemed to fit in well. No one who did not know Sam's background would have said he was a farm boy. He picked up his mother's poise and charm easily and was very intelligent. Wednesdays and Sundays were the days that Sarah truly looked forward to.

She thought, "These days when we are just at home together are what I missed when Sam was young."

They had time to talk and Sam asked many questions about his father and Sarah's side of the family. But Sarah told him nothing that would disparage his father or the Elwood family.

Sam's questions about her family prompted Sarah to realize that her mother hadn't seen Sam since he was a baby and she herself hadn't been to Minnesota for about four years. Even though she was not excited about sharing her time with Sam, he deserved to go visit his other Grandmother. It was time for a trip, and Sam seemed excited about the idea. He had never been to Minnesota, or seen the town where he was born in South Dakota.

The train ride north was really an interesting time for Sarah as Sam continued asking questions about her family, and he was old enough to understand many things she had not previously told him.

"Why did my grandfather come to this country? Do you love this country or Norway more? Was Grandfather Petersen rich? Sarah was happy to answer his incessant questions until he came to the important one. "Why did you and my father get a divorce?"

"Well, Sam we didn't have the same values and interests as we had when we married." said Sarah as she immediately turned the conversation to an unrelated subject.

"Do you read many books? I haven't noticed you looking at the ones I put in your bedroom."

The question about their divorce basically went unanswered by Sarah, but the rest of the Petersen family history was explained.

Grandmother Petersen and Sarah's brother Peter, who had driven a horse- drawn buggy to greet them at the station, met them as they alighted from the train in Brookings, South Dakota. As they rode to Grandmother's house, Sarah mused that horses were still better transportation than automobiles. Sam enjoyed going through the small town of Verde as it reminded him of Colo, Iowa near the farm where he grew up. When Sarah's father died, her mother had moved from the old family farm where Sarah grew up. She now lived in an unimposing three-bedroom farmhouse at the edge of Verde, not really very far from Pete who lived on the old farm with Sarah's sister, Petrina.

Sam was very much at home in the surroundings; however, Sarah was ashamed of herself because she was not comfortable in this rather primitive atmosphere. Her present life and environment were very stylish and elegant while her family and old home were on the opposite end of the spectrum. She tried to remind herself, "This is who you are and where you came from." But it didn't help. Her mother was kind and very happy to see her, but she sensed Sarah's discomfort and was disappointed by it.

While Sarah and Sam were visiting Grandmother in her house in Verde, they saw all of the family who still lived close by; Sarah's sister Nina and her husband also lived in town, while older sister Petrina and brother Pete who were both unmarried ran the farm. Pete, who was just four years older than Sam, took him around to meet some of Sarah's old neighbors in Elkton and to see the house where Sam was born. Sam loved the tour and was enjoying himself immensely.

Sarah stayed at home with her mother and was forced into having conversations that were a bit uncomfortable for both of them since they had nothing in common except for the fact that they were related. Sarah had always been close to her father, but never took the opportunity to get familiar with her mother. She was cordial to her, but did not know her. As mothers do, Grandmother Petersen tried to impart wisdom and morals to Sarah.

"Sarah, it's so nice to see you with Sam. I can't imagine why you haven't taken him to live with you all these years. I guess you were wise to divorce Charles, but I think I would have stayed with him and made sure that he behaved himself; then the family does not get broken up. Why didn't you take Sam from the Elwoods?"

Swallowing both her anger and her guilt, Sarah responded patiently to her mother's judgments which Sarah realized came from love not blame.

"I wanted to be sure Sam had a safe home before he lived with me full time. Circumstances seemed to be against us. I feared to take him when I was alone and then when I married William... and well, we were too busy building his career. I always thought we would bring Sam to Decatur in a couple of months, but that never happened. I believed I was doing what was best for him."

Her mother drew a breath, and replied.

"My advice is you must be a good moral person. Love your husband and your son. And you must never forget where you come from."

"I'm trying to do just that, Mother," She replied softly.

Sarah and Sam stayed for two days; then everyone came to see them off on the train. Sarah was glad they had made the trip as she had been feeling guilty about not seeing her mother, sisters, or brother for a long time. Sam happily chatted about their visit all the way home. Sarah knew it was her fault that she had felt like a stranger to her family, but after her father's death, she had known that Minnesota was no longer home. Though she admired her family for what they did, she could no longer be a farmer.

Back in Decatur, it soon became apparent that everyone loved Sam; older adults, middle aged, and younger people. He almost immediately had "oodles" of friends his own age and yet was still spending quite a bit of time with Sarah and with William. He seemed so perfect that Sarah questioned whether or not anyone could be that good.

Her question was answered one hot evening in July as she looked out the window in her sitting room and saw Sam staggering up the street on his way home from a friend's house. He had obviously been drinking and Sarah confronted him as soon as he got in the house.

Sarah's voice was harsh and disapproving, "What have you been up to, Sam? You have had too much to drink! And you shouldn't be drinking any liquor at all," Sarah stepped closer to him and not only smelled the alcohol but also smoke. "And you have been smoking as well."

"Don't spoil my evening, Mother. It's no big deal. Bob, Frank, and I do this almost every evening," retorted Sam, realizing as soon as the words were out that he had confessed to something that he didn't mean to.

Making matters worse, he blurted out, "Why are you so concerned about me now? I am old enough to make my own decisions."

Telling herself he was trying to justify his behavior by putting the blame on her, Sarah refused her guilt for a change and simply said, "Go to bed, young man. We'll deal with this tomorrow when you will be feeling better."

Sam bowed rather saucily and took off for his bedroom. Sarah was devastated. This was a side of Sam she had not seen before and was not prepared for. As wonderful as the summer had been and as close as she had felt toward him recently, she acknowledged that she really didn't know him. Very little of her time had been spent with him over the years. She had gone twice to Iowa to visit him on the farm, but those visits weren't satisfactory because Grandmother Elwood was closer to him than she was and Sam treated Sarah as the visitor that she was. She had sent him gifts, written to him, but only on holidays had he come to Decatur to visit and each time for no longer than a week. Sam's father never had time for him. Charles visited his family farm once in a while, but Sarah knew he didn't go often and, when he did it, was only for a day. Sarah had to come to grips with the fact that she had been an absentee mother and Charles an absentee father. Though she loved Sam, she felt she had had very little influence on his character. He was Grandmother Elwood's boy and Sarah had missed his growing years.

William came in late from a business meeting only to see his wife scowling.in the semi-darkness of the library.

"Is something wrong?" he asked.

And Sarah poured out the story along with her disappointment and worry while he listened attentively.

William leaned back and placed his hands on the arms of the chair as he began, "I am so sorry Sarah but I believe that Sam does indeed have a wild streak. After all, a soft-spoken Grandmother who was fairly elderly raised him. She taught him to show love, which is a wonderful quality, but she did not teach him the discipline that he needs to be a successful adult. His father has indicated he wants Sam to go to college and I don't think given his present circumstances he will be ready to go in two years. I have a suggestion that you won't like, but nevertheless give it some consideration. I think Sam should go to a Military School. There's a first-class one in Indiana. It is a very prestigious school, which would teach him the discipline he needs and also help him to get accepted at a first-rate college."

Sarah felt her world crashing, "Send him away – again?"

William seeing the shock and confusion on her face continued, "Since Sam really doesn't have a full time father around him I feel he has gotten wild and I don't know if I can solve this problem. I think he needs the stern discipline of a father every day. I think you can help, but I don't know if you can turn his thinking around in another month. Sam is such a loving and outwardly obedient boy, but I now see in him a stubborn streak that I don't know how to handle."

She knew William was right, and, as a woman, she was not equipped to give Sam what he obviously needed. She loved him so much and wanted to ensure his success as an adult. If that meant sending him away again, she would agree for his sake; despite her feelings, she would do what was best for him.

"Please, William, you talk to him in the morning and I will write his father a letter to try to convince him Sam should go to military school. Actually I think Charles might be for it. I know he wouldn't want full time responsibility of Sam."

The following morning William confronted a sleepy Sam in his bedroom. "Wake up. You have to learn if you drink too much alcohol in the evening you still have to be up and going in the morning."

"Mother told you?"

"Of course she did. I may not be your father by birth but I think of myself in that capacity and furthermore, I care what happens to you. You are not of an age where you can hold your liquor and besides you must realize that to be successful in life you must do everything in moderation. For the rest of the summer you will have a curfew. We will insist that you are in the house by nine o'clock every evening – sober."

Reacting to William's rather harsh tone, Sam only said, "Yes, sir."

"Also, I have to tell you we are considering sending you to Howe Academy this fall. It's a military school in Indiana with a really terrific reputation for helping get their students into first-class colleges. You do want to go to college and learn a profession?"

Sam nodded his head in agreement.

With William's discipline and Sarah's determination to make up for lost time, Sam did behave himself for the rest of the summer, and he and Sarah continued to bond like mother and son should. Sam was not averse to going to military school. He saw it as an opportunity to become more independent, and, even though he loved his Grandmother Elwood, he did not want to go back to the farm, especially since he had had a taste of living a faster paced life in the city. Sarah wrote Charles and Clara a very business-like letter describing Sam's behavior over the summer and the need she felt to have Sam in a disciplined environment. Stating she and William would be willing to pay half of his expenses, she asked for his financial participation in military schooling. A letter came back almost immediately from Clara stating they would be happy to pay half of his expenses and they concurred that military school would be best for Sam.

During this time Sarah had been writing religiously to Ed and he to her sometimes four times a week. In her letters to Ed, she told him about Sam's exploits and her concerns about him. Her thoughts of Ed were constant, but Sam was taking up most of her time and effort; therefore, she made no plans to see Ed. Even William had seen fit to require less of her this summer so she could spend her time with Sam. Week after week she relied on the postal service to carry her words to Ed and dutifully the hotel box delivered his replies. Sometimes Ed would send a telegram, faithfully he sent his letters, and once in a while he chanced calling her on the phone. The phone was risky, but if William answered Ed could always make him think the call was for him.

A week before the Gradys were to take Sam to school, Ed did call and William happened to answer. The result of that conversation was William asked Ed and his family to join Sarah and him at French Lick in Indiana after they dropped Sam off at school.

William hung up the phone and said, "Guess what? Ed and his family are going to join us at French Lick after we take Sam to school. We should really have a good time with them, and Ed and I can even get a little business done."

Inwardly, Sarah cringed. How in the world could she spend several days with Ed and not be able to see him alone or be with him? She had not seen him all summer and now this. She said, "Sounds like you are planning to drive Sam to school. Are you sure that is a good idea? And who is driving? You don't like to drive, so it will be me. You can be certain the car will have some kind of a problem on the way. I think it's easier if we just put him on the train," Sarah reasoned to William, desperate to find some way to spoil the plans he had made.

William thought for a moment and then replied, "You are right. I probably would rather you drove than me and that's not fair. Sam is independent. Let's allow him to go by himself on the train. We can also take the train to French Lick to keep our engagement with the Rockafellows."

Sarah nodded in resignation as she thought of Ed awaiting her in Indiana.

"Alright, William. An engagement with the Rockafellows would be wonderful."

The week flew by. Sarah shopped with Sam and helped him pack. In spite of their difficulties, the summer had been the nicest time she had ever spent with Sam. For his part he had loved being in Decatur and he had gotten to know his mother. Wanting his independence, he was excited to go away to school. When the Gradys put him on the train, he was reflective but in high spirits.

"Thanks for a great summer, Mom and William. I guess I caused you some trouble and I'm sorry for that. I want to be on my own and I think this school will be fun. I'll miss you, but I'll be home at Christmas." Sam seemed to be giving himself a pep talk before he stepped on board. At the last minute he leaned over to Sarah, gave her an uncharacteristic hug and jumped on the train.

When Sam was out of sight, Sarah started sobbing. Both William and she were depressed watching the train pulled out of the station knowing that the next time they saw him he would be a young man not a child. As they headed home, Sarah consoled herself with the thought that Sam would still be able to spend his vacations in Decatur. But Sam's summer in Decatur was over and Sarah had to get ready to go to French Lick and be with Ed from a distance.

Before leaving for Indiana, Sarah received another letter from Ed:

> *My Precious Sweetheart,*
>
> *Please don't despair at the thought of being close to me while William and Florence are present. We will have to be cautious, but we WILL find time to be alone together. We must back up hope with deeds. We must be willing to work for what we want – we must definitely plan to have what we want and we mustn't be faint hearted about it either.*
>
> *When I fell in love with you and realized it --- It was your prayer that decided me -- you were the one Nature intended for me and you are right about my being your chum lover. As long as you are in my presence – my soul seems satisfied and I am content, but when you change suddenly I am at a loss to know what to do or say and then it is hard to be natural. Let us take the difficulty of being with our spouses at French Lick in stride, attempt to be natural, and think only of the time I know we can be together-- just the two of us.*
>
> *I hardly know what to say about Sam. Youth must have its fling, and sending him to military school should be just the thing for him. I'll write later about him.*
>
> *Would give worlds to see you this moment and know how you felt and at the same time I would give you a lovers kiss. I wonder if you know what it means to be alone in New York – the temptations I mean – the visitors to the great city that I must entertain want to see its shady side. For years I have kept out of it by avoiding or excusing*

myself from the society of people seeking excitement on the seamy side of things. This summer I would be under duress again but how happy I will be thinking of you and with your beautiful letters next to my heart. There will be no possible temptations or tempters. Love or rather true love is in my opinion but little understood even among intelligent people. It is made too commonplace a word and becomes hackneyed from misuse. One lesson has been learned by me and this is I will never again scoff at people similarly afflicted as I am and I'll furthermore know how to disseminate between the real and the dross – the wheat and the chaff. Having plighted my troth I can feel for others – and that is what I have learned – but how I preach.

Today my business associates from Omaha were here and we worked all morning. At noon we had a swim in the tank at the University Club. A little more work, then we went to the ball game to see the Cubs play the champions. How I wish you had been with me.

After the game came the real excitement of the day – losing my companions so that I could be alone and commune with you. So here I am alone in my room rereading your letters (six of them) -- packing up and getting ready to leave to meet in a few hours the woman I truly love – my soul mate

I Love You, I do

I am sending an accounting of our stock market purchases. We have been doing very well.

CHAPTER 11

⚜

The Couples' Weekend

French Lick, Indiana Fall 1915

Sarah loved going to French Lick. It was so easy to get there. She could board a train several blocks from her house and get off right at the door of the resort where a bellhop would grab her trunks and take them to her room. The resort was up to Sarah's standards with its extravagant lobby, large and well-appointed rooms and extras like the bowling alley, beautiful golf course, expansive grounds and formal gardens. This year there was a new resort that people were raving about a short walk from French Lick. Sarah had to see the publicized building…. that was it! That's how she could get to be with Ed. Neither William nor Florence liked to walk, so she could get Ed to walk her to West Baden to see the new resort. Sarah was pleased with her plan.

"As Ed says, I must appear to be natural toward him and adoring of his wife. Poor William. He wouldn't understand that Ed and I are meant to be together. He must never find out. But, he has to learn the truth because Ed and I will be together at some point," Sarah argued with herself.

Ed, Florence, and their ten-year old daughter Gwen were already in the lobby when the Gradys arrived. Sarah brushed right past Ed and warmly greeted Florence who responded with a sincere welcome. Florence was not pretty, but she was attractive because she presented herself well, as any well-bred woman would. She seemed kind and had no put-on airs, making her seem natural but not very appealing. As Sarah stood within the group exchanging pleasantries, she assessed every detail of the woman who had captured her beloved. The similarities between Sarah and Florence were almost non-existent even in their physical characteristics as one was rather

87

tall and slender and one was rather short and dumpy. Florence wore her muted brunette hair pulled back severely in an old-fashioned bun, while Sarah's shiny blondish hair was pulled back loosely so that some curls hung softly around her face reflecting the current style.

"We're nothing alike," Sarah mused, pleased with her conclusion.

She then greeted Gwen who immediately seemed to respond to her warm greetings.

"Gwen, I have heard a lot about you, but no one told me what a beautiful young lady you were. Do you think you will enjoy spending a few days at French Lick with us old people?"

"You don't look old and I have plans of my own. For one thing my father says I have to learn to play golf and I know that the resort has activities for young people so I expect to get acquainted with some children my own age. You are very pretty too," chirped Gwen.

Sarah offered her hand formally to Ed and said in a cool tone, "How nice of you to meet us here. I'm sure we all will have a wonderful few days of relaxation."

Their eyes locked briefly and quickly Ed turned his gaze away as he acknowledged Sarah's greeting by giving her hand a slight squeeze as he held it. Dinner and dancing plans were made for the evening and both couples retired to their rooms to prepare for the night's entertainment.

Back in the room William inquired of Sarah, "Is there a problem between you and Ed? You seemed a little tense and slightly cold when you greeted him. He is a good friend and very valuable business contact. I can't have you being at odds with him."

I'll have to be clever at hiding my feelings thought Sarah, but maybe William's astuteness will be just the thing I need to help me through this vacation.

"I'll do my best to impress him while we are here. I have nothing against him. I'll work to keep your friend happy," she replied.

That night, true to her word, Sarah engaged Ed in conversation at dinner and loved it. William was amazed at Sarah's knowledge of the war in Europe, the theater and of several recently written books. Ed and Sarah began to talk about *Of Human Bondage* and soon they both realized there were similarities between that narrative and their own situation. Trying to change the subject Sarah quickly asked if Ed had read *The Good Soldier*. Immediately realizing that book was more sexual and risqué than their first discussion of Somerset Maugham's newest, Ed got Sarah out of the situation by asking her to dance. They hurried onto the dance floor, leaving Florence and William a little befuddled at the dinner table.

Having already had two dances with William, she enjoyed the rest with Ed as Florence seemed content just listening to the music and William was happy that Sarah was charming his friend. Sarah had a wonderful evening as she and Ed had their alone time dancing. Sarah noted how comfortable she was being in Ed's arms and how effortlessly they moved together with the beat of the music. Even though their conversation could not have been overheard out on the dance floor, they were silent, happy to be together without any sound except the music.

Later back in their room William said, "Thank you for engaging Ed this evening, Sarah. I dare say he appreciated the feminine attention."

The next morning Sarah had to sacrifice her golf because Florence did not like to play. She stayed in the dining room and participated in a game of Whist with Florence while Gwen went to a golf lesson and the men played their sport on another Ross designed course. Getting to know Florence was easy. Sarah encouraged her to talk about her trips. "Tell me about your last voyage. I have never been abroad, except of course, I was born in Norway."

"Norway. Near Italy, correct?" inquired Florence.

Knowing how many trips to Europe Florence had taken, Sarah was almost dumbfounded. Trying to simplify the map for her she said, "It's north of France and Belgium."

"I've been to those places, I know. I just never care to bother with the geography of it all."

After several more attempts to discuss Florence's trips, Sarah was amazed to discover that Florence loved to go on ocean cruises, but she knew nothing about the world in which she traveled. Being a world traveler did not come with knowledge of the countries she visited. Also, Florence had no idea which of these countries was involved in the war overseas.

She confided to Sarah, "I'm lonesome. Ed doesn't spend much time at home and I'm really looking forward to this small vacation. He works so hard and I know he does it for us. Now, finally we will be together for a few days."

Sarah swallowed hard and only nodded in response.

After spending the morning with Florence, Sarah's fleeting guilt passed and she thought it was no wonder that Ed spent so much of his time with his club friends who were cognizant of world affairs and no wonder he enjoyed conversing with her because Florence's world was very limited.

When the men returned from golf, Sarah attempted to carry out her plan to be alone with Ed. Brightly she said, "Let's all walk to the new resort, West Baden, and look it over."

As she had anticipated, neither Florence nor William wanted to walk that far. William said, "Why don't you three go. I'll stay here and entertain myself."

Florence suggested, "Sarah, I don't like to walk and that's pretty far away. How about William and I playing cards while you two walkers go to West Baden?"

Ed acknowledged that was a splendid idea, as he wanted to see the new structure that his friends in New York were talking about. So Ed and Sarah walked off alone with Ed complimenting her on her brilliant strategy to get them time alone and Sarah smiling a mischievous smile.

Once out of sight of French Lick, they held hands and enjoyed being together. Ed turned to her as they walked.

"Darling, I wanted to ask if you would mind being a sort of mentor to Gwen. It should be easy because she is very taken with you. Florence loves her children, but doesn't teach them the things I want them to learn. I want Gwen to grow up to be more like you and learn to swim and to play golf. I want her to have a bright positive attitude on her life. You would be a wonderful influence on her. In short, I want another you."

"I'm not sure I can accomplish what you want, but I would be happy to try. She is such a sweet girl and I think we could have fun together. She could spend her summers with us if Florence didn't mind. And maybe some holidays too."

"Thank you, Sarah. It really means a lot to me and I think Florence would be happy about it too."

When they got to West Baden, they were genuinely impressed with the structure. The lobby with an atrium that spanned two hundred feet and a fireplace that burned fourteen-foot logs was more open and grander than anything Sarah had ever seen. Everywhere you looked there was stained glass and brilliantly colored tile. Someone said it took a crew of twenty men three years just to lay the floor tile. The resort had originally been built in 1855 and had been popular because of the health benefits the springs brought to people. In 1901 it had burned to the ground and the rebuilding began a few years later in the image of a European castle. Both Sarah and Ed marveled that something as fine as this building had been completed three years ago and they had never seen it.

After walking the grounds, the couple sat in the ornate wooden chairs in the lobby and pretended to be just another pair of visitors, perhaps honeymooning. As they sat the only words that were spoken by either were "I love you." Finally realizing they had stayed too long, they headed back to reality and their respective spouses.

William met Sarah in the lobby saying in a slightly disgruntled voice, "Where have you been? Florence and I didn't think it would take you this long to view West Baden. You are almost late for dinner. I thought this trip was for us so we could spend time together and I've hardly talked to you since we got here."

Sarah shot back at him, "You were the one who invited the Rockafellows to come with us. And you were the one who encouraged me to be nice to Ed. You can't have it both ways." Sarah hated to feel anger at the moment because she had just had such a wonderful afternoon with Ed and didn't want to spoil the mood, but she knew her secret was safer if she played it this way.

After realizing their error, Ed and Sarah attempted to distance themselves from each other; yet the next afternoon both spouses declined a game of golf, so again they were able to be together. After golf they walked the formal gardens and then sat for a while on a bench. The flora around them, so similar to that which surrounded them on their first evening together, was intoxicating for the pair. Only moments after sitting on the bench, they were embraced, kissing passionately as they both wished they had on that first night.

Suddenly, Ed pulled away from their embrace and Sarah followed Ed's widened eyes to the top of William's head above the bushes. They straightened themselves and in a moment, William had rounded the corner and was standing before the couple.

"Oh, William," said Ed, "sit down with us. This is just a perfect place to enjoy these gardens. We were just commenting on the birds that are in this area. Some of them are very colorful."

William looked a trifle concerned but said, "I really just came to find Sarah. Sarah, I have made plans to have a special dinner with my sweetheart this evening."

Sarah, feeling relieved that their kiss had not been discovered, said, "That is quite thoughtful of you, William."

She turned to Ed but he was standing before she could speak.

"We will probably be gone in the morning before you two are bustling around; so I'll say good bye now. William, wonderful to see you again," Ed said in his easy, charismatic tone.

"Sarah," he finished with a slight nod, already exiting.

As they walked back inside the resort, William said, "I told Florence that Gwen would be welcome to spend time in Decatur with us any time she wanted. She's ten now and at her age I thought it would be good for her to spend time out of the big city environment. Also, Sarah, I do appreciate you spending so much time with Ed."

But to himself he had a fleeting thought. Sarah looked "funny" when he came upon the couple. No, jealousy was not called for. Sarah was just doing what he, her husband, had asked her to do.

"Heaven help me," thought Sarah to herself. "This is getting very complicated."

Dinner that night was indeed special. William had gone to a great deal of trouble to have a romantic dinner with his wife. She looked at William across the table and remembered why she had fallen in love with him. He was handsome and could be very kind and considerate. As of late he had been so focused on his work that he had not taken the time to enjoy Sarah. Yet, when he was away from 3 Millikin Place like this and could just be her William, he could be so loving, so attentive. In these moments he allowed her to be his partner rather than his business asset.

"If he could be like this always," Sarah thought, adding, "I shouldn't resent him so. We both have made many sacrifices for his position; the stress, the perfection have made raw both our nerves."

Sarah went to bed confused. Ed provided the kind of love that only comes along once in a lifetime. However, when she was able to be with the true William, her husband, her partner, she realized she couldn't hurt him this way.

"I do love him," she said with resignation. She had to break it off with Ed.

Back at home in Decatur, Sarah's torment continued. The thought of never seeing Ed again made her angry at the world and gave her that crazy feeling in the pit of her stomach. She loved Ed so dearly and had never experienced this particular emotion when she was with another man, not with Charles and not with William. Ed was hers. She could finish his sentences. She knew just how he would react to news of the day. She knew which plays and books he would like. Giving him up was not an option. But Sarah had an ethical and a practical side. William was her husband whom she had promised to love until "death do us part" and she took her vows seriously, especially after the way she had been treated by Charles. Also, being practical, there was no way at this time that Ed could divorce his wife and marry her and the options for single women were not many. William had been good to Sarah. Yes, he was dictatorial and did demand a superhuman effort from her many times, but mostly he was kind, he helped her with Sam, and he had given her one of the nicest houses in the city. Her life with William should be almost perfect. No matter her feelings for William, for her own betterment she needed to end her liaison with Ed.

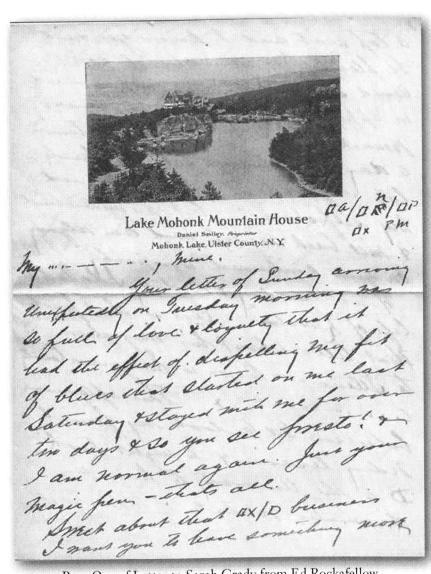

Page One of Letter to Sarah Grady from Ed Rockafellow
Written from Lake Mohonk in 1916

CHAPTER 12

Living for Letters

Decatur, Illinois Winter 1916

Despite Sarah's determination to end the relationship with Ed, each week her postal box favored her with one, two and usually three letters, which she dutifully reciprocated. She rationalized that just writing to him was not harmful. Ed in the meantime was perplexed, as one day he would get a letter stating that she could not go on seeing him, and the next day he would get a letter telling him they needed to put more money in their account so they could be together sooner. Yet, no matter what the state of their affair, they both enjoyed writing to each other.

They had all sorts of codes; the Morse code, one made up for numbers, and symbols they fashioned to refer to their spouses. This subterfuge did not really disguise the writer of the letter, but added to the intrigue of their affair.

The letters also served the purpose of determining which stocks and futures Ed should buy to grow their joint account. Sarah was fascinated by the stock market and expressed interest in having Ed take her down to the curb market the next time she was in New York, knowing she would enjoy the excitement of watching the outside trading. Much of the detail in their letters related to which stocks they should be purchasing. He asked Sarah's opinion before buying or selling and always bought the stocks she suggested as well as those he felt would be profitable.

Ed knew his way around Wall Street; he had been buying stocks and futures for years, but Wall Street was not friendly for the small investors in 1915 when Ed and Sarah opened their account. Competition was fierce.

Bull raids (when everyone is buying) and bear raids (when everyone is selling) were prevalent and investors caught in the middle suffered badly. Ed told Sarah that Wall Street manufactured panics to make money on the clean-up operations that followed. The war was also affecting the market. Because of the unsettled conditions overseas, the markets were closed in the last quarter of 1914, but when Wilson decided not to go to war, investors celebrated and the markets skyrocketed. Ed had caught the swing upward and Sarah seemed to have a real knack for choosing stocks that were going to boom, so in spite of it all, their account was doing splendidly.

In his letters, after the initial declaration of love, Ed would describe the places he was going and the people he was seeing, leaving Sarah totally fascinated. Her life in Decatur was eventful but not on the scale of Ed's.

> *My Sweetheart,*
>
> *What is there about nature that is so mysterious in the sense of where love strikes two people as it has us. My awakening of the soul was over a year ago. I must have been asleep before that – but the spark struck and it has been ignited ever since and yet some scoffers say there is no such thing as love. We can testify to the contrary for never was I more in love than this minute. I am missing you so much. I comfort myself with pictures, letters and mementos of what has happened and then it is that personal effects like a handkerchief or a book or something my loved one has had count for so much. I need more. Send me some little thing - - if only a handkerchief.*
>
> *Some friends arrived this afternoon and took me to a ball game (the Cubs played the Champions) and then to dinner, but I balked at Winter Garden. I wanted to be alone to commune with you and write you. The Winter Garden and its gaudy beauties are as flat to me as stale beer – so instead of seeing The Passing Show of 1916 I am reading over your last seven letters which show me the faith of my*

true love. You call it 'the depth of life'. It is life to know you, but the parting is so long.

I hope William has seen some light and will lessen your burden now that the holidays are over, but I doubt if it will be for long as he does not appreciate you in the right way and is too self-controlling and selfish. You well know how it galls me to know you are a slave to such a tyrannical person. To see you abused as I have is the worst thing I experience.

Went to a private gathering at the White House a few days ago given for Wilson's new bride, Edith. He didn't want a public party when they were married, but decided to have a small celebration after the fact. There were still many people there and the surroundings are always impressive. Our country is blessed to have such a structure for our President to live and entertain in. Edith is not a great beauty, but is substantial looking. She is well bred, intelligent and has a strong personality. I believe she will be an asset to the President.

Save all your love for me as I want it all. Every last atom of it and can't spare any of it for anyone else.
Your Ed, I Do, I Do Do Do

The whole country was wondering what the President's new wife would be like, but Sarah knew. For his part, Ed felt Sarah's letters gave him a pulse on the Western part of the country which helped him sort out the war situation by knowing what most of the American people in that area were feeling. To him the "West" (as he referred to the Mid-West and beyond) was a better barometer of the country's mood than the East was. Sarah also would give him opinions on the books she was reading as well as political matters. She too expressed her undying love much of the time.

Since Ed traveled the country, Sarah never knew where his letters might be coming from. One came from the Illinois Athletic Club in Chicago soon after a business conference, which she and William had attended as well as Ed. At this meeting Sarah and Ed only managed a few minutes alone. Ed wrote:

My Sweet Love & Mate of My Heart,

I have known a few hours of happiness today. Your voice, the letter that awaited me yesterday – for somehow or other after reading your beautiful letter, the most wonderful I ever read, in its simple statement of actual condition & facts pertaining to your affection for me, - it didn't seem true that I had actually seen you since it was written. It seemed as though I had been dreaming.

How selfish I am to be as unreasonable as I was because I thought you didn't want to see me and yet as I wrote you in my last – if your letter had been received before the holidays – my holidays would have been different. – My Sweet – you with your keen analytical mind, and you have such a mind, explained it all – that William would have been suspicious of us if you had come east for the holidays and that you would have given anything to have seen me on New Year's. With your verbal explanation – that you took the obvious for granted and thought I did and that was the mistake. Love insists on dwelling on the obvious and any neglect brings heartaches. If it didn't then would the obvious be commonplace. So love demands its toll, and has its code – as in other things in life that are less vital.

Oh, how I was hurt Sunday night – when you treated me so coldly, but I understand now – for the look in your eyes, even without the verbal explanation cleared it all up and all is forgiven for I know now where your heart is. And then again in your letter you say that something is slowly but definitely forming in the back of your head and I know it portends to our happiness for the future. So may we never again have such a misunderstanding and live definitely for each other for the future.

Tonight I took two men to the theatre and I chose to see "Come out of the Kitchen" because you had seen it and

I enjoyed it very much. Would that I could make love to my sweetheart the way that the hero did & whom you said I resemble.

How easy it would be for me to step back into the military. Monday night I went to a drill of Company I 1st Illinois N. Y. as a guest of its Captain and found myself correcting some mistakes of command given by its officers – It seemed second nature and I haven't drilled in 25 years so I am convinced I have a memory. Thursday afternoon am going to talk to our men and am going to try and do a good job and inspire them if I can – as I used to. Do you know I think I'd have no trouble at all living in the West for I have always been successful in getting along with Western people, where other Easterners in my line have failed. I used to think Southerners were my special forte – but having won the love of a Western Sweetheart – my sectional allegiance, has changed.

Next week will go to St. Louis and Kansas City and then back to Chicago. It will take all of next week until Friday.

Did you read the President's message on World Peace? It is as usual a masterpiece and worth reading.

Darling it is late 2:35, so I will close and go to bed – with a prayer that my beloved will not contract a cold as she did last year and get sick – I want my next visit to be a happy one for us both and not marred by sickness. Here's to the success for your wish when burning the wreath on the log fire the other night and may we be with each other until Mother Earth claims us.

I love you and send kisses

Good night, Ed

You did not give me a haf (handkerchief).

Wear one and give it to me when I see you.

Sarah was ever excited to get Ed's letters; she couldn't give them up. She inevitably retreated to her spot on the third floor of the house and sat in the little chair by the window before she opened the envelope. Divining from this last letter that Ed believed she did not want to see him during the holidays, she was surprised by his sensitivity.

Thoughts trailed through her mind: "Even for Ed this was too emotional. I gave him no reason to think anything like that. He is over perceptive imagining feelings that are not intended... I do so adore that he writes me about his daily activities. It really makes me feel close to him. He almost sounds like he is bragging when talking about the drills he attended, but that's not the Ed I know, so I suspect he was just surprised by how much he remembered..." She had been depressed during the busy Christmas holidays because she wanted to see Ed, but she had the letters.

The two families drew closer together with Ed's daughter Gwen adopting Sarah as a surrogate mother. Gwen came to stay with the Gradys on her school breaks and Ed visited Sam at Howe Military Academy when he was in the area. William and Ed did more and more business together because Ed saw that as a way to see Sarah, even if her husband was with her. After French Lick, Sarah and Ed saw each other at two more business conferences during the year and were able to sneak a few minutes each time to be alone. 1915 had been a substantial beginning for their love affair, but Sarah was trying hard not to continue their relationship. This locked Ed in perpetual turmoil. He wrote:

> *My dearest darling,*
>
> *Before me are two letters –about four days apart. One is full of love, life & hope & made me the happiest I have been in months. The second received today crumpled me up so that in addition to being sick I feel like the meanest dog living. One phrase burns in my mind 'There are times dearest I wish we had never met" and 'will I help you to forget' and here I am I suppose playing the part of the mean dog you may rightfully call me by saying I can't!! As long as I feel that I am such a dog, it ill becomes me- or does it*

become me? To be a supplicant for the love I thought was mine until death do us part.

What has influenced you to change so in four days? Where am I at? I feel half crazed with grief at this writing for what has come over you I cannot imagine. My heart tells me to call you for an explanation – but your letter pleads practically, to leave you alone as you would live your life all right if I would cease my attentions. If I do call you it will be with the feeling of an intruder at a party and yet. I had already promised I would call at four and it is now five or six Eastern Time. Perhaps if I try I can't get you anymore on account of storm delays. Oh – but I am very weak – for if ever I wanted to drink it is this very minute. I can understand this minute why people under a fit of depression take to it or anything else – to forget... As I have said in the past it is a fearful handicap to overcome to be so many miles away and if I was saner I would realize the possible truth of it - that I cannot compete under such circumstances and expect -- well I had better stop now as I do not feel like going on for the present. Will try again when I may be more collected... Will put in a call. If I get connection may have a peaceful night. If I don't – then the light will be dim.

I do, I do, Ed

After reading Ed's letter Sarah felt hopeless. Thoughts raced through her mind: "I know that he really loves me and I am making him miserable. He is my soul mate and by making him share my struggle, I am causing him much grief. Giving him up does not seem to be something I am capable of; he is my happiness. But, what about William? He is my husband and we have done well as a team. I don't wish to hurt him."

Sarah's dilemma was never-ending.

As the year 1916 dawned, William began a campaign in earnest to become both secretary and treasurer of Faries Manufacturing feeling that appointment would be the best path to become company president. His next-door neighbor, E. P. Irving, was presently the treasurer and as much as he liked and admired Mr. Irving, William wanted his job. As the child of an Irish immigrant whose family was not accepted into middle-class society, William had determined in his teen age years that he would someday become an important industrialist and nothing was going to get in his way; however, he was raised to be an honest and ethical person and to have compassion for others, so he was attempting to use the proper channels to gain his business positions, even though his dictatorial personality got in the way at times.

Mr. Faries the founder of the company was Mr. Irving's father-in-law and lived with them, so William knew Mr. Irving probably would become President, but still he felt competitive. The Irvings had no live-in servants and with several children living at home, Mrs. Irving had to do much of the household work. Sarah because of her live-in help was free to concentrate on social and community affairs, as a proper, well-off lady should. In addition, Sarah was probably the most prominent socialite in Decatur and the most gracious. When Faries Manufacturing needed to entertain their most important clients, they asked Mr. and Mrs. William Grady to host. William felt he was winning the competition.

William attributed this advantage partly to his home. He was confident that his house outranked the Irvings. Yes, the Irvings had contracted Frank Lloyd Wright to build their home, but Wright was unable to finish the project and William felt the Grady's California architectural style was superior to Wright's prairie-style any day. Their California shingle style house actually looked similar to Wright's own home in Chicago.

William couldn't help trying to "outdo" people, which is one of the reasons he married Sarah. The first time he saw her at a friend's party in Chicago, he thought she was the most stunning woman he had ever seen. A huge crowd of men both single and married had gathered around her and she was deftly charming them all.

As the hour grew late and the crowd around her had not diminished, William thought he might take a chance that she was getting tired and might enjoy being saved from the throng.

Striding up to her he said to the men standing close by, "I must claim my date now. It's getting late."

Taking Sarah by the arm, he led her to the coatroom and told her to get her wrap. Sarah's eyes twinkled as she mouthed the words "thank you" and obediently left the party with William.

Immediately he was captivated by her and for several months they spent most evenings together whether it was just the two of them or a group of William's business clients. It didn't take long for William to see what an asset Sarah would be to his business success. He gave her credit for his increased sales. His company, Faries Manufacturing, decided he would be more valuable to them in their headquarters than in Chicago, so they promoted him and brought him back to Decatur.

Not being able to imagine his future without Sarah by his side, he proposed. For her part Sarah was ready to get remarried. She loved that William included her in his business dealings. Amongst a room of businessmen she was able to shine for William, garnering great success for them both, the kind of success she had bitterly let go of after Charles's betrayal.

She could feel how much William admired her and she asked herself, "What's not to love, a handsome, rising business star that many other women are chasing?"

Since this was her second marriage, Sarah did not want a big wedding. Several of their friends went to a Justice of the Peace with them in Chicago and in February of 1903; they were married, a year after Sarah's divorce.

It was after the wedding that Sarah started to think of Sam. Even though William knew about Sam and had visited him, little had been discussed about what they were going to do with him. William said he was not averse to having Sam come live with them, but he thought they should wait until they were settled in Decatur and had a suitable house for him.

Sarah was anxious to have him living with her. Since her divorce, she had only seen Sam twice. He was fine with Grandmother Elwood, but Sarah missed him. At this point he was five years old, getting ready to begin school. Not wanting to argue with her new husband, Sarah accepted William's point that it wouldn't be wise to bring Sam into an unsettled situation. She would get comfortable in her new marriage and a new town and it shouldn't be long she thought before Sam could come to Decatur and live with her.

But it had taken eleven years for Sam's lengthy visit of last summer to come to fruition. Sarah admitted to herself that she had been selfish and had put William and his needs before Sam's welfare. She should have insisted that Sam come live with her, but events, parties, trips to California, all had delayed Sam's reunion. He had come at holiday times but only for a few days or a week at a time. William had been very kind to Sam and Sam liked him.

Occasionally, the Gradys had talked about having a family of their own, but how could Sarah justify more children when Sam was not with her? Even though she loved children, she had not had an easy birth with Sam and the doctors told her it would be unlikely that she could have another baby. In addition, she wondered if her life would be calm and stable enough to raise a child, even if one were possible. After all, it was obvious that William's thrust in life was to be a success in business not in raising children, and Sarah could be of no use to William if she were busy raising a young family. But as she reflected on their choices, the thought that Ed enjoyed his children crept into her mind.

CHAPTER 13

Revolution

Decatur, Illinois Spring 1916

WITH WILLIAM'S CAMPAIGN well under way to add the title "treasurer" to his position in the company, Sarah was beginning to feel abused. Her life consisted of William greeting her in the morning and checking her schedule for the day and even what she planned to wear. "Put on the blue dress with the white circles on the blouse for this afternoon and don't waste your time going to the woman's golf meeting at the club. Go to the orphan's home meeting instead."

She wanted to scream, "Leave me alone. Let me do something I want today," but she said nothing.

She felt almost at the breaking point. When life seemed too much, she would sit down and write to Ed who would write back encouraging her not to be a slave to William and not to do too much entertaining. Emboldened by Ed's letters and furious at William's normal dictates during breakfast, Sarah determined that on this day, she was going to do what she wanted.

William left for work and she went upstairs to her sitting room, prayed that the phone would work (which it did) and cancelled her day's planned events. Tonight William had no special entertaining planned so she was going follow her own desires for the day -- - beginning with a long ride on Midnight.

Her ride on Midnight was special today. She didn't even try to solve problems while riding as she usually did, but felt free and it was a glorious sensation.

Back at home she began thinking, "If I didn't have my long hair to worry about, my morning and nightly routines would be much easier and quicker." She dressed for the street and hurried to the beauty shop. As she sat in the chair, the beautician let down Sarah's hair as usual and prepared to trim the edges before her shampoo. Sarah looked at herself in the mirror and thought of the brushing one hundred strokes every night, the combing and twisting she had to deal with every day, and determined that actually she would look better with shorter hair. The result would be less bother and her appearance would be improved.

She said in a strong voice, "Cut it off."

The beautician repeated, "Cut it off? Maybe an inch. You feel it is too long? It actually isn't …"

"Cut it off to just above my shoulders," Sarah interrupted.

The beautician tried again, "You know it will take over a year to grow back to the proper length."

Sarah had had it with convention and what she was expected to do, and said with authority in her voice, "Cut it off, please."

Viewing the results in the mirror, she knew she had made a good decision. Her hair was naturally curly and the short cut softened and enhanced her appearance. Even the reluctant beautician said she looked amazing.

Leaving the shop, she bounced down the sidewalk feeling at least ten pounds lighter. Next, she needed a dress that she liked, one that reflected her personality.

Oh, she was really having fun! Almost running into the department store, she found the clerk that always waited on her and asked what she had that was a little more daring than her usual purchases.

The clerk looked approvingly at Sarah's short hair and said, "Perhaps a dress to match your new hair style? I have just the thing for you. We just got these in from our buyer in New York and I'll warn you they have a different look; the waistline is down and the skirt is up. They are much shorter than what you usually buy but I think you'll like them."

Sarah slipped into the first dress the clerk brought her and turned to the mirror. The length of the soft blue dress was just below the knee and the waist sported a layer of ruffles way down on her hips. She gasped when she saw image in the mirror. What she saw in her reflection was not Mrs. W.J. Grady, but was finally *Sarah*. She had found herself.

She told the clerk, "Please put my old dress in a sack. I love this one and will wear it home." The clerk smiled approvingly and Sarah left the store.

Noticing that both men and women were staring at her as she sauntered down the street, she couldn't have been any happier with her new appearance. The feeling was exhilaration.

"Today I do as I wish," said Sarah out loud to the passersby. Not paying much attention to where she was going, she bumped into a young woman.

"Sorry," said Sarah.

Then, realizing who the woman was, she said, "Mrs. Rogers? I've been thinking about coming to see if you needed some help with the Woman's Suffrage Group. Are you still in charge?"

Sarah had wanted to join them for a long time as she really believed in their cause. The idea that women couldn't vote was appalling to her partly because she knew more about politics than most men and partly because it just wasn't fair.

"Yes, I am, Mrs. Grady, and certainly we would be thrilled to have you join us."

Mrs. Frank Rogers, the leader of the group, was a young matron who had an abundance of enthusiasm. Sarah knew by reputation that Mrs. Rogers was well organized and an able leader. After hearing of the accomplishments of the women in Decatur and realizing the movement was organized all over the country, Sarah wanted to join in the fight to win the right to vote for women. Most of the groups William wanted her to join were not very active and their causes were not always relevant to Sarah. With this organization she could make a difference. So delighting in her new found freedom, she told Mrs. Rogers to call her when they were to have a meeting.

Now late afternoon, Sarah had to rush home to be sure to beat William. Her day or not, it wouldn't do to be gone when he arrived home from work. As she scurried along, the impact of what she had done hit her. What was William going to say about her dress and her hair? Maybe he would like what she had done, but no --she knew he wouldn't.

"He'll get over it though," she thought smoothing her cropped hair. "And he doesn't have to know about the women's suffrage group yet."

Practically running in the back door of her house, which she noted was much easier in her short skirt, she charged into the front reception hall and stopped abruptly. William was standing there with three other gentlemen.

The look on William's face turned Sarah to stone.

Instantly recovering his poise, William smiled and said, "Mr. Schultz, Mr. VanWinkle, and Mr. Rouland may I present my wife, Sarah."

Also regaining her composure, Sarah held out her hand to each of the men and said, "How nice to meet you. What brings you to Decatur?"

"At your husband's request we have come to look over the products that Faries Manufacturing creates here. William has bragged about everything in Decatur, including you. He said he had a beautiful wife and now we know he was not exaggerating," responded Mr. Rouland to Sarah's greeting.

Sarah was happy to see Sadie bring a tray of drinks for the guests and William herd them into the living room. Without another word Sarah raced up the stairs and into her sitting room. Her stomach flipped with dread. The look on William's face when she bounced into the hallway had told the whole story. No doubt William had brought these guests home to meet her so she could do her magic to impress them. Not only was she not home, but also she was dressed inappropriately. William was a stickler for the correct social customs and attire. Sarah sat on her window seat and contemplated what she should say to her husband. She could think of nothing. It was an hour and a half before she heard the men leaving and William saying good-bye.

Immediately after hearing the front door close, she heard William's footsteps on the stairs. He was not in a hurry but climbed them slowly and deliberately. Sarah felt her heart jump with every footstep. Standing in the doorway to the sitting room, he just stared at her. Time stopped for Sarah.

Finally, not being able to take the silence any longer, she whispered, "I'm sorry, William. I should have been home when you got here."

"What in God's name have you done to yourself? And why did you do it?" said William quietly.

"I was so tired of giving parties and going to events, I wanted to do something I'd enjoy," said Sarah pensively, "and I did enjoy my afternoon."

William exploded, "You don't enjoy this beautiful house I built for you? You don't enjoy having ladies in Decatur envy you your position in society? You don't enjoy having a husband who takes you to the finest resorts in the country? You don't enjoy your country club membership? Why do you believe you need to look like a scarlet woman to enjoy yourself? I was trying to land these men as customers. I brought them to my home so they would be impressed with my house and especially with my wife. You straggle in through the back door looking like a damned floosy!"

And that was it for Sarah. Her years of frustration came pouring out. She didn't care what William thought of her or her hair and dress. He had been using her for years and she was not going to be used like that any longer. Ed called him a slave driver and Sarah decided Ed was correct.

Sarah spat at him, "I am tired and I'm not going to entertain for you any longer. I deserve to wear the dresses I feel are right for me and the new hairstyle in the East is short. I even joined the Woman's Suffrage Group this afternoon! And ..."

Beet red, William strode over to her, grabbed her by the arm, stood her upright with one hand and slapped her as hard as he could with the other.

The world spun and Sarah realized she was going to pass out.

The next thing she remembered was a dull ache in her head and throbbing pain on her cheek, and then nothing.

She woke up in her bed an hour or so later and William was sitting next to her holding a cool, damp cloth to her face.

"Sarah, I'm sorry. I didn't mean to hit you, whether or not you deserved it. I lost my temper, which I never do."

William repeated his apology and rambled on and on. Sarah was calm but her face hurt badly and she didn't wish to hear his regrets, so she asked hurriedly said he would be in Chicago in three days and stay at the Palmer House. Sarah realized that Chicago posed a threat for them as it was not out of the question that one of her Decatur acquaintances could be in that city at that hotel at the same time she was, but she wanted to see Ed right away and going to Chicago would be the quickest way to accomplish a meeting. If William found out about them, it would serve him right to know that his wife loved another man. They intended to divorce their spouses anyway and she needed to discuss this with Ed.

After hanging up the phone, Ed reflected on this conversation with Sarah. Something was wrong. He knew Sarah well. He also was aware that she made quick decisions and sensed that at this point in time she was serious about the two of them being together forever. Actually he would like nothing better. He was so in love with Sarah and both he and Florence felt their marriage was one of convenience, but it would jeopardize his job if he should leave Florence as her family was good friends with the president of his company and politics played an important part in his position. His social clubs were a result of friends he made through Florence and membership would be lost if he divorced her; not having a social position would weigh on his future promotions as well. Divorce still was considered a "no" even in the relatively immoral upper classes, "free love" was being touted as the way of the world, but divorce still held a stigma. Ed played through the scenarios he could visualize if he and Sarah were together permanently and he realized, as much as it pained him to admit it, the time was not right. Maybe, he thought, if he and Sarah could make enough money in their stock trades...

Telling William she needed to sleep alone so nothing would disturb her painful face, Sarah occupied the front guest bedroom and made it a point to see very little of him. On the second day after the incident, she told him a visit to Chicago would help her feel better and as soon as her bruises could be hidden with powder she was going away for a few days.

William was feeling horrible about striking her, so he immediately agreed with her arrangements. Every time he looked at Sarah he was mortified that he could have done such a thing to her and longed to take it back. She was a trophy to him. She had charm, wit, elegance and was clever too.

"How could she have done that? Driven me to strike her with her antics and hysteria?" he thought.

He hoped a trip into the city would give her time to reflect and remember who she really was, Mrs. William J. Grady. Regretting harming her, yet confidant that was what she needed in that moment, he swore it would not come to this again. He would strive for more control and be watchful, and she knew now that he would not tolerate her humiliating him.

CHAPTER 14

Respite

Palmer House Chicago Spring 1916

HAVING SPOKEN LITTLE to William in the days following the physical attack, she had James drive her to the train station without a goodbye to her husband, perceptive enough to know this would upset him. She didn't care. Actually, she was feeling very free. Telegraphing Ed to meet her at the station, Sarah couldn't wait to see his reaction to her new haircut and short dress, which she was wearing. She imagined that winning smile spread across Ed's face, the utter antithesis of William's reaction. Checking her appearance in a compact mirror as the train neared Chicago, she was pleased the bruises no longer could be seen through the powder she had meticulously piled on her face. The swelling had gone down enough that she surmised her appearance would look normal to Ed. She did not intend to tell him of William's cruelty.

Foggy and chilly, the aptly named "Windy City" blustered upon her arrival. Sarah pulled her coat tightly around her as she stepped off of the train. Ed was standing on the platform waiting for her. Showing his military training, he appeared to be at attention as he stood watching the passengers disembark. Dressed perfectly in his fashionable dark blue suit and light blue tie, his sober face was scanning the crowd. The minute Sarah came into view Ed's solemn look turned to sunshine. Oh, how wonderful he looked. He threw his arms around her and smothered her with kisses. The enthusiastic warm welcome and the frustrations of the past week flooded over Sarah and she began to cry. Ed took her face in his hands and looked her straight in the eyes.

"I thought you might be glad to see me. I am not accustomed to tearful greetings from my Sallie," he said humorously.

As he gently started to inquire if something was wrong, the sweetness in his countenance dissipated as he looked at her tear stained cheeks, which were now pink, yellow, and red since the tears had washed away the powder.

"Sarah, what happened to you?" he choked as he turned her face one direction and then the other. "Never mind, I know what happened. I have feared this all along. Is William suspicious of us or is he just mistreating you?"

Bringing up her hand to cover her tear-streaked face, Sarah cursed how easily she cried. Why must she always sob like a young girl? Feeling mortified, she reminded herself that Sarah Grady was not a weak woman, but was strong, poised and confident. How horrid she must look. She hadn't meant for their reunion to go like this, for him to know what had happened.

Tears were still flooding down her cheeks, "I was hoping to hide this from you. I don't think he knows about us. However, I read your lovely letter, Ed, and I decided you were right; I need to show my true self. I wanted my appearance to follow my new mindset, but when I came home from shopping and greeted some of his business clients with my hair cut off and my dress shorter than usual, he…"

"I can't believe he would do this to you. That scoundrel! I know he thinks more of his business than he does of you, but I really didn't think he would get so physically violent. This is more than a slap in the face."

Ed finally realized they were still standing outside in the inclement weather. "Come on let's get a cab and check in at the hotel. We'll get you warm and order room service as I know my Sallie is hungry."

Within an hour Sarah was comfortably resting in a soft chair in the hotel room with a blanket tucked around her waiting for the feast that Ed had ordered. Ed was perched on the other chair in the room, looking very concerned.

"Your face is also swollen, Sarah. When did this happen? He must have struck you with all his might. I'm not sure you should go back to Decatur. He is obviously dangerous if he can do this over a haircut and a dress, both of which, by the way, are entirely becoming to you. I've noticed the fashionable ladies in New York are wearing dresses like yours now."

After a wonderful supper in their room, Sarah was relaxed and had re-gained her composure. Ed on the other hand was tense and upset, pacing back and forth at the foot of the bed, and finally falling back into the chair across from it. Looking into his eyes Sarah could see disgust and repul-sion, which she assumed, was targeted at William.

Thinking she needed to calm him down or he'd get both of them in trouble, she said, "We have to have a serious talk about our future. When our few days here are over, I have to return to William and you to Florence, and I am resigned to that for now, my love, but when are we go-ing to be able to be together? Darling, I …"

Ed interrupted, "I don't think you are safe in Decatur and I don't want you to get hurt any more than you already have been. You can't go back."

"And what would you have me do?" she asked, raising her brow.

Ed stammered, "How about getting an apartment in New York where I could watch over you? Or, well, you could… oh, Sarah, you are my world and I love you so, but I guess we do have to be practical. When I think that I only get to spend a few days here and there with you when I want to be with you every minute of every day…and the thought of sending you back to that selfish, dictatorial, and dangerous man… I almost get physically ill."

Tears gone and mind clearly set, Sarah rose from the bed and knelt beside him, "We can, my love, we can. We are both smart, industrious people. Look at where we both came from. Compared to that, this is noth-ing. We will just have to use our gifts to make the life we want."

Sarah now being the calm and more practical one rattled on, "We have to have money to live on. If I divorce William, I won't get much money from him. I have some land and some money of my own, but not enough to finish raising Sam and to last the rest of my lifetime. We have been doing really well in our stock market dealings, but we don't have enough in that him to leave her alone. When he left, Sarah began to sort out what had happened to her that day. She had made some decisions that she knew William would not approve of and yet these were decisions that she felt she had a right to make. If she were ever to have a satisfactory life, she would have to be free to evaluate what was good for Sarah as well as what was good for William. Ed had warned her that if she didn't stand up for herself, she would not be happy and he had warned her to be careful of William. She wanted Ed to be with her now. All her feelings about being untrue to her husband were gone, replaced by the throbbing pain she now felt and her desire to be with Ed who would have loved what she had done today.

The next day Sarah cancelled her activities for the rest of the week because her brown, red, and yellow bruises showed up vividly and were so wide spread across her face, rather mimicking a handprint. She knew that all who saw her would view a story of being struck by Midnight's hoof with suspicion. Ashamed, William left for work quickly in the morning with a sheepish look on his face. That was fine with Sarah as she really did not want him around. As soon as he left, she picked up the phone and tried to get a New York connection. In about five minutes she had a clear connection with Ed.

"Hello, my darling," said Sarah in her most nonchalant voice.

"Are you alright?" said Ed. "You don't usually call at this hour."

"I need to see you. Can you come to Chicago?" said Sarah trying to hide the urgency in her request.

"What's wrong, Sarah? I can tell something is amiss."

Sarah was afraid to tell him what William had done for fear he would come to Decatur and confront her husband which would not help any of their relationships, but she needed Ed, so she replied, "I can't go on being separated from you. I love you. We need to discuss what we have to do to be together."

Ed was very happy to hear Sarah say that she loved him because her letters of late had been indecisive. Not wanting to miss this mood he account to last us if you are fired from your job. We need money. I can try to get a patent on my invention and hopefully our stock trading will pay off handsomely."

Ed smiled, "You are my smart little Sallie. You're right. I can always get a job, just not of the caliber I have now and we could not live in New York or Decatur, but we could be together, just not living in the style we are both accustomed to. But, Sarah, my children … Florence would probably keep me from my children if I divorced her."

After a period of silence, they looked at each other and said almost in unison, "We can't yet."

Sarah, looking Ed straight in the eye and smiling, said, "Well then, you will just have to keep your promise not to drink. I need you to have a long healthy life if I must continue to wait for you, Ed Rockafellow."

They renewed the pact they had made to give up drinking in order to keep them physically fit for each other and planned how to save more money and what stocks they were going to buy when Ed got back to New York. Ed said, "I believe steel is going to have a huge run-up in price and I think we need to be heavy in it."

Sarah agreed, "I think you're right but don't ignore wool. I'm sure it's a good buy."

Ed approved, "I'll buy both of these when I get back to New York."

After the money discussion, their thoughts turned to planning how they would spend the next two days in Chicago. Never was there any dissension on that score. They decided on an uplifting musical show for their theater trip, *H. M. S. Pinafore*. For high tea the decision was to remain at the Palmer House because it was easier to just go downstairs. An afternoon at the art museum was a must, as was a long walk in Grant Park, then dinner and dancing at the brand new Edgewater Beach Hotel. Having made their plans, they stretched out together on the bed and held each other closely thinking how heavenly it was to be with their one true love.

Their two days in Chicago were fantastic. Sarah forgot the pain William's angry blow had caused her both emotionally and physically. She laughed and talked and ate, and they even had time to include a silent movie, *The Cheat*, in their itinerary.

Ed said, "The plot of this movie shows how someone who has great love for another will go to great lengths to protect them. Sarah, I will protect you as you are the most important person in my life."

"I know," Sarah quipped with a smile.

The fear that they would bump into someone from Decatur, or a New York friend of Ed's, did not materialize. Sarah threw caution to the wind telling herself it didn't matter if someone discovered them together, because being with Ed was the chief thing in her life at the moment.

As they packed up their belongings on the morning of the third day, Ed could see Sarah needed cheering up. He said, "There is a conference of electric suppliers in Ottawa in a month. Insist that William take you with him and I'll see that we have a chance to be together," he said.

"Alright, Darling, William owes me that, at least."

Deciding that their letters would be the only connection they could have for a while, an agreement was made that if they couldn't write every day, they would at least write three times a week.

"My Sallie, I will come to you any time you need me... no matter when or what the problem. Please promise you will call if you want me."

With this assurance from him, they parted ways at the train station. One headed south and one headed east.

Back in Decatur, William was feeling very unsettled. He had not wanted Sarah to go off to Chicago by herself, but knowing how disturbed she was, sensed it best not to argue about it when she told him she was going. He had let his temper get away from him and when he thought of the mark of his hand on her delicate face, he cringed. His mind wandered back to times in Springfield as a boy when he had seen some of the Grady's neighbors beat their wives. The "drunken Irish" some of the other neighbors had called those guilty of physical aggression. Upon these occasions

William's mother would take him aside and explain to him that the Irish had a reputation for excessive drinking. She said he needed to work very hard to dispel that reputation when he grew up. Drinking to excess was one of the worst behaviors he could ever exhibit according to his mother; then her stories would turn to the brave and glorious feats of the Irish people and how proud William should be to be an Irishman. The Grady family had always made sure they did everything in their power to be accepted as Americans in this new country they called home, even going so far as to change their name from O'Grady to Grady. William knew that at present his mother was satisfied with his accomplishments, but would be chagrined if she knew he had reduced himself to such a state.

On the second day after Sarah left for Chicago, William tried to call her and see how she was feeling. He realized she had left without telling him where she was going to stay, but she always stayed at the Palmer House, so he put in a call there. No Sarah Grady was registered there. He called several other hotels, but still no success. The phone lines were not being very cooperative so he gave up in frustration. Since Sarah was not talking to him before she left, he didn't know when she would return. After the second day, he came home early hoping to find that she had returned-- but no Sarah.

William's thoughts turned to fear, "What if she does not come home? What will my business associates say? What excuse could I give for her not returning? Should I go find her?" Dealing with the social embarrassment would be devastating.

The next day, determined that she would return on the afternoon train or he would set out for Chicago himself, he anxiously waited at the station. Like an incantation, Sarah swung down from the train onto the platform in one fluid motion looking like a fashion model. She was dressed in her normal travel attire so the only remnant of the ridiculous episode was her hair cut and, looking closely now, William had to admit that her coiffure was extremely attractive, soft blondish curls framing her face and the back of her neck. William immediately put his arms around her and gave her a welcome home kiss full of passion. He was delighted to see her.

"Sarah, I'm so happy you are home. I've missed you so much. Let's put everything behind us. I tried to call and make sure you were okay, but the Palmer House said you weren't there. Where were you?" asked William.

Inwardly Sarah cringed and thought, "Good Heavens! I didn't even think to get a room in my name. How dumb of me. What to do now?"

Playing for time to decide what to say, she dropped her travel satchel on the ground so William would have to take a moment to pick it up. What to say? Her quick mind made a decision to bluff through it with nonchalant remarks,

"I was at the Palmer House. They didn't have their records straight? Well, they had no trouble taking my traveler's checks when I checked out. I'm sure it was just a clerical error that has been straightened out. It was good for me to get away, but I'm glad to be home," she said, biting her lip with her last words.

Relieved to hear so, William didn't push the discrepancy. He was happy to have her back and determined he would make her forget his bad temper by spoiling her as he always had.

Despite having had a wonderful time with Ed the last few days, Sarah felt her words come true as they rode along in the Reo. She was happy to be home. Decatur was her real existence and there was much good in it. She loved her house; she loved her dear friend June, and, although taxing, she did love her position in the community. Right now William would be easy to live with as Sarah was sure that he would coddle her at least for a bit. Ed was her dream life. She had enjoyed every hour she had spent with him and was already looking forward to his next letter. But she knew that for now, William was her reality; in spite of his recent actions, she understood that William loved her and was the security and stability she needed right now. Seeing him so repentant, she resolved to forgive him, but not to let him make all of her decisions anymore. She would decide when and where she would go, what clothes to wear when she went, and even which charities she would support. She would be an excellent, but not obedient, wife to him while getting great pleasure from Ed's niche in her life. Yes, for better or worse, she had to keep both men.

CHAPTER 15

❧

Dearest Friends

Atlanta, Georgia Fall 1916

In the fall of 1916, still vowing to do as she pleased, Sarah attended meetings of the suffrage group on the sly because William still did not approve of women being franchised. In Illinois women had achieved a limited right to vote in 1913 but her group worked for full federal approval in the form of a constitutional amendment and many women from her group had attended the march in Washington in June to promote women's rights. Sarah itched to go to Washington and join the march, but did not have the will to fight with William, so she contented herself with helping to organize the activities from Decatur. However, at this point in time the majority of her fervor was directed to the accelerating war overseas.

Sarah saw Ed three more times before the year 1916 ended. The Electric Companies had a conference in Atlantic City, one in Montreal, and one in Atlanta, and of course, William wanted Sarah along with him at all these meetings. Always Sarah and Ed found some time to be alone, but they had to endure their spouses being with them for most of their free time.

In the Georgian Terrace Hotel in Atlanta, Sarah and Ed were seated directly across from each other at dinner with Florence and William being next to them in the same position.

Florence was chattering excitedly, "I went to the most wonderful flower show last week. The sponsors were educating people on how to grow gardenia plants. Do you know they had a plant there that was fifty years old?"

Sarah shot a glance at Ed that required action from him so he dove right into the conversation, "William, is Faries Manufacturing having trouble getting their shipments to France?"

"Not too much, but transportation has been more of a problem since the Black Tom incident. Many believe that was sabotage," replied William.

"Yes, that was horrible. I was working late that evening so I had a ringside seat to see the explosion. I had just walked into an interior office to put some papers on Mr. Potaka's desk when my window blew out in my room and millions of chards of glass covered my whole area. All of the office furniture was hopping around like I had seen once in a Californian earthquake. I suppose I am quite fortunate."

Florence looked shocked. "You didn't tell me about that. What is a Black Tom?"

"I wasn't hurt so I didn't want to worry you needlessly. Black Tom was a munitions plant," said a patient Ed.

"The authorities haven't been able to prove yet that it was the Germans who did it. I really am disgusted with President Wilson. He refuses to believe that our enemies did this. I wouldn't vote for him even if I could," said an animated Sarah.

"I agree with you that it seems like the Germans were to blame, but Wilson really believes we can stay out of the war and blaming Germany for this without proof would be very confrontational," Ed replied.

"We should have declared war months ago, right after the Lusitania was sunk," she reiterated, nodding with enthusiasm.

"Sarah always jumps into things without knowing the facts," said William who seemed more interested in eating his dessert than talking.

Sarah and Ed went on with their substantive conversation about the actions of the European countries, which Sarah followed closely. Feeling the storm gathering, she wanted the United States to join Britain and France to defeat the Kaiser. Ed on the other hand followed President Wilson's thinking that we should stay out of war, noting that business was flourishing and that this country was not prepared for war.

Florence went on with her discussion of gardenia plants, directing her comments to William, and Ed winked at Sarah across the table, shocking Sarah who glanced immediately at William to see if he noticed. Even with their spouses seemingly occupied, Ed's boldness was made Sarah uncomfortable.

Feeling devilish Ed again winked at her and said, "Sarah, are you finding enough to do while we men are working?"

"Yes, I'm enjoying myself. Atlanta is an amazing city," said Sarah while giving Ed a stop this nonsense glance.

Ed winked at her again, so Sarah turned to William, interrupting his conversation with Florence.

"Mr. Grady, would you care to dance with your wife?" she asked.

As William led Sarah out onto the dance floor, Ed smiled and was able to throw one more wink in her direction. Sarah was left to bemoan the fact that Ed and William were best friends and she could do nothing to stop the unfortunate positions in which she was placed.

Circumstances left Florence and Sarah together much of the time at these conferences. Sarah found her company tolerable, but not desirable, especially since she really wanted to be with Ed, but she was a good actress and Florence determined that Sarah Grady was her best friend. As the men started their business meetings the day after Ed decided to misbehave (in Sarah's opinion), the two wives sat at a card table in the lobby of the hotel. Florence decided to share with her companion intimate details of her life.

"Sarah, it's so nice to spend time with someone who can understand my loneliness. I try to make Ed happy, but I always seem to do the opposite," said Florence. "Just the other night I tried to make myself available to him, but he was more interested in reading his book than coming to bed with me. Do you have any suggestions for me? Do you have similar problems with William?"

Sarah prayed to some higher power to set the building on fire or send a bolt of lightning down on their table. But silence reigned. Florence was looking at Sarah waiting for her to deliver the secret of married life. With an earnest expression on her face and a sincere tone of voice, Sarah tried to answer her.

"I'm certainly not an expert on marriage. William and I have our troubles and you know that this is my second marriage."

Florence continued, "You are always so poised and know what to say, and you're … well, so pretty."

Sarah could take no more of this conversation. "Forgive me, but I didn't sleep well last night and I have a headache. I hate to leave you but I need to lie down for a while."

Florence responded with a sympathetic look, which made Sarah feel culpable, but she had to get away from Ed's wife.

While in Atlanta, William did note that Sarah seemed to spend an inordinate amount of time with Ed.

"You two are always taking long walks, dancing most of the evening together, and talking in the lobby. I don't think I like the way I have seen him look at you sometimes. Is there something going on that I should know about?"

Sarah didn't even bat an eyelash, as she said, "Of course not. It's just that I like to have fun and do things. You don't like to walk, you don't like to dance and your conversations always revolve around your business. What is going on in the rest of the world, William? And why aren't you interested like Ed is in what I have to say?"

Sarah huffed off before William could answer; she hadn't even needed to lie, her response to William was the truth. And in knowing that truth, she certainly wasn't going to give up her time with Ed. However, the frequency of occasions that the two families were spending together, did give her concerns.

William considered Ed his best friend. To his associates in Decatur he referred to Ed as "my true friend and loyal buddy". That phrase was repugnant to Sarah, but making matters worse for her was Ed's daughter Gwen who was eleven years old and had adopted Sarah as a second mother. She was spending most of her vacation time at the Grady's home with her father's hearty approval. Ed repeated again in one of his letters to Sarah that he wanted "Gwen to grow up to be just like his one true love, independent and spunky."

Without malice, Florence also remarked to Sarah, "Gwen seems to prefer you over me as a mother. She begs all the time to go to Decatur and spend time with Aunt Sarah. She idolizes you. Instead of doing her homework, she sits down to write you a letter." Florence chuckled.

Gwen had a sweet, but strong personality and, in spite of the confliction it caused her, Sarah enjoyed having the "little girl she never had" around her. Last summer Gwen had spent the entire time in Decatur and Sarah had taught her to swim and play golf, finding that like her father she picked up physical skills easily. Sarah compared Gwen to Ed all of the time; she couldn't help herself because Gwen was so like Ed. She looked like him, having the same thick brown hair, the same taunting smile, and even speaking with the same intonation.

Gwen had said, "I enjoy being here so much more than going to Maine with my mother. You are so much fun and mother doesn't do anything. Can I come to live with you all of the time?"

When Gwen verbalized this thought, it struck Sarah right in the heart because she fantasized that this darling girl belonged to her and Ed.

Sarah had answered by giving her a big hug and saying, "I love you, Gwen, and I enjoy having you here, but your mother also loves you and you need to find what both of you like to do so you can be together more. When you go home I'll write you lots of letters and maybe you can come visit at Christmas."

It was somewhat a chore to keep up with writing at least two letters to Ed each week and also correspond with Gwen, but she always made time, as Ed did for Sam.

Ed who was constantly traveling to Indiana on business visited Sam at his military school more than Sarah and William did. Ed applied to Princeton University on Sam's behalf and with the help of President Wilson, William, and Charles Elwood, Sam's application was accepted. He started his college life in the fall of 1916 with Ed being a frequent visitor to the university.

The lives of the two families were intertwined much more than Sarah considered healthy. There were times when she actually felt sorry for Florence because Ed did not love her. The affair was getting more complicated, and their plan of being together forever did not seem to be gathering any steam even though their stock account was growing.

Sarah wrote to Ed that they needed to be more careful since William seemed to be a little suspicious, but she encouraged him to keep writing thinking their letters were still undetected. Ed wrote back:

> *Darling Sweetheart,*
>
> *Is William still suspicious? Should I write William anything or isn't it wise just now? I do so much want to see you. Can't you find a place somewhere around you? Have you looked?*
>
> *Has Sadie come back yet? Write me everything. Will mail another letter Thursday. One of the pictures I sent you was enlarged by Deming. It is pronounced good. Do you want me to save it for you?*
>
> *My heart is full of love, Ed*

CHAPTER 16

❧

The Food of Love

Warm Springs, Georgia February 1917

SARAH'S LIFE BEGAN to change in January of 1917. William's friend and neighbor, E. P. Irving, told him with pride that Mrs. Irving was working with the prohibition group in Decatur and how successful they were becoming in outlawing liquor in the community Therefore, William's attitude softened a bit on the organizations Sarah could belong to; if Mrs. Irving could be part of those groups, so could Mrs. Grady. He came to terms with his wife being what the press called the "New Woman". Short hair was stylish and hemlines were up. He "got it". He was now aware that she belonged to the Woman's Suffrage Organization. Giving in to the tide as a few more states endorsed the women's' right to vote, he no longer begrudged Sarah the time she spent working for them. He still forbade her to march in their parades, however.

Besides her work with the poor farm in Decatur, she had joined several groups to help prepare supplies to send to the men overseas that were fighting for the Allies; some were Americans, but most were French. In January Germany declared unrestricted submarine warfare, which meant they would attack the ships of any country anywhere. This declaration Sarah recognized was the final straw and America's entrance into the war was eminent. Even Ed agreed for a change. They both couldn't understand why President Wilson didn't formalize the United States' position.

In addition to her war activities and charity work, Sarah was working on her own projects to make money for her new life with Ed. Having developed several natural lotions to be used on the skin to prevent wrinkles, she was trying without William's knowledge to form her own company to manufacture a line of natural cosmetics. He had made clear his opinion that women, at least women of Sarah's social stature, should not be in the work place, and he felt his position as an officer of the company would be less secure if his wife went into business as she had often threatened to do. Ed was trying to advise her from a distance, but forming a manufacturing company was a difficult task and took up a great deal of her time. And that wasn't all. Sarah had an invention she was working on. Being an avid golfer and seeing how many people who enjoyed playing golf had a difficult time walking around the course, she envisioned a small cart with an automobile engine that would transport golfers around the course. Sarah's neighbor Mr. Mueller manufactured automobiles and every chance she got she would pump him for information about how his engine worked. Never telling him what she had in mind, Sarah seemed to him a strange woman who was obviously a frustrated engineer.

Writing at least three long letters to Ed a week was her secret reprieve from various and endless daily tasks, and she knew how much he needed them. As love-starved as William left her, she knew that Florence left Ed doubly as cold. Through the hours, nights and months that they could not be together, those letters were their sole nourishment.

To add to her busy life were her regular duties such as hosting the dinner parties William still gave and attending the countless frivolous country club events. Sarah was doing too much and was physically paying the price. Always having been slender, Sarah was now what people called thin, too thin. Her face was drawn and white; bones were beginning to show through even her loosely draped dresses. She tried to disguise her pale face by using her own products of brightly colored lipstick and rouge, but to no avail. Anyone looking at Sarah would say she was ill. She was breaking her promise of keeping healthy for Ed.

While at the dinner table one evening, William did notice that she wasn't looking well. He did not want to slow down his demands on her to help him entertain because he was anticipating his appointment to treasurer very soon, so he told Sarah he couldn't afford to have her sick right now.

"Sarah, you need to get more sleep and stop those dangerous night rides on Midnight. Your charity work isn't as important as helping me obtain my position as Treasurer at Faries, so maybe for a while you could stop taking on those frivolous responsibilities. You are looking dreadful; your bones are showing through your dresses. You aren't much of an asset to me when you look so sick. Besides giving up some of your activities, you need rest. What is it you do all day? You could take a nap in the afternoon then it wouldn't be so difficult for you to stay out at night for our parties."

Sarah quietly looked at the uneaten food before her and played with the peas chasing them around the edge of her plate. Inside she was seething and wanted to scream out that she was tired of his parties and tired of him not paying any attention to her except when he needed her for something. But not feeling up to a confrontation she managed to avoid an ugly scene with William by saying, "I need to go to Warm Springs and relax for a few days I don't seem to be able to eat much right now but maybe I could enjoy their food and gain a few pounds. I know you need me to be at my best so I'll try to get myself back to normal. You'll have to excuse me right now. I think I will go to bed early."

William was happy to agree, "Warm Springs sounds like a marvelous suggestion. Would you like for me…"

He let his final words slip away as he looked at her pitiful face. "No," he thought, "she doesn't want me with her."

"Thank you," said Sarah, "I'll make the arrangements myself."

As Sarah climbed the steps to her bedroom too worn for excitement, she knew whose company she needed. As Sarah began plotting how to call Ed that evening, William called up the stairs, "I'm going to a board meeting at the Decatur Club. The club has called a special meeting to take care of some urgent business. I should return in about an hour or so. Please go to bed and get some sleep."

"Fine. Be careful. Have James drive you."

As soon as Sarah heard the car leave the driveway, she hurried downstairs to the phone. She would have to call Ed at home at this hour and there was no assurance that he would be the one to answer. According to his last letter, he should be at home tonight and usually he was the one to take the calls. If, however, Florence should answer, Sarah would have to make up some excuse to authenticate the call. The phone rang and Sarah held her breath.

Finally, a deep voice said, "Hello."

Sarah let out a sigh of relief, "Oh, Ed. I have a chance to go to Warm Springs by myself. Could you get there sometime in the next week?"

Ed's excited voice came through the crackling line in a staccato rhythm, "Unbelievable. I have … go … Atlanta…Thursday on business … will take me two days … was planning to …a couple of days off. Perfect timing. Shall I … us reservations?"

Sarah was frustrated that the lines were not clear, but she understood what Ed was saying and responded, "No, please don't. Let me … my own room … you get yours. William is unpredictable … now. I don't know … he might do."

"Your voice … not clear, but I … enough to get the message. I'll … my reservations for Saturday … and Monday."

Further conversation was not possible because the line was making louder and louder noises and drifting in and out, but Sarah had accomplished her mission. Now, acknowledging she was sick and needed sleep, she went off to bed before William came home. She hoped Ed wouldn't notice how poorly she looked. What she needed was her soul mate and lover and then she would feel better. She collapsed into bed and went to sleep easily, dreaming of gardens and feasts.

Arriving in Warm Springs a day before Ed was to come, she hoped to get some rest and improve her appearance before he saw her. The Georgia weather in late February was warmer than usual and spring flowers were already blooming.

"This is what I need," thought Sarah, "Part of my problem is the gloomy weather back home. I will begin to feel better immediately in these sunny, peaceful surroundings."

In Sarah's opinion, Meriwether Inn in Warm Springs was an architectural mess. It was a huge four-story structure that included every building accessory known to man. It possessed arches, columns, round turrets, pointed turrets, steep gables, all sorts of gingerbread, covered porches, and the list went on. Regardless of the building, the mineral springs were relaxing and healing, always warm at precisely eighty-eight degrees. She had chosen to come here for several reasons, one being she felt the springs would rejuvenate her tired body and spirit, and secondly none of her friends would be here because Warm Springs was not considered fashionable anymore. In the 1890's it was *the* place for the socially prominent and famous people to spend their leisure time. The inn was accessible, just sixty miles from Atlanta and could be reached easily by train. One was sure to run into a well-known person of some sort when staying there. At the turn of the century when cars began to be popular, it was more fashionable to drive somewhere obscure than to stay at places that were on the train runs. Now in 1917, the Meriwether Inn was a bit forlorn appearing, but still clean and quiet, not too many people around, perfect for Sarah and Ed.

Sarah signed up for an attendant who, as the receptionist said, was there to take care of all of Sarah's physical and mental problems and make her feel better than she had ever felt in her life. Sarah chose to believe her and commenced her regimen. Soaking in her bath, she became aware of the virtues of the warm spring water. How good it felt! Everything else seemed to fade away as she allowed the warmth to spread over her entire body. And then... she was floating on a white fluffy cloud in a silent world.

After struggling to get her heavy, sleepy body out of the deep copper tub, she was encouraged to drink a potion that the attendant assured her was concocted from all natural ingredients. Since Sarah was always trying to be "natural", she drank and found the beverage, whatever it was, to be excellent. The last event for the day was a massage after which Sarah hardly had the strength to walk to her room. Dropping on the comfortable bed, she fell into in a peaceful sleep that had been denied her for a long time. Room service brought her a delicious supper after which she again went to sleep, not to awaken until the sun streamed into the window in the early morning.

Sarah jumped out of bed to start preparing for Ed's arrival. Looking at her reflection in the mirror, she noted how much better she looked today. The bones were still protruding, screaming "too thin, too thin", but her face had some color and a sense of well-being reflected in her eyes. Sarah felt free. Away from William she could breathe. Ed's words drummed a theme into her head, "You are a slave and no more to William Grady." She smiled at her new found autonomy.

Ed and Sarah spent their time at Warm Springs relaxing and absorbing the healing water of the springs. They had three glorious days just being together, spoiled only by the fact that Ed was worried about her. Upon his arrival he had to sit down quickly in a chair because he was so taken aback by her appearance.

"Sarah, you're ill. Why didn't you tell me? I would have come to you no matter what if I had known. What is the matter?"

Sarah had anticipated his reaction and responded very matter-of-factly. "I'm not really ill. I am just a little run-down. All I need is three days with my lover and I will be fine."

Ed was somewhat reassured by her comments. "We will eat and eat and then eat. Somehow we have to fatten you up. Next month I want us to be worried about you getting too fat." said Ed joking with her.

Sarah looked healthier each day and both of them forgot her condition and concentrated on making lover's memories. Suggesting that they leave the weighty subjects of conversation to discuss in their letters when they went home, Ed talked only of when they would be together forever. He knew that was just what Sarah needed.

They rode the train together back to Atlanta and then as usual one went one direction and one the other. Renewed by Ed, Sarah felt strong enough to endure all her work, William included.

CHAPTER 17

A More Perfect Union

Decatur, Illinois Spring 1917

MARCH 1917 SAW the end of the myth that America could stay out of the war abroad. The American citizens began shouting, "No more isolationist policies" as Germany attacked and sank three U.S. ships that were carrying supplies to the Allies. President Wilson began trying to evaluate whether or not the country was prepared for war and Congress started working on a conscription law. By this time many young American men had volunteered for the armed forces and some were fighting overseas already, but it was clear that this country did not have the trained man power needed to fight a war. As much as Sarah believed we should go to war, she was beginning to think of Sam. He was finishing his first year at Princeton. Anxious as she was to go to war and deal a deathblow to Germany, Sarah worried about the draft being instituted soon and Sam would be nineteen next year. It was not that she wouldn't want Sam to do his duty, but she wanted him to get his college degree first. It was a concern.

As the country's thoughts turned to war, William turned his thoughts to his marriage during Sarah's absence. Witnessing Sarah's blatant unhappiness only increased his misery. He loved her, but he just couldn't seem to do whatever it was that she needed or wanted. It frustrated both of them. He found himself studying Sarah's reactions to him and reluctantly determined that she had to be her own person and could not think of herself as merely his wife. This was a total contradiction to his belief that a wife should always do her husband's bidding and strive to make him successful in whatever endeavors he undertook. He decided that was the problem, but the way to make their relationship right eluded him.

His values could be traced to generations of Irish ancestors who believed that women should stay at home, make a comfortable life for their husband, and take care of any and all children they had. Sarah disagreed. She had made clear that she thought a woman should be free to follow her own interests and her husband should consider his wife as an equal partner. And yet for all her independence, Sarah was always complaining that William never spent enough time with her. How could she be so conflicted? How could she decide that all the work in which he had allowed her to assist and the involvement in his business he had shared with her was suddenly worthless? For years she had blossomed and reveled in it. And now he was forced to watch her wither. How could she do this now when he was so close to success?

Several board members of Faries Manufacturing Company had just told William that he was to be named Secretary/Treasurer of the company in a matter of months. Having achieved a prominent level in his company, he did not need as much from Sarah as he previously had expected, so he determined that now he would be able to fix the rift between Sarah and himself by having time to pay more attention to her. He could take her on more trips that were only for pleasure not business and actually spend quality time with her. They could play golf together; he could learn some of the newer dances; and, if Sarah wanted to walk in the gardens, he would walk in the gardens.

As a start, he congratulated himself on already letting her join the group in town that was organized for the purpose of rallying for Prohibition. William was not a heavy drinker and felt he could give up alcohol if it became unlawful to imbibe, but could not believe that prohibition was the way to improve a society that was becoming immoral. Drinking, he was sure, would continue whether or not the law prohibited alcohol, so he saw no future for a prohibition group. But if Sarah wanted to join them, he would allow it. These changes in his behavior he believed would repair his marriage. He was resolved to succeed with her once again, as he had done in all previous endeavors. William Grady would not tolerate failure.

Sarah noticed the change in William when she returned home from Warm Springs. He met her at the station and gave her a warm kiss.

"How much improved you are. You're looking beautiful and so rested. I would go down south too if I thought I could come back looking like you do," William said softly in her ear. "I've had Dorothy come to the house today and she's been cooking your favorite foods all day. I thought a nice quiet dinner at home would be just what you would want. I've missed you."

Sarah responded positively to the difference in William. He seemed like the man she had married. When they got home from the train station, William had James take her luggage upstairs and he ushered Sarah into the living room.

In his most pleasant voice, William began, "My dearest wife, sit down and relax. Train trips are tiring and I thought maybe a cocktail before dinner would help you feel better. I know you are working for Prohibition, but maybe you would allow yourself one drink. If not, I'll have Sadie get you something non-alcoholic."

Sarah could hardly believe what she was hearing. William was actually paying attention to her needs and asking her what she wanted instead of telling her.

"I think I will celebrate my homecoming and the new William by having a cocktail. Tell me what has come over you. You seem like a different man," she replied to her altered husband.

William stood close to her and put his hand on her shoulder, "Sarah, I know you have been unhappy. I see it and I want you to know I will allow it no longer. It is foolish, because in truth I love you and I'm going to strive to be your perfect mate, or at least as close as I can come to that ideal."

Sadie served their cocktails and Sarah set down on her big comfortable sofa covered in a gold and blue Chinese print and sipped her Rob Roy. As Sarah surveyed the room, she wondered if she might be dreaming. There were fresh flowers on the end table, her favorite, daisies. A spunky fire was burning in the fireplace making the large room feel cozy. The room was bathed in soft light stemming from the wall sconces sending small golden beams up to the ceiling. Sarah felt special. William had gone to all this trouble just for her and she was speechless. William set down beside her on the sofa, put his arm around her and they sat in contented silence as they drank their cocktails.

Still enjoying the moment, Sarah hardly noticed that Sadie brought them another drink. This one went down quicker than the first. Then the chimes on the dining room wall were struck to call them to dinner. He seated her and the feast began. William had not exaggerated when he said Dorothy had fixed all of Sarah's favorite foods; there was beef stroganoff, mashed potatoes and gravy, oysters Rockefeller, baked pineapple, and the dinner wine was Pinot Noir. The individual dishes that were served did not go well together but they were all Sarah's favorites. The conversation during dinner was light and enjoyable.

Feeling a little sentimental after the cocktails and dinner wine she had enjoyed, Sarah told William about her dinners on the farm when she was growing up. With a faraway look in her eyes she related that her family worked hard physically, so there was always tons of food on the table, mostly beef, bread, cheese, and garden vegetables. She went on dreamily remembering that the dinner meal was always at noon and they ate lightly for supper. She could still see all the family and the hired help sitting at the long harvest table and could almost hear the conversation taking place and people laughing. How happy life was then when she was young.

Sarah stopped and apologized for monopolizing the conversation and fell silent again as William just sat back in his chair and smiled, happy to see her enjoy herself. How much of her enjoyment was real and how much was alcohol induced he couldn't be sure.

A Spanish liqueur rounded out the meal and resulted in Sarah feeling lightheaded. As William led her upstairs to their bedroom, she thought, "When he acts this way, I remember why I married him." Her eyes followed their clasped hands and rested on the face that had turned back to her.

Her eyes sparkled as she whispered, "You're really quite a man. I love you too."

For a moment William was taken by her sweetness, "Sarah, I…"

She broke into a fit of giggles and William carried her the rest of the way to their room.

The remainder of the evening did not go exactly as William had planned, for Sarah was drunk. He did not recall ever seeing Sarah drink too much before and he realized he should have been counting her drinks if he wanted her to participate in a romantic soiree. As it was, Sarah just stood in the middle of the bedroom and waved her arms around like a windmill.

"Well this is a fine state," thought a frustrated William.

"Sarah," he said, ducking quickly as her arms were on the upswing, "how about getting ready for bed?" He couldn't seem to get close to her as the rotation of the windmill continued.

"How about we dance, Darling?" shrieked Sarah. The windmill stopped and she flew across the room and dived at him. Luckily he had quick reflexes and caught her in midair. He carried her to the bed, sat her down, and asked her to sit still while he got her nightgown. It took him less than thirty seconds to find a nightgown, but when he returned to the bed Sarah had toppled over and was sound asleep. He rearranged her with her head on the pillow and covered her up with a blanket. For a moment her paused and stared down at her. In her sleep, she looked youthful and free.

But he set his jaw again, with the realization he was not what made her happy tonight.

The next morning Sarah was not up at 5:45 a.m. as usual. William had left orders with Sadie for Sarah not be disturbed and she didn't wake up on her own until closer to 8:30 a.m. When she did sit up in bed, it was very unpleasant.

"What happened?" she wondered, trying to remember. Last evening was a blur and her head was pounding. Since Sarah had never had an over-abundance of alcohol before, she was not familiar with the symptoms of a hangover. Still sitting in bed, she called for Sadie who was immediately before her, bringing James's very own remedy for hangovers.

"Sadie, I'm really sick. My head is throbbing badly and my arms feel like they could fall off. Maybe you should call the doctor."

"Hmmm," said Sadie in a rather uncompassionate voice. "That's not necessary, Mrs. Grady. Just drink this and you'll feel better."

Sarah looked at her in a skeptical manner. Sadie sighed and said with a little more feeling, "I know you don't feel well, but this concoction that James made will really help your headache. And, oh yes, it's made from all natural ingredients -- just like your cosmetics. Drink it down."

Sarah took a sip and made a terrible face, "I won't drink this stuff. It would probably kill me."

Not having much sympathy for those who drink too much, Sadie muttered under her breath a few choice sentences and then said aloud kindly, "Come on, drink it down fast and I promise you'll feel better. You are not ill, you are having a hangover and this will help your head."

"Sadie, I'm not having a hangover, for heaven's sake. I'm not a drunk." Sarah raised her voice and immediately regretted it. With her head splitting in two, she drank James's brew and to her surprise, she immediately began to feel better.

It took Sarah the rest of the morning to put together what had happened the night before, but when she did, she remembered what William had done for her and how nice he had been. Smiling at the memories, she realized how hard he had been trying to incur her favor and how happy that realization made her. But she had just returned from a marvelous three days with Ed, her soul mate. She loved Ed more than she had loved any other man. How could one love two men at the same time? When her head stopped hurting she would decide what she should do. Giving up either of them did not seem like an option.

She spent the rest of the day resting and reading a novel that Ed had given her. When William got home, he found her with her book in the library curled up in an overstuffed chair in a comfortable but unladylike position.

"Well look at you, the picture of relaxation. I see more life in your eyes than I have seen in a long time. For someone who had too much to drink last night, you look absolutely beautiful. I never thought I would see my wife imbibe to that extent. I was so glad to see you that I paid no attention to how much you were drinking. How do you feel?" said William.

"For some strange reason James and Sadie knew just what I needed this morning and took excellent care of me. Did you tell them I had a problem?" inquired Sarah.

"My dear, I didn't have to tell them. After we went upstairs you thought you were a windmill I guess, and windmills are rather noisy. Then you ran across the room and jumped at me, shouting that we should dance. I believe anyone in the house last night would have guessed your problem. Luckily, besides me, Sadie was the only one in the house," joked William.

"I am sorry. I don't know what came over me. See, this is why I work so hard to get alcohol prohibited. People lose their sanity when they drink to excess and most people seem to drink too much. Just look at the parties at the club. Almost without exception the men and lately even the women drink more than they should. The men get flirty and the women don't cut them off like they used to," preached Sarah as she pushed away the nagging inner voice that reminded her of her own indiscretions.

"Let's spend another evening together, but perhaps you should only partake of one glass of wine before dinner. I have cancelled my meeting tonight so I can stay at home with you," proclaimed William.

Sarah was a bit incredulous at the change in William, but nevertheless very pleased. She had her "old" husband back and she loved it. The evening went as they hoped it would, both enjoying the other's company. William talked of the two of them taking a vacation with no business meetings scheduled. He told Sarah about the expected promotion at Faries Manufacturing and vowed that they would go away, just the two of them, to celebrate. Sarah went to bed without writing to Ed or even thinking about him.

However, the next day she found herself before the mailbox at the hotel knowing a letter would be waiting for her there. Though she vacillated between continuing to see Ed or telling him she needed to be true to William, she couldn't give up those letters. He was such an intelligent man and so involved in America's affairs; he was an outstanding historian and businessman; he knew the stock market and how to maneuver it. Ed saw all the new shows and read all the latest books. His letters opened to Sarah a more sophisticated world than she was able to perceive in Decatur, Illinois. He told her what he was doing almost minute by minute, thus giving her an education she could get nowhere else.

Upon opening the mailbox, she smiled and nodded her head. Ed had not disappointed her. She grabbed the letter and charged home with it. Once in the house, she took her place in the third floor room that she had fashioned into a secret reading room to specifically give her a place to read Ed's letters. She had taken a chance on asking James to put a hook on the inside of the door to the room so she could lock the door, feeling that he would not tell William what she had requested. Sarah relied on James to protect her privacy as he had always done.

After the door was secured, she surveyed her covert area. It was a huge space three quarters the size of the entire first floor. Both she and William had decided not to turn this space into a ballroom, but to use it in a practical manner. The machinery for their central vacuum system was installed practically in the middle of the floor and the central water tank was nearby. The room was sparsely furnished with a discarded little chair she had taken up there from the basement and a small table that James had placed by it, its pedigree unknown to Sarah. She had never seen it before. The meager furnishings had been placed by the big front windows so Sarah could view her entire realm from this vantage point. Older houses used to have a Captain's walk on top of the roof where the man of the house could go to survey his domain, but modern houses didn't include this feature. Sarah, however, had fashioned her own Captain's walk up here in this third floor room by the large windows where she could relax, read Ed's letters, and dream of --- whatever she wanted. Even with the primitive furniture, the room seemed like an inviting place to be because it was here that she was able to read his correspondence in peace and privacy and daydream. Eagerly she opened the latest letter that he had written the night he got home from Georgia:

Darling Mine,

Am anxiously awaiting your next letter to know if you are well, and to get the news & to know what is on Sweetheart's mind. Oh! how I love you, - more and more – is the true way of putting it.

Darling, I cannot thank you enough for the new picture –To me it is grand and was needed so much. Am indeed proud of it. Every new one and every one in fact is treasured so much and helps lighten the burden – so never fail to have one taken when opportunity offers – for remember – it is for me & I need them. You are the truest mate in the world and I would trust you to the end of the world as our symbol indicates.

Tomorrow I have a man-sized job on my hands. Want to hear a little business?

Well – the electric light companies- ever since the introduction of the Mazda or Tungsten Lamp as it was called, (8 years ago), on account of their revenues being cut in two had to make it up in some way – so they started out to get new business – so they organized commercial depts. and started selling merchandise – such as vacuum cleaners, heating appliances and what not. Not being able to sell them fast enough and overlooking the important point that they had not yet created a demand through advertising, etc. – they started to sell at cost – then cut prices and in lots of cases actually gave goods away – then following installment plans and every resource was called in to get devices on their lines – to sell current. Of course – no dealer or jobber could compete in the sale under these circumstances. So the majority of the dealers and jobbers just did nothing and protested of course.

In some cities like Cleveland for instance – the lighting company cooperated by advertising and doing other creative

*work and the dealer and jobber made its sales and every-
thing was OK. –But Cleveland cases were rare. Now the
Electric Light Assns. Committee have the temerity to go to
the Manufacturers directly and demand better prices than
the jobbers are getting – or as good and use the argument
that the dealer and jobbers are not an economic factor in the
scheme of things – which has got us up in the air and we are
going (3 of us) before the August Body of Capitalists who
control the lighting business (their Executive Committee)
and tell them what we think about it & the writer, Lover,
is to be the spokesman – I suppose I should tremble at the
thought of talking to Mr. Sam Insull and others of his ilk-
but somehow or other I don't & no proverbial cold beads of
perspiration are as yet running down my back. The job is
to be done tomorrow morning – so I am studying it now –
hence this dissertation.*

*Have got to go to a dinner dance at the Astor Saturday
night with the Liens. Two or more likely three dances will
be Sweethearts share How I will commune with you – you
will know it and feel it.*

*With love and kisses, Sweetheart, as of yore – I close –
as ever and ever thine own – (and more), I Do.*

Baby

Sarah thrust the envelope into her pocket, reread the letter and then
opened the small door that led to the attic space. Ducking her head and
getting down on her knees, she crawled a few feet until she reached a box
she kept on the far side of the chimney. She kissed the letter and lovingly
placed it into her secret box. Downstairs Sarah destroyed the envelope
by tearing it into a hundred pieces and disposing of them in the garbage.

William wouldn't be home for hours so Sarah felt secure in conducting
personal correspondence in her sitting room at the comfortable, elegant,
woman's writing desk. Sarah set down and lovingly ran her hands over the

smooth mahogany surface of the pullout writing board. The desk was one she had purchased in Chicago. Her country club friends without exception had "family" pieces of furniture they showed off as Grandfather John's desk and Great Grandmother Mary's china cabinet, but neither William's nor her family had nice furnishings to pass on. Sarah's farm family, although well off, acquired practical, not elegant, furniture and William's Irish tribe with their six children bought what they needed and could afford, which was not a great deal. Sarah thought about telling visitors to her home that this was Grandmother Elsa's desk, but decided to just be proud that she could afford to buy it. Maybe Sam would have children and then she could pass it on.

Reaffirming the beauty of the desk she began to write, first to Ed telling him that William was allowing her to slow down the entertaining a bit. Not that he had slowed down on his desire to be first in command at Faries Manufacturing, but at present, he had a new strategy that didn't require as much effort on Sarah's part. He had simply decided to become closer to the Irving family next door. During the 1910's, Mr. Irving effectively was in charge of the company and William felt his friendship would pay off by at least being awarded the position of second in command. First William had gone into partnership with Mr. Irving and two of the Mueller's sons to buy the land on which they all built their houses; therefore, the Irvings and Gradys were next-door neighbors. In 1914 the Faries moved in with the Irvings giving the Gradys an opportunity to be close to the whole family. William encouraged Sarah to organize social trips out-of-town with the Irvings, which she did; but now, William planned the trips for just "the boys" and Sarah smiled a little as she conveyed to Ed her relief at the lifting of part of her burden.

Sarah did not have an abundance of news to relate to Ed, especially since she and William were getting along well, but she did tell him her love for him was abiding and that she was already looking forward to their next meeting. Sarah sat back in her chair and surveyed her letter. Momentarily being honest with herself, she did believe Ed was her soul mate and wished she had met him before she married William, and also admitted the intrigue of their affair made life exciting.

Next she wrote to Sam who was doing well in his first year at Princeton. He had been able to come to Decatur for all the holidays and had only returned to Iowa to see Grandmother Elwood once since he came to live with Sarah. Knowing how petty her feelings were, Sarah still couldn't help being glad he chose to spend most of his time with her and William. She felt that finally Sam was *her* son. And William had always treated Sam as his own. Occasionally when Charles's business trips took him to the east, Sam's father went to visit, but Ed, with encouragement from William, went to see Sam more than any of the others and formed a tight bond with him.

As Sarah wrote the chatty letter to Sam she reflected, "How lucky he is to have all these people care about him."

Things were going well between mother and son, easing much of Sarah's former guilt. Soon Sam would be home for the entire summer, and then, back to Princeton in the fall for his sophomore year.

COUNTRY CLUB HOUSE
DECATUR, ILL.

The Decatur Country Club
1915

CHAPTER 18

Wilson's War

Decatur Country Club April 1917

ON APRIL 6, 1917 it became official. The United States was at war with Germany. President Wilson's efforts to keep our neutrality were a failure. No longer could America ignore the acts of war being committed by Germany. When the news was announced, Sarah was at a luncheon at the Country Club. The women at Sarah's table each had a comment on the news, the main statement being that it would not be possible now to take a trip abroad. One of Sarah's lunch companions complained that not only would she not be able to travel to Paris, but probably couldn't even have a dress shipped to Decatur in a timely manner. She showed great dismay that the season would be over before she could get a dress. The group chattered on and on in this fashion until Sarah finally jumped up from her seat and glared at the seven other women seated around the table.

Surprising even herself with the intensity of her feelings, she shouted, "Be quiet! You all sound selfish and silly. Do any of you know what is going on the World? Even though President Wilson promised to try to keep us out of war, it has been very clear for the last several months at least that we would be at war with someone. You had to see this coming. Look what happened in Mexico a few months ago."

"What happened in Mexico a few months ago?" queried one innocent, wide-eyed woman.

Sarah took a deep breath and tried to get her frustration under control. She knew this group of friends spent no time on reading the newspaper or any nonfiction book, only fashion news. They really did not know what was happening in the world away from the country club.

"Don't you ever read the newspaper? We have a real problem with Mexico. Have you ever heard of Poncho Villa? Not one of you? Well, he is trying to usurp the power of the legitimate government in Mexico and take over."

Looking at the group Sarah saw no understanding or signs of agreement.

Trying again she said, "His army took seventeen American engineers off a train and shot sixteen of them in cold blood."

At last there were some changes of expression on the faces of the women. Encouraged, she continued.

"Do we as Americans ignore this or should we retaliate?" she demanded.

Realizing she was getting too upset for the circumstances, Sarah sat down and tried to get back to a quiet discussion, but all eyes remained on her, so she stood up and continued tempering her comments to the level of her friends' understanding.

"It seems the whole world is in turmoil. You remember the Lusitania, and you do know that many of our young men are already overseas fighting in France and Belgium with the Allies against Germany. These men are in trenches which they had to dig, live in, and then get shot at. The Germans are killing them with guns and poison gas as well."

The lunch group was now paying close attention to Sarah and what she was telling them and began asking questions.

"How could you live in a trench?"

"Where could you go to the bathroom?" asked one very serious woman.

"How do they get their showers?"

One excited woman had read something in the newspaper which upset her, "Do you think our children will have to wear wooden shoes like the English children do?"

Another wanted to know, "Why do they have to wear wooden shoes?"

Again quietly Sarah said, "Leather is scare because the government is trying to keep shoes on the soldiers, so this is one way the general population can help save leather.

Sarah was able to answer their questions as she was very well informed and she painted for them an accurate picture of trench warfare.

Finally the question was asked, "Can we do something?"

Looking around the table at the women listening carefully to what she was saying, she began to see that her patriotic enthusiasm might be able to help her country during the oncoming war. Maybe she could inspire people to help with the war effort.

Encouraged Sarah went on. "Of course you can do something. Most of you know that I've been training with the Red Cross to learn how to assist nurses who are dealing with traumatized patients. You all could do that too."

"Oh no, Sarah. There's no way I could do that," said Jolene, one of the younger ones of the group. "You are so good at things like that. You don't seem to be afraid of anything. Remember when Anna Millikin was dying, you stayed with her for days to help her pass."

"Well, I did that because she was my friend and neighbor and wanted me to be with her. That certainly wouldn't qualify me to help clean up a gunshot wound, or help with an amputation."

"Why would you have to do that? You aren't overseas in the trenches," said Jolene.

"I am thinking of going to France with the Red Cross for a tour of duty."

Again Jolene spoke up, "For heaven's sake! Are you crazy?"

"Goodness," thought Sarah, "no one knows me or understands me."

She looked at Jolene's face, still pleasant in her concerned frown.

"I am just as afraid as any of you, but we are called to do what we must— I do what I must," she said.

Looking around the tables Sarah again saw only confusion. These women could do so much, change so much, if only they were given the information, not kept in the ignorance of their privilege. Sarah looked to June, unsure of how to continue. June rose from her seat, stood beside Sarah, and with the poise and determination engrained in her personage, addressed the group.

"Ladies, are we not Americans? To fail to take the action Mrs. Grady calls for is to fail to care for our own families. We are matriarchs within our homes, let us also be so within our community. Mrs. Grady, the only naturalized citizen among us seems to have more patriotism for her adopted country than any of us that were born here. I for one am going to join her at the Red Cross."

Sarah clasped June's hand as the women around them began to nod in agreement.

Sarah went home from lunch feeling very satisfied. She had given the girls a whole list of activities in which they could participate to help the war effort, and they were excited to feel that they could help. Knowing that war was inevitable, she had been writing to Ed asking what she could do to help and he had supplied her with a directory of actions she could take; but Sarah had noticed that Ed's suggestions would involve her in very safe activities and that was not necessarily what she wanted. She hoped to make a difference, not just be safe, so Sarah began to form her own plans. After her success with the girls at lunch, she was sure that she could mobilize many women to help with necessary chores for the armed forces both overseas and at home. She sat down and wrote Ed a letter asking him to help her get a commission to go abroad as an assistant nurse.

Focusing on the war, Sarah was much less concerned about William and his promotions. Almost immediately after the declaration of war, parties were being cancelled. The thought was that these events were frivolous at this time of need in the country. Even William was not as concerned about his standing in his company as he was about helping deliver goods for the war effort. This attitude made things easier for Sarah as she did not have to entertain on the massive scale that she had been accustomed to.

Her time was consumed with war, taking on one activity after the other. Three days a week in the afternoon she stood outside the Millikin Bank soliciting money for Liberty Loans. She led a group that consolidated the charities in the county so less money would be spent by each one on administration as people's generosity now was more concentrated on giving for the war effort. Five mornings a week she spent working for the Red Cross.

Sarah received a response from Ed on her request for help getting a commission for an overseas tour of duty with the Red Cross. Pulling strings would be easy for Ed, but his response was quick and firm:

> *Your proposal for becoming an applicant for the post the clipping describes acted on me like a cold douche. Darling, you ask what I think. Frankly it strikes me as sheer madness. Why should you go to such a post of danger? Why should you think of such a thing? It was never mentioned in our original plan. If you stick to the plan then there might be a chance of our reunion – but to enter into such a dangerous occupation is unspeakable and would tear your Ed to bits.*
>
> *You wanted me to promise to not discourage you – but I did not promise on a proposition like this last one you put up. No, darling, you must defer any action until I see you.*
> *From your loving and adoring, Baby*

Sarah's chances of seeing Ed at William's business meetings were increasing, as the electric groups were getting a little more active because of increased production of materials needed for the war. William went to at least one meeting a month and, when Sarah could get away, she went with him. She and Ed always managed to spend some time alone, but Sarah thought that William was a little more watchful of her than he used to be.

Sarah told Ed, "I believe that William is still slightly suspicious of us, but since you are his best friend, he can't convince himself that you would act inappropriately. Therefore, he tells himself that you and I are just friends and continues to invite you and Florence and Gwen to visit us –often. He and Florence are friends and he knows that Gwen likes being with me. Those visits are extremely difficult for me because I can't be with you as I would like."

Ed responded with sympathy, "I know how hard it is for us to be together when our families are around, but Sarah, our love is strong enough to withstand any and all obstacles. We are strengthened by overcoming our barriers."

Sarah was beginning to wonder about their promise to be together for the rest of their lives. There was always something getting in the way. First it was money – now it was the war. What would it be next?

CHAPTER 19

Wartime Life

3 Millikin Place Summer 1917

WILLIAM NO LONGER had to insist that Sarah arise at 5:45 a.m. in the morning. She had to be up at least by then to start her many tasks for the day. Wartime in America was busy. William totally ignored Sarah as he was occupied trying to keep his business current with the government demands and participating in the war efforts his clubs were promoting. Trying to single handedly make Decatur the Midwestern center for war activities, Sarah again over extended herself, and, as she was disposed to do, lost too much weight. Her slender figure became extremely thin and the color left her face. William did not notice. His relaxed demeanor had vanished with Wilson's declaration of war, and he insisted Sarah do certain business related chores for him in addition to her own work.

When she was totally exhausted or depressed, she would sit down and write to Ed or steal away to her sanctuary on the third floor and reread some of his old letters. No real privacy was needed for her reading or writing because William was never home. Within Ed's letters Sarah found her salvation. Why, she asked herself, did she feel compelled to work so hard? Ed was entreating her to come spend some time with him in New York or in their special spot at Hot Springs. Maybe she should go and relax a bit. She was longing to see Ed – alone. Always.

Sitting by the window in her room on the third floor in her old chair, she made a decision to go to Hot Springs.

"Who knows how long this war will last and I am wearing out," she proclaimed to a bird perched outside on the windowsill.

Picking up one of Ed's letters that she especially enjoyed, she pretended to read it for the first time even though she could recite it word for word:

> *My own darling Mate,*
>
> *How you are longed for. Dearest, how I love you – you must take this one on faith – I Do – more and more. When I was before that august body last Friday your image was before me every minute and thereby my courage was kept up. You are always my inspiration. When I see you at the next meeting don't overdo your acting as though I'm an unpleasant stranger and make me too miserable. I want to enjoy the meeting and if you put into effect too much acting – your poor mate will have a hard time.*
>
> *We will know in about two weeks I suppose whether we will have war or not. It will depend on whether our armed boats as they enter the war zone are attacked or not – if they are- then we are in for it and all of us will have to decide what to do – that is what part we individually will play in it.*
>
> *President Wilson certainly showed LaFollette what he and his ilk of Senators are - and Wilson upset all precedents by making the new Senate change their rule – so that it can't happen again. No longer can one Senator block the whole game as anyone could since the Senate was established.*
>
> *Do you know that this was what destroyed Poland as a nation? They had some such rule in their parliament, which was worse than a select body as our Senate is supposed to be. So jealous were the Poles of this liberty that if one man in parliament objected the thing couldn't go through – so this proved to be their weakness and they were gobbled up and partitioned into three parts Russia taking 1/3 – Germany 1/3 and Austria the other 1/3 – all because of a silly rule such as our Senate has into effect.*

Wilson will be given his true place in history by posterity. He will never be appreciated in contemporaneous life.

Enclosed is a cartoon from "Life" that caught my visibilities. It reminds me of Americans in London and Paris hotels – Every American goes to the most fashionable hotels and thinks all the people he is looking at are Londoners or Parisians – when as a matter of fact – most of the people he is looking at are from his own country. I found this to be true when I was overseas some years ago and changed my hotel at both places and so fell in with the real natives – who were visitors from their own provinces or cities. This cartoon was so funny to me because the other day at the Knickerbocker Hotel – some people at the next table mistook the others for residents of 5th Ave. and it turned out the curious ones were from WilkesBarre, PA. and the alleged New Yorkers were from Scranton.

Well, Darling, am praying for the 14th when I can fold you in my arms once more.

With my heartfelt love and affection, I close with the usual kisses
Ever and ever your mate, Ed

After rereading Ed's letter, she almost ran for the telephone to try to call him on the phone. Sarah immediately decided to go spend at least a week in Hot Springs by herself, but hopefully Ed could join her for a day or two. This quick decision came as she found herself actually longing to go back to the days before the war when all she had to do was give parties for William. The stress level from her war activities was so high that she was becoming really ill. She needed to relax with Ed without having to worry about William.

The sacrifices the American population was expected to shoulder were really not that terrible in Sarah's opinion and she wanted to do everything she possibly could to help her country, but, nevertheless, life was a little harder under the war rules and just trying to keep track of everything was quite a job.

Planning meals was time consuming. Dorothy still did Sarah's cooking, but insisted Sarah plan all the meals because keeping track of "wheatless" Mondays, "meatless" Tuesdays, and "pork-free" Thursdays was too much extra work. So in addition to her other work for the cause, Sarah planned meals and organized the Victory Garden that James worked. Sadie was in charge of reducing electric usage; the War Police, as she called them, allowed only one light to be turned on in the house at night and no outside lights. Somehow, Sadie never seemed to be around when excess lights were left on, so Sarah had to pay attention to Sadie's job too.

Sarah still had her golf when she could take time to play, but that was not very often. Her new appointment by the Red Cross to Regional Coordinator of the War Effort meant that almost every waking hour was spoken for. Ed had convinced her that she could do more good staying in the United States rather than going overseas because certified nurses were going abroad leaving a shortage over here. She had completed her nurse's aide training and could help those medical personnel tending to people in this country, especially since wounded soldiers were being sent home from the front. The territory Sarah had to cover with her new job took in many miles of Central Illinois, from Bloomington to Springfield to Effingham to Champaign. Usually she traveled on the interurban, but occasionally she had to drive her own car. Breakdowns were so frequent she had taken an auto mechanics course to ensure she could be responsible on the road. Sarah often wondered if going overseas would have been easier than staying home. William commented that he would have to buy her a car of her own soon because of all the miles she was putting on the family's present one.

Sarah recognized she had to leave for a few days relaxation or she would "blow up" as Ed told her. That was why she decided to risk phoning Ed at his office hoping that he would be there. Sarah held the receiver tightly as the phone rang. Ed's secretary answered and Sarah was pleased that the connection was clear. Crossing her fingers she said boldly, "This is Sarah Grady, a friend of Ed's from Illinois. May I speak to him, please?"

Sarah held her breath as the second of silence seemed an eternity.

"Just a minute. I'll see if he can take your call," said the secretary's crisp voice.

Again Sarah waited having time to reflect that calling him at work was a bad idea, but momentarily Ed's strong voice came through the line, "Sarah, what's wrong? Are you all right?"

"No, I'm not. I can't take any more pressure or responsibility. I need to get away and have some fun. I haven't even played golf for a month or ridden Midnight. Can you get away for a few days and go to our special place?" Sarah's words tumbled out.

"Oh, Sarah, I've been warning you that you were taking on way too many responsibilities. You sound really bad. Just tell me when you are going and I will be there for at least a couple of days. I promise you I will get away," Ed said in a concerned voice.

"Next week. I'll be at Hot Springs on Wednesday and plan to stay for a week. I'll reserve a suite in my name so William can call and check on me."

Ed agreed and they hung up.

Without checking with William, Sarah made her train and resort suite reservations and started making arrangements with her groups to be gone for a week. June who was a part of most of Sarah's volunteer work, agreed to take over for her in her absence. Sarah was grateful not only her support socially, but for her unending loyalty. Faithfully, she had remained the keeper of Sarah's secret life.

William made it home for dinner that night. It was a Wednesday so Dorothy had prepared most of the foods that were prohibited on the other weeknights. William gobbled his food down as though he hadn't eaten for days and Sarah picked at the little bit of food she had put on her plate.

William took second helpings and started a conversation, "This food is delicious. It's amazing how we take for granted that we will always have anything we want to eat. I don't want to deprive our troops of food, but I do miss my meat."

Sarah continued the small talk, "You know I really miss not being able to buy the shoes I want. The stores, all of them, just don't have many to choose from."

As Sarah spoke, William took a recess from shoveling food into his mouth and looked up a Sarah.

"Sarah, you aren't eating much. You look ill. You need to go to the doctor – tomorrow."

This was Sarah's opportunity to tell William of her plans.

"I've decided to go to Hot Springs for a week by myself and play golf and rest. I'll be leaving next Wednesday."

With visible relief William said, "That's a great idea Sarah. You need a rest."

The next day she got a telegram from Ed saying he would arrive on Thursday and spend the whole weekend with her. My, how she was looking forward to this trip; it was time for fun. Sam was home for the summer but Sarah didn't think he would mind her being gone for a week.

When she told him, he said, "That's okay, mother. I have a golf match scheduled every day next week and on Tuesday and Thursday evenings I have a meeting of my group that mails supplies overseas to our troops. I'll be busy. And besides I have to start getting my things ready to go back to school."

"I do hate to spend time away from you. It seems that we have so little time together, but I have to have some rest or I will be down sick and no good to anyone."

Sam gave her a tender look and said, "I'm happy you are going because you do look ill. I'll be here when you return."

Pleased that Sam was so mature in their interactions, Sarah thought about the assessment Ed had made about Sam stating that he still was wildly independent, but was an honest and intelligent young man. Sarah was very proud of him.

Hot Springs was biblical for Sarah and Ed. Besides playing golf, bridge, and dancing every evening away, they took long walks. Walking through the beautiful, well-manicured gardens of the resort, they held hands, sometimes not saying a word for hours and sometimes talking animatedly for long intervals. One evening Ed told Sarah about a couple he had seen while playing golf.

"They stopped their automobile at a place where two roads crossed. The couple was about fifty some years old. The lady fascinated me. Her face was like yours would be if you were her age. Something white like lace hung from her hat and her hand was in that of her companion who I fancied as her husband. As the machine stopped a moment, I couldn't take my eyes off of them – for they appeared for all the world so engrossed in each other that I fancied them as my dream of what you and I would be like when we get to that age. I have always had the feeling that we would be so deeply in love with each other that we would never tire of caressing even in old age and would make people gasp at our boldness even in public. Such is the power of late love, my dearest."

Sarah listened with delight at Ed's story. He knew how to tug at her heart and he had such a way with words. Sarah could picture Ed and herself in old age still madly in love as an old couple.

"You are my soul mate, Mr. Rockafellow. I didn't know I could love anyone the way I love you."

Sarah was eating ravenously and could feel her weight coming back to normal as she enjoyed her food. After two days, Ed remarked that the color was returning to her face. Neither of them read a newspaper or tried to get any news. How wonderful it was to totally rest from the war.

Sarah called William on the phone every night hoping the call would forestall any notion he might have to drop everything and come to join her. William could tell by her voice that she was getting better – little knowing the real reason. Sarah had all the attention and love she could ever ask for from Ed and it was just what she needed. Ed was always there for her. Sarah didn't want to ever go home, but Ed brought her back to reality reminding her that the time was not yet right for them to leave their spouses and be together.

"You know I have to go home now, but we are coming closer to being a married couple. I want you to know that our investment account now totals about $14,000," Ed said, adding, "I think we need double that amount before we obtain our divorces, but the way the stock market is going now, I estimate in a year we will hit our goal. And this damned war is keeping us so occupied that it is difficult to think of anything else, even us."

"Ed, I would go with you anywhere, anytime – without money," said Sarah.

"I love you so, my Sallie, but we must be practical."

When Ed left to go back to work, Sarah didn't really mind. She was a dreamer and needed alone time to make her plans and solve her problems. She and Ed were so right together, therefore, she needed to be free of William and Ed needed his freedom from Florence. However, the war was in the way right now. She was sure they would already be together if it were not for this war, but she could be patient.

CHAPTER 20

Bright Blue with Red Rims

3 Millikin Place Summer 1917

THE MORNING AFTER she returned from Hot Springs, Sarah put on her riding clothes when she arose because as soon as breakfast was over she wanted to take a ride on Midnight. Not only had she missed Sam, but it had been over a week since she had seen her horse. As she sat down to eat, she noticed William seemed a little nervous. He cleared his throat and spoke softly, "Midnight isn't here, Sarah."

"What? Where is he? Is he sick?" boomed Sarah.

"Calm down. He's fine. In fact, I think he's happier than he's been for a long time. I took him to my farm."

"You did what? Why? Midnight is happy and I want him here," screeched Sarah as her voice formed a shrill echo in William's ears.

"It was a practical decision. You have been too busy to ride him very much. We no longer need him for transportation and we need the space in the garage because I bought you your own car. With all the traveling you're currently doing for the Red Cross, you need your own vehicle. Hopefully the car will be here by your birthday next week."

"I don't want a car. I want Midnight here," pouted Sarah, "and now how can I go for a ride at night when I can't sleep?"

"You can't and that's the good news. I've told you time and time again, you shouldn't be doing that. It's too dangerous. I'll take time today to drive you to the farm so you can see him. It only takes about 25 minutes to get there."

"No, thank you. And you can keep your car. I want my horse not some silly new motor car," ranted Sarah as she thumped upstairs.

Sarah plopped on the window seat in her sitting room and stared out the window as hot tears streamed down her face. What horrible thing could she do to William to punish him for taking Midnight away? After about five minutes of imagining the worst punishments possible, Sarah reclaimed her adult status. Telling herself she had been acting like a spoiled brat who didn't get her way, Sarah Grady the dignified, sophisticated, society belle came back to reality. Her thoughts had a little trouble finding their way through her anger, but as they did pass through her mind, Sarah had to admit that possibly Midnight was happier on the farm where he could run around more. Also, she really could use her own car and it would need a garage. And yes, she hadn't found much time to ride lately.

"It probably was the correct decision," thought Sarah, but her stubbornness prevented her from telling William. She found James and asked him to leave the car in the driveway after he took William to work, as she was going to the farm.

James nodded and smiled, "He's doing fine, Mrs. Grady. A horse really likes being out in the country where he can be free to run, and you'll enjoy your ride out there more than you do in town."

Since there were no people to disturb and the scenery was more pastoral than the park in the city, Sarah did find the country atmosphere more pleasing. William's farm had a creek running through the fields and one area was nothing but trees. Actually, she could see that Midnight was relaxed, not as jumpy as he was in town. She decided the arrangement would work out and she really did want her own car, but never would she give William the satisfaction of knowing she felt this way. William again had ignored her in his decision making. If only he could be more like Ed she thought. They would have sat down together, weighed all the "pros" and "cons", and then reached a conclusion that pleased both of them.

On Sarah's birthday when she came home at noon from her Red Cross duties, William was there and escorted her outside to the garage.

"Shut your eyes." He raised the garage door and shouted, "Happy Birthday!"

Sarah opened her eyes and there sat a beautiful, bright blue Packard roadster with red rims on the tires, the most luxurious car the company made and it was all hers. She walked around the vehicle touching parts of it as she went. All her friends were going to be incredibly jealous. In spite of her desire to punish William for taking Midnight to the farm, she couldn't contain her excitement.

"It's gorgeous. Thank you, William. May I drive it now?"

"Soon. There's a salesman coming over to show you how everything works. After that it's all yours," William replied in a rather smug voice. He knew Sarah would love the car and he would be back in her good graces.

Since returning from her vacation, Sarah had plunged into her war work with renewed energy. She and Ed continued their banter about the war, their love, and general day-to-day activities through their letters and the occasional phone call. Disagreements between them, and there were many, tended to strengthen their bond rather than pull them apart. For instance, Sarah complained about the states in the East not meeting their draft quota, while the Midwest always met or exceeded the federal goals. She felt something had to be done to improve the draft ratio in the East. Rather than taking exception to her position, Ed tried to explain the situation to her as he wrote,

> *Your reproaches against the East for failure to fill their quotas in the army are apparently justified by the returns here. Never was any question about the number we were drafting when the talk started last fall*
>
> *You recall how severe was the patriotism of the West at any time. It was their seeming indifference as to the*

criticism of our President all last year because he didn't lead us into war. In retrospect one can see now how well he realized that the country wasn't prepared to declare war, let alone fighting one – and let me add right here, Dearest one, that this is a war of mechanics– or machinery whichever way you want to put it. There will be no hand to hand fighting as of old – no charging up hills – no cavalry, etc. It is all mechanics and the most scientific will become the victors. This means that shops, laboratories and farms will do the work heretofore done by the men in camps. We have nearly 500 engineers in the shops working for the government alone and every one of them will be rated the same as an enlisted man with a gun on the firing line and will wear a badge or uniform so that people will not be able to call them slackers, so my dear mate – I do not fear for one moment that in the final count the East will show up favorably, for after all, we are one people no matter what locality we may be living in Unfortunately for the east – we have the congested population and an ever increasing horde of foreigners and Jews added to which is the preponderance of factories attracting them, so we do not shine when compared with other parts of the country. One thing we know is holding up our regular army recruiting and that is that Roosevelt has thousands tied up from enlisting in the guard or army because with him they expect to go to Europe. Some 180 thousand he has from all over the country, but the big majority are from the East ...

With all my heart and soul dearest you are mine for life,
I Do, I Do

Every time the draft was mentioned Sarah thoughts turned to Sam. He was the right age to be taken into the army, but if he remained in school, he might be exempt at least for a while. Princeton was the most prestigious school in the entire country and the students enrolled there had to study diligently to get acceptable evaluations. His grades as a freshman were adequate, but not outstanding; Sam was not giving all his effort to his studies. Her prayer was that he would do well and remain eligible to stay in college, knowing that after graduation, he would go do his part for his country. For now Sam had two more weeks left of his summer vacation and Sarah intended to be with him every minute she could.

CHAPTER 21

❖

Our Neighbors Are Spies

Millikin Place Fall 1917

THE SUMMER WAS over and Sam enthusiastically left to go back to Princeton. Sarah was delighted to accompany him so she could help him get settled and have a change of pace for herself.

As they got off the train in Princeton, Sam said, "Mother, you really don't have to help me get settled. All I have to do is make sure my trunk gets into my dorm room. I guess I can take you on a tour of the campus after that."

"I'd like to help you arrange your room and I want to see where you'll be living," she said, "William had to pull some strings to get you into Campbell Hall and I want to see what it looks like."

Sarah ignored Sam's protests, as all mothers do when they take their sons to college, and organized his room while Sam sat quietly on the bed. The room had the essentials; a bed, desk, book shelf, wardrobe and a chair. Sarah noted that the window had no curtain or drape on it, but quickly chided herself remembering this was a young man's dorm room. After the mother in Sarah was satisfied with the living quarters, she accepted Sam's offer of a campus tour. First they went to an upscale "eating club" of which Sam was a member and had lunch, then walked around the rest of the campus. Sarah experienced a reverent feeling as she stood looking at the tall towers of the Gothic buildings and felt as though she should bow her head. Many of the brick buildings were fairly new, but looked old, as though they had been there for centuries. Never having been to England, Sarah felt she knew what Oxford or Cambridge must look like. What a tribute to the architects. Ed had told her which of the buildings had been in Wilson's plan for the college, which made the whole area even more interesting to her.

After touring the campus for several hours, Sam said, "Why don't you go on to the city and maybe have dinner with some friends?"

Perceiving that her settling services were no longer required as Sam was very outgoing, greeting old friends and trying to make new ones, she determined she was not needed and took a train to New York. The next day she managed to spend the afternoon with Ed who promised to see Sam as often as possible and report on his progress. Sarah experienced "Mother's Anxiety" over leaving her only son and a nagging thought kept rising to the surface of her consciousness: Sam was now nineteen and could be taken into the military. Sarah wondered how patriotic she could be if he were drafted and sent overseas.

December of 1917 brought the holidays. William decided to have several parties, one on Christmas and one New Year's Eve, rationalizing he had contributed generously to the war effort for the year and it would be good for people's morale to have some fun for a change. That meant Sarah had to go into action in order to make William's events, as they always were, the talk of the town. Because of the two galas she was hosting, she informed Ed that she would be tied down for the holidays and would not be able to see him until after the first of the year. She read with interest his response telling her what he thought of New Year's Eve parties.

> *Dearest,*
>
> *Am planning to go to the seaside on Jan 1st. How to get by New Year's Eve is a problem – of all the nights in a year – this New Year's Eve celebration is the limit. It is the most disgusting orgy ever conceived and if National*

Prohibition ever comes – it will be because of the disgraceful exhibition that occurs at New York and Chicago and elsewhere in imitation of what goes on in these cities. The liquor people are doomed unless they do two things d---d quickly: 1ˢᵗ – abolish the corner saloon, 2ⁿᵈ -- Get the hotel people to cut out the New Year's bacchanalian orgies of the – so called – bourgeois.

To go out to get deliberately drunk is the most supremely senseless thing I know of. In olden times these New Year's jags were conducted on lines that could at least be defended on the more reasonable score of sociability - you called on your friend and took a social glass with them – and if you get drunk – you were in the hands of your intimates – if that has any merit to it – and so from these abuses – the matrons in society abolished it – but ye Gods – what a substitute they gave us in the form of these New Year's Eve affairs. Ugh! I have been out of them for ten years until last year when I was dragged into one ...

To hear me preach, Darling, in the above fashion one would think I was a teetotaler wouldn't they – well I am not I love a social glass – but excuse me from the New Year's Eve type with strangers, but I may have to go through another one to satisfy my boss.

Busy as I am, Love, not a conscious moment passes without thoughts of you – you are always with me no matter what I may be doing – and oh Sweet – keep well for me, won't you? ....Keep on the brakes – don't attempt too much and rest When things are coming too fast think of me and what I want you to do and then you will act for both of us. Save yourself for the one who loves you best in all the world.

With all my love and kisses,
I Do, I Do

As Sarah watched the hounds of Decatur bourgeois pour into her house for a New Year's Eve party, she thought of Ed's letter. How she wished that she could spend a quiet evening alone with her soul mate. But putting on her party face, she greeted everyone with a welcoming smile and spent the evening making William proud of his perfect wife.

As the calendar turned to 1918, the war raged on. Often it looked like the conflict would be over quickly, but sometimes it looked like there was no end to it. Most people in Decatur embraced patriotism, even the Irish population who forgave Britain just enough to be their ally as they supported destroying Germany. Citizens were so full of fervor for the war that they even denounced the German- American families who were not allowed to participate in the war activities for fear they were spies. Neighbors now viewed the "Huns" next door, with whom they had been friends for years, as suspicious defectors at best and full-fledged spies at worst. Many of these people were pillars of their communities but were now shunned and watched carefully.

In Decatur, everyone who was not German was intent on blaming these American families with a German heritage for anything that was going wrong on the war front.

Sarah was astonished one morning when a neighbor called her and said, "Mrs. Grady this is Mrs. Beal. Do you think we should turn the Muellers over to the government for espionage? I saw Mr. Mueller outside in his back yard yesterday and it looked like he was burying something in the ground... or maybe digging something up. I think we better take action. It really looked suspicious."

Sarah's astonishment turned to anger as she absorbed what the caller was saying. Her first thought was to ridicule Mrs. Beal, but then she realized that Mr. Mueller's accuser was simply scared.

"Do you suppose that Mr. Mueller could have been digging up a bone that his dog had buried? Or maybe he was planting a bush. I did that a few days ago. I planted some flowers that I wanted to get in the ground before it got any warmer. You know what a beautiful garden the Muellers have every year. We should watch carefully and see how they accomplish that," she said.

Sarah's patience worked and Mrs. Beal began thinking about her spring garden. Before she hung up the phone, Sarah assured Mrs. Beal, "We don't need to keep an eye on Mr. Mueller because he is such an honest and trustworthy man. If I find anything amiss in our neighborhood, I'll call you."

"Thank you so much, Mrs. Grady. You always know just what to do."

Sarah didn't believe her neighbors the Muellers were spies; in fact, their company was doing a great job furnishing the army with needed supplies. At the few events the country club was still sponsoring, Sarah made it a point to talk to the Muellers because they were being noticeably ignored. No one questioned Sarah's loyalty to her country so her sympathy and belief that this attitude towards German families was wrong, eased the tensions towards these citizens in Decatur.

At one of the parties at the country club, Sarah noticed that the two Mueller families were sitting in a corner all by themselves. Unbelievably their friends were ignoring them. Sarah stepped into action by grabbing June and William and telling them the rest of the evening would be spent with the Muellers. Since everyone wanted to be sure to spend time with Sarah, the crowd soon gravitated to the corner where she sat … with the Muellers. The partygoers forgot their suspicions and had a good time with all of their friends. Both Mueller families that lived in Millikin Place were forever grateful to Sarah Grady.

In her quiet moments at home Sarah took stock of her time with Ed. Their secret had survived the nearly three years since that night in the garden. Both felt their love was genuine and were willing to go to great lengths to keep it from their spouses. Sarah was agitated because William had started leaving her at home when he went to his business conferences and she was not able to see Ed as much as she desired. In a letter Ed tried to comfort her.

> *I agree with you that it is a mean selfish thing for him to do – to come and leave you at home. His policy seems to be to keep you in a state of subjugation – or putting it another way – submerge you – through terrorism or something else – a fine policy indeed to adopt toward a high spirited*

woman - but darling – for the hundredth time – let me remind you of our statue and symbol and bide your time. Follow up on your invention and work for some freedom for the future.

Every once in a while Sarah's conscience bothered her and she would write to Ed saying she could no longer see him. Then, two days later she would realize life would be unbearable without him and she would declare her undying love for him. The next week, she would question why they couldn't be together immediately, and then she would try again to bring a halt to the affair, but she could never follow through on her scruples. For many reasons Ed felt, more than Sarah, that they could not be together until their joint stock market account could make them independently wealthy. He was trying hard to make their stock purchases pay off and Sarah was doing her share by putting money into the account.

The biggest problem Sarah had with the status quo was that William insisted on inviting Ed, Florence, and their daughter Gwen to come and spend as much time as they wished in Decatur at the Grady's house, and Florence wished to come often. Also, Florence was encouraging William to stay with them when he came to New York on business. Even though Ed told Florence he would rather stay at a hotel when they were in Decatur, Florence insisted that she preferred to stay with Sarah and William. It drove both Sarah and Ed to distraction when these visits occurred. Sarah especially found it impossible to act normal when Ed was a guest in her home, causing Ed to complain that she was too cool towards him, which might cause William to be suspicious.

Ed wrote Sarah an account of one of William's visits to New York:

William showed up at 10:30 in the office and from then on things rushed and I got caught in a jam so that I didn't get time to write you much of a note but I got one off to you anyway and in the evening I sent you a telegram when I got the opportunity.

Last night I took William, Florence, and Sam to the Justin Johnston's Club -- Just we four – to dinner and William and Florence had an old-fashioned time of it dancing (I didn't have ¼ of a half of a dance) – Just got up once and started to going once a round but we couldn't synchronize and so I left it all to William and both of them were happy while I talked to Sam who looks fine. Finer than I ever saw him look – both of them are coming up to dinner to day.

All our friends went to dinner at Crafts, but Florence backed out of it and preferred to be with William and I didn't particularly care where I went to, there you are. William didn't report to Florence until yesterday – I don't like the role of tattle tale – but will assume it for once. I judge from his talk he has seen one of the 'popular' women that live above the restaurant. He wanted to bring her down for me to dance with about 11 P.M., but I balked and would have none of it. He says he will be here all next week and I think it a crying shame that you are not here. Isn't it possible to come? It makes me rail at my helplessness in not being able to bring you here.

Florence is surely pleased with William and William certainly had a good time last night. He likes them all and I think I have truly named him "Squire of Dames"... William made Florence last night several cigerets – I did not object – but William tried to make you out as an inveterate smoker, what for I do not know, nor can I imagine – but as far as I could go told him I didn't believe it – then he wouldn't bet me on it and etc. but I didn't go on with the discussion.

Darling, I do not believe it, but even if it were true – it would not affect the degree of my love one iota. Even if you have smoked, I don't believe it was ever a habit so that you *become "inveterate". My position, Sweetheart, is simply this – personally I hope you don't – but if you ever do – don't become a fiend at it.*

Am about to go down town to mail this on the fast train and leave Florence abed and Ning (maid) washing in prep for William and Sam.

With a long lover's kiss, Your own, Ed

After reading Ed's letter Sarah felt vindicated somewhat by William's actions while in New York. The double standard – what men could do that women couldn't – seemed grossly unfair to her. William's principles for her were quite high, but he clearly no longer abided by them.

"Squire of Dames, indeed," she thought, "But after everything with Ed, how can I blame William?"

No matter his actions with other women, she couldn't suppose what he would do if he ever found out the truth about her and Ed.

CHAPTER 22

⚜

Sam Takes Control

Princeton, New Jersey Early 1918

SARAH WAS KEPT abreast of Sam's activities through Ed's letters. She worried, but her war work kept her occupied so thoroughly that she saw little of her son and she rationalized she saw him as much as any college boy would want to see his mother.

Sam's father Charles went to see him at Princeton once during the year and wrote him the occasional letter. Charles professed to love his son, but was a busy man and somehow Sam did not take priority. The greatest concern about Sam from William, Ed and Charles was that he didn't take his schooling seriously enough. Sam was seemingly more concerned about having a good time than pursuing a career, drinking and gambling more than studying. Ed and William felt it was not their place to dictate rules to Sam, but insisted that he would be fine if he would choose a career path to follow. Sarah wrote to Charles who said he would go see Sam just as soon as he had a break in his business schedule.

In the meantime, Sam also worried about his grades and somehow managed to keep an acceptable grade point average. He really didn't have a clue what he wanted to do for a vocation. As he saw many of his classmates leave school and join the armed forces, he made a decision to drop out of school and become a navy pilot. He had inherited his patriotism from his mother and flying seemed to him like an exciting way to participate in fighting for his country.

The response to Sam's decision to quit school came quickly from both his birth father and mother. None of his family or mentors wanted to talk him out of being a navy pilot; they just wanted him to finish school first. Ed went to see him and gave him all the reasons he should stay in school and William wrote to him.

At the beginning of his second semester in January of 1918, about two weeks after Sam's proclamation of leaving school, he received a letter from Charles. Sam took his time opening the letter because he knew exactly what the letter would say and did not want to hear it. Unfolding the pages slowly, he noted that the correspondence was twice as long as he would have anticipated. This was going to be unpleasant reading.

Dear Sam:

Your letter at hand and I will plead guilty to having neglected to write you very frequently since the Holidays, although I wrote you a few days ago my attitude toward your entering the war at this time.

We all see the terrible situation our country is in because of lack of proper preparation for this war, and if it teaches us anything at all, it should teach us the value of preparation, not only in national affairs, but it should teach us that in our private affairs proper preparation is invaluable.

College education is simply a proper preparation for a man's life work, and without it he will be crippled all his life, and it is on that account that I have wanted you to continue your college work until you graduate, for I am confident that if you once leave college to go to war and once get busy in the outside affairs of the world, college life will look too narrow and you will never want to go back to complete your education. On the other hand I know that to be successful and to have a properly cultivated mind, one that enjoys literature and art and the beautiful things of life, that you should complete your education.

...I regard it important that you build a proper foundation under yourself. You must be well grounded in history and philosophy and in languages and mathematics and in

the culture of civilization generally before you attempt to erect the superstructure of actual business life.

I agree with you that the time may come when you should enter the service, but as I wrote you a few days ago there are hundreds of young men dying from pneumonia in our cantonments because they lack proper buildings, sanitation and clothing, and if they were in France, we still lack sufficient guns and other war material. I believe the government has all the men it can possibly use at the present time. It appears that we are not going to have enough flying machines within the next year. It is all right for you to practice aviation, and I am glad you do it, and I am willing to pay the $200.00 for you to secure an aviator pilot's license, and I note you could then earn $300.00 a month as a civilian instructor, but Sam, remember that $300 a month is only $3,600 a year, about the price of a first class clerkship, so don't allow yourself to be lured by the money you think you can earn at it. Big business men earn from fifty thousand to three or four hundred thousand a year, and an aviator's license will be of no value to you in big business, except as training in self-control.

I really appreciate the lonesomeness at Princeton, and also the feeling that other boys may look upon you as unpatriotic because you have not entered some branch of the service, but I advise you to pay no attention to that. Cultivate your mind as I have always told you to do. Don't let the war confuse you or alter you plan of work. The war won't last but a few years, but your life may continue for fifty or sixty years yet, and you will be worth more to your country as a man with a matured mind – a man of education and culture – than you will as an aviator. Of course the time may come where it is so apparent that every man is needed in the service to whip the Germans that you should

go, and when that time comes I shall not object to your going. And it is all right for you to begin to prepare for that
day by learning aviation at this time, but don't allow the
training however take your mind from your college work
any more than you can possibly help. I can realize that all of
you boys spend your evening talking war talk and aviation,
and you entirely forget your studies. Look upon the war as
only temporary. I realize too that as you say, the college life
looks narrow and small with such gigantic operations going
on in the world, and that you are eager to get into the fray,
but as I said before, you must be properly equipped before
you leave college for any other line of endeavor... I realize
that your college professors don't like to be unpatriotic, but
I know that deep down in the heart of every thinking pro-
fessor will be found the same opinions that I hold regarding
your preparation and the advisability of continuing your
studies to the very last moment.

The fear that you may be obliged to enter the service
for the safety of the country before your college course is
completed is why I advise you to look ahead in the junior
and senior studies and get as much from them as you can
so as to at least get an outline of what those studies will
bring you and to at least imbibe the philosophy that those
years will teach.

I note you say you have been up in a machine a few
times and were going to fly again on the day you wrote me.
How do you like it? What is the sensation? Do you get
dizzy or attacked with nausea? Before I ever drove an automobile, I was afraid I would be too nervous to drive, but
now I enjoy it immensely, and I imagine a man's experience
in learning to fly will be the same. You want a quick brain,
absolute self-possession and a complete co-ordination of
your mind and muscles.

I note you say your mother suggests that she pay your half years college expense. I suppose you are referring to tuition and books and board amounting to about $300. And that I furnish the spending money, clothing, etc., which you say would cost a little more than $300. This will be all right with me and I will write your mother accordingly. Please write me, therefore, what you need in clothing, and indicate at what stores you want credit, as I do not wish to give you miscellaneous credit everywhere. Also how much per month in spending money you require, and I will pay it to you in a lump sum each month. I think the clothing and expenses of that kind should be taken care of on the credit system, sending me the bills and you merely be furnished cash what you require for your personal expenses, which I imagine will largely consist of cigarettes. Don't make too many trips to New York.

I had planned to make a trip with Clara to Florida and come back by way of New York during the winter, but I felt it would be unpatriotic to spend the money for pleasure when I had better buy Liberty Bonds with it, and I am today subscribing for $1,000 worth of Thrift Stamps. Then too the weather had been rather mild out here and I have had a good land business all winter. Think I have probably made twelve or fifteen thousand dollars since the day before Christmas and I did not want to go away when the land business was good, for this business usually moves in periods of eight or ten years of poor business with two or three years of good business and consequently the last year and probably the coming year will be my harvest, and the only one for perhaps the next ten years to come, so I don't like to go away. But I caught a severe cold about New Years and have been nearly laid up ever since, and think that within a couple of weeks I may run down *to Excelsior Springs to exercise and rest up and then get back to work. I am on a large land deal with some Buffalo people and had thought I might take a run down there and then on to New York to see you, but I have just received a letter from my party there that he will be here this week. It is also really necessary that I make a trip out to Seattle late this winter or early this spring on my business out there, and it seems I simply have more to do than I can possibly attend to, but I don't want you to leave school to come to see me, and yet I am going down to see you if I can possibly get away. Of course you and your welfare are more to me than anything else, and if I really thought it was absolutely necessary I go down to New York to set you right in your ideas, I certainly would do so, but I am trying to make my letters do the business rather than personal conversations, no matter how much I would like to meet you. So think the thing over and if you still feel that you and I should have a personal conference, and that it is so important that I should leave my business matters to do it, then write me and I will get down there some time probably in March.*

I note you say your club elections are in March and I hope you will be able to make some one of the offices. Now, my boy, think it over. Think it over a great many times, and think it over looking from every side of the proposition, looking at the long avenue of years ahead of you and what a proper mental training and a proper education will do for you, and how it will be more and more valuable to you as time goes on in your competitive struggle against other men more poorly equipped. Try to get the big thing from your mind that you must go into service now at this time. Remember, I am not advising you this way to keep you out of the war, or because I am afraid for your personal safety, or because I am a coward, but because I want you to be properly equipped not only for this battle, but for all of life's battles for years to come and that is why I urge you to complete your course, if possible. After you have thought this matter all over from every angle, let me hear from you again, and if you insist or believe I should come down to see you, I will do so in March. Talk it over. Talk it over with Dean McClanahan and Dr. Fine the things I am writing you. Show them this letter, if you like. Get their point of view on it, for I don't want to advise you wrongly.

Awaiting your letter in every confidence of your ultimate good judgment,

I am.

Lovingly, Dad

Trying to digest every bit of wisdom his father conveyed to him, Sam felt fatigued. Not feeling he could fight the pressure from everyone in his family, he decided to stay in school until his semester was concluded, although he intended to continue his training to be a pilot at the same time. He sent a telegram to Charles and one to the Gradys informing them that he would remain in school until the end of his semester in May, but at that point he was going to join the navy. Being twenty years old, he was certain he knew what was best for him. Charles again wrote a letter near the end of Sam's second semester, but did not take the time to go to New Jersey to see him.

Dear Sam,

Your wire at hand saying interested leaving college at once and entering officer's training camp for Naval aviation.

I wired to inquire if Clara and I could not visit you in camp latter part of June instead of now for I am having a fine business now but expect it to drop off last of June. Clara expects a lady from California to arrive June 1st to visit her for two or three weeks.

Also, a guy is moving here from NYC June 1ˢᵗ and I need to put in couple of weeks with him, helping organize his new business as I have a half interest for he is a stranger here and will need my help awhile in getting established.

But if no visitors are allowed at training camp I will go at once for you are more important to me than business although you are expensive and it keeps the old money busy to keep you in funds.

Now, I have been wondering especially if you feared you were not going to pass your finals in this college year and were trying to get away from it by going into navel service –am I right?

If I go latter part of June you better have your mother visit you before I go as I wanted to take Clara with me, as she has never seen the East in summer time, but also it would do my old heart good to visit you and your mother alone – Just us three – still it hurts – oh how it hurts! To open up old wounds – so perhaps your mother better visit you first.

Now write to me fully at once telling about your finals at school – when you go and when you go to officer's training camp – and if I can visit you at camp last of June.

Also, if you become an officer what your duties will be - whether to go abroad and fight or to remain here and instruct students in flying.

I rather expect my business will let up latter part of June for 30 days so I can get away then other than now.

Now write fully at once. I sent you a check for $75.00 few days ago – I now enclose you $50.00 to go to camp with – the U.S. will take care of you after that I suppose.

Goodbye and write soon.

Lovingly,

Charles O. Elwood

If you could get 20 or 30 days off – why couldn't you come back, visit grandmother a couple of days – me a week and your mother a week without our going east?

After his finals in May, Sam went immediately into the naval aviation training camp in Chatham, Massachusetts. Sarah did manage a few days with him in New York before he went into training. Since William had a business meeting in New York, Sarah went along and took advantage of being in the east to see both Sam and Ed, and even spend some time with William so he wouldn't be too irritable with her.

Sarah and Sam had a memorable time. They went to the opening performance of *The Good Men Do*, dined in Sardi's Restaurant and walked the busy streets of New York City. Mixed emotions gripped Sarah as she came to terms with what Sam had done. He was now in the armed forces and would be subject to be sent anywhere they needed him as soon as his training was over.

As they walked briskly down the wide, bustling Fifth Avenue, Sarah suddenly had a premonition of something evil, but couldn't put her finger on what it was. Just a feeling inside of her that inspired dread on this beautiful sunny day in the busy city. Was it just because she was worried about Sam fighting in the war – or was it something related to Ed – or William? She panicked. Feeling suddenly cold and clammy, she stopped walking and grabbed Sam's arm.

"What's the matter, Mother? You are awfully pale," said Sam.

It took Sarah a minute to answer as she fought for composure.

"I don't know what it is. Maybe something I ate for lunch. I think I am fine now, but let's take a ride in Central Park instead of walking. The carriages are right over there."

Sarah, who always felt better around horses, scolded herself for letting something stupid get to her and settled back to enjoy the carriage ride. Central Park was beautifully green, very peaceful in spite of all the people there, and the ride produced a gentle breeze. Her recent episode, however, made Sarah stop and think retrospectively about her life and Sam's. Even though young, he was grown now and would probably be going overseas to

France to fight in the war. What did a mother say to a son who was walking, or in this case flying, into danger?

She took a deep breath, found Sam's hand and grasped it firmly as she spoke in her most serious voice, "Sam, I love you so much. I know I haven't always been the best mother to you and sometimes I might have done things for me instead of for you, but I always wanted to be there for you. In many ways I regret leaving you with Grandmother Elwood, but look what a really good job she did in raising you. I never wanted you to get tangled up in the problems your father and I had so I never talked about it, but I think you know that I felt he was more interested in his business than he was in you and me."

"Why don't you just say it, Mother? My father had an affair with Clara. I've suspected that all along."

Sarah held her breath a moment wondering how to deal with an adult Sam. Having hidden the truth from him all his life, as did Grandmother Elwood, she exhaled and felt an enormous sense of relief because the truth was out.

"Yes, Sam. He had an affair."

"Why did you leave me with Grandmother in the first place?"

"My intention in leaving you with your grandmother was that your father and I would bring you to a nice home in St. Paul in just a matter of months when our new business got off the ground. Instead, the business became of prime importance and then your father fell in love with Clara and that was the end of our marriage."

"Why didn't you come and get me after you divorced father?" asked Sam who was listening intently to these things about his life that he had never heard before.

"I really wanted to, Sam, but you have to understand what it's like to be a woman, especially one alone with a small child. I had to think of how I was going to survive on my own. I inherited some land from my father, and got a generous settlement from Charles, but not enough to keep me going forever, so I had to think about what kind of a job I could get that would pay me enough to raise you. Therefore, I felt it best that you stayed with grandmother on the farm while I tried to get my life in order. I went to Dixon, Illinois where I owned some land and tried to plan my next step. I soon saw that Dixon was too small a city to afford me a good job, so I went to Chicago, thinking there I could probably find decent employment with my business experience. Trying to forget my trauma, I found a nice group of friends and then I met William." Sarah found herself smiling as she remembered her time in Chicago. "He was so attentive, handsome, and seemed to be an up and coming businessman. In fact, I was able to help him entertain some of his business customers while they were in Chicago. We fell in love and, I don't know if you realize, but we were married only nine months after we met."

"Mother, that was a great thing for you. William is a fine man and your marriage meant that you didn't have to worry about money any more. But why didn't you come get me *then*?" persisted Sam.

"Well, I was going to, Sam. In fact, William and I came to Colo to see you right after our marriage so William could get to know you. Do you remember our visit? You were only five and might not remember. Right after we returned home and began planning to come to get you -- William received a promotion and his company moved him from Chicago back to their headquarters in Decatur. My new life there was so fast paced I determined it would be best to wait a little more before I brought you into the whirlwind. When we got to Decatur, I saw that I would have to work very hard. You know William has an enormous desire to be successful at his business and I have an active role in pushing him forward into bigger and better promotions. I was happy to help him and he was pleased with my assimilation into Decatur's society. However, I was throwing a dinner party every other night, going to country club affairs, doing charity work and getting hardly any sleep. It didn't seem like a great atmosphere to bring you into on a permanent basis, and your life seemed fine. I grew up on a farm and was always glad I had to work physically hard to help make it successful. It was good for me and I thought it would be good for you as well."

"Why didn't my father take me to live with him and Clara? I only saw him five or six times when he came to visit the farm and never at his home. He wrote to me on my birthdays, but always seemed too busy to come see me. I love Grandmother, but she was getting rather old and even I could see that it was difficult for her to have me around. I was happy to come live with you when I was sixteen. Finally, I was with at least one of my parents. Was it acceptable to William for me to come and stay?" mused Sam as he was deep in thought.

"William has been wonderful about you. You are our only son and he loves you like his own. I was so happy those few times you were able to stay a week or so with us, and that whole summer spent in Decatur, and I really hated to send you off to Howe Academy. I cried for a week, but William, his friend Ed in New York, and your father all felt that the discipline of a military school was needed. As great as grandmother was, they all sensed she had been too lax with her discipline and you would grow up to be a better man if we sent you away to a disciplined school. It did make you grow up, Sam, into a fine young man. I am so proud of you. Proud of your patriotism, but at the same time wishing you had elected to finish college before you joined the navy. I will be praying for you and all the other boys every night."

"I had to join, Mother. You are the one who taught me to love my country and to not take a backseat but to get out and do something to help. I truly feel that by becoming a pilot I can do important things for the war effort. I look at you and the things you are doing for the Red Cross, Liberty Loans, the canteen, the motor brigade, and the list goes on and on. How could I sit idly bye in school when you are working along with so many others to make things right in the world?"

Sarah gasped, "But, I didn't mean to make you quit school. I hadn't realized that my beliefs and attitudes had that much of an effect on yours. I'm flattered, but scared. I will worry so much about you. Now, you can see how weak I really am."

Settling against the back of the carriage, Sarah felt drained. She tried to put their conversation into prospective and couldn't. She had told Sam everything about his past and hers as well and didn't know how he would react. In telling her story, she could see her selfishness in keeping Sam with Grandmother Elwood. Sarah knew she could have disparaged Charles more, but that was wrong, after all he was Sam's father no matter what and Sam deserved to be able to have respect for him.

Just as guilt was totally overwhelming her, Sam put his arm around her and said, "Mom, I really, really love and admire you. I know your life hasn't been easy and I know you always wanted the best for me. I'll try to earn your respect now as a naval pilot and a fighter."

Unable to speak, she saw that Sam didn't need her words of wisdom. Already he knew about respect, love and determination and yes, even sacrifices. He was grown up. Giving him a big hug, she forgot about her premonition and snapped back to her usual vivacious self, seeking a good time with her son.

Although she was traveling with William, after Sam went to his training camp, Sarah was able to steal a little bit of time alone with Ed. She and Ed got to play golf together one afternoon because William wanted to rest after an exhausting morning of business meetings. Being in charge of the conference, Ed saw to it that William had many extra meetings to attend, leaving him free to see Sarah.

Sarah was beginning to discuss the future with Ed more and more as a small kernel of doubt had begun to creep into her mind, a little suspicion that Ed was not trying as hard as he could to bring them together permanently. Their stock investment account had its ups and downs, but had grown to a substantial sum. Surely Ed would not lose his job if he divorced Florence, although he would lose some powerful friends. Blaming Ed for their separation seemed logical yet Sarah had her own reservations that dealt with her fears of a third marriage for her, and how Sam would feel about losing another father. Her feelings for Ed were firm. She loved him and felt that he was her soul mate, but even in Sarah's circle, divorces were rare and a second divorce was not very acceptable. Yes, she needed to be careful. Thus, poor Ed had to endure Sarah's change in attitude toward him from time to time. Sometimes the affair was over and sometimes they needed to discuss their future. Their present discussion of the future made Ed declare that he thought he could find a way for their union to take place after the war and all its problems were over.

"After the war," Sarah consoled herself. After the war she could have both Ed and her Sam, safe.

❧

CHAPTER 23

Interrogation

3 Millikin Place   Summer 1918

AT HOME ONCE more Sarah tried not to think about Sam and what he might be facing, and struggled to concentrate on her own daily activities. William did not provide a diversion from her busy schedule as their relationship became cordial but more distant. Nor were social engagements an interruption to war work activities as fewer and fewer people planned parties thinking them to be too extravagant for war- time. The highlight of her life was still the letters she received from Ed. Not only did they overflow with love and admiration for her, but also they fed her desire for knowledge. He spelled out his opinions on the war, politics, literature, and business with certainty and related general information that kept her up to date. Through Ed's eyes she had a much broader prospective on the world than was to be found in the Midwest. When she had an extra hour or so, she would retire to the third floor room, bring out the box from the attic space, and randomly pick out letters to reread. One afternoon she dipped her hand into the box and brought out the following letter:

> *Did you know that the mails must reach Post Office one to two hours earlier now – beginning on Monday?*
>
> *Slowly and surely the war is getting us- soon all of the Nation's resources will be subordinated to fostering the war – which is as it should be --- for instance- to conserve sugar – the non-essentials will have to give way first, a food commissioner told me that Hires Root Beer people were*

told last week that they would have to stop manufacturing Root Beer and give the sugar to the Government and if they fail to do it, transportation by the rail roads will be denied them -- and so it goes.

Sarah smiled remembering how upset she was with Hires Root Beer because they weren't as cooperative as they should have been for the war effort. But she did miss the root beer.

Carefully returning that letter to its place, she picked another from a different stack:

It is a glorious satisfaction my darling to me to read your letters once more – telling me you understand the President. Always did I feel you would come back to see things Wilson's way, but it was hard during the time you temporarily strayed from the fold. Why your very nature is in revolt against materialistic Republicanism – you prove it by your interest in the lowly and in your last letter you tell me that you are again in the saddle in social service work and I am elated over it.

"Now wait a minute," she told an absentee Ed, "I only said the president did the right thing when he finally got us into the war and -- not all Republicans are materialistic. I don't remember properly chastising you for your remarks in this letter."

Sarah was enjoying rereading the letters almost as much as originally receiving them. Next was another war dissertation.

What do you think of the Huns being on our shores and what do you think of the big city with all lights out at night. It seems odd to be in darkness – but the police are enforcing the edict and all lights are out and blinds are pulled down and when it isn't done a policeman calls and compels you to do it.

Curious minds the Huns have – they admit their idea is to terrorize non-combatants, so they will ask their Government to make peace. When they first raided the peaceful sea towns of England and successfully killed some school children the English campaign for a volunteer army was languishing. The immediate and instantaneous effect was to stimulate recruiting so that 500,000 Brits enlisted in a few days.

As soon as it was heard that the Huns were off the New Jersey coast and the damage that was done, recruiting started at our naval stations with an unprecedented rush. In other words instead of terrorizing as intended it stiffens the resistance. I wonder if the Huns logic is that if a similar thing happened to them – they would yell for peace – if so – then one can figure out that that is what they think should happen with all others that they attack.

Ed also kept his eye on Sam at his naval camp for Sarah:

Now to my last visit with Sam – Darling, don't worry about him. He is OK. He just sort of acts as though for the first time in his life he had to do things at a time when he didn't want to. I said, Sam, what do you miss the most? And the reply was – not being able to go where I want to! So you see, Sweet – it is the discipline that has got him. And it is just the sort of thing he needs. I think you will see him before long because as soon as he begins to spruce up at inspections and obey willingly they will let him off.

This letter made Sarah feel optimistic about her son. Like it or not, Sam did need to be subjected to strong discipline.

In some of his letters Ed allowed Sarah to reminisce with him about his childhood.

As I look back to childhood days – my memory can carry me back to when I was 5 years of age which brings me into the year you were born. The first recollections begin in '76. I can remember a train all bedecked with flowers leaving the county town I lived in for Philadelphia where the centennial was being held. It was the last I ever saw of my father. I also remember it was the year of a Presidential election and they had a night parade in the town and I was allowed to sit up and see it - The men carried torches on their shoulders and wore blue oil cloth capes and yelled for Hayes and Wheeler, the Republican candidates who were afterwards installed in office – but never elected. Perhaps this incident may have made me of the opposite political faith – or at least it was the germ of it. Other things I can remember from this year for it was the beginning of memory for me. Perhaps now I know why and will be pleased henceforth to connect it all up with you. So you see I am getting ready to claim you as far back as memory will permit. If it pleases me to do it and makes me happy – you won't make fun of me will you?

"I love this letter," Sarah reflected. "It gives me an inside look into Ed's character and draws me closer to him. He is really a self-made man, strong but so sensitive." Sarah placed the letter back into the box with extra softness and removed another.

In August of 1918, Ed wrote his outlook on foreign affairs, and since he was privy to much of President Wilson's thinking, Ed's opinion on the war was usually accurate.

This may sound strange to you – It is not that I believe the Allies will score a military victory – but the economic pressure on Germany is becoming very severe. The Neutrality

Embargo Act has hurt more than is generally known. There are today 50 Dutch ships in New York harbor that cannot sail to Holland with foodstuffs that have heretofore been going to Germany and to a less degree this applies to Scandinavian Countries.

The recent peace proposals of the Pope are inspired by Germany - Put these together with other things we know about and it makes for my belief.

Not only did Ed write about war, but sometimes Sarah was instructed in literature through Ed's letters.

I have just finished the 'Life of Lincoln' series by Ida Tarbell and am ready to tackle 'Bracebridge Hall'. Have you started it yet? You realize don't you that it is not a novel – it is only a narrative of characters met at a Christmas Wedding in an old English manor house of long ago. Irving is noted for his beautiful style of English. I read his 'Life of Washington' and 'History of New York' and 'Alhambra'. The latter is beautiful and tells all about life in Spain after the Moorish conquest and I think the best of the lot. 'Bracebridge Hall is not exciting as I remember it – but is entertaining nevertheless and we will read it together and exchange notes on it when we meet.

I do wish you would read 'Vanity Fair' by Thackeray for me sometime -- to me this is one of the greatest books on English life and then imagine Mrs. Fiske playing Becky Sharp in the dramatization of it and George Arliss as the Marquis Stayne. I saw them in it and it was one of the treats of my life.

Upon receiving that letter, Sarah had immediately made a list of books to read. How inspiring Ed was! Sarah had read most of the books Ed had discussed; the only problem being that she had no one with which to discuss the literature except Ed. She wrote him her feelings and ideas but longed to have a personal dialogue with someone on these fascinating topics.

Ed's focus was not narrow. He wrote on a wide variety of subjects, even giving Sarah business updates.

> *Yesterday I attended a hearing before the Chamber of Commerce in regard to the new tax bill up before congress. You see it is to raise $200 million to run the government. We have no imports now because of the European War hence no revenue from tariffs. It is proposed to raise the money by taxing corporation or partnership profits and the tax will fall largely on Eastern manufactures where it belongs. The debate was great. One chap blamed the South for saddling it on the North. So another fellow gets up and says that he never heard such croaker in his life. A few weeks ago – all of them were parading the streets, shouting and carrying flags for preparedness and denouncing the administration and Congress for not giving it to them - Now as a result of these country wide demonstrations- centered in N. Y. and Chicago – Congress passed the bills as desired and now that the money is wanted to pay the fiddler with and the burden naturally falls on the only people that can stand it – and they are the people that shouted the loudest for the big army and navy – the business people, - it is amusing to hear them kick and want to pass it along to the farmer and laboring man. I enjoyed the meeting hugely!*

Sometimes Sarah wondered whether she loved Ed or his letters best. Ed wrote without fail twice a week, and most of the time, three times; the usual length of his documents was eight pages of stationary paper. Sarah wondered if she needed a bigger box to hold them. Was her stash safe from William? She recognized that he suspected that she was having an affair, but did not guess whom it was with.

Only yesterday, William unexpectedly confronted her at the door when she returned home from picking up Ed's letter at the hotel.

"Come in. Where have you been?" he queried.

Sarah realized she was in for a grilling. Trying not to look guilty as she felt the lump that was Ed's letter in her skirt pocket, she forced a cheerful response, "Oh, I just went downtown to the drugstore to get something for my skin. It seems to be drying out a little."

"Where is your purchase?" said William.

Sarah steeled herself as she realized this was to be a real inquisition, "Since when are you so interested in my skin lotion?"

William seemed determined to catch her in a lie and took a gruff tone, "Don't play with me. I asked a simple question. Where is your skin lotion that you bought downtown at the drugstore?"

Now anger took the place of guilt for Sarah and she lashed back at him, "Why are you grilling me like a fugitive?"

"Because I believe you have been lying to me lately and I want to find out why."

Sarah decided she better get her anger under control or she might give away things that she did not intend to. In a very measured tone, Sarah answered his question, "I said I went to get something for my skin, but I didn't say I bought anything. I couldn't find what I wanted so I didn't buy anything. Now may I go or do you want to put me in the dungeon?"

William, convinced that he had caught Sarah in wrongdoing, persisted, "Let me see your purse."

Thankful that she had put Ed's letter in her skirt pocket, she flung her purse at him and stomped upstairs yelling that she would not be intimidated like this ever again.

Since William was unable to prove his suspicions about Sarah, he dropped the matter with a slight apology as he brought her purse upstairs.

"What is it you think I have done?" asked Sarah.

"I thought maybe you were having an affair with someone. You certainly don't act like you care for me anymore."

"That street goes two ways. The only time you even know I am around is when you need me to do something for you. And I never question your actions when *you* are not in *my* presence. I can't forgive you for what you just did to me," she said closing the door behind her as she exited the room. William was left dumbstruck in their empty bedroom.

Eager for distance from her husband, Sarah tried to be outwardly angrier with William, but was unsuccessful because a small inner voice kept rearing its head telling her that she was actually at fault. Being aware that he was still suspicious, Sarah carefully picked up Ed's letters at a time when she knew William would not be around and read them, as she did now, while he was at the office.

Her guilty inner voice confirmed that, as long as Ed was around, her marriage was in trouble, but no matter now she vacillated, she always longed for Ed.

CHAPTER 24

A Mother Knows

Chelsea, Massachusetts September 1918

ONE MORNING IN September after Sam had been training as a pilot for three and a half months, Sarah received a telegram from the naval station in Chelsea, Massachusetts informing her Sam was critically ill with the flu. William read the telegram first and immediately said they both should go to him. Even though the flu had not reached epidemic proportions in the Midwest at this time, William and Sarah had heard how thousands were dying from it out East. William wrapped up his business affairs quickly and they were on the afternoon train.

On the train Sarah was overwrought. William tried to be supportive and comforting, but she kept returning in her mind to the premonition she had in New York when she last saw Sam.

"He's going to die. That's why I had that feeling in New York. I know he's going to die."

"Now, Sarah, we don't know anything yet, except he is sick with the flu. I know several of my associates in New York that have had this flu and are now over it," said William.

"But, William, this is something a mother knows. He's going to die," repeated Sarah.

"He's a strong young man and I'm sure he will be good as new in a week or so. Please don't borrow trouble," consoled William who tried to remain optimistic.

Upon arriving at the makeshift naval hospital, even William lost his positive attitude. The building the navy called a hospital was primitive at best and consisted mainly of row upon row of cots - all full of flu victims. The room was not partitioned and the outside walls looked to Sarah as if they were composed of cardboard. No electric lights shone down on this horrible scene. The only light in the area streaked in grudgingly from two open doors and a few lanterns tucked away in the four corners of the big space. Flies zoomed around Sarah and headed for the ceiling avoiding the sick ones as though they were shunning the stench that was emanating from the cots.

As she surveyed the terrible image before her, Sarah couldn't help but think, "If one of these boys survives maybe they all will, but if one dies, it is likely that the rest will follow."

A woman at a scarred, walnut desk gave them each a mask for their protection and identified Sam's location. Sarah leaning on William's arm set out to find her son. Feeling as though she was floating in a nightmare, she allowed William to lead her to Sam's cot.

"I am afraid to look at him," thought Sarah, but pulling strength from the tips of her toes to the top of her head, she looked down at her son.

Holding tighter to William's arm, she saw a grotesquely thin young man with a face the color of his white sheet. His cheeks were totally sunken into his face and his eyes -- the eyes told Sarah the story, there was no life left in them. However, a glimmer of recognition flashed through those lifeless eyes and as Sarah took his hand, he was able to faintly squeeze hers.

At that point Sarah knew he would not survive, but she fought back her tears, sat in a chair that had been provided by the bedside and gave Sam a big hug. She and William stayed with him until an overworked nurse told them they needed to leave, but could come back tomorrow. The Gradys did as they were told, cheerfully telling Sam they would be back in the morning and they were sure he would be feeling better then. Sam nodded his head.

Stopping at the desk as they left, William inquired if it would be possible to move Sam to a regular hospital, thinking he might get better care. The woman to whom he made the inquiry gave him a sympathetic glance and told him the hospitals were all overflowing and did not allow families to visit their sick ones, so there was no chance of moving Sam. She added that the care he was getting at the naval base was as good or better than he could get elsewhere and here they did allow visitation. The Gradys stepped out into the fresh air and went to get their hotel room.

William knew as well as Sarah that Sam would not survive. He had gone to talk to one of the doctors while Sarah sat with Sam and was told that Sam now had pneumonia and it would be a miracle if he could overcome it. Still giving Sarah hope, William held her in bed and told her everything would be fine as she cried herself to sleep.

Sitting with Sam all the next day was somehow a bit comforting to Sarah. Even though Sam was unable to speak and Sarah knew that most of the time he was unaware that she was there, twice when she held his hand and said "I love you, son," he nodded his head telling her he knew she was beside him.

When evening came William expected that they would be asked to leave again, but this time the doctor came by and took Sarah's hand saying, "I'm sorry, Mrs. Grady, Sam isn't going to make it through the night. You may stay with him."

At this point Sarah was numb. Some way she had felt since that day in Central Park that this was to be Sam's fate. Looking around the hospital she noticed for the first time how many other loved ones were still there sitting with their dying sons or husbands. The world was not supposed to be this way. Poor Sam. At twenty years old, just becoming a man. If he had stayed in the better environment of Princeton, his chances of getting sick would have been greatly reduced. But no, she mused, he felt he needed to go to war to prove himself and his father didn't do the job of discouraging him. Sarah immediately blamed Charles, but then went on to hold herself liable. William was next to be held responsible until she comprehended what she was doing. All of Sam's family would be as devastated as she was and no one could be blamed. Looking down on Sam's face, she saw his eyes were closed and he had a peaceful look on his young thin face.

"William," she cried, "he's gone."

"Yes, he is," said William as he took Sarah's hand.

They stood in silence for several minutes, holding hands and neither of them moving. Finally William, realizing that Sarah was incapable of moving on her own, covered Sam's face with his sheet and quietly led her out of the hospital.

As Sarah sat immobilized in a chair in the hotel room, William began handling the plans. He telegraphed Charles, Grandmother Elwood, and the Irvings who as neighbors and friends he asked to help with the funeral arrangements; then he tried to get Sarah to eat and rest, but she would have none of either.

When William had taken care of all the little details, they caught the train heading home. Sarah sat in the train car, dazed and unseeing. Turning toward the window, she heard the noise of the train in its rhythm repeating, "Sam is dead, Sam is dead." William – what was he saying?

"You have to eat something, Sarah. Just a bite or two."

He put a bite of meat into her mouth, but she couldn't chew it.

"Please let the world just leave me alone," she thought.

William attempted to comfort her. "Sarah, you have been wonderful through all this. Aren't you glad you are a nurse's aide? You knew just how to make Sam's last minutes comfortable."

It wasn't until much later that Sarah realized the validity of William's statement. She had instinctively known what to do.

Back home the Grady's friends pitched in to help. The funeral home only took a day to get Sam's body ready for visitation and the Irvings made all the arrangements for the service and burial. William purchased a lot at Fairlawn Cemetery that would be suitable for three interments, his, Sarah's and Sam's. Sarah tried to prepare the house to receive the body, but couldn't come to any decisions. Where to put Sam on display? Should it be in the reception hall – or in the living room – or in the library? Incapable of functioning, she wanted Ed, who couldn't be there to comfort her, and she wanted her best friend, June Ewing, who was still working for the army in France. William, however, was with her so he became her rock and she let him make all the choices.

"Sarah, let's put Sam in front of the fireplace in the living room. There'll be many people who will come to view him and I think the traffic pattern will work best from the living room. You can sit in a chair nearby."

Sarah couldn't even manage a response. It was all a bad dream.

As the day of visitation dawned, William called a doctor to come look at Sarah. She didn't have the strength to get out of bed. The doctor gave her something to help her mood and talked to her rather gruffly.

"Sarah, it's time to think of Sam not of yourself. Doesn't he deserve a brave mother who will give him a hero's funeral? After all he sacrificed his life for his country just as much as those overseas that are fighting in the trenches. Pull yourself together and bury him with dignity."

Partly due to the medicine she had been given and partly due to the doctor's stern words, Sarah snapped out of her self-imposed dream world and began to act like the compassionate, charitable lady she was, focusing on her son. She had a job to do and she would grieve once Sam was at peace. By the time Sam's body arrived, she was giving orders on how things should go, what foods should be served in the dining room and where the numerous bouquets should be placed. To add to her comfort, June Ewing made it back to Decatur the morning of the funeral and was able to help with the details. June came straight from the train to Sarah's house and found the grieving mother trying to organize the funeral arrangements.

"I got back from France four days ago and was being decommissioned in New York when I got the telegram from my sister that Sam had passed, so I got here as fast as I could. Oh, Sarah, I'm so sorry. He was too young. Just a boy," said June as the tears rolled down her cheeks.

Sarah rushed to June, hugged her tightly, and let out all the tears that she had not yet spent.

When she could find her voice again, Sarah said "You have no idea how badly I needed you to come. I thought you were still in France working for the Red Cross. Oh, June, help me make Sam's ceremony one that a hero deserves."

"I will, Honey," said June and they got to work.

The funeral was serene, but with an unprecedented veil of sadness hanging over the room. The emotion was not just for Sam who was so young and had so much potential, but for all the young men who were dying while fighting in a tragic war. More than seventy bouquets of flowers stood beside the coffin making the room appear celestial. Several impressive singers, procured by the Irvings, added to the heartbreaking tone of the ceremony. As one of Sarah's good friends, a forceful contralto, began singing "Amazing Grace", Sarah gripped the sides of her chair afraid that she was going to pass out.

"My heart is breaking and the music just makes it worse. I can't take this," thought Sarah as she started to panic.

William, who was sitting next to her, saw her increased distress and tightly held her hand.

"You can do this, Sarah. I'm right here. Just lean on me," he whispered. Sarah held William's hand on one side and reached for June's on the other.

As the minister's remarks began, they seemed soothing and comforting, but, when he said that Sam was in a better place, Sarah began to shut her mind down, internally singing "la, la, la" so she would not hear anything else the preacher said. Sam was not in a better place. He was just gone.

As a distraction, she stared at Sam in his coffin, noting that he looked handsome in his navy uniform, also noting how much he looked like Charles. Silently she thanked Charles for not coming to the funeral. He had sent flowers and a telegram saying he thought it would be awkward if he came, and it would have been. She was also grateful that the Rockafellows had sent their condolences, but decided not to come. Ed knew it was better this way.

The parade to the cemetery was six blocks long. Sarah was pleased with the lot William had chosen for them in Fairlawn since all the important people in Decatur were being buried there now. Greenwood, the old cemetery, was showing neglect and Fairlawn was now the prestigious place to be in the hereafter. As Sam's coffin was settled in place over the grave, Sarah visualized the large monument she would erect for him. Suddenly Sam's coffin was lowered into the ground and it was all over.

CHAPTER 25

⚜

Grandmother Elwood

Colo, Iowa October 1918

THE FOLLOWING DAY, bereft and alone, Sarah busied herself answering letters, sending thank you notes, and making sure she had notified everyone. Upon Sam's death, both William and Mr. Irving had immediately sent Charles a telegram, but Sarah also included him in her correspondence as she told herself he would be devastated and had a right to have a description of the service. In fact, she was really grateful to him for not coming to the funeral and putting that extra burden on her. She had not seen him since the day she had thrown him out of their apartment, and it would have made things terribly awkward during the worst moments of her life. She also wrote to Grandmother Elwood telling her she would make a visit to Iowa soon. Sarah was not planning to notify Charles when she intended to visit Colo, but she did want to see Grandmother and get some of Sam's things.

William had notified Sarah's family in Minnesota of Sam's death. Since Sarah was not close to her family, she had not expected any of them to attend the funeral. When her younger brother was killed fighting overseas about six months prior, Sarah had not been notified in time to go to his funeral, so she didn't feel it necessary to inform her family about Sam in a timely fashion. She sent several pictures to an old friend in Elkton instructing her to keep one and give the others to Grandmother Petersen who lived nearby.

A week after the funeral Sarah received a letter from Charles.

Sam's Mother,

Your card received saying you were sending mother two pictures of our dear little Sam's grave so I could have one and hasten to thank you for your thoughtfulness – and hope when you visit mother you will take her some of the flowers from the floral tributes left on Sam's grave – and enough so mother can give me some of them – for when I die when- ever it may be, there will be found among my effects – a package containing Sam's letters, bills, pictures, newspaper clippings – poems and trinkets and his baby shoes grandma kept for me and the flowers from his grave you're taking to my mother – and that package, you may be sure will be tear stained – oh so tear stained – and over that package many, many prayers will be said – prayers for Sam's soul – prayers of repentance for my own sins – prayers for the happiness of Sam's mother and for the salvation of the whole world.

Oh, if God could only have taken me instead of poor Sam – I am old – my life is mostly spent – I have seen the world – anything else I might do would be more or less only a repetition of things I have done before – while Sam had the whole world yet before him. It was so cruel to take him, but I cannot question God's plans.

I have lived so wholly for Sam all these years – more than you can guess- far more than most fathers love their sons - for interwoven with my love were prayers of repen- tance and the hungry hope to yet atone my sins through Sam in watching him develop and in guiding him watchfully and tenderly to a fine free successful moral life and then I have him turn to me with his arms around me to freely forgive me my early wrong to him and his – oh how I have looked forward to that day, for when it came as I was so sure it would, I would then feel my life's work was complete and I would go serenely to my grave – but now- oh now- I feel like an unforgiven sinner- but I shall hope on and labor on and do all the good I can – I have been seriously considering Red Cross or YMCA work, but will take on perhaps a year to respectably arrange my business affairs – for I have mother and so many others dependent on me – I must not leave them helpless-

But time is a great healer and while the world will never again be the same to either of us, we must find some activity to occupy our minds now over time – oh if I could only have talked to Sam before he died – I think of him a thousand times a day - and away into the night after all the world is still I am still thinking ......a thousand thoughts come rushing through my mind – but we must be brave – for thousands of fathers and mothers are daily losing their darling boys in this terrible war – one spirits must not weaken – the war must be won so no other outlaw will ever again try to overrun the world.

Perhaps it is wrong for me to write you but I know Mr. Grady will forgive me if he but knew my heart and that I only try to help sooth you in your great loss.

He has been very kind to Sam and I appreciate it and I know he will comfort you in your sorrow as no one else can.

I want you to visit poor mother – she is utterly heartbroken but her Christian fortitude is her staff – and I would like to see you when at mothers for she has all of Sam's baby clothes – baseball bats and mitts – his books and play things and she wants us to divide them - part for her. So if you desire it, I will meet you there any time with a few days' notice.

My wife is heartbroken too for she more than anyone else, knew the depth of my love and hopes for Sam ..... – why did our son – such extraordinarily brilliant prospects – so fine an aviator – so fine a mind – why, why, why? And

*for an answer? Only the mournful sighing of the soft wind
through the trees. Oh, I could go on and on forever writing,
wishing and praying – but I must control my emotions. I
must get busy – and help some poor mortal worse off than
I – and now poor Sam is only a memory – a sweetly sad
memory –*

*When I see you I want to talk about building a monu-
ment for him one at Elkton his birthplace – one at Colo
where he spent his boyhood.*

*I have thought of drinking fountains on the leading
corner of the two towns – a monument to him and to all
the brave boys who fall in this war – a monument that will
inspire patriotism and loyalty to all boys for years to come,
who look upon those remembrances of our fallen heroes*
... Please thank Mr. Irving for his kindness to me.
Sam's Father

After reading Charles's letter, Sarah sat staring straight ahead at a blank
wall in her sitting room, thinking "that's how I feel, blank." Except for a
slight tug of her heart at the salutation, she felt nothing except contempt
for the man who was all talk. He refused to take time to visit his son to
help him with his life's decisions. However, she did not have the strength
to bolster her contempt into an emotion.

Sarah dreaded the thought of going to see Grandmother Elwood. She
knew it had to be done and it was certainly on her mind, but she couldn't
make herself go.

As she and June sat on Sarah's veranda a couple of weeks after the funeral each quietly absorbed in their own thoughts, June suddenly blurted
out as if making a proclamation, "Sarah, this is no way to remember Sam.
He was a 'doer.' First, we are going to Colo to see Grandmother. Yes, I said
'we'. I am going to go with you and we are leaving tomorrow. And secondly,
when we return we are going to get back to our work for the Red Cross. I'm
not going back to France; I'm going to stay in Decatur. There is as much
work to be done here as there is overseas."

"Oh, June, thank you. You have been the best friend anyone could possibly imagine. You are so right. For Sam's sake I need to get back to work and help others that are still here. Sam would not have appreciated me sitting around doing absolutely nothing."

June and Sarah were on the train the next day with William's blessing. He was happy that June had gotten Sarah moving again. He had been unable to help her, being almost as devastated as she, but he was able to lose himself in his work.

Grandmother Elwood sent John, Charles's brother who still lived at home, to meet them at the train station with the horse and buggy. Sarah was rather enjoying the buggy ride and thinking how pretty the Iowa countryside was until he turned into the lane that led back to the farmhouse. At that point, Sarah began crying uncontrollably.

"Sarah, you can do this. What can I do to help?" said a concerned June.

"You can't help. I went down this lane and left my baby boy behind. June, I just left him – for business. What a horrible mistake and I have no way to make it up to him."

The pain Sarah conveyed in her voice was beyond human capacity for understanding. June just let her cry and told John to stop the buggy for a minute. Sitting there in the lane, Sarah suddenly composed herself and like she had been struck with a bolt of lightning, finally understood where she was in life. She had made mistakes with Sam and there was no going back. Sam was gone and she would never see him again on this earth. She still had a life and could do some good for others who were fighting a war for their country and others who were also losing their sons.

"Drive on, John, I'm fine now," Sarah said.

Grandmother Elwood was overjoyed to see Sarah. She was a strong woman who had lived seventy-five years and survived without her husband on a farm for the last thirty. Grandmother's grief was masked, but Sarah could feel the older woman's compassion and sadness as she looked into her eyes.

"You know, Sarah, I did not take sides when you and Charles divorced. I know what he did and I certainly do not approve of his actions, but he is my son. I was not worried about you, my dear, because you were a young, beautiful, spunky lady and I knew you would find your way. Sam was my concern. I didn't want him to suffer because of the actions of others and he didn't. His boyhood here on the farm was all a child could ask for. Every day I loved him for both of you."

Somehow Sarah felt better after talking to Grandmother Elwood. She gratefully accepted the division of Sam's belongings as Grandmother had ordained. Charles, as Sam's father, maybe did deserve some of his things. She couldn't help but note though, that grandmother had given her the most important articles, his christening dress, the lock of hair from his first haircut. Charles had gotten the bats and balls and other toys that a boy would play with. Sarah presented grandmother with several pictures and the day slipped away into night.

CHAPTER 26

✤

The Beautiful Letter

3 Millikin Place Fall 1918

ONCE HOME, HER resolution in Iowa to get back to living a normal life dissipated quickly into depression. Her friends all tried to get her to go to lunch, or play bridge, but "not today" was the response. Even the golf committee at the country club could not get her to finish the tournament she had been winning before Sam's death.

She unenthusiastically continued her Red Cross work and other activities she was doing for the war effort. The sooner the war was over the sooner other young men could stop being placed in harm's way. She often did not get home until 9:00 or 10:00 p.m. in the evening because as Regional Coordinator for the Red Cross she was on the road a great deal. When she couldn't travel on the interurban, she would drive her car. William tried to tell her how dangerous it was for her to be driving at night between the central Illinois cities she was responsible for, but Sarah paid no attention. What did it matter if she was lost on a dark, sparsely traveled road? Nothing worse than Sam's death could befall her, there was only work and war.

In the endless moments of her grief, she abhorred thoughts of Ed. Her memories and obsession with him now seemed a child's dream. How could she have been so focused on Ed, William, and even begrudging Charles rather than on the one young man that mattered? The only one that truly belonged to her. She hated herself, hated their stolen love affair, and even hated Ed.

Meanwhile Ed was suffering terribly in New York. He had received a telegram from William telling of Sam's death, but thought he should remain on the sidelines and not come to the funeral. He sent a telegram back with his condolences, addressing it to the family, and then waited for Sarah to send him a note, or call. Nothing. So he started sending his letters as usual, hoping in that way to help her through her grief. First he wrote about Sam and how he would be happy to do anything he could to help her get through her mourning.

> *Oh, my darling – to not be with you now in the hour of your greatest sorrow and grief is one of the greatest trials I have ever had to undergo. My heart is bleeding for you, and every fibre of my body goes out in sympathy for my darling in her bereavement. Would that I could share it with you and console and comfort – but alas the letters that bind make that impossible and it is maddening to think of my impotency and helplessness.*
>
> *When you become composed and rested – will you, sweetheart, write me something and indicate in what way I can help you bear your burden. Gladly and willingly will I come to see you or do anything to help – only command.*
>
> *My love is as constant as the North Star. I will do what-ever you say – come out – write you every day or anything – only remember, I love you and am yours.*
>
> Ed

No response to his letters came from Sarah. Writing to her as usual, Ed felt he was doing all he could to ease her sorrow, but many of his letters lay unopened in Sarah's postal box.

In October, William came to New York for a business conference, but did not bring Sarah. Given that Ed was also in attendance, the two friends met for a drink in the hotel lobby.

"Ed, I am really worried about Sarah. I wanted her to come to this conference thinking it would do her good to spend some time in New York, but she won't go anywhere or do anything except work at the Red Cross and a couple of other organizations that were set up to help the war effort. I have tried, but I can't seem to help her through this rough period. Any suggestions as to what I can do?"

Ed bit his lip and tried to find his normal voice.

"I'm terribly sorry, William. I don't know what to tell you, except to listen when she wants to talk."

To himself Ed thought, "And ease up and love her for once, you tyrant."

A month after Sam's death William erected a monument over his grave. Sarah knew that William did not want to build that big of a structure, but to please her, he spent a small fortune on it to honor Sam. Daily Sarah sat before the arch shaped, reddish monument with the image of doors carved out in the center and allowed the granite to become a physical barrier between her and her three men. Would those faux doors ever open?

At 3 Millikin Place, Sarah climbed the stairs to the third floor, intent on writing her final letter to Ed. She locked the door, and dragged her box of letters out of the attic space.

"I must throw these away," she thought.

Opening the box she pulled out one of his letters and despite warnings to herself, she unfolded the papers and began to read... It was one he wrote to her the first year of their relationship. As she began to read she remembered the letter.

"How could I have pulled this very letter out of so many others? This was the sweetest letter he ever wrote to me."

> *My Dearest,*
>
> *Six months ago I wrote you about the wonderful impression a woman I met at a resort two months before had made on me – how I journeyed out to see her at her home in the West, not once but twice, yes three times. Of course*

I reasoned it all out that it couldn't be that it was only a temporary infatuation, etc. I analyzed and analyzed – but always to the same conclusion – no such woman had ever come in my life before. It was impossible day or night to get her out of my mind. Until her face was close to mine, I never realized what love might be.Until my lips met hers in the kiss that sums up all life, I never knew what love was. Therefore if she be not mine – she is nothing – If I do not attain to her level – I am nothing.

That she loves me I have boundless proofs. At first – supreme happiness and contentment that I had never known before were mine. Our families occasionally met and on such occasions we had many delightful days together -- Once her mood changed and continued until late in the day – in what I thought was indifference or shall I confess it – antagonistic – a sort of mental fight was going on against me. Tortured beyond description – I demanded an explanation and what she told me made me cry for the first time in sixteen or seventeen years – it was an awful shock – she explained that she woke up that particular day with the idea that a gross flirtation was at the bottom of my attentions and that my love wasn't real – while hers was. We quickly made up – but oh the agony I went through took the sunshine out of me for many a day.

After separating from her on this particular trip – I became melancholy and kept getting worse – during this spell we met again and I half told her my condition – she then proved to be the best tonic a man could have. Her subsequent correspondence was of a nature that brought me out of my 'slough of despond' as it can be called. Her letters to me were philosophical, full of love and tender solicitation and under her guidance and inspiration – I recovered my normal condition in about a month. Looking back at it now

I know I had a narrow escape and owe my recovery entirely to her loving solicitude.

She proved that she had the mental mind qualities that I divined in her when we first met. No one need ever debate with me the difference between infatuations at the age of twenty-five and the real adult love of the forties. The latter is the real 'Depth of Life' as she would call it. There isn't the slightest doubt in my mind that if she had been my mate that I would have attained my highest ambitions long ago – she is an inspiration for me in everything - for instance her presence is so strongly felt by me – that after the receipt of one of her letters that I will walk in to a business conference feeling the power to put some proposition over that has been hanging fire for a long time and which has been op-posed because I apparently had lacked the power to impress my own convictions on my associates and often after the receipt of such a letter I'll go in and gain my point.

Again at night in my library alone I have been studying something and not be making much headway with it and when suddenly the answer to the problem will come to me clear as a bell.. On one particular occasion she seemed to be by my side – I could see her – but – I suppose this will be answered by scientists someday.

What a wonderful thing to come into the life of a man past forty. The love of a magnificent woman. What a renewed interest in life it gives. And to think that the woman combines all the qualities that you have theorized or idealized on ever since you cut your wisdom teeth. The adored one of mine possesses physical charm – mental and intellectual ability – affection – and above all, poise and self-possession. What a comrade she is. And she possesses another quality that few women have – at least I have never met any who did – and that is a sense of humor – and she talks understandingly with you on any subject that it suits your fancy to bring up – be it history, politics, war, sport, religion or stocks – by which is meant everything in a business way. She would have made a good business-woman or a teacher in anything she seriously undertook. She is liked by all who come in contact with her. My serious male friends like her and invariably comment on her knowledge of what is worthwhile in contrast with the artificial chatter and emptiness one meets with in the daily run of woman. She is apparently liked by all the women – but I suspect – that down in their hearts – it is a kind of respect for her intellectual attainments. She is an individualist of the first order and the women can't compete with her at that – so they decide she is all right and let it go at that – a little mystified with all.

And this paragon is mine. I know she is otherwise I wouldn't be so happy and lighthearted. Have just spent four beautiful days with her and am now a few hours later in a hotel where we were a few months ago. Every nook and cranny looks different to me because she has been here. Oh how I love her and always will. She knows it and reciprocates my love. Her power over me is stupendous. She is an inspiration and guiding star in everything I do – such is the influence of my soul mate – for she is that in every sense of the word. I wonder how many men really appreciate the influence of a talented woman. I never did until the last few months. My credulity would be put to a severe test – if anyone ever attempted to tell me that time would ever dim my memory of her – of my love be lessened this side of the great divide.

Sarah wiped the tears from her eyes after reading the letter and folded it, gently placing it back in her special container. Picking up the box she carried it to its position behind the chimney, crawled out of the attic space and quietly closed the little door. As she sat down in her chair and stared out of the big window, she told herself to listen to the voice of grief no longer. Her Ed, like her Sam, had not been a childish error. Ed had always cut through their artificial world of politics and cocktails. And it was him she needed to witness her grief if she was to continue in this life.

But she knew that as of present, she was not the woman that he so beautifully recalled and was in no condition to attempt their future together. After the war was over, she would again cloak herself in his love. Right now, however, she could not bring herself to write.

The Millikin Mansion was a hospital during the flu epidemic. The basement became a morgue.

The James Millikin Homestead

CHAPTER 27

❖

Nurse Sarah

Millikin Homestead October, 1918

SARAH COULD HARDLY look at the causality lists. Most families in Decatur were suffering the loss of a loved one. In fact, she couldn't think of anyone she knew that had not been impacted in some severe way by this war, and many more projects were being added to her work at the Red Cross. Ed kept writing her about the President's plan for peace and according to the news Germany seemed to be falling, but still the fighting went on. The home front was suffering not only from the problems overseas, but Sarah had been noticing some of her friends and co-workers were coming down with the flu that had killed Sam.

One October morning, Sarah's supervisor at the Red Cross called on the phone and informed her that there was no need to travel for a while because, if she would agree, they needed her in Decatur.

"What I am going to ask you to do is different and dangerous. We need nurses and nurse's aides to take care of flu patients. I'm calling you for two reasons. One, you are a nurse's aide and two, we need you to work right across the lane from your house," said the supervisor.

"I don't understand. Why are these patients not in the hospital?" Sarah asked.

"The hospital rooms are all full and so are their hallways. We are out of nurses and space, so we have had to find other facilities to house our flu patients. One of our most useful buildings is your neighborhood's empty Millikin home. We are starting to convert it to a makeshift hospital and you could be of great assistance. Your organizational skills are well known, as are your nursing abilities. It would be dangerous, Sarah. This flu knows no boundaries."

Like the retired old fire horse who runs when he hears the bell, Sarah did not even pause to consider the dangers. This would help with her grieving. She could help other families maybe avoid the tragedy she had to face with Sam.

"Of course, I'll do what you need. I had no idea the flu was that bad here in the Midwest."

"Thank you, Sarah; somehow I knew you would help us. It's not only bad here, but it's getting worse literally by the minute. In a few days I don't believe anything will be open. They are going to close the schools, churches, the YMCA, actually any place where people gather, and ask them to stay at home for a bit. I know you are familiar with the Millikin homestead and will be respectful of the building as well as helping adapt it to function as a hospital. We have no time to waste. I'll meet you there this afternoon and we'll get started."

Sarah phoned William at his office and informed him of her decision to help with the flu epidemic. Initially William started to rant at her for making such a rash decision, but hearing the passion in her voice, relented. He said, "All right, Sarah, if you need to do this -- be careful. Be sure to wear a mask and use caution when taking care of the patients. Hopefully since you took care of Sam and didn't get sick, maybe you are immune to this thing."

Turning the Millikin homestead into a hospital proved to be relatively easy. It was a grand house with five rooms downstairs plus a kitchen, a big hallway, a bathroom, and five usable bedrooms upstairs. That afternoon the Red Cross, the YMCA, and the hospital began delivering cots and various supplies. About the time Sarah began to feel they were getting organized, the hospital started sending sick people to them.

"We aren't ready for patients yet," choked Sarah, but she had nine very ill people almost before she could finish her sentence. The harried supervisor asked Sarah if she could borrow the Grady's home phone, then ran across the street to call and see if they could get a doctor and a registered nurse.

"You are sending us sick people and we have no medical staff, only one nurse's aide," the supervisor told the hospital manager.

A sympathetic voice on the other end of the line said, "I'm so sorry, but we only have three registered nurses for the whole hospital and two very tired doctors on duty right now. The other staff are home getting some rest."

When the supervisor got back with her bad news, Sarah too ran across the street to phone her friends and ask them to bring her all of their big linen tablecloths and extra pillows, blankets, and sheets. By the end of the day the Millikin home had been turned into a makeshift hospital with patients and one registered nurse. Sarah realized she was as competent as the nurse because of her experience with Sam. She had cared for him and also observed how the medical staff out east had managed this pandemic. Most of the patients the hospitals were sending to the homestead were those whose flu had progressed to pneumonia, just like Sam.

Late that afternoon one of their patients died so Sarah again rushed across the street to phone one of the funeral homes to come gather the body. Another very sympathetic voice told her all of their vehicles were busy taking sick people to the hospital and then transferring bodies from the hospital to the funeral home.

"We will get to you as soon as possible, but it will be awhile," said the compassionate woman on the telephone.

Discouraged, Sarah returned to the makeshift hospital that used to be one of the nicest homes in Decatur. She placed a linen tablecloth over the lifeless man and went on with her work. Three more patients were brought in during the night, but the ambulance drivers couldn't take the deceased body because they had previous calls to get people to the hospital. Sarah stopped a moment to look around at the once beautiful surroundings and wondered how the Millikins would react if they could see what their house looked like now. Knowing how hard both husband and wife worked to help charities in the community, thinking specifically of Anna Millikin's home for orphans and widows, Sarah was certain that they would have been anxious to help and would be pleased.

Sarah looked at her watch and saw that it was 3:30 a.m. William had walked over to the homestead about 8:30 p.m. and insisted that Sarah come home for the night. She told him she would be home very soon. She had experienced so much trauma getting the hospital ready and taking care of those who had been brought in, that she did not really feel tired. Maybe in the morning they would get some additional help and she could go home for a bit.

William had sent Sadie over about 11:30 p.m. to bring Sarah home, but Sadie would not go into the hospital for fear of contracting the flu. Standing outside on the porch she tried to get the attention of someone inside the house. She knocked on the window. She knocked on the door.

Her efforts achieved no results except someone yelling: "We're busy, it'll be a minute!"

Waiting in frustration for about five minutes, she decided no one was going to come. Why couldn't she get Sarah's attention? She wasn't going in and become exposed to the flu, but she didn't feel like going home and telling William that she was afraid to carry out his orders. Feeling she had no choice, she went home and lied to William, telling him that Sarah refused to come. She rationalized that was what Sarah would have said if she had talked to her.

In the early morning hours another patient died. Feeling surrounded by the dead, Sarah realized something had to be done with the deceased bodies and it was obvious that they were going to need the beds. The ambulances and hearses were all otherwise engaged.

"Nurse Alice, come help me with these bodies. We are going to take them to the basement," said a decisive Sarah.

Alice looking up from her work seemed about to aggressively protest Sarah's suggestion, but after a second she sighed and said, "I'll be right with you."

The two women wrapped the deceased persons separately in tablecloths and then each took an end and began to drag one of the bodies down the steps to the cold basement. The ladies were not strong enough to lift their load off the ground so the body bumped onto each step on the journey and with each bump Sarah felt a pain in her heart. Just like her Sam, this was a person who had a family that would grieve for him and -- Sarah felt sick and almost dropped her end of the tablecloth. Then, thinking of the many ill people upstairs that needed help, she gathered all her strength and held her end of the sling high enough that it no longer bumped on the steps.

Luckily there was a wooden platform on the floor of the basement room where they felt they could leave their lost patient. As they laid the first body down, Sarah and Nurse Alice looked at each other in silence and in unison bowed their heads for a moment. Alice removed the tablecloth for reuse since their supply was finite and headed upstairs.

Climbing the stairs slowly, Sarah felt dizzy. At the top of the stairs a man identifying himself as a doctor stopped her.

The doctor took one look at Sarah and exclaimed, "Are you a nurse or a patient? You look as though you need to be in bed."

"I guess I need to go home. I do need to eat and sleep for a bit. It's been almost 24 hours," said Sarah glancing at her watch, "I'll be back as soon as I sleep awhile."

Sarah staggered across the yard to her house. She was greeted by Sadie who took one look at her and immediately felt guilty about not going into the homestead last night to bring Sarah home. Not wanting Sarah to bring her germs into the house, Sadie removed all her outer clothes and grabbed the arm of a barely upright Sarah.

"Let me help you upstairs. You get in bed and I'll bring you some soup to eat," Sadie barked. But by the time she returned to the bedroom, an underwear-clad Sarah was sound asleep on the bed. Trying to wake her proved fruitless, so Sadie left the soup beside the bed and went downstairs. She needed to burn the clothes she had removed from Sarah.

Sarah woke up ten hours later famished. Going down to the kitchen, she found Dorothy whose day it was to cook.

"Dorothy, I'm hungry. How about some eggs and bacon and toast?"

Dorothy delivered, but after three or four bites Sarah could eat no more. At Dorothy's urging she stayed at the table, but really just played with her food. Coming into the breakfast room, Sadie told Sarah that William had given strict orders that she keep Sarah home for the day, even if she had to sit on her. Sarah smiled and said that she would only go across the street to see how they were progressing.

Strangely, Sarah was feeling pretty good. Yesterday had been a nightmare, but she had survived. She would take a shower, and then return to the homestead to see how they were doing.

Her shower always refreshed her. It was a special one she had insisted that they install in the master bath, a round enclosure that spewed water out of the layers of rounded pipes that surrounded the bather. Standing on the low porcelain tray and letting the water hit her from all sides she relaxed and thought of Ed. He must be going crazy by now because she hadn't written to him as yet. She must write and tell him – something. Brought back to reality by being dosed with cold water, she realized she had been in the shower so long that the hot water had been used up.

Sadie protested but Sarah scurried across the street to the Millikin home which her supervisor told her yesterday was now to be called the Red Cross Hospital. As she went toward the side door two ambulances pulled into the circular drive. Sarah found herself at work as soon as she went in the door. Trying to find beds to put the new patients in, she discovered there were only three cots left. There were now twenty-one patients in the hospital.

Her supervisor yelled across the room at her to come to "her office". Sarah was confused. There was no office only cots, people, and supplies. Working her way through the cots, she understood when she got near the front door. The supervisor was sitting at a chair pulled up to a battered oak table with stacks of papers on it. This was the office. No matter what the circumstances, paper work had to be done.

"Sarah, will you please find us some help. We can pay the nurses and the doctors, but we also need volunteers that will have to work for free. Also, could you please try to get us more supplies? Your tablecloths have been a god send to cover up the dead and to double as sheets for the cots," said the supervisor. "Maybe you could get us more."

About that time, one of the nurses now on duty, called to her, "Please come help me remove this patient, we need his bed."

So Sarah again picked up her end of the tablecloth and helped to remove the body. Once in the basement she noted there were now five bodies on the wooden platform.

As her foot hit the last step coming up from the basement, Sarah almost cried as the doctor called out to her. "Aren't you an aide? Come over here and help me with this patient."

Feeling like throwing up her hands and running home, the urgency of the situation won out and Sarah forgot her other orders and hurried to the doctor's side. What she saw when she got there made her fight hard to hold back the tears. Lying on the cot was a boy, maybe six or seven years old. His face was drawn and totally white except for the blood that kept dribbling out of his nose. Eyes that were almost swollen shut still showed pleasure as Sarah said, "Hello, my name is Sarah, and I'm here to help take care of you."

The doctor took Sarah aside and informed her about the boy.

"His name is Thomas and his flu has progressed to pneumonia. However, he still is strong and, with care, possibly can be saved. You'll find him agitated because his father, mother and a sister have already died. The only relative he has left is a brother who is ten years old. He doesn't fully understand the situation, but he knows he will never see his family again except for his brother. Do what you can."

"What is this flu doing to us?" thought a tearful Sarah who could not even comprehend the pain Thomas must be feeling, but she knew she had to help nurse him back to health. Finding a chair Sarah sat beside him for the rest of the day and talked to him, ignoring the rest of her patients.

"Thomas, I have a little boy named Sam who likes to play baseball. Do you like to play ball? Sam plays in the outfield because he can run fast. One time he caught a ball way out in the field and threw it all the way back to home plate. Everyone watching thought it was impossible for a little boy like Sam to throw a ball that far."

Sarah was not conscious that she was speaking of Sam as though he were still alive. She was thinking of the time he had come to Decatur in the summer and had played ball with some of her friend's children. Without stopping her narrative, she chattered on realizing that Sam was gone. "My Sam isn't here now, but he will watch out for you from where he is. I told him that you were a fighter just like he is and he will help you fight, Thomas."

Interrupting Sarah's stories, the supervisor came over and asked her how she was doing gathering supplies. Sarah said she would not leave Thomas alone to take care of that, but gave her names of people she thought would be able to help.

When William got home from work and found Sarah was across the street at the homestead, he was heartsick and went to the hospital to talk to Sarah. He was not allowed inside, but the volunteer at the door searched out Sarah who did leave Thomas long enough to talk to William. She stepped outside onto the porch to talk to him and breathed the welcome fresh air.

"Where is your mask Sarah?" asked a concerned William.

"I haven't been wearing it because Thomas likes it better when he can see my whole face."

"And who is Thomas?"

"Oh, William, he is this six year old boy who has lost almost all of his family and he is very ill – just like Sam was. He is so sweet. I have to help him."

"Sarah, my heart goes out to him too, but you are going to kill yourself doing this work. You are physically and emotionally drained. You aren't eating. You aren't sleeping," chanted William who knew he was defeated before he even asked, "Will you please come home with me?"

Sarah was moved by William's concern and the fact that he was really giving her a chance to make up her own mind.

"You know I can't. I'm touched that you are so concerned, but please don't worry. You know I have to do this for myself and – for Sam."

Sarah went back to her chair by Thomas's cot. Through the night she rubbed Vicks Vapor Rub on his chest. She kept cool rags on his face and tried to stop his nosebleeds.

Sometime in the early morning hours she fell asleep in her chair. As she entered her dream world, she saw Sam in his navy uniform standing beside an airplane and waving to her with a big smile on his face. She felt him putting his arms around her and helping her on board the plane. Then, they were up in the air with no air craft to hold them as they sat on the fluffy snow-white clouds and drifted through the blue sky. Pleased to see Sam so happy, Sarah closed her eyes and glided through the heavens. When the sunlight streamed through the shutters in the morning she snapped awake and looked down at Thomas.

"Hi, Sarah. I feel better. Can I go home now?" he asked in a weak voice.

Surveying him Sarah felt gleeful. He was going to make it. His fever had broken and his chest was not rattling like it had been. His eyes were not swollen and he asked if he could have something to eat.

"You are better, Thomas. I suspect the doctor will let you go sometime soon. I'm going to find him and let him look at you," Sarah said happily.

On her way to find someone to declare Thomas ready to go home, she suddenly came to the bitter realization that while he probably had a physical home the only person in it would be a ten-year old brother. Her work was not over. She had to find a guardian for the little boy.

After the doctor confirmed Thomas was ready to be released, Sarah sat by his bed again and started asking questions. Did he have an Aunt or an Uncle? No. Did he have a grandma or grandpa? No, but there was Aunt Teresa who was not really an aunt. Upon further examination Sarah determined that Aunt Teresa was a neighbor with whom Thomas and his family spent a lot of time.

Leaving Thomas's bedside, she took his address and went to the neighborhood to see if she could find someone who would agree at least temporarily to take him and his brother. Sarah started knocking on neighbors' doors and soon found Teresa. When Teresa came to her door, her set look told Sarah that she was expecting the worst news.

Immediately Sarah said, "Thomas is much better and is ready to be released if we can find a place for him to stay."

"Oh, do bring him here. His brother is with me and I don't know of any family that they have. Luckily my family doesn't have the flu, so we will be fine."

Sarah could tell after talking to the woman for a few moments that she cared deeply about Thomas and Sarah felt that she would take good care of him.

"Come to the Millikin Homestead and pick him up. I'll see that he will be ready to go home with you."

Back at the hospital Sarah saw to all the details for Thomas's release then sat with him until his neighbor came.

"Thanks, Sarah, for staying with me," said Thomas.

Not being able to find her voice, Sarah nodded her head as she watched him grab Teresa's hand and go with her out the door. Breathing a peaceful sigh, she squared her shoulders and went back to work.

For the next few weeks, Sarah spent most of her waking hours at the hospital. It was the worst nightmare she could imagine, but at least she could help. As her supervisor had predicted, everything did close, the schools, churches, theaters, in fact, any place that people would potentially gather. Thirty-five was the most patients the makeshift hospital ever had at one time, but the beds were constantly full. The bodies in the basement were piled up until the hearses could come retrieve them, which usually occurred every couple of days. The death rate was much higher than the medical staff thought it should be, but everyone was doing the best they could.

Finally, on the ninth day of November, the health department declared the epidemic over and reopened the public places. The new cases of flu were admitted to the real hospitals and the Red Cross hospital closed. For the first time in almost a month, Sarah went home at five o'clock in the evening, ate supper, went to bed, and slept soundly.

CHAPTER 28

After the War

Atlantic City, New Jersey November 1918

SARAH AWOKE THE next morning feeling tranquil for the first time since she lost Sam. Since September she had been to hell and back several times. Now the flu epidemic was winding down and everyone praised her help in making that happen. The Red Cross made her "Heroine of the Month" and hosted a luncheon for her where they encouraged anyone who wished, to stand up and praise her work. Many people rose and told a story showing her dedicated work.

Thomas and Teresa attended the affair and everyone in the room had to wipe the tears from their eyes when Thomas stood up and said, "Thank you, Sarah, for getting me well."

Sarah sensed from Ed's letters that were still coming faithfully three times a week that the war was also coming to an end. Exhausted from the work at the hospital, she recognized that it was time to think about her own health and renew her own soul. Checking the mirror in her bedroom and not liking what it reflected, made her determine to take care of herself. She perceived ugliness about her person when she was so thin, and she wanted to be pretty again. Resolving for the hundredth time to stop giving in to her grief, she vowed to live for the good times and make her husband part of that life.

For at least a month she and William had barely spoken. What they needed was to go on a trip; when he got home, she would ask him if they could go somewhere. So when William came into the house that night, he saw a changed woman sitting in the library reading a book. She looked up and smiled at him.

"Sarah, I haven't seen that smile since Sam died. It makes me so happy." said William.

Sarah ignored the dull pain in her stomach that ached at the mention of Sam's name and replied, "I know that he is gone -- I am alive; I have my passion again, doing what I can for others is my life's work now. To achieve this I'll have to take care of myself, but my intention is to have a good time while doing it."

William leaned over and kissed her saying, "This is the first time you have verbalized that Sam is gone. That's real progress. I can't believe how well you are doing right now. I almost had given up thinking you would ever be my Sarah again."

They sat together and planned a trip out east to Atlantic City. William had to go to a business conference there in a week anyway, so he thought they could mix business with pleasure. Sarah agreed with some trepidation because she realized that Ed would probably be there and wasn't sure what she should do about him. She had not talked or written to him since Sam died two months ago, but had leaned on his letters to help her through her tragedy. She had to face him sometime so it might as well be at the conference.

More reason for celebration came the next day, November 11th. The war was over! As soon as the news of the signing of the Armistice reached Decatur, people started pouring out of their houses, out of their businesses and out into the streets wildly yelling and throwing objects up into the air. Much of the public kept celebrating outside throughout the night, while some planned a big parade for the next day.

Sarah and William went to the Country Club and celebrated by having a few drinks with their friends. Many stood up and made a toast or two.

Even Sarah rose from her chair, raised her glass and said, "I wish to give an inadequate thank you to those brave young men who gave their lives for their country, whether on the battlefields of France or in the hospitals of a naval base." Sarah's voice cracked but she finished softly, "The world owes them a sincere debt of gratitude – it will be a better place."

She surprised herself by being able to give the salutation without totally breaking up in tears. When she sat back down, William placed his hand over hers and nodded his head in appreciation of her words. Sarah now realized that she could go on with her life, but things were different and never again could she be solely Mrs. W.J. Grady, the obedient socialite that she was before the war.

The next morning the newspaper described the Armistice as being effective on the eleventh hour of the eleventh day of the eleventh month. Sarah, being a stickler for details, couldn't help but note that the peace agreement had been signed early in the morning of the eleventh and wondered how many men had been killed between that time and the eleventh hour when the ceasefire took effect.

A few days later, buoyed by the end of the war, the Gradys set out for their trip to Atlantic City. Following their arrival, however, Sarah was quite disappointed as the supposed vacation trip, turned into nothing but William's time with his business associates. Now that the war was over she had hoped that life would become easier than it had been the last two years. Sarah wished the Gradys could reinvent themselves and seek more pleasure in their lives. Instead, throughout the trip, William's priority, as usual, turned out to be business. Harking back to the time before the war, he became suspicious and grilled her every time she danced with or spoke to another man. She was trying to help her husband as she had done in the past, but it was not possible with his distrustful attitude. It was as if nothing had changed for him since before Sam died. Sarah was baffled and frustrated by his regression.

"How can I help you with your business dealings if you will not allow me to be social with your contacts?" said Sarah.

William replied in a gruff voice, "I don't believe you have my interests at heart when you are socializing. I think you are just out to have a good time and garner as much attention as possible."

William could sense Sarah's displeasure with him, but did not know how to overcome his feelings. He couldn't put his finger on it, but knew something was amiss. He had brought Sarah with him so they could enjoy the resort together for a few days, relax and have a good time; but since his business associates were there before the conference began, he expected Sarah to help entertain them. In his opinion, she was carrying on with the men more than she had in several years, and it bothered him greatly. Sarah had never given him any clear cause to question her loyalty, but his doubts remained.

Sarah sighed. There was nothing she could do that would please William.

She mused to herself, "I deserve this attitude from William. I don't give him all my love. He used to be attentive, but now we have nothing in common. He doesn't look upon me as a worthwhile individual, and I see nothing in him either. I tire of trying to love him."

She thought of the love that came easily into her life. The love she had ignored now for months.

"Ed is all the things I need and admire," she told herself, "The war is over and, if anything, it has taught me the brevity of life. I will suggest to Ed that we not wait any longer, but divorce our spouses immediately so we can be together."

Later, as Sarah she anxiously watched the rest of the businessmen William was courting arrive in Atlantic City, she realized that Ed was not in the group. Since the families were such good friends, it was a natural question for Sarah to ask when she inquired where the Rockafellows were.

"Ed could not get away, but you and I are going to New York Thursday and spend the week-end with them. Ed and I still have some business to accomplish and I figured you would enjoy the city with Florence for a few days," said William.

Sarah was both delighted and disappointed. Ed had to be beside himself since she had not written a word to him since Sam died. The war over and expectant to see him here, she was now overwrought with longing for him.

"In New York," she told herself, "we'll form our plans."

Ed met them at the train station in New York and Sarah melted at the sight of him. Oh, how she had missed him. When his eyes met hers, for just a second, they were lovers, Ed and Sarah. He quickly gained his composure and extended his hand to William. Sarah was having trouble regaining her poise. With her emotions showing all over her face and knowing her husband would sense something was off beam, she feigned illness. As Sarah intended, William decided it would be better for her if they got a hotel room instead of staying with the Rockafellows so she could recoup. Ed took them to a hotel, which removed a little pressure from Sarah, as she didn't have to see so much of Florence or Ed. It was too difficult to see Ed when William was close by.

After William left for his meetings the next morning, there was a knock on the door of her hotel room. Sarah's mind jumped back to the time in Hot Springs when there had been a knock on her door around 2:00 a.m. Feeling very nervous she opened the door, welcomed Ed in, shut the door, and then fell into his arms. They held each other tightly for at least two full minutes. Sarah cried, as was her wont to do, and Ed smothered her in kisses.

"I have wanted so much to be with you in your sorrow. If you had called, I would have come, but I thought you wanted me to stay away. I couldn't help writing to you. I've waited so long to hear from you," said Ed.

"I've just now been able to get my feet on the ground and return to normal living," said Sarah.

They had an hour while William was at a meeting and they packed everything into those sixty minutes. They talked, made love, and tried to make plans. Ed was terribly upset at Sarah's appearance as she still showed the effects of the last several months.

"I can't believe that you worked all that time in the hospital right after Sam passed. I know you felt the need to help others, but I suspect you almost killed yourself. I can't live without you, Sarah. You have to learn to take care of yourself."

As he expressed his concern, something snapped inside of Sarah. She realized their affair had gone on for almost four years, and, although Ed professed his love almost daily, they were no closer to being together than the first time they met. What if she was just his mistress? She thought unwittingly of Charles and how he had affected her with his affair. But at least he married Clara.

"You can't live without me? Oh, I do love you, Ed, but are we ever going to be together? Ed, do you really love me? For almost four years you have told me we would be together soon. I am beginning to believe that this was a flirtation, nothing more. Maybe we should say good bye and just hold on to our beautiful memories. Our situation is just too complicated. I'm tired, Ed. The war is over. It is time."

Sarah surprised herself with her practical attitude.

"Oh, my Darling, you are so wrong. I do, my love, I do love you so. I love you enough to be with you the way you deserve. Please, my Sallie," he said, taking her in his arms, "Love me enough to wait for me a little longer."

She looked up at him as he pulled his watch out of his pocket.

"But, Dearest, please forgive me, I cannot discuss this now. I have to dash to pick up William. I hate to leave you with this hanging over our heads."

He shut the door behind him and Sarah was left to fret over her own unexpected proclamation. During the rest of their stay Sarah and Ed were not able to be alone again.

CHAPTER 29

Unfashionable Love

3 Millikin Place Spring 1919

CRESTFALLEN AFTER ED'S hesitation to make permanent plans with her, Sarah continued her routine with William and her charity work. She threw parties, entertained out-of-town guests, and worked diligently on the nursery she had started for underprivileged children. The Red Cross was still in dire need of assistance, so she helped. Ed's letters kept coming and in spite of her determination to break off with him, she wrote to him as well. How she wished she could have the strength to tell him goodbye, but the temptation of finding his words waiting for her in the postal box always won out.

Following their return from New York, this letter awaited her.

> Darling,
>
> It is so hard to speak with the specter of that awful talk of last night to haunt one. I haven't had a happy hour nor have I been free from mental anguish since we talked. I was so happy to see you – but it was short lived and my wonderful Sarah seemingly ended with all sorts of imprecations heaped on me like coals of fire.
>
> Perhaps I am wholly to blame. When I die – I want to remember the happiness of when I basked in your supreme love and the smiles and alternate tears that went with it.
>
> If you could know the torture I underwent when you left New York, you would have some idea of my feelings and then you would know whether my love is genuine or not.

No, I suppose it is not the fashion for a love like mine to exist in these days – therefore it is easy to reproach me – as mine is not understood from such a point of view. – But my darling, it will last to the grave and that means it will stand the test of time which fashionable loves will not.

I must not keep putting all my burdens on you – God knows I don't want to – but my future depends so much on your attitude toward me – that I must beg you to help me – by not crucifying both of us as you often threaten.

I want no other I care for no other and therefore I deify you - Please I beg do not reject me. I want to be a living, breathing thing in your life and not a memory. Tell me darling – where do I stand? Can we not continue to love? It will probably be my only happiness for the rest of my life. Wouldn't it dear heart, keep you too – to make up your mind to keep me as yours, come what may and someday we will be together to end our days.

I love you,
I Do, Do you?

Sarah continued to write to Ed telling him that she did love him, but, until they could be together, she had no choice but to be a good wife to William. The Gradys traveled as most well-heeled families did in 1919 and vacationed in Florida, California, and Texas. The stress of war was over and those who could afford it were trying to have a good time. William, obsessed as ever with success, attended to work while others celebrated, and the divide between he and Sarah only grew.

Their vacations were tolerable for Sarah, but she no longer enjoyed her husband's company. His mind was singular in focus and that focus was business. The vacations they took were arranged around which trade associates would be present at which destinations. He couldn't even enjoy a game of golf unless it could further his business ventures. Sarah often suggested that they go to the theater and William would not inquire what was playing but he was concerned with who would be there. If the colleagues that he was currently trying to impress were not going with them, he was not interested. Sarah watched silently as month after month he wound himself tighter and tighter. His hair grayed more daily and the lines deepened on his face. To Sarah, he embodied joylessness, and she avoided his company and mounting temper.

Again Sarah found herself longing for Ed's company, no matter what the status of their relationship. She continued her practice of going alone to resorts of her choice for a week or two when she desired and, of course, she coordinated with Ed for these vacations and was able to spend days at a time with him. This was her salvation.

When Sarah was not with Ed, she had his letters. This correspondence not only kept Sarah sane, but also tuned her into the broader world and provided spirited debate as she answered his letters. The highlights of her week were his opinions on politics. She usually agreed with the Republicans and was not a great Wilson fan, but she really enjoyed hearing Ed's defense of the President and his policies.

He wrote:

> *I have always tried to keep you posted on the merits of the 'League of Nations'. You have perhaps heard a lot about Great Britain having 6 votes to our 1 and how Wilson sold us out, etc., etc. Really Great Britain has but one vote the same as we have in the council or executive committee. In the house all self-governing nations and colonies have a vote, but that doesn't count for much so why not let them have it? I only wish you were by my side and would let me interpret more of these things to you. In my studies of these things – it is easy to get at the bottom of them – if you understand the reason and necessity – then you get the motive and if you are open minded – I mean are not prejudiced – then understanding follows. One of the questions or issues I understand (not from hearsay but from ten years study) is the Greek-Balkan*

or Bulgarian question – Thrace or Macedonia has been the cause of 3 Balkan Wars. Greece wants it – but it belongs to Bulgaria by racial inheritance and blood descendants since the 12th century - The peace Conference rights a wrong of 7 centuries by giving it to Bulgaria and all Europe and the world agrees – excepting our own, cantankerous Senate who in their ignorance or hatred for Wilson want it given to Greece. It is enough to make the angels weep. Am now glad I am not in politics, much as I would like it. Still when you think about it, it was always thus, because Geo. Washington when he negotiated what was known as the Jay Treaty at the conclusion of our war with England was according to his own biography accused of everything from burglary to petit larceny by the Borahs, Lodges, Shermans and Johnsons of his day and he hadn't a shred of character left and twas the same with Lincoln in his day...

As William became deeply absorbed with a new business he had purchased, he became more verbally abusive toward Sarah. He complained about her clothes, her hair, and even the fact that she looked too tired. One night as they were getting ready to go to the country club to meet some of his associates, he literally ripped a dress off of her and told her to wear something more flattering.

Sarah angrily retorted, "I'm sorry you don't find me pleasing, William Grady, you damned fool, but others seem to find no fault in my appearance. Maybe I will spend the evening with one of them!"

William slapped her. Then, throwing another dress from her closet on the bed, he said gruffly, "Now put on this dress and fix your face. How dare you threaten to humiliate me!

"You're nothing but a scorned farm girl without me beside you, and if you think another man would have you, you're the fool."

Even though she wanted to show strength, Sarah couldn't help crying, "I won't go with you tonight. Why do you treat me this way? You will have to tell people that I am ill – and that isn't far from the truth."

William left the room slamming the door behind him. Sarah sat in her favorite spot on the built-in bench in her sitting room as she held her swollen cheek.

"Enough! I'm too old to live like this, too worn by these last years. Ed must take me from this now," she mentally determined.

She and Ed could live happily together and make a place for themselves some place other than Decatur or New York. They both loved California. It mattered not whether their stock account was large enough to support them; they were intelligent and resourceful people and would figure it out. Her grief over Sam had made her look at life differently. You did not just sit and wait for things to happen; you made them happen. Yes, it was time. She couldn't live with William any longer, especially since her true love and soul mate was out there waiting for her. Ed would now have to leave Florence so they could be together, whether he was ready or not.

She dashed down the stairs to the phone. Looking around she determined that Sadie had gone to the movies on her night off and James was in his room above the garage. She was alone. Now if only the phone line was clear enough that she could have a conversation with Ed, she would tell him that it was time for them to be together as a couple. Sarah fantasized that Ed would be so happy that he would immediately drop everything and be on a train headed for Decatur.

Sarah dialed the phone number for the Union Club hoping that Ed would be there and not at home. The reception desk answered and Sarah asked for Mr. Ed Rockafellow.

The phone line was clear and within a minute Ed answered.

"Our time has come," blurted out Sarah, "I am going to leave William – just like we have talked about for the last four years."

"What has happened Sarah? Did he hurt you?"

"Of course he did … the coward. Ed, please, William is absolutely crazy and I cannot stay here another minute. I want to live again, with you."

"My Sallie, I've waited a long time to hear you say those words."

"What should I do – come to New York or just stay here and get my divorce?"

"Love, you should go to bed this evening and in the morning plan a trip East so we can be together and plan our strategy."

She was disappointed at the wait Ed was suggesting. The happiness in his voice made her long for him.

"Alright, my love, I'll meet you at our sacred place."

CHAPTER 30

The Impressionists

Hot Springs, Virginia Fall 1919

WILLIAM DECLINED TO talk Sarah out of her trip to the East. Frustrated and exhausted by her constant displeasure, he mused.

"I'm glad she is out of the house for a while. Maybe more time away from Decatur will help. She doesn't attend luncheons or bridge games with her friends, and, though she is still an avid charity worker, her sparkle is gone and she doesn't seem to enjoy her work. Sarah is not the partner that I need anymore. I do love her, but can't understand her. Why won't she behave herself? Is this attitude all due to Sam's death?"

Excited about her decision to divorce William, Sarah was giddy as the train approached Hot Springs and eager to feel the welcome of Ed's arms. William had not questioned her destination, so she planned to book just one room for her and Ed. Soon they would be together all of the time – after four years of eluding their spouses and friends. She envisioned her life would consist of going to the theater, reading books, visiting museums, playing golf, discussing politics, and riding Midnight. It was fitting that they would make plans to be together for the rest of their lives in the place where they first met.

Ed joined her about three hours after she arrived, and they left the lodge to take a walk. The weather was perfect, a warm fall day. They walked to a spot where there was a small bridge over a clear, swift running creek.

As they stood for a moment on the bridge Sarah said in a low soft tone, "This is what I have waited for all my life. The world is perfect. Just look around you, Ed. Don't you feel like you are standing in middle of an impressionistic painting? The sky, the grass, the water are all bright colors mixed with the subdued fall color of the leaves, and you and I are not totally defined. We are spirits who are twisting together in the wind. Finally, after all this time, we will be together."

Ed admired his love in her wistful euphoria and then darkened as he wondered how long her joy would last when their days were not stolen moments encapsulated in their beautiful hideaways. Ed knew if they were to truly create a life together, it would be their ruin. His own ruin he could carry, and would, for her, if she still wanted him then. But hers? If it were *him* to break her after all she had endured, that was a burden he would not fashion for either of them.

In a voice just above a whisper, Ed said, "Sarah, my darling, finally we will be together, but we have to do it correctly or we will not be happy. The minute you divorce William, you will get a settlement from him, but it will not be a large one since you are the one initiating the separation. On the other hand, I will have literally nothing. If my friends feel I have wronged Florence, they will desert me and I could lose my job, my club memberships, and my influential connections – not to mention the money I would have to pay Florence. Also, have you noticed that our stock account has been going down quite a bit lately?"

"Ed, I don't care. We can be happy on very little. I'm sure you could get a job and so could I for that matter. I own some land in Colorado, Minnesota, and Illinois. We could build a house on one of those properties. And besides isn't the coal strike the reason our stocks have gone down? Coal strikes don't last forever. I'm sure they will settle and then our stocks will go up."

"No, the coal strike is not affecting stocks. That's not the cause of the present decline. The banks are determined to put the brakes on futures speculation; so to accomplish this, they are raising the money and interest rates to a prohibitive rate -- for instance, Saturday call money was twenty percent..."

Sarah interrupted, "I don't care anymore. I just want to get away from William and be with you. Don't you want that too?"

"Of course I do. But, Sarah, the timing is dreadful. Just last week I was told by my company that I was getting a promotion, which is good news. The bad news is they want me to take care of something over in France for six months and Florence wants to go with me. All week before your call I have been trying to decide how to tell you this. If only you could go with me – but that won't work because Florence will be there and I will be extremely busy with work. My Sallie, we will have to postpone being together for just a little while. By the time I get back, we will have everything figured out and our stock account will be better. I worry about William hurting you, but I don't know what I can do. Maybe if you follow his dictates, he will leave you alone."

Sarah choked back her disappointment.

"*Follow his dictates?*" she thought, "You have always encouraged me to do the opposite. This is not how it is supposed to be. I thought you would be tripping over yourself to get us together. Do you truly love me?"

There was little else in her life but him. What could she do?

Aloud she said, "I did not think anything could keep us apart, but if this is the way it has to be – it will be." She hoped her voice sounded strong and resolute, because inside she felt like a piece of broken glass, shattered into a thousand chards.

"I am so disappointed too, but, Sarah, I promise you we will be together. Please, just have patience."

As they walked off of the bridge, Sarah quickened her gait, damning her hopefulness, and then turned back and stood before him with a wistful smile.

"Let's forget everything and have a good time," she said running her fingers over his heart, as the painful thought ran through her, "for the last time."

For the two days they were together, they were soul mates, lovers and nothing else. Sarah could not shake the little voice that interrupted her activities with Ed. Outwardly, she was Sarah having a good time, but that voice inside her kept saying, "This is the last time I will kiss him. This may be the last time I will ever see him."

Ed couldn't help but notice that Sarah was having several cocktails of an evening, breaking their pact not to have any alcohol. But he refrained from chastising her. The timing of his promotion and the overseas work that went with it was terrible, but hopefully Sarah could be patient just a little longer. If his love could only wait for him, all their days could be like these. He was not ready yet, nor was she.

Back at home, Sarah prayed every night for Ed to hurry up and get overseas so he could come back to the states and they could carry out a plan to be together. Her prayers always ended with a plea to help her hang on until he came for her; yet, her heart mourned the future that became more distant with each new day.

CHAPTER 31

Blighted Love

3 Millikin Place December 1919

Sᴀʀᴀʜ ꜱᴛɪʟʟ ᴡʀᴏᴛᴇ to Ed faithfully and he to her. He was not scheduled to leave for Paris for at least another four weeks but there was no chance of her seeing him before he left. Both of them were busy. William asked Sarah to help with the books in the business he had just purchased and Ed had a multitude of work to do before he left the country for six months. Ed's letters came regularly and were in the same vein as before Sarah asked him to leave his wife and be with her. Sarah still enjoyed hearing from him as he described his daily activities from the most prestigious resorts in New York, but she read his mail with a sense that their affair might be over. Not believing every word he wrote anymore, she nursed her inner doubts, but in spite of herself, she imagined being by his side as he composed his letter. From Lake Mohonk Mountain House in upper New York State, Ed wrote:

> *Darling,*
>
> *Being without you day by day is becoming unbearable. I resort to all sorts of expedients to click away the days from Wednesday to Saturday which seem to be all I look forward to. Today for instance I was not at the office but was attending a meeting in another part of town. Had a special messenger bring your dear letter to me and I stole out and read it and then came back to the meeting. Got through at 2:00 and then met Mr. Shreeve and went up*

to Mount Hope in Westchester where the oldest and of course the first golf course in America was laid out. It was backed by Andrew Carnegie and is named the St. Andrews after its prototype in Scotland. It is beautiful but would be called an old man's course. About 10 holes are flat but the other eight are difficult. It is located in a very secluded and inaccessible place and visitors are not numerous. It is cozy and comfortable and you would love it. I went through the usual mental picture which is a daily habit with me of imagining you by my side and enjoying it together.

When I got home found Florence very cross and envious of my trip. It is hard for me to understand her no matter what she does – or anyone else I seem to feel that way. She has a car and now doesn't use it. So what is one to do? It is probably like this - we haven't one single thing in common that we like to do together...

Oh, I forgot to mention that on Tuesday noon at a luncheon I heard Cardinal Mercier speak and tell about his trials under the German invasion which was great to hear...

It gave me a thrill of joy to read in your letter today that you were constantly willing us to be one which is what I have always wanted you to do. Now we have our minds working in harmony and therefore the time maybe shortened. Do not think I am unmindful of the time slipping by but the money we must have and I am devoting some energy to that phase of our situation...

Always your loving and adoring, Ed

Sarah tried to keep her letters to Ed upbeat and interesting even though she was not feeling cheery. Knowing that Ed was still very involved in politics, Sarah wrote to him often about her political viewpoints. The only cause she was excited about at this time was the minimum wage for women. New York had a bill in its legislature that would force businesses to pay women a minimum salary. The bill was considered revolutionary and other states were watching New York carefully hoping it would not pass. Ed was not against this bill although he could foresee many problems stemming from its passage. He was however concerned about the Republicans (of which Sarah was one) destroying Wilson's peace plan and thereby the whole government. Sarah rather enjoyed goading him. Aware of Sarah's mounting impatience for their future, Ed's letters focused more and more on his political dealings. Hoping to hold her attention and help her to feel needed, he responded by passionately explaining to her why she should not take up the banner of the Republicans:

> *You are correct in surmising my disgust at the contemptible action of a political party that will go so far in their partisanship as to block the appropriation bills to run the different departments of the Govt. It is one of the reasons I have never since a kid joined any political party. Where they put party advantage above their country as Americans are prone to do – they differ from all other nations for they wash their dirty linen always in public. No matter what party is in power abroad, the people of England, France, etc. stand behind their Govt – even behind a Socialist Premier as they did in France before Clemenceau took office. In England the Conservatives (who are akin to our Republicans) hate to the marrow the Prime Minister Lloyd George – but are patriotic enough for England's sake to stand behind him until the job is finished. When that is over they will probably rend him from limb to limb – as they threatened to do before the war started - because he has opposed their class schemes which are characteristic of the wealthy i.e. to keep the poor poorer and not raise them above their environment.*
>
> *I wonder if you can recall that only a few years ago about (7 Or 8) there was almost a revolution in England and*

the power of the House of Lords was curtailed so that now they have no power or influence as peers in politics. If the Govt. now puts a bill through the house (parliament) which the people elect and the Lords should turn it down - it goes before the people direct and if they back it up - it becomes a law without the approval of the Lords. Since this change in the British Constitution, the Lords have never vetoed (nor have they dared to) a single bill.

Now I predict if our Senate continues to block what Congress or the Govt. wants -- it will suffer a similar fate as the House of Lords. Mark the prediction from little me...

Finally Ed left the country, but assured Sarah the six months he would be gone would fly by. His regular three letters a week were slower getting to her from overseas but they did come. But Sarah was finding that his correspondence did not seem to be enough for her. She wrote to him occasionally but not often as it was not as easy for him to receive her letters as it had been in New York. The philosophy she adopted after Sam's death began to repeat itself daily to her; "life is too short to postpone taking actions, live for the present."

She found herself daily questioning the depth of his devotion to her and began to realize that the chance of him ever leaving his wife was not very good. She needed to analyze her feelings and answer her own questions about her relationship with Ed without emotion. A decision had to be made -- to keep the affair going or drop Ed out of her life. She was accustomed to knowing what she wanted, and her indecisiveness with Ed was a daily drain on her thoughts, heart, and energy.

About a month after Ed's departure, Sarah climbed the stairs to her third floor room and locked the door. Intending to have a rigorous self-inspection, she sensed that whatever her decisions would be about her future, her evaluations would be setting the course for the rest of her life.

She sat on her little chair by the window and stared at the familiar landscape.

"Okay, Sarah, let's have it," she said out loud. "Why did I marry William?"

"I liked him and thought that he would be a good provider for Sam and me," she answered herself.

"Was I happy with him? Did I spoil our chances?"

This was a difficult one for Sarah and she cautioned herself to answer truthfully.

"Yes, for probably ten years. I was happy, but then William seemed changed. He no longer paid attention to me except for what I could do to help him obtain higher levels of responsibilities in his job. His obsession with becoming President of Faries Manufacturing Company trumped anything else, including me. He overworked me and instead of being grateful for my efforts, he only commanded me to do more. Sometimes I think he would have rented me out if he thought that would have gotten him a promotion. But it was my choice to take up with Ed. By our twelfth wedding anniversary, William was dictating all of my daily activities, and when he did not like my efforts on his behalf, he became both physically and emotionally abusive. We had nothing in common. Never did he take me to a theater, concert, or art show unless business prospects were involved; nor did he support me pursing my own interests. He thought my wanting to learn French was a frivolous activity. My participation in various women's causes was forbidden for a long time. He ruled me. And did whatever he wanted with whomever he wanted. I hated my life."

Sarah noticed that a bright red cardinal was sitting outside on the windowsill. As Sarah paced up and down in front of the window, the bird cocked his head and seemed to listen intently to her.

"Yes, I was very unhappy and then, I met Ed. He told me I was a beautiful person both inside and out and said so over and over again. When I expressed an opinion on a subject, he listened intently. Although he did not always agree with me, he was able to see the merits of my argument and without patronizing me, explained his point of view. We had everything in common as though we were soul mates. And, yes, he was handsome and I was physically attracted to him as well. And, now, I will admit it. Having an affair was exciting. It brought an element of danger into my life that had never been there before and I liked that as well.

"What do I do now? Ed seems more distant. Our future seems so far, like it will never be, like it was never meant to be. Do I wait for Ed to be free? Or do I go out on my own? Can I leave again? I am forty-one years old and without my darling boy to find a life for. No William? Perhaps even without Ed?"

The cardinal cocked his head to the opposite side and then flew away as if to say, "This is too deep for me."

Sarah couldn't come up with answers to those questions, but, at the same time, she told herself she had to decide. She loved Ed, but still had some feelings for William. Now that Sam was gone, she felt differently about her own life. Somehow she felt she had a right to be happy for the rest of her life and now that she was over forty, she could feel her days slipping away. Of course, she would be happier with Ed, but the reservations she had since telling him she was leaving William, kept her upset. He should have jumped for joy and planned immediately to quit his job and divorce Florence, but – he procrastinated. He went ahead with his company's plan to send him overseas and said they would make plans when he returned in six months. There was little doubt in Sarah's mind now that this was a stall tactic.

Sarah went downstairs and decided to have just one little cocktail before William got home for supper. An emptied tumbler in hand, she found her problems still inhabited her mind.

One afternoon Sarah sat with June on the veranda of the country club having tea. Their work with the Red Cross was complete, and they were now free to resume leisurely afternoons in one another's company. Sarah was delighted to have her back in Decatur and eager to discuss her troubles with her confidant.

"After four years, Ed is never going to be ready to disrupt his life and marry me. I know he loves me, but not enough to go away with me and be happy with the existence we could forge out for ourselves. There will always be some reason we can't get together as a couple. June, this is a devastating blow for me to absorb. If I want to continue with Ed, it will be as we are now. Forever his mistress. William is getting more suspicious which makes it more difficult to see Ed, even when returns."

June looked at her friend and could see the turmoil on her face.

"Sarah, you have to go on living. Life after Sam is terribly difficult I know, but your life is truly your own now. You can live apart from these men that cause you so much pain. Maybe it is time for us to just behave ourselves."

Sarah looked at the familiar face before her; the creases around June's sweet smile had deepened. It had only been four years, but they had been the most difficult years of both their lives. Sarah placed the teacup back in the saucer, looking up at June.

"You are so right. Please excuse me, dear friend. I've got to go home. I have to do something."

At home Sarah once more went to her space on the third floor. She crawled into the attic and retrieved the box with all of Ed's letters and trinkets in it. Resisting the urge to reread the letters, she picked up an old newspaper off a pile on the floor. Lovingly and carefully she divided the letters into several bundles, wrapped them in the papers and placed them into the box. Tightly closing the box, she hesitated a moment trying to decide between destroying it or putting it back behind the chimney in the attic. Convinced that William would never get into this space, she carefully tucked the box out of sight behind the chimney and crawled out of the area shutting the door tightly and with some resolve. She would never again see Ed as a lover. All she had left of him were these letters, trinkets, and beautiful memories.

Her sitting room beckoned her as she came downstairs from the third floor and she sat at her desk with tears flooding the stack of papers on top. She quickly penned a letter to Ed telling him that she would no longer be writing to him and he should stop writing to her, explaining that she felt they would never be together because he did not love her more than he did his position in society and in the business world. She told him how hurt she was and how she would never forgive him for having his flirtation with her for four years.

She had made her decision and would stick by it. Perhaps William's tirades had been her doing all along, the tantrums of a neglected husband. The holidays were almost upon them and she would try to make these festive days the best celebration of Christmas that she and William had ever had; she determined to have the best New Year's Eve party ever given in Decatur Illinois. 1920 was going to be a good year for the Gradys.

Right now she had to make her tear stained face look presentable for her husband as he would be home soon.

CHAPTER 32

The Good Life Is Over

Decatur, Illinois January 1920

WANTING TO KEEP her vow of having the most successful parties in Decatur at Christmas time, Sarah was spending all of her effort organizing them. One day close to Christmas, as she picked up her mail and started sorting through her Christmas cards, she noticed a card post-marked Paris, France. Her heart skipped a beat, but then she realized Florence was the originator not Ed, and it was addressed to both she and William. Trying hard not to think of Ed since packing up his letters and ceasing to write him, she realized she had not closed the postal box at the hotel. The rental fee was paid till the end of the year, so the timing was perfect to close it. There might even be a couple of letters in the box that would have been written before she told Ed to stop writing her. She immediately got into her car and drove downtown.

Confronting the hotel clerk who could have cared less what she wanted, she told him she wished to close her postal box. Lazily he looked up from behind the desk and finally said, "Have you paid up-to-date for it?"

"Yes, I paid through the end of the year."

"Well, we don't refund money you've already paid," said the clerk who was finally warming up to his job.

An impatient Sarah responded, "I don't want any money. I just want to close the box. It's in the name of June York."

"Are you Mrs. York?"

"No, but I rented it for my friend."

The dialogue continued for several minutes with Sarah cleverly getting around giving her name.

"I'll need the key," said the persistent clerk.

"As soon as I empty the box, I'll give it to you," said Sarah.

Feeling there could be one or two letters inside, she opened the box and retrieved four of them. By the time she got back to the clerk's desk, he had disappeared, so she put the key in her purse and left. As she walked away from the hotel, she couldn't help turning and looking at the building where she had eagerly retrieved Ed's letters for four years.

"How could I have been so gullible for so long?" she asked herself, "just some pleasant diversion for him – nothing else."

Now she had to decide whether or not to read the four letters he had written. Her inner voice said "throw them in the garbage." However, another voice full of curiosity said, "Read them and put them in the box as an end to your affair." She of course listened to the curious voice and after arriving home, retreated to the third floor to digest them in private and perform her ritual once more.

Reaffirming to herself that Ed had never really loved her, she read the letters. The first one she opened read:

> *This has been a miserable day for me. Just blank despair and no ambition to do anything. A sort of inertia took hold of me. Then toward noon I felt physically sick and the cause of it all is what? Even from a distance a voice – the voice of my beloved chilled me to the marrow. No magician in the practice of legerdemain can change like my sweetheart – that is the cause of my woe today. Am denied the consolation of even writing a letter to her let alone seeing her or talking to her. A complete reversal in a few brief weeks. When I am frozen by these moods, a paralysis of fear seizes me and I sit in fear of losing myself.*
> *What a fearful thing – blighted love is. Never will I ever again treat flippantly, in fact I haven't for a number of years, the passionate love of one person for another. It is a terrible*

thing for a person in the prime of life to be entangled in a hopeless love – to carry around day after day, week after week, month after month, year after year – a heart of lead and a sick soul – that cries out for something to heal you. Nothing however helps in such cases – no philosophy can. You can't eat, sleep, or read – all you can do is think, think and think by the hour over what might have been if fate or destiny or life had treated you differently. Verily, there is no anguish equaling that of a hopeless love.

It is said that nature will in time heal the aching voids in human hearts. I seriously question if it will cure the serious and passionate love of an adult well along in the prime of life, if that person knows life and has been in turn loved by the object of his passion. Little consolation was afforded me by the receipt of a beautiful letter couched in terms of deepest affection to inform me that we could no longer see each other...

After reading three of his letters, Sarah could no longer read his words without telling herself, "He had a chance to be with me forever and didn't take it." Opening the last letter, she steadied her hands.

After you read my afternoon letter you will indict me as the pinnacle of selfishness. You will immediately say that I 'do not think of your position, etc.' but I certainly do. Sweetheart, the defect of your logic is – that when you dispose of me as you did in the letter just received, you do not allow in your plans, where you say time will cure all, that my age is against it. It is a mistake common with all writers, especially modern writers of fiction. Now if I was between 20 and 30 things can be done - but when love such as mine comes at my time of life nature does not heal the breaks as it does to youth – so the wounds do not respond to heroic treatment ...

Well, Sweetheart – I have given you my love – all that there is – is yours – there is nothing else. There is no more – so it is up to you. I am always ready to do your bidding day or night.

Sarah could take no more. She wondered were her hands trembling from grief or anger as she held in her palms the letters containing the last words she would ever hear from Ed?

Sitting in the small old chair she had placed on the third floor to make a comfortable spot where she could commune with him, she gingerly wrapped the four letters in a single sheet of newspaper, opened the little door to the attic space, dropped to her knees, tearfully crawled over to the chimney, and brought into the room the special box that contained four years of correspondence and mementos of her time with Ed. She placed the letters with the others, tightly wrapped the whole container in more newspaper, and secured it with twine. Crawling back into the small area, she stuffed it behind the chimney that protruded through the attic. Reaching deep into her soul, she heard a voice telling her to burn everything, but she quieted the sound knowing she was incapable of destroying all that was left of her life with Ed. Maybe someday, she reasoned, someone would find these letters and bear witness to their love and to the wonderful years they shared together -- but she would never touch the box again.

Wiping her eyes, Sarah determined she had shed her last tear for Ed Rockafellow. Holding her head high, she descended the stairs stopping on the second floor to stare into the sitting room. Slowly approaching the built-in window seat that was constructed just for the purpose of looking out the window and ruminating over all the important parts of life, she realized, at this time, that was exactly what was needed. A place to think, to ponder. Where had she gone wrong? Or had she? William wouldn't be home for hours from the office, so she had time to sit and contemplate what she had done and what the next step in her life would be.

Sarah snuggled into the cushioned seat, looked out of the window and remembered that it was only four years ago that she had curled up in this exact spot on the same puffy pillows. She closed her eyes as 1915 bloomed within her mind's eye.

✤

Sarah snapped back to reality, realizing she had been sitting for hours on her window seat and reliving her last four years. She had an empty feeling in the pit of her stomach. No more letters from the East. No more Ed.

She stiffly rose from her seat to check on dinner. William would be home soon.

CHAPTER 33

※

A Face in the Clouds

The Grady Farm Early Spring 1920

TRY AS SHE might, life with William held nothing for Sarah. Sarah soon found that removing her lover from her life did nothing to revive her marriage. Void of all she held dear, Sarah only pretended to continue living and the days slipped past her, one into the next, meaningless. As she retreated from her responsibilities in various organizations, she received honors and awards for her previous service. Honored by the day nursery for the underprivileged children as their founder; she acknowledged their award graciously, but had no feeling of pride. She accepted awards from the Red Cross for her work during and after the war; she attended a dinner to honor those who had worked tirelessly during the flu epidemic; and she received a pin from the woman's suffrage movement for her service to their cause.

Not alone in her withdrawal from the world, Sarah realized society, in general, was different after the war; many people led their lives more privately because the "War to End All Wars" left them depressed. This knowledge did not, however, repair her emotional voids. The public did not notice Sarah's abandonment of her duties in Decatur's organizations except for a few "friends" who used this opportunity to propel themselves into Sarah's vacated prominent positions. People seem quick to forget the good things about others and when one was as active as Sarah had been, envious opportunists celebrated her absence. Sarah still had a position in the community, but her groups placed her unofficially on an inactive status and others stepped in to take her place. Since she had also stopped playing golf, her newspaper publicity declined as she no longer won trophies.

Sarah had been Decatur's number one woman activist, leading many organizations during her time in the city; but as the spring of 1920 dawned, she was no longer a force within her causes. She didn't care. The life had been syphoned out of her. Her thin frame held up her bones; her shiny hair turned a listless dead, brown color, and her eyes no longer sparkled. Those who had not seen Sarah for a while barely recognized Mrs. W. J. Grady.

June set up golf matches for Sarah at the country club, but Sarah always found an excuse to cancel them. Lunch dates with Sarah's closest friends were arranged, but she never appeared. June told her the home for orphans, which had been Sarah's most cherished organization, was faltering and needed her help, but Sarah was unresponsive. June was worried.

Sarah considered June part of the problem, as June's life bounded forward, Sarah's stagnancy was all the more clear. June became engaged to an old friend, Corwin Johns, and spent her time preparing for an upcoming wedding. The impending nuptials forced Sarah into thinking about reality. Trying to come to terms with helping her best friend, she informed June she would host a dinner for her the night before the wedding, but could bring herself to do no more.

She felt happy June was marrying an exceptionally nice man who belonged to the second oldest family in Decatur, June's family being the first.

"It will be a good marriage," thought Sarah, "not as perfect as my marriage to Ed would have been, but at June's age of thirty-nine it will be a healthy relationship."

Even though she wanted to hear about the wedding, Sarah experienced great agitation with the situation as June had very little time for her now, when Sarah needed her the most. Not wanting to hear June go over and over the details of a wedding that she herself would never have with Ed, Sarah tried to ignore June. When she could stave off June's invitations to tea no longer, Sarah allowed June to ramble through the endless details of a wedding, all the while imagining they were her plans with Ed. She sipped her tea, bitter in the cup, as she grew to dislike one more person she had held so dear. June was now just another loved one not fulfilling their role in Sarah's life.

⚜

One evening in early spring of 1920, Sadie summoned Sarah to the phone.

"Mrs. Grady, this is Gerry at the farm. I think you should come out here, maybe pretty soon."

"What's the matter, Gerry? Is something wrong with Midnight?" said Sarah.

More or less ignoring the question, Gerry said, "Just come soon, Mrs. Grady."

Following Gerry the foreman's phone call that suggested she needed to come right away, she drove into the countryside knowing in her heart she would find a problem with her beloved horse.

Arriving at the farm, she found Midnight lying down in a stall in the barn on the soft hay. When he saw Sarah he tried to get on his feet, but could not. She fell down on her knees and settled close to her stallion's side. Gerry told her that the veterinarian had been summoned a few hours ago and had diagnosed the problem as an infection caused by a blockage in his blood flow. His organs were failing. There was nothing to be done.

Sarah thought she would break in two. How much more tragedy could she endure? Tears streamed down her face; she had not cried like this since she was at Sam's bedside. Certain a horse heaven existed, she prayed to God to take him quickly.

For five hours, well into the night, she sat beside Midnight and rubbed his nose, offering water in her cupped hands once in a while. It was a cool night, but the hay made the temperature bearable. The cold helped Sarah to focus solely on Midnight.

"Take me away with you, old boy," she whispered in his onyx ear.

Gerry came out to the barn, "Please, Mrs. Grady, come to the house and let me fix you a cup of tea. Then I can stay out here with Midnight for a while."

"I can't leave him, Gerry. He has been a friend and companion to me for all his life. I need to be here," said Sarah wiping away more tears. You can do one thing for me though. Call William and tell him where I am and what is going on."

At last Sarah felt the big creature shudder. He stopped breathing. Gone was the last truly meaningful thing in her world. For almost an hour, Sarah laid her head on his body and sobbed. Finally, Gerry came out to the barn, picked her up, and took her into the farmhouse. Sarah could not remember the rest of that night.

The next morning as she opened the door to 3 Millikin Place, she found William standing before her in the foyer.

"You should have come home last night. It isn't that safe for you to be running around alone at night," he chastised.

Sarah, exhausted, looked at him through red-rimmed eyes, "Where were you, William? Why didn't you come to be with me?"

He shrugged, "There was nothing to be done for the poor beast."

"There was something to be done for me," she spat.

Sarah had nothing left inside but emptiness and anger. Before William came home in the evenings she would fix herself a cocktail, or two, so she could appear to appreciate spending the evening with her husband. The alcohol did its job, but Sarah knew it was a sham. She seldom left the house. At night, she would lie awake and think of all her five men, finally slipping into dreams of rocking ships and darkness.

No one paid attention to Mrs. W. J. Grady, and she welcomed the obscurity. William did not need her as a business promoter any more. He had solidified his reputation with his company, and he expected the presidency as soon as he had saved enough money to buy in as a partner. William did notice that Sarah looked sickly all the time, but thought that she was just getting older. Besides he was too busy to focus on her.

Sarah arose one morning, had her breakfast with William as usual, and got ready for her weekly visit to Sam's grave, which she scheduled religiously even in the colder months. It was now April, and she could feel the dreariness of winter waning. Getting into her beautiful blue Packard with all its expensive features, she no longer reacted with the pride she used to feel as she paraded around the town, but drove mindlessly to the cemetery.

The day belied Sarah's mood as the warm sunshine brightly shone down on the few graves in this new cemetery. Upon kneeling before Sam's large monument, she looked down and saw a yellow daffodil just barely peeking its head through the dirt.

Aloud she cried, "Sam, I don't even like flowers any more. I no longer think they are pretty -- nor is anything else pretty. Sam, I want to die. I just want to be with you."

As she continued talking to Sam, dark clouds began to form in the sky. Sarah took note of them, but did not interrupt her conversation with her deceased son. However, the sky turned darker and the wind began to gust aggressively. Sarah looked up at the threatening sky as she awaited the rain. A flash of lightning zigzagged down and hit hardly three feet away from Sarah. The ground trembled and she felt a tingling go through her body. Dazed, she realized the lightning bolt had thrown her flat onto the ground.

"What's happened?" She asked aloud. "Was I struck by lightning? No, then I'd be dead and I don't think I am."

As she lay disoriented on the ground, she looked skyward again and noticed a break in the darkness that revealed a snow-white cloud. Staring at the fluffy mass, she imagined a face. The sky seemed to be moving quickly, but she envisioned Sam's likeness--or was it her father's? As quickly as it had formed, the visage dissipated.

After a minute she composed herself, and, looking at the monument, she saw a blackened crack in the corner of the stone. Yes, she wasn't dreaming, lightning had hit about three feet from her. Her whole body was still tingling, but she felt basically unhurt. Checking the sky again, she looked for the face. Nothing but black clouds was above now.

"Was the image I saw my father or Sam? Were they trying to tell me something?" she questioned. The face had appeared to Sarah to be frustrated and angry.

"Oh, Sam. Oh, Papa. What a disappointment I must be to both of you. You each lived for the day and did it with such gusto."

Sarah picked herself up off of the ground and brushed her clothes off.

"I am going to live again. I will not let anyone get in my way, not Ed, not William." She looked skyward, "Papa, Sam, I love you both."

The Dining Room
3 Millikin Place

CHAPTER 34

✦

Round One

Decatur, Illinois Fall 1920

STILL TRYING DESPERATELY to keep the resolutions she had made part of her psyche since the incident at Sam's monument, Sarah did everything William asked of her without complaining. She planned and executed his occasional dinner parties, his golf matches, housed his guests, and anything else he asked of her. But after breakfast each day, both she and William were ready to go their separate ways. She would no longer spend her energy solely for him.

Eager to keep her vow of living life to the fullest, she scheduled a get-away to Chicago with June. Since June's marriage, Sarah did not see much of her and was looking forward to this trip that they had been planning for weeks.

Having seen on his calendar that William had no planned engagements on the dates she would be gone, Sarah waited until two days before she was to leave to tell him of her plans. As usual, the main conversation they had with each other during the day was at breakfast.

"William, I'm going with June to Chicago on Thursday to see a play. Neither June nor I have ever seen *Over There* and it's going to be in the city this week. We're going on the morning train and return on Friday," said Sarah.

In a matter-of-fact tone William said, "Let's see… that won't work. I think I'll probably plan to entertain Mr. Prentice and Mr. Lockhart on Thursday and I'd like to do it at home. I'll need you to plan dinner and be present when we eat."

"What do you mean 'probably' you'll entertain them on Thursday? If you decide on Thursday, you could take them to the country club or I'm sure Dorothy could fix a suitable meal here without me to instruct. June and I planned around your schedule and I'm really looking forward to seeing this play."

Continuing to read his paper, William said, "Sorry, I need you here."

"I haven't done anything I enjoy for a long, long time, William. Don't you think you could do without me just this once?" pleaded Sarah.

"No. You may go to Chicago some other time," mumbled William still with his nose in the paper.

That was the end for Sarah. Seventeen years of being married to a man who had abused her, never put her first, and only cared for his business -- that was enough. The earth shook and so did Sarah's voice as she raised her hand and brought it down on his paper as though it were an axe at a guillotine.

"I AM GOING TO CHICAGO ON THURSDAY!" She wailed.

William was stunned and reacted by grabbing her flailing wrist with one hand and striking her with the other. Sarah did not even feel the blow. Everything that had gone wrong in her life exploded in the form of her anger at William—Charles's infidelity, William's disregard of her feelings, Sam's death, Midnight's death, and Ed's delay and her rejection of the life they had planned together. All the anger inside her body burst out and Decatur's most prominent society lady engaged in a fist-fight with her husband.

William, who was far superior to Sarah in height, weight, and knowledge of common brawling, quickly pinned her to the ground and immobilized her.

"You have gone crazy, Sarah! What is wrong with you?" he managed through gritted teeth.

As she lay flat on the floor of the breakfast room, Sarah started smiling, and then came a hardy laugh as she gazed up at William, "You have a big shiner! Your right eye is already turning black and blue. How will you explain your injury to your business associates?"

Unable to see any humor in the transpiring events, William released Sarah and turned to retrieve his crumpled newspaper, saying, "You have lost your senses. What in the world prompted that behavior? I should have you committed!"

Having run the gamut of human emotions in the last forty seconds, Sarah, empowered, picked herself up off the floor and carefully chose her words.

"The fact that you don't know why I am disturbed is exactly why I am upset. At one time I loved you deeply, William, but you have killed that love by using me as a slave to your wishes. I have been a business asset to you and little more. I don't care what you do to me. I quit. Divorce me if you like – or not, but I no longer am your slave."

Sarah marched up the stairs and clung to the pillows on her window seat in her sitting room. She was free and the elation of the thought bounded in her chest.

"I did it," thought Sarah as she hummed "Break the Tie that Binds You".

Sarah felt physically and emotionally strong. His blows were better than his blindness and belittling, and far better than continuing the life she was being forced to lead.

William was still downstairs trying to sort out the situation. He had to deal with Sadie who luckily was in the basement and did not decide to come upstairs until the event was over. William made up some story when she inquired about the noise and James was outside in the garage and heard nothing.

What had come over his wife? He didn't understand what she was talking about. A couple of times in the prior two of three years he had felt that maybe she was having an affair, but she always dutifully returned from whatever mood plagued her. She was a little headstrong and often had wild ideas, like her golf mobile invention, and her membership in the Woman's Suffrage movement, but she did so much for him that he could not doubt her love. This was different, however, what choice was there but to hit her? It was only a reaction to her behavior. He decided he had better go put some meat on his eye. She had quite a swing and he could feel the swelling getting worse. His injury could be difficult to explain. After he cared for himself, he would check on his lunatic wife.

By the time William got upstairs, Sarah was packing her trunk.

"Now what are you doing?" said a tense William.

Sarah's actions were slow and deliberate as she placed more clothes in the large wooden trunk that bore her name on the top.

"Well, I am packing my clothes for my trip to Chicago with June. I am taking a few more things because I have decided to stay an extra day and do some shopping."

William understood that Sarah was baiting him and did not fall for her trap.

"Since you are so upset that is probably a good decision. Maybe there you can settle down."

Sarah continued to pack silently.

"Damn it, Sarah! I won't tolerate these outbursts!" he cried at her.

Sarah smiled, "Outbursts? I am not upset, William. I have just obtained my freedom and that is cause for celebration not depression. I intend to enjoy myself with June."

William strode from the room, slamming the door behind him.

Once at his office, William sat in his well-worn black leather office chair and stared at the haphazard pile of contracts on his desk. He was always able to lose himself in his work when personal problems arose; that was how he solved them. Today, however, he could not focus on his business. He recognized that something serious had happened that made Sarah's reactions different, but he had no idea what made her behave like she did.

"I thought she shared my dream and wanted my success to be her achievement as well," he told himself as he rummaged aimlessly through the papers in front of him.

"I have done everything I could think of to make her happy and have given her more freedom than most wives enjoy. I buy her clothes, a car, her own horse, and give her vacations to the finest resorts in the country whenever she asks. She has a prominent position in the community because of my influence. What more can I do for her? She knows I love her and she damned well better get over whatever this is. I will not allow her antics to ruin decades of work."

William put his thoughts aside and started shifting through his papers. Some of these contracts needed to be dealt with immediately.

CHAPTER 35

---- ⚜ ----

Financial Intrigue

Chicago, Illinois Fall 1920

IN THE DAYS between their fight and Sarah's impending trip with June, Sarah reveled in her newfound freedom from William's commands. But for the first time in her life, she found herself unsure of the direction in which to set her sights. This emptiness, Sarah filled with evening cocktails and steals from William's brandy snifter.

On Tuesday afternoon as Sarah sat reading a book on her window seat she couldn't help think how much Ed would love this particular novel and wondered if he had read it. Always trying her best not to think of Ed, she was quite taken back when at that exact minute Sadie called her to the telephone saying that Mr. Rockafellow was on the line for her. Sarah sat frozen in her seat.

Again Sadie called, "Mrs. Grady, Mr. Rockafellow is on the telephone and wants to speak with you."

With her heart pounding, she slowly walked to the telephone and softly said, "Hello, Ed."

"Sarah, I know this is awkward and you never wanted to speak to me again, but I need your direction as to the disposition of your stocks. You know half of our profits are yours and the amount is fairly substantial. I can liquidate our account and send you half or I can send yours in the form of certain stocks. Do you have a broker in Decatur?"

Sarah couldn't think. All she wanted to know was how was Ed doing? Did he still love her? Was he sorry he didn't leave his wife? It totally undid her to hear his voice.

"I hadn't thought about it, Ed?" she found herself answering. "What do you think I should do?"

"I believe it would be best if you got a broker in Decatur and let me deal with him. That way I can liquidate the stocks I don't think are terribly good ones and send him the ones I think you should keep. You know I will be generous with you. I'm sorry this has taken so long, but I kept hoping you would change your mind and still see me. I am back from overseas now. My Sallie, I am terribly unhappy. I really—Sarah, I need you." said a serious Ed.

Her desire boiled to anger. How selfish he was. "That's not enough, Ed."

Sarah continued stiffly, ignoring his declaration of love, "I will get a broker and send you his name and address. Thank you for taking care of this. Goodbye, Ed."

Sarah slammed the phone down with shaky hands. This time she knew her unsteadiness was from anger not from grief. Ed, her soul mate had put his career and his position in society above her, and he had the audacity to still want her. All her life, she would believe they could have been happy having very little worldly possessions and very few friends, but having their everlasting love. He hadn't her faith.

Every moment with him flashed before her eyes as she stood beside the telephone. His hands, his dark eyes, the sound of her name from his lips, the way he looked at her when she spoke, the saved dances, the refused cocktails – all in the name of their love. All had been good and beautiful, all surrendered so easily. But now Sarah imagined her passionate, vivacious heart turn to granite in her chest.

"I'm such a fool," she agonized, biting back tears, "There was never anything there – and what am I left with? Just a box of empty words."

She picked up the receiver and flipped through the phone book. William knew almost everyone in town; it could be difficult to find the right brokerage firm. Then she remembered someone at the club had noted that there was a new brokerage in town with the firm name Scanlin, Totel, and Smith. When she called, she asked for an appointment with Mr. Totel, not having any idea who he was. The appointment was made for the following day and Sarah crossed her fingers that this broker would be what she needed.

Disturbed by the realization that their stocks were the final piece holding Ed and her together, Sarah picked up the receiver again.

"5491, please," Sarah spoke into the line.

"Johns Residence," June's maid said cheerfully.

June was soon on the line, but before Sarah could begin recounting her troubles, June said, "Sarah, I'm so glad you've phoned. I'm afraid I cannot accompany you to Chicago…"

Sarah gave short replies to June's words, and hung up the phone feeling more bereft than ever. The rest of the afternoon Sarah gave to one of James's hidden bottles of Whiskey.

As Sarah walked into the brokerage firm's office the next day, she was pleased that it was new and small. New meant that the brokers might not be friends of William's and small meant a little office staff and less chance of someone recognizing her. In dealing with the stocks, it was imperative that she give her correct name.

So she bravely said to the receptionist, "Hello, my name is Sarah Grady and I have an appointment with Mr. Totel."

Just then a tall, good looking, well-dressed man in his early forties strode up to her with his hand out and introduced himself as Roger Totel. He ushered her into his office, gave her a charming smile and said, "Please sit down. How may I help you?"

Assessing that he appeared to be a pleasant and trustworthy man, Sarah decided he would serve her purpose.

"I need someone to handle a private account. I have some stocks with a New York firm and I want to have my account transferred here. But – I will be frank with you - I don't want anyone else to have access to my information."

Without batting an eye, Roger assured her that every bit of information would be private. Flashing his charismatic smile, he declared, "I'm sure we can do business. I will take care of you – I mean of your stocks, of course."

Sarah looked quickly at him to see if she should read anything else into his words and determined that all was well. His eyes twinkled but he still gave the impression of being trustworthy. She returned his smile, knowing that a bit of flirtation might garner better efforts with her portfolio.

"I'm taking the train to Chicago tomorrow, but I will be back in a couple of days and I should have some information for you by then," quipped Sarah.

"Really? I'm headed for Chicago tomorrow also. I have a meeting with the owners of our firm. Maybe I'll see you on the train, but I know you want your privacy so I won't address you if you are with someone," said Roger, cautiously.

"I am just going shopping so I'll be alone, but I appreciate your sensitivity." Sarah replied, knowing she had found the right stockbroker for her account.

The next morning as she sat down with William for breakfast, she said, "You remember that I told you I'm leaving for Chicago today to shop and will be back on Thursday."

"Alright," grunted William as he turned the page of his Decatur newspaper. "It looks like the city is going to attack the problem of cars parking downtown at all different angles to the curb. They are considering painting lines on the street so everyone will park in the same direction. It's a mess down there. Sounds like the city has a good idea."

"I'm going to meet my lover in Chicago and have the time of my life. Okay?" said Sarah in a disgusted tone.

"That's great, Sarah," said William without ever lifting his head from the paper.

Sarah had James grab her trunk and drive her to the train station.

"Please tell William when he discovers I'm gone that I'll be back on Thursday. You come pick me up then, James. Thanks. Unlike William, I know you and Sadie will miss me."

James gave Sarah a pitying look and just said, "Yes, Mrs. Grady. You be careful in Chicago."

Since she was only going as far as Chicago, Sarah was riding in the coach cars. Settling herself in a seat by the window, she got out a book and started to read. A gentleman settled himself in the seat beside her, but she did not look up. As the train lurched out of the station her seat companion said, "May I address you, Mrs. Grady?" Looking up from her book, she saw Mr. Totel.

"Oh. Of course, Mr. Totel. It will be nice to have company on the trip."

"Please call me Roger. I will be pleased to get to know you a little. That will even help me manage your account."

Sarah had a feeling of des je vous. Why did his words sound familiar? She had never talked to him before. Sarah started the conversation by telling him the things she liked to do--play golf, ride horses, and go to the theater. "Well, the things I used to enjoy," she thought.

Roger interrupted her by saying, "I have two tickets to a musical tonight. I'd love it if you would go with me. It's been a hit in New York for the last month and is just now getting to Chicago."

"Why not?" thought Sarah, "That's what I intended to do with June anyway."

Without hesitation Sarah said, "I'd love to go with you. I'm staying at the Palmer House Hotel. If you are sure your wife won't mind –"

"I'm not married and I hope Mr. Grady won't mind. I am also staying at the Palmer House."

Sarah assured him with certainty that William wouldn't mind.

"And call me Sarah," she added with a smile.

They got to know each other better as the train took them to their destination.

Sarah had just enough time in the afternoon to buy a dress specifically for the evening. Marshall Fields had what she was looking for, something that shouted "happy" and "fun". Finally the designers were putting some color back into their fashions. For two years after the war, black was still the popular color, but today as Sarah looked she easily found a bright red evening dress, a little shorter than last year's models and a little lower waistline. It was exciting to find something new that she felt would emphasize the good points of her figure. She wanted Roger to be proud of his evening date.

Back at the hotel, she determined that her plan to eat a small supper wasn't going to work out because shopping had taken too much time. Digging through her purse she discovered a package of Nabisco biscuits that would have to suffice as a meal. She would be ravenous after the theater, which was when she would get dinner, but it was more important that she look her best and spend all her time on dressing for the night's affair.

When she went down to the lobby to meet Roger, she noticed several men turned their heads as she went by. This was how it was supposed to be. She knew she looked good and Roger confirmed it.

"You look beautiful, Sarah. I'll be very proud to have you as my companion this evening."

"Thank you. What play are we going to see?" asked Sarah.

"It's a musical titled, oddly enough, *Sally*. Has anyone called you Sally as a nickname?" asked Roger.

Sarah paled a little as she thought of Ed, "My Sallie" he had written so often.

"In another life someone called me that," Sarah breathed.

Quickly changing the subject she declared, "I love musicals. I'm not ready for a complicated drama. This should be a wonderful evening, Roger."

And it was. Sarah enjoyed the musical and Roger proved to be a perfect escort, handsome and witty. Returning to the Palmer House, they had dinner in the dining room. The food arrived just in time because she was starving and Roger had taken a flask from his pocket to add some zip to her ginger ale. The pre-dinner cocktail had made her very dizzy. Sarah had a couple more glasses of Roger's brew during dinner and was feeling good. Roger was so captivating and so available that an inebriated Sarah decided she would take him as a lover.

"What's to stop me?" she happily thought.

After all, her marriage to William was a sham, and Roger had begun to dismantle the only product of her life with Ed. She was free. She began to flirt outrageously with him. All he needed to know, she was sure, was that she was available.

"If you are through with your dinner, I'll take you to your room," said Roger.

This is working out well thought Sarah. It's nice to be desired by men again.

When they got to Sarah's door, she was quite pleased when Roger accepted her key, opened the door. Sarah leaned against the entry, allowing him space to pass into the room.

Roger cleared his throat. "Thank you for a lovely evening, Sarah. I'll be delighted to see you again in Decatur."

"Aren't you coming in for a while?" asked a surprised Sarah.

"No, thank you. I have to get up early in the morning for a meeting."

Roger bowed and walked down the hall to the elevator. He was looking forward to having Sarah as a client, and suspected it would be best if that were the extent of their relationship. Like William, he saw Sarah as a very charming business asset.

Once in her room Sarah burst into tears from total humiliation. Even though she had had too much to drink she was well aware of what had just happened – rejection from yet another man. Not stopping to consider his reasons, she thought she was no longer a desirable woman. All her life people had gone on and on about how beautiful and charming she was, and now that was gone. Even golf no longer held accolades for her. Some of the younger women at the club could now beat her. Sam was dead, as was Midnight. Her one true love and soul mate did not think enough of her to want to spend the rest of his life with her. The organizations in which she held high offices were now taking in middle class people who had risen in status due to positions they held during the war. William still paid no attention to her. What was there in life for her? Blackness rescued her from her misery, relieving her from her blunder until morning.

Upon awakening, she ordered breakfast sent to her room then stepped into the shower. As the warm water splashed over her, the headache and fuzzy brain began to dissipate. Still the disappointment of the previous evening dominated her disjointed thoughts.

"I can't even seduce an unmarried man. What is wrong with me?" She pictured Ed standing before her. "Could I even go back to him?" She shook the thought from her mind. "What can I now say to Roger? Should I find another stockbroker?"

The phone was ringing. Sarah answered it as she stepped out of the shower.

"Good morning, Sarah, this is Roger. I just want to apologize to you for my behavior last night. I should have known the amount of liquor I put in your drinks would be too much for you to handle. I'm used to going out with men who drink a lot. How are you feeling?"

The realization hit Sarah that Roger blamed everything on the alcohol and considered the whole event his fault. Maybe her behavior could be attributed to the amount of liquor she had consumed.

"I am beginning to feel better. I am sure after I eat breakfast I'll be fine."

She started to say that it wasn't his fault and knew better than to drink that much, but she decided to leave the fault to him.

"I'll see you in my office when we get back to Decatur. I'm anxious to get started on your account. Have a good shopping trip, Sarah."

Roger hung up. Sarah felt relief. It was Roger's fault not hers and now she would not have to get a new stockbroker. Taking the time to write Ed a short curt note with Roger's name and address, she gave it to the hotel clerk to be posted. She rather liked the idea of it being postmarked from the Palmer House as she and Ed had stayed at this hotel many times.

The 3 Millikin Place Drive

CHAPTER 36

The Speakeasy

Decatur, Illinois Winter 1920

WRETCHED AFTER HER failure in Chicago, Sarah's mind was plagued with flickers of the past. As she starting planning for yet another holiday season, the growing recklessness within her deepened.

William busied by the purchase of another company, giving him two small ones in addition to his position in Faries Manufacturing, brushed away his wife's moods with business. His main goal was still to become president of Faries, but two factors were hindering progress for that dream to become a reality. One thing that had to happen was that E. P. Irving had to either retire or die and secondly William had to have sufficient funds to buy into the company. It was a waiting game.

While she resigned most of her positions in the various organizations, Sarah kept active only in those groups that she wanted to promote such as the orphanage. As far as outsiders were concerned, nothing had changed for the Gradys, as they still entertained and joined in the parties at the country club, but amidst her obligations, Sarah insisted on keeping her freedom to come and go as she pleased.

William was very unhappy and tried several times to reconcile with Sarah, but to no avail. For months after their big fight he offered many vacations to the finest resorts, trips to New York, or trips to anywhere she wished.

"Let's go to California for a month. Remember how happy we were out there. I promise to give you all my attention and we will go to as many plays as you like. Would you rather go on a shopping excursion to New York? I'll go sit in a salon all day and watch you try on dresses."

Sarah would answer, "Not right now, William. I'm too busy. I'll let you know when my schedule gets lighter."

William sensed he deserved some rebuke, but he could not understand why Sarah continued punishing him. The amends he was trying to make were going unnoticed and he missed his wife. On the other hand, Sarah did not understand why she was not happy as she had William under control. No longer did she have to endure his dictates. Again she began searching for "fun" in her life to fill that empty space in her heart.

One night she and June were having dinner at the St. Nick Hotel. It was Sarah's favorite place to eat because it was a combination of good food, good service and good atmosphere. It was an old hotel with an abundance of Lincoln history. Sarah liked to draw mental pictures in her head of Abe Lincoln carrying Jane Johns' piano into her suite at the hotel from the wagon that moved her to Decatur. Now that June had married into the Johns family, the images became even more vivid as June told the family stories. Lincoln had visited the hotel several times and even been in this room where the Republican Party was born.

This evening as they sat down at their preferred table in the middle of the room, Sarah noted, "June, it looks like we have a new waiter. Isn't he adorable?"

June replied, "Sarah, you don't call your waiter who is obviously in his thirties 'adorable', but he is good looking."

As the waiter approached their table, Sarah flashed him a coy smile. "Would you mind bringing us a glass of water? I'm really thirsty."

Totally unflustered by Sarah's flirtatious overtures the waiter said, "Of course, Madam. My name is Charles and I'll be your server this evening."

Sarah watched as the waiter retreated to fetch her water.

"Do you think I still appeal to a younger man?"

"Oh, Sarah, why would you want a younger man?" said June with an exacerbated sigh.

"I just want to have a little excitement and what's the harm in flirting with our handsome waiter?" said Sarah as she batted her eyes to tease her friend.

June shook her head as Sarah brought out her flask and poured whiskey into the water that Charles brought to the table along with the menus. June, uncomfortable with Sarah's antics, chided her, "What's become of your 'no drinking pact'?"

Sarah shrugged. "That's all over now. He's gone, why should our foolish pact remain?"

"All I know is that you did not take any alcohol as a rule and you were a better person for it," June replied, curtly.

Refusing to succumb to her devastating unhappiness when her thoughts turned to Ed, and immediately feeling the effects of the whiskey she had put in her water, she quipped right back.

"My goodness, June. You are only just married. Don't worry, your husband will soon tire of you and you'll slip from grace as easily as I did. Everyone does."

As the conversation began to take a bit of a heated tone, the waiter walked briskly to their table filling Sarah's water glass for the third time as Sarah winked at him.

June, disgusted, said, "You'll have to excuse me, Sarah. I can't bear to see you destroy yourself like this. I'm leaving. I drove--"

"I'll call James." Sara interrupted, with a smile. "Don't worry about me."

The waiter was at the table with their food as June quickly left the room. Standing there with a plate in each hand, he was totally at a loss as to what to do. Sobered by June's fleeing, Sarah instructed him easily.

"Put my food down here. My companion has been called away but I will have dinner. Take the other plate to the kitchen and eat it yourself if you wish. I will pay for both of us. By the way, my name is Sarah."

Sarah ate her dinner and enjoyed it. She liked watching the other people in the room, some of whom were acquaintances, and she continued flirting with the waiter since June was not there to chastise her. Sarah finished dinner and several more glasses of "water". As the waiter brought her the check, he asked if she might be interested sometime in going to a place where they had great dancing.

Taking only a moment to assess the situation, Sarah inquired, "What time do you get off work tonight?"

"I'm off early tonight at 9:00 o'clock," said Charles.

"I'll pick you up down the street behind the dairy."

The hotel clerk called James who came to pick her up in her car. William was at a meeting at the Decatur Club and Sarah estimated that he would be very late getting home, but he had his own car. James drove her home and Sarah informed him that she was going to take her car and go for a ride.

James frowned and almost insisted that she let him put the car in the garage.

"Now, James, you know how I used to go for rides at night by myself on Midnight. I am perfectly capable of taking care of myself and I really miss those rides. I'll only be gone a few hours," said Sarah.

James started to say something but thought the better of it and just shook his head and walked away.

Sarah started to back out of the driveway. She soon found herself in the middle of the side yard... She was feeling a little light headed and admitted to herself that she had had too much whiskey. She should probably switch to gin. Gin didn't seem to affect her as much. Trying a second time to navigate the driveway, she missed again and ended up facing the house.

"James, could you come here a second?" she called.

James came and asked if she would like him to put the car away, but Sarah replied, "Oh, no. If you could just get the car out of the drive for me, then I'll be fine."

James said, "Mrs. Grady, I'll not be party to you driving in your condition. Please let me take you into the house."

Greatly angered, Sarah threw the car into reverse, turned the wheels and lurched forward taking out a piece of the house and leveling a rose bush., but now she was facing the street and thus successfully out of the driveway. Muttering about firing James, she jerked her way down town to the dairy and drove behind it without any further mishaps. Her watch said it was 8:45 p.m. so she would have at least fifteen minutes to wait for Charles. While sitting in the car relaxing, she wondered how mad June was...

The next thing she knew Charles was gently shaking her. "Sarah, are you okay?"

Immediately snapping into adventurous Sarah mode, she said, "Get in the car and we'll go to that place you were saying had great dancing."

Evaluating Sarah's condition, Charles said, "How about I drive? You don't know where we are going anyhow."

That proposition sounded like a good idea to Sarah, so she slipped over into the passenger seat, Charles hopped in and they were off.

Charles drove down some streets that Sarah was unfamiliar with, then down a dirt road and stopped in front of a rundown house with boarded up windows. There were two other cars parked in the front and Sarah could hear ragtime music drifting out of the door. It certainly was not the caliber of establishment to which Sarah was accustomed.

She thought, "I came to have an experience and I'm sure I'm going to get it."

Charles knocked on the front door. It was opened by a burly, rather rough looking male who immediately smiled when he saw Charles and let them in. The lights were so dim that she could hardly make out the outlines of people and the noise of the band was deafening. It was a very small room and although there were only two cars parked outside, the place was full of people. Charles took her hand and pulled her deeper into the room. Sarah caught her breath. The aroma-- It was unlike anything she had ever smelled before. The air hung heavy with cigar smoke making her gasp for air and the other aroma ...what was it? As her eyes grew accustomed to the dim lighting, Sarah carefully looked around the room to be sure she didn't know anyone. She did not think so, but it was so dark that she couldn't be sure. Even in her drunken state, she realized it would not do to run into anyone who knew her or William.

"Come have a drink. You'll need a few minutes to get used to the surroundings, but it's really a fun place," declared Charles.

Sarah did as she was told and began to sip her drink. Spitting out her first sip, she choked, "Charles, what in the world is this I'm drinking."

"It's moonshine whiskey," said Charles proudly. "Not bad, huh."

Sarah who was accustomed to imported mellow whiskey did not answer. She glanced around trying again to assess the crowd. The dim lights made it impossible to distinguish faces, but, as she did with all the ladies at the country club, Sarah was able to evaluate their dresses. Even in the dim light she could see that fashion was not uppermost in these women's minds, but the price tags dictated what they would wear. These people all looked like they were having a good time and she was now sure that none of her friends would be in attendance.

Most of the crowd was in the middle of the floor attempting to dance. It was so congested that people were actually just moving where they stood in their square inch of the dance floor. The band was obviously composed of neighborhood talent and there were some sour notes, but all in all, they sounded pretty good and kept a heavy beat going. There was a singer, but she was off key and Sarah hoped that she would sit down. Charles sat their drinks on the makeshift bar and wiggled her out onto the tiny wooden floor. They began to move to the ragtime music bumping into people with every step they took. But it was fun.

Sarah had the time of her life for about a half an hour before she collapsed. Charles got her in the car and drove back to the dairy where she had picked him up. Telling Sarah to sit tight, he ran to the hotel kitchen where he worked and got a large cup of coffee and ran back to the car.

"Here, Sarah. Drink all of this and you should be capable of getting home."

She felt terribly sick but drank all the coffee and in a few minutes did feel a little better. With as much grace as she could muster she said, "Thank you for a lovely evening, Charles. We'll have to do it again sometime."

Charles smiled and said, "Anytime, Sarah."

The road looked wavy and strange, but Sarah managed to stay on it and eventually turned into her driveway. She sat in the car for a minute and James came out of the house.

"Let me help you upstairs, Mrs. Grady. Mr. Grady is not home yet. He called to say he would be late as he was playing cards with some friends."

"This is good, James. You may help me up the stairs because I don't feel very well."

"Probably not, Mrs. Grady," said James.

The next thing Sarah knew was Sadie was shaking her saying, "It's almost time for breakfast and I believe that Mr. Grady wants to be sure you are downstairs this morning. Here drink this."

"Is this one of James concoctions?" said Sarah holding her head between her hands and squeezing.

Sarah drank the whole awful cup of stuff that James fixed for her and watched Sadie laying out her clothes.

Just then becoming aware of Sadie's tone of voice when she got her out of bed, Sarah snipped at her, "What's wrong with you, Sadie? It almost sounds like you were giving me orders."

Sadie opened her mouth to speak but thought the better of it and merely mumbled, "Yes, Mrs. Grady." Then left the room.

Slowly Sarah finished dressing and went downstairs. Was there a problem about last night she wondered? William wasn't home when she came in and James would never tell. Maybe Sadie-- could that be what is wrong with her?

Sarah sat down at the breakfast table and William looked up from his newspaper to survey her. Putting his nose back in the paper, he said, "You look pretty bad this morning. Obviously you had too much to drink last night. Where were you?"

Sarah started to retort that it was none of his business, but decided against confrontation this morning. She wasn't up for it. So she answered matter-of-factly, "I had dinner at the St. Nick with June and I probably had a little more to drink than I realized."

In an uncharacteristic move, William put down the paper and reached across the table to grab Sarah's hand.

Holding her hand between his, he said softly, "Sarah, I love you. When can we put all our nonsense behind us and be together as a husband and wife should? We once had such a good time together. What happened?"

Sarah's answer was on the tip of her tongue, but did not come out. She wanted to tell him it was all his fault; he only loved her for what she could do to enhance his standing in the business world and he never paid any attention to her needs and desires as she worked to make him prominent in Decatur. Besides, she wanted to say, I fell deeply in love with one of your good friends and it's difficult to equally love two men at the same time.

Instead she looked straight into his eyes and said, "I feel you have treated me badly, William, and I do not love you as I once did, but if you want me to remain your wife, I'll try to make you pleased with my social performances on your behalf. I need my freedom to come and go as I please, however."

William slowly withdrew his hands, sighed heavily, and went back to his newspaper.

He knew his Irish temper had flared up on occasions, but he had also given her most of the things she had wanted throughout the years. Giving up didn't fit his personality, but he did not know how to regain Sarah's love.

Sarah went about her duties for the day with Charles on her mind. He was not an Ed, but he was young, good-looking, and lots of fun, always laughing and smiling. Despite having had too much to drink, choking on the cigar smoke, inhaling that unidentified smell, and drinking the horrible whiskey, she had had an exciting time at his little speakeasy last night. Even though the atmosphere inside the club was something Sarah had never experienced, the neighborhood band did an acceptable job playing ragtime music which Sarah loved. The people were there to have a good time and did not care that Sarah was in a different class than they were. No business associates to entertain, no country club ladies trying to decide how old your dress was, where you obtained it, and how much you paid for it. What fun it was! Sarah determined to see Charles again.

As if on cue, an opportunity presented itself. June called on the phone and said she regretted abandoning Sarah and wanted to buy her dinner to make up for it. Yes, thought Sarah here is my opportunity.

"Sounds wonderful, June, let's do make-up at the St. Nick again. How about tomorrow night? Don't pick me up. I'll meet you there at seven."

Giving herself a night to recover, Sarah was eager to see Charles again and make plans to go dancing.

CHAPTER 37

---—✦—---

Another Charles

St. Nicholas Hotel Early 1921

SARAH MET JUNE in the lobby. Upon entering the dining room, Sarah asked the maître de to seat them at the same table they had previously used. Across the room Charles spotted them and came immediately to their table with water.

"I recall that you ladies want your water right away. Again, I am Charles and I will be your server this evening," said Charles as he slyly winked at Sarah.

Sarah mused as she watched him. Her first Charles had been good-looking, considerate, and sweet tempered just like this one. Remembering how the previous relationship had turned out, she wished this Charles had a different name. Maybe she would call him something else.

Sarah ordered ginger-ale so she wouldn't have to drink her whiskey with water and June, predictably, started chastising her for using alcohol.

"Can't we just talk and laugh like we used to. Why do you have to drink? I'm worried about you, Sarah. I know what a blow it was when Ed refused to leave his wife for you, but you have a pretty great life to lead without him. It seems like you always think you need excitement and danger to be happy anymore and --- I know that you really aren't happy," said a concerned June.

The mention of Ed made Sarah stop pouring from her flask and stare at June.

"You know that we do not mention his name."

Her eyes moistened and she dropped her gaze.

With head bowed, she continued, "I made a mistake. I should have stayed his mistress and continued the affair because I love him so. But I wanted it all. I knew we could be happy even if we didn't have much money, but he couldn't see it. Being a mistress seemed so sorted. I wanted to be kosher."

Raising her head she cheerfully said, "But –such is life. Right, June? What is there besides having a good time?"

Dinner was enjoyable for the two friends until Charles slipped as he served dessert and called Sarah by her first name. Sarah giggled and June threw up her hands. When Charles walked away, June looked at Sarah, aghast.

"You went out with him the other night, didn't you? Don't even answer. I know you did. I thought there were looks between the two of you this evening. Oh, Sarah, please stop this behavior," pleaded June.

"Don't worry about it, June. I'm really free. William thinks he cares, but he really doesn't. All he desires is to be President of Faries. And besides, he'll never know about Charles, because where we go William doesn't know any of the people or even about the places. I am going to go with him again tonight and no one will be the wiser except you. June, he took me to a speakeasy the other night. It was great fun and I will go again."

"Sarah, please. That is so dangerous. For one thing the police here in Decatur have declared a war on those establishments and have been raiding them. You know the Chief of Police is a friend and he told my husband the other night how many of those places they have shut down recently. Please don't go with Charles-- goodness, he is just a waiter."

Knowing that she might as well be talking to the proverbial brick wall, June left Sarah at the table in the hotel when their dinner was over and went home feeling frustrated. June didn't seem to be able to help her stay out of trouble.

Sarah on the other hand was feeling elated. Adding the prospect of a raid by the police simply included another dimension to Sarah's planned evening. After June left, Sarah motioned Charles to the table and asked if he was up to another evening after work. Charles took stock of Sarah's condition and determined that she had not consumed as many drinks on this night as she had before.

Leaning in, he said, "I think we'll have a better time tonight than we did the other evening. I'll meet you at the same place, the same time."

Sarah had asked William about his schedule before she left for dinner and was told that he would be home early. Pleased by the thought of him sitting in his den alone, she asked for a telephone. Sarah made a call home and told Sadie to tell William that she was going to have some drinks with friends and would be late getting home.

Aloud to her empty plate, she said, "Turnabout is fair play, if he can go out with friends until all hours of the night, then so can I."

In the car on their way to the "dancing place," Charles and Sarah had an opportunity to get better acquainted.

"I want you to know I've taken a sales job with a car dealership. You know, to improve my lot in life," he said with a laugh and a swig from her flask.

"Great," thought Sarah, "June can't say I'm running around with a waiter; now she will have to recognize he's a salesman."

Tonight in the speakeasy, Sarah was more alert. It was still full of people having a good time. They all looked alike to Sarah, with no specific qualities except they all had on the same inexpensive clothing that Sarah had noted previously and happy smiles on their faces. The lighting was dim, emanating from bare light bulbs hanging from the ceiling. Gay ragtime music was mediocre and echoed off the walls in the small crowded room. Clouding the air, cigar smoke hung heavy and thick -- and that aroma...What was it? Another drink of moonshine whiskey and Sarah was having a grand old time.

After several dances Sarah suggested they sit awhile, so Charles guided her to a dark corner table. Leaning over close to Charles so she could converse with him, she said, "I thought speakeasies were supposed to be quiet places where people could go and not be noticed. You can hear this racket from a block away. Why haven't the police shut it down?"

"Oh, they will someday. Really they are after the larger ones in town that compete with the two Al Capone owns in Decatur. He doesn't want any competition. Some of the police in your town are corrupt and cater to Mr. Capone, but they go after the small ones like this when they have time."

No sooner had those words come out of Charles's mouth than the front door was kicked in and the room began to fill with police in their blue suits with badges shining even in the dim light, their sinister looking guns drawn and all of them yelling, "Everyone get against the walls!"

It was total chaos as screaming people started running in all different directions. Charles grabbed Sarah's hand and propelled her to a nearby basement door. They stumbled down a rickety dark staircase, across an uneven dirt floor, and quietly he opened an outside cellar door. As they popped outside in the back yard, there was a policeman coming from around the front of the building. Charles almost threw Sarah down behind a large bush and put his finger to her lips, gesturing her to be quiet. The policeman went to the cellar door they had just exited and looked around. Deciding it was too dark to be able to track those who had escaped, he went back to the front.

Charles whispered, "We'll stay here for a bit. I don't believe they'll look around the grounds too carefully. They really want the owners, not the customers so much."

Sarah was so energized that she answered in a rather loud voice, "How long do we have to wait?"

"Shh!" he urged, but when their eyes met, Charles reached over and gave Sarah a fervent kiss. She was confused by the relief she felt as he drew her close to him. How wonderful to be wanted again by anyone, by this younger man whom she imagined could have any attractive girl he wanted. But as the kiss deepened, disappointment washed away the excitement. These lips were not the lips she longed for. They were not her lover's, her Ed's.

After about fifteen minutes, Charles decided it was safe for them to go to Sarah's car. Everyone seemed to be gone. As they got up from behind the bush and brushed themselves off, Sarah recognized that her thoughts of Ed had sobered her greatly. She asked Charles if he thought they would have taken her car, realizing that at the very least, the police would know whose car it was and would be aware of her presence at the establishment.

"I don't think they would take your car, but they will be aware that it is possible you were here. I think you may be a suspicious person in their eyes now. I hope you don't mind being a marked woman. They will be looking for you," said Charles jokingly.

"You don't seem to mind if the police catch you. I'm rather afraid of that possibility," said Sarah, frowning.

She waited around the side of the house while Charles checked the front of the building.

After a moment he said, "It's all clear and your car is still there."

They jumped in the car and drove away hoping no one was the wiser. Sarah relaxed telling herself that no one could prove she was in that building even if they did know her car was parked in front. She returned Charles to the back of the dairy and they discussed when to meet again. He told her to wait a few days because starting a new job at the car dealership would take most of his time for a while.

Sarah, who was always full of bright ideas to perpetuate her ends, said, "I know. I'll tell William I'm going shopping for a new car. Mine does have some scratches on it now. That way I can talk to you and we can decide when to meet. And who knows, maybe I'll get a new car."

Charles gave her another powerful kiss and she drove home.

Not wanting to deal with William who she saw reading in the library, Sarah tiptoed up the servant's stairs and into the bedroom without William hearing her. Undressing quickly, she hopped into bed and feigned sleep.

An hour later when William crawled into bed, Sarah was still maintaining her pretense. As William pulled up the covers he said, "I know you aren't asleep, Sarah."

And he curtly turned away.

At breakfast the next morning, William suggested to Sarah that they take a trip to California in a week or so.

"Wouldn't you like to get away for a month? I believe I can arrange to be away from the office for three or four weeks. The weather here is so dreary in February and March. How about it?"

"Let me think about what I have going on and I'll let you know. If we went, you would miss the annual St. Paddy's Day celebration at the club and I know you love that party."

William exhaled slowly and folded his paper.

"Sarah, if I could get you and me and our marriage back on track, I would miss anything," said a somber William.

Sarah did think about it. In fact she spent the afternoon considering what William had said, and what she thought he had not said. Being a good judge of his character, she knew what he was really saying was: "This is our last chance to make things between us right."

Did she want to be married to William or did she want to be free to go out with Charles, or anyone else, and just have fun?

Already married twice and having had a four year affair, it was obvious to her that she should settle down and spend the rest of her life as Mrs. W. J. Grady, prominent society woman. William with all his faults was a fine man and he was good to her most of the time.

"But I want to be loved," Sarah interjected into her righteous thoughts, "just like I thought that Ed loved me. I want someone to care whether or not Sarah wants to go golfing or to the theater. I want to be able to help poor people instead of taking my time to give business dinners for my husband. Above all, I want to be able to laugh at something really funny instead of seeming to enjoy William's business associates' bad jokes. I am over forty years old and I want to have fun like I do when I go out with Charles."

Suddenly she realized what that aroma was in the speakeasy – it was people, common, ordinary, everyday people. It was sweat, dirt, soap, perfume, and anything else that makes regular people have a fragrance. That was real humanity and Sarah wanted to be part of it. Her world as Mrs. W. J. Grady was fake and scripted. One must wear a hat and a certain kind of dress for each occasion; one must say certain phrases at specific times and speak with an assured society accent; one must raise their little finger when consuming a cup of tea; one could laugh, but not too loudly.

With Ed, Sarah had been able to be herself. If she wanted to say "damn," she could. She didn't have to pretend to be dumb on foreign affairs and, best of all, Ed listened to her opinions. What she missed most of all was the pure enjoyment they had just being together.

Her thoughts continued on Ed, as they did most every day, and once every so often, Sarah would decide to phone Ed, but always stopped herself before she placed the call. Even after Roger had called from the brokerage office with the news that Ed had sent her money and stocks revealing that it was quite a substantial sum, she had denied herself the sound of his voice, even just to thank him, because he had surely sent some of his money along with hers. Anger stopped her each time she lifted the receiver, as she would remind herself that Ed used her for four years as a mistress and never had any intention of making her his wife. Between the money and land she had inherited from her father, the settlement she had from her first husband Charles, and the money she now had from Ed, Sarah was a wealthy woman, independent of William.

For an hour Sarah mulled over her future. What should she do? If she could only discuss everything with Ed --as angry as she was with him, as badly as his rejection had hurt her, she longed for his counsel.

As Sarah came downstairs after her grueling self-examination, the phone rang.

"I'll get it Sadie. I'm right here."

"Hey, Sarah. It's Charles, your friendly car salesman. We just got a car on the lot that would be perfect for you," said Charles.

Silence.

"It's blue. A touring car. And it's all electric. Practically drives itself. Wouldn't you like to take a look at it?" continued Charles.

Sarah hesitated, but said finally, "Well, I guess it wouldn't hurt to look at it."

Thinking to herself that a new car might be just what she needed, she made an appointment for the next day to look at the car.

CHAPTER 38

⚜

The New Car

Bloomington, Illinois April 1921

THE NEXT DAY Sarah awoke thinking of Charles. He was very good-looking, about six feet tall with sandy brown hair and deep blue eyes that captivated Sarah. She thought him to be in his early thirties, maybe eight or nine years younger than she. Would he make a good lover, or husband, or just a friend to have fun with? As she pulled up to the dealership in her car, he approached her with his winning smile. She decided that he would be an excellent lover and that was all she needed right now – a bit of fun.

Walking into the building she immediately saw the car Charles was talking to her about. It was a new 1921 bright blue Packard. The blue was a nicer color than the one she presently owned and this one also had red on the rims of the tires. It was a touring model, not like the roadster William had bought for her before. There was nothing practical about this car and being partial to blue Packards, it was just what she wanted.

"Perfect," said Sarah. "I'll tell William I have to have it."

Lowering her voice she said, "And to celebrate your sale you will take me to a special place of your choosing. Can I pick up my new car tomorrow evening?"

"When it's paid for, it's ready to go."

"Then I'll pick you up behind the dairy at 7:00 o'clock tomorrow evening in my new car."

Once home, Sarah phoned William at work and said sweetly, "I have found a new car that I really want, William. Would you mind going to the Charles Bradley Motor Company and paying for it?"

"Sarah, I'm really busy right now. Can we talk about this at home this evening?"

"No, someone else is interested in buying it and it won't be there tomorrow," lied Sarah.

William had two clients in his office that he was trying to sell on Faries Manufacturing Company so he tried to get rid of Sarah.

"How much is it?" He asked quickly.

"Only one hundred and fifty dollars more than my last one. And mine is getting old and shameful looking. I need this one, William."

Looking at his clients who seemed to be losing interest in his project as he sat there talking to his wife, he said, "Tell them I'll instruct the bank to pay them tomorrow morning."

"Thank you, William," said Sarah happily.

That night at home William protested that Sarah should not call him at work and he was not sure that she should have a new car.

Sarah merely retorted, "To uphold your image in the community you need to have your wife drive around in a fancy new car, not an old one with scratches and dents on it. People will talk," she assured him.

"You're right, Sarah. People do talk. You may have your car if *you* continue to uphold my image in the community as well."

"I always do, William," she replied, already exiting the room.

The next day Sarah picked up her new, bright blue, Packard touring car with the red rims and drove around town showing it off. She loved the car and was pleased with herself that she had managed to get William to pay for it.

"I deserve it," she yelled at some people on the street who stopped to look at her.

That night she and Charles went to Bloomington to an illegal establishment that was certainly more chic than the Decatur speakeasy. It was larger, clean, and the band was more professional. The lighting was still dim, but the electric bulbs cast a cheerful light onto the lively crowd. Smoke was still thick in the air, but Sarah noticed it was not just cigars; many were smoking cigarettes, including the ladies. The whiskey was more refined, imported from overseas and gin was also another option.

They danced and stopped often to take another drink. Sarah really liked the gin.

As they danced and he held her close, she drifted into a dream world, and said, "I'd rather dance with you than anyone else in the whole universe, Ed."

Snapping back into reality, she realized what she had said and looked up at Charles expecting an unfavorable response. No change in a pleasant expression on his face. The music was so loud he had not heard her.

They continued to drink, laugh, dance, and mingle with the people until Sarah asked to sit down. While sitting, she noticed a particular man alone at another table kept staring at her. He was middle-aged and fairly well dressed. Did he know her? No, that wasn't it, but when their eyes met he quickly looked away. Sarah had had too much to drink to worry about a strange man, so she forgot about it.

Suddenly, the front door burst open and the room filled with police. As Charles grabbed her hand and pulled her towards a back door, Sarah thought, "This can't be happening again." Another raid didn't seem possible. Luckily Charles was deft at hiding from and evading the police, but again Sarah realized her car was out front and could be traced back to her. As they were driving home Charles warned Sarah, "It would not do for you to get arrested for drinking. We'll have to be more selective about where we go. In fact we'll need to hide from the police in the future."

When Sarah pulled into her driveway, she realized it must be one or two o'clock in the morning. What story should she tell William? Breaking through her sleepy, intoxicated mind, she found nothing, no lie, no story, nothing-- so she went in the house and up the stairs. She found William in bed asleep. Donning her nightgown, she slipped into bed and sleep came immediately.

At breakfast the only thing that William said was, "You are very prominent in our city and people in the community look up to you – and to me."

He was veiled by his newspaper and went on reading as though he was not concerned.

Sarah sat before her untouched plate as foggy thoughts formed in her mind.

"What exactly does William think I am doing? What do I care if he does know? He doesn't even care to stop me. He only cares about his reputation. His reputation be damned!" She fumed silently.

Over the next few weeks, she spent blurred euphoric nights with Charles and wretched silent mornings with William. As she read more and more books about free love, she was sure that she was doing the right thing for her self-preservation. Being with Charles made her feel whole and that life was worth living. Charles enjoyed her money, her car and her company, in that order. Damaged and careless, they were well paired.

For several months they dodged the police by going to different hotels and sometimes going to Charles's room which was in a building downtown. Sarah never parked her car too close to where they were spending the evening. The couple delighted in their ability to elude the police.

Several months passed, and Sarah no longer pretended that she was William's dutiful wife. When the spirit moved her, she spent the evening with Charles and never felt that she owed her husband an explanation as to where she had been. When she was home, she enjoyed her wine or cocktails and barely spoke to him. Occasionally she wondered what William was thinking, but she told herself that as long as she kept up his image for Faries Manufacturing, he would not care what she was doing. She and Charles were careful not to let any of the prominent Decatur people see them together.

William began to stay out with his friends until the wee hours of the night, seemingly not caring where Sarah was or what she was doing.

She finally wondered if he suspected her affair, but she thought, "This is not a big deal. If I want to, I will just divorce him."

When he came home one day in the middle of the afternoon, she was nervous, but not terribly surprised when he said calmly, "Sit down, Sarah. We need to talk about getting a divorce."

He had another man with him that Sarah assumed was a lawyer.

"Actually, this will be a good thing," she told herself. "Let's get this over with."

Then, she looked carefully at the man who was sitting next to William.

"I've seen him before … but where?" thought Sarah.

William continued, "I know you have a fair amount of money from your father and from your first husband, so in light of that I am proposing a settlement that I consider fair. I will give you thirty-six thousand dollars either in monthly payments for ten years or in a lump sum. The house and all the contents will remain with me."

A flash of recognition came to Sarah. The nameless man sitting in her living room was the one who had been staring at her in Bloomington. Now it was clear. This man had been hired by William to follow her, which explained why William had said nothing to her in these last few weeks about her behavior—he already knew from his private detective. Trying to take in the situation, Sarah realized she had not heard what William said.

"I'm sorry, William, I didn't hear what you were saying," said Sarah, reeling from her new knowledge.

William repeated his terms and then said, "Sarah, whatever it is that you want out of life, I obviously can't give it to you. You have self destructed with your drinking and I am not capable of helping you, although God knows I have tried."

Sarah listened to his conditions and mini lecture and began to comprehend that he was really going through with divorce proceedings.

"I better get myself an attorney. His financial terms do not sound unreasonable --- But wait a minute! What did he say about the house?" She thought.

"You would keep my house?" choked Sarah.

"*My* house," retorted William.

This was a blow that Sarah had not considered. She could not wrap her mind around losing her beautiful home.

"But what about my things like ---ah, ---my pillow on the window seat in my sitting room."

That really sounded stupid she realized as she tried to compose herself. William just shook his head and did not reply. Where was the beautiful, intelligent woman he had married eighteen years ago?

After a few moments of silence, she recognized leaving town was her only choice in order to be really free, so giving up her house made sense.

In a city where William Grady was prominent and had founded nearly every existing civic and social organization, she would be a persona non-grata as the divorced wife. People would not recognize that she was the one who had made him successful.

"William, I don't care. I just want to get away from you. I'll accept your terms. I'll get an attorney and file for divorce against you," said Sarah heading for the library to fix herself a drink.

As William escorted the detective out of the room, he called over his shoulder, "Wake up, my dear, I will be filing the divorce decree. You will be the defendant. You are a disgrace to me and to the community and I want everyone to know whose fault this divorce is."

She remained alone in the library and drank as she cried.

"Divorce should be *my* idea. Why had William thought to hire a detective? He's ruined everything," she commiserated to herself.

❦

Mr. Whitley's Office

Decatur, Illinois April 1921

THAT AFTERNOON SARAH phoned her attorney making an appointment for the next day. She was happy to already have a lawyer who had helped her out with a disagreement on the sale of a parcel of her land and who had handled the divorces of two of her friends at the country club. Even with the reports from that unfriendly detective, William could not possibly know all about Charles and her indiscretions, so winning a divorce from him should be simple. She would declare that he had struck her (which was true) and was mentally cruel to her. Sadie could be a witness. The judge would see that she was the injured party. William didn't have a chance of smearing her name. She would smear his.

The next morning she came downstairs to a quiet house. Where was Sadie? William was already long gone to work, so Sarah was alone and had to fix her own breakfast, a piece of toast.

As she was nibbling on her small feast, James came into the kitchen from the back door.

Sarah called to him from the breakfast room, "Where is Sadie?"

Coming to her table and hanging his head so he did not look her in the eye, he said, "I'm sorry, Mrs. Grady, but Mr. Grady fired her."

"Why? Why would he do that?"

"I don't know, Mrs. Grady. But she and all her things are gone."

"Where would she go?"

"I don't know that either, Mrs. Grady."

Sarah quickly realized that William had sent away her only witness, and besides he would not want to pay for Sarah to have a personal maid.

That night as she and Charles spent the evening in his room, she admonished him that they needed to be very careful not to be seen together as her divorce was eminent and William suspected her of having an affair.

"My car can't be seen parked close to your room and no one can see me enter your building," she told him.

The two of them devised a plan whereby Sarah would leave her car at the dealership for Charles and walk to his room. Charles would come later, driving her car and parking two blocks away. She would use the rear stairway that came up from the alley. It was a foolproof plan.

With plans set for continuing their affair, Sarah decided it was time to go home. She had to be sharp tomorrow to talk with her attorney. Besides Charles was acting a little strange after hearing about William's decision to divorce Sarah. She was sure that Charles would be fine after the court proceedings were over and he would return to his normal fun-loving self.

The next day Sarah kept her appointment with her attorney. Fortified with two glasses of wine, she sank down in a dark brown leather chair in the small reception area. A tiny marble topped table, a green plant in the corner and two more leather chairs were the entire furnishings for the room.

"Why," she wondered, "did all lawyers' offices have big brown leather chairs to sit on?"

She was not getting nervous because she remembered how easy her first divorce had been, but she didn't like having to wait in small rooms. Soon an efficient assistant ushered her into the private office of Mr. J.T. Whitley.

Rising from behind his desk he said, "Hello, Sarah. Have a seat and tell me what brings you to my office."

"I want to get a divorce from William."

Mr. Whitley took time to settle into his chair behind the desk, stared at her over his glasses, then started speaking slowly, "Oh, no, Mrs. Grady. You two are pillars of our city and such a great team.

"You don't really want to separate from Bill. Are you ill? Frankly, you don't look well. Your skin is so flushed and you are so thin."

Angered by his too familiar comments, Sarah decided she could use his observation to bolster her case and replied, "Thank you, Mr. Whitley, for your concern. It is well-placed because I have been mistreated by my husband and I'm sure that has altered my looks. I want a quick divorce. This has been coming for the last six or seven years."

"Have you given William any reason to want you out of his life? Do you think he is being unfaithful to you? Be honest with me. What you tell me doesn't leave this room."

Sarah was slow to answer, "He thinks I am being unfaithful to him."

"Are you?"

"Well, he treats me so badly that I do go out once in a while to have fun. He doesn't pay any attention to me and he sometimes hits me, and…" Sarah poured out the many things that she felt were wrong in her marriage and finally, relented.

"Yes. Yes, I have been unfaithful," Sarah looked at her gloved hands.

Sitting quietly for a few minutes, Mr. Whitley finally asked, "Sarah, do you have a drinking problem?"

"I do drink—socially—I don't have a problem," said Sarah indignantly.

Taking another minute to absorb what he had just learned from Sarah, finally he said, "I will take your case, but I am not confident that you will be spared the indignity that comes from dragging your reputation through every sordid fact of your life. I'll try to do a great job for you, Mrs. Grady. Now you need to go home and stay there -- and stop your drinking. Please help me by being good."

Sarah did as she was told, went home and vowed to be perfect until this was over, thinking then she could go out and have fun again, all the fun she wanted as a free woman.

Later Mr. Whitley called on the phone and said, "Sarah, I will handle all the court proceedings, but William has quite a bit of information on your activities as he hired a private detective who has been following you for several months. It is going to be a rather tough situation."

Attorney Whitley said he would try to counteract the information and bring in witnesses in her behalf. Sarah told herself not to worry that William would never make his information public because he would be afraid of hurting his own reputation. However, the news that the detective had been following her for several months gave her cause for concern. She thought, "I guess he knows everything about Charles and me."

Her court date was set for May 21st, a month and a half away. William and Sarah signed an agreement on the financial terms of their separation with Sarah coming to grips with losing her house.

Left alone to dwell on her impending divorce, Sarah was getting very antsy. Staying home was not to her liking and she wanted to have another exciting adventure with Charles, but during the day he was engaged at the car dealership. Instead, she called June and made a lunch date with her.

"Let's go to the country club," said June. "We haven't been there for a long time."

Thinking about the remark her lawyer had made about her appearance, Sarah said, "Let's go to Greider's Cafeteria. We can talk there without being interrupted by a deluge of friends. I have a gob of stuff to tell you."

Since June was the only friend Sarah could really talk to, she poured out the whole story to her, including the fact that she had been drinking too much. June was devastated but not surprised. She loved Sarah, who had been her best friend for about sixteen years. In June's estimation, Sarah, who was so pretty, so intelligent, and so compassionate—had utterly ruined her life.

Knowing nothing she could say to her friend would change the circumstances, June took Sarah's hand in hers and replied, "I will help you get through this period in your life, my darling friend. It will be alright soon."

CHAPTER 40

Court Proceedings

Decatur, Illinois May 1921

THE DAY SHE was to go to court finally came and Sarah was as nervous as she had ever been in her life. Mr. Whitley said she should appear at the proceedings, as it might help her case if she were present. He promised her that he would not call her to testify. William was in Chicago for several days and she was glad, thinking it would be easier if he were not there.

The trial began with the detective's statements revealing Sarah's behavior of the last several months, enumerating the exact dates and times she had been in a hotel room with Charles. Sarah was dumbfounded – how had he gotten all that information? As he testified, Sarah glanced around the courtroom and was mortified to see it packed with members of the community. Drawing on every bit of strength she had to keep calm and poised throughout his testimony, she kept her appearance outwardly sedate, but inwardly she was destroyed. She felt dizzy and couldn't even hear what the detective was saying after a few minutes. Every sound in the courtroom sounded eerie and faint. After what seemed an eternity, Mr. Whitley arose from his chair and called June and several other friends to the stand as character witnesses, but as pledged did not call Sarah. Then it was over. The judge's ruling was to be delivered in July, but Sarah knew the judgment of God had already been placed upon her.

June asked Sarah to come and stay with her for a while, but Sarah could not face any of her friends, not even June, so she called Charles and they resumed their plan to hide from the public for the evening. Sarah was to drop off her car at the dealership for Charles in the afternoon, then walk to Charles's room, enter by the back stairway, and wait for him to come after work. He would park her car almost two blocks away.

Sarah contemplated, "With William gone, I could even spend the entire night with Charles."

Then she almost laughed at the ridiculousness of her thinking. What difference did it make now what William thought?

Alone in Charles's room Sarah wondered what she would do all afternoon until Charles came home. After her morning in court she felt totally drained and empty with no feelings left for William, Charles Newlon, or even-- Ed.

Making her mind focus on something, she looked around the small studio area thinking, "This apartment isn't very attractive. In fact, Sarah, what are you doing here? The places I have been and the things that I have done – and now I am reduced to this?"

Sarah had been in the room before, but never while she was sober and never for a lengthy period of time. Her gaze fell on the sofa that was the sole piece of furniture for the area.

"Why, I wouldn't even give that to the Salvation Army," she thought.

Turning around slowly, she absorbed the rest of the tiny space.

"It doesn't smell fresh in here. How could it? There's only one window and from the looks of it, no one could get it open. I hadn't recognized that he has no kitchen --- and --- not even a bathroom."

She remembered there was a shared bath at the end of the hall.

"How could anyone use a shared bathroom? I bet he has never made that bed because it is so squashed into that corner that no one could get around it to change the sheets."

The reality of Charles's living quarters swept over her like an ocean wave clearing her mind and drowning her with the same force.

"Sarah, what have you done? You've allowed William to ruin you, beat you, take your home."

She sucked in a breath, "I wronged him though."

She admitted to herself, "And, oh Ed. What a wonderful marriage we could have had if you had loved me enough. I wronged my Ed too."

Sarah sat down on the sofa which could no longer support even her slight weight and determined she was close to sitting on the floor.

"After my first marriage, I should have known that anyone named Charles would not be good for me. How did I get here? What have I done? I need a drink."

Fixing herself a drink with the ingredients she had brought from home, she gulped down the whole powerful gin cocktail.

"That's better," she reflected while mixing another drink.

Staring through the clear liquid swirling in the glass of her next cocktail, she saw a reflection of a very thin, rather sickly looking, sad, old woman. Was this really her true image?

Her eyes filled with tears. The eyes that Ed used to tell her twinkled so brightly.

As the tears flowed down her cheeks, she thought, "William's obsession with becoming president of Faries Manufacturing Company was the root of our problem. Never did he put me or my interests before business. Ed on the other hand always put me first and our values and interests were the same. If only Ed had not been so practical, or maybe, if I had waited just a little longer, we could have been together. I miss him so much."

In her grief, she hurled the glass against the wall.

Sarah clumsily emptied the bottles down the small rusty sink on the wall. Aloud she almost shouted, "I will not be an alcoholic. I promised Ed I would not drink and I will now keep my promise. How low I have sunk. I have broken my marriage vows just like my first husband did. I pushed away the only man I really loved and have taken up with a man that has no ambition, little knowledge of the world, and nothing in common with the former Sarah Grady."

Sarah's remorse became deeper and deeper.

She decided, "I will not spend the night here. I want to go home and be there in the morning when William gets back from Chicago. I need my things. I need to tell him how sorry I am. When Charles gets home I will tell him that I can't see him anymore and I will go home as soon as Charles brings my car here."

Charles arrived home with a bowl of soup he had picked up at the hotel for their supper and was looking forward to having the entire night with Sarah. He noted she looked like she had been crying. Sitting on the sofa with her while they ate their soup, he tried to determine what the problem was.

Fondly he asked, "Sarah, what can I do to make you feel better?"

"He has been so nice to me, how do I tell him I can't see him anymore?" questioned Sarah to herself.

Putting his arms around her and already kissing her, he said, "Let me make love to you."

Numb to the outside world, Sarah relented.

"Just this one more time," Sarah told herself as he slipped off her dress. "Then our affair will be over."

At that moment –a loud knock on the door.

"Police! Open the door right now or we will break in!" yelled a gruff voice.

Charles who had just finished getting undressed stood still trying to absorb what was happening. As he stood there in the middle of the room, the door came crashing inward and almost simultaneously a heavy arm clamped down on his shoulder.

"You are under arrest," said a loud, large policeman.

Another officer grabbed Sarah off of the bed, as three others stood by making sure the couple would not attempt to flee. Sarah could hardly comprehend what was happening. All she could think of was these men were standing in the room where she stood with very little clothes on. So what could she do? Hysterical tears and shrieks flowed from her.

One of the policemen took pity on her and suggested the men all turn their backs while she dressed herself. Quickly Sarah grabbed her clothes and put them on. She put her dress on wrong side out, but it had to do. The police then escorted them downstairs through all the interested observers and put them in the paddy wagon.

All the while Sarah continued to sob and say, "But -- I wasn't -- going to do this -- anymore."

Two policemen rode in the back of the paddy wagon with the couple. Charles tried to comfort Sarah, "I have been arrested before. It will be okay. They will let us go. Don't worry."

Sarah wailed between sobs, "But someone might see us in this wagon… What if some of William's business associates see us? Oh, how did this happen?"

Sarah couldn't ever remember being this scared before. She didn't know anyone that had ever been arrested. Would they lock her up in a jail cell?

The ride to the station was short. Inside, they were questioned as to their names, addresses and ages. Not being able to accept the situation for what it was, Sarah tried to lie her way out of the charges giving her name as Sarah Gray of Maroa, Illinois, age forty-four. Charles knew better and gave them his correct information.

The couple was ushered into a courtroom and there sat Judge Noble. Sarah's worse fears were realized because she knew that the Judge was a friend of William's. He would recognize her and know that she had given false information to the arresting officers. Her crying was so profuse that their hearing was delayed in order for Sarah to compose herself, which she finally did by imagining herself on a cloud high up in the sky and looking down on the events in the courtroom. She convinced herself that she was not in the room.

Charles whispered to her that they should plead guilty and there would only be a fine to pay. Having no other advice to follow, she did plead guilty of unbecoming conduct, disturbing the peace, and consumption of alcohol, and, as Charles said, they were fined. The judge admonished them that as soon as the fine of $74.80 was paid they would be released. From her perch in the clouds, Sarah almost let out a squeal of delight. She had that much money hidden in her car. Finding her voice she told the Judge that she needed to get the money out of her car which was a few blocks away. A policeman was dispatched to bring her car to the station and Sarah was allowed to retrieve her money and return to the courthouse.

After paying the fine, the Judge said they were free to go and Sarah, still in shock, ran out of the police station with Charles. Coming upon the car, they saw someone leaning on it.

"Good evening, Mrs. Grady. Do you have any comment on your arrest this evening?"

His appearance gave Sarah back her spunk and determination. She suddenly realized that she would be the headline in the newspaper tomorrow, but this reporter would not see Mrs. W. J. Grady being remorseful.

"It was nothing. I just had to pay a little fine."

She and Charles jumped in the car and drove away.

"I can't stay at home, but, since William is not there, I'm going to stop by the house to get some clothes and a couple of other things. Then I'll get a hotel room and plan what to do next."

As Sarah turned into Millikin Place, she could see lights on inside her house. James would be in his room above the garage and not in the house. Sadie was gone and William could not have gotten back from Chicago yet. She was confused until she saw the police car in the driveway.

Instantly, like a flash of light, she understood what had happened. William's detective had notified the police when she and Charles got together so they could be arrested. This circumstance would give William revenge by humiliating her, and now he was not going to allow her into the house to take her clothes or anything else. William was in total control.

"Charles, I'll drop you off in the next block. I'll be leaving town," said Sarah as she backed out of her lane.

"Am I not going with you?" said a surprised Charles, "I think we could be happy, Sarah."

"No, we couldn't. It's a bit ironic that I decided this evening that I would never see you again and then we got arrested for being together. I have been willful, spoiled, and immoral and now I have to pay the price, by losing everything."

Charles tried to protest but she stopped the car and said, "Goodbye, Charles. I'm sorry I brought you into this. I wish you luck in this life; I wish you the kind of love I had for a time."

Charles rose from the Packard's seat with a shrug.

"Well, thank you for the good times at any rate, Honey. I'm likely finished in this town anyway. Chicago may prove to be a bit more appropriate for me," he replied closing the heavy car door behind him.

Eager to be away from him, Sarah drove off wishing she could have gotten back into the house just for the few moments it would have taken her to retrieve Ed's letters, her Grandmother's rose maul box, and her doll from Norway. These were the only things she regretted leaving behind. Once the police left tonight, she would go back for them before she left town. That was all she needed. All the possessions, but not all the people.

Abruptly, she pulled over to the blue postal box pillar on the corner of Main Street and Pine. From her handbag she drew out a pencil and the paperwork from her court proceedings. On the back of the papers she wrote:

> *My Darling Soul Mate,*
>
> *Forgive me, my love. I have broken so many oaths to you, which we once made with such soul-binding fervor. As you can surmise from the papers on which I write to you, in your absence I have torn away all that I am, all that once was your Sallie. On this night, as I answer for all that I've done and dare to contemplate what I shall do, I think of you, and must have you know that I vow to be the woman you saw in me once more. Tonight I will claim the few things I need in this world and then go to our special place. There, I pray God will restore me and perhaps even restore our love.*
> *Forever I Do, Do You?*

She scratched Ed's office address on the envelope, found a stamp in her hand bag, and dropped her mail into the postbox, sending her last letter to her lover.

Sarah's head was spinning. The fiasco of her arrest had taken away the effects of the alcohol she had spent the afternoon consuming, but a gigantic headache was left in its place. But, never mind. She had to go. She drove away in the beautiful Packard that William had been persuaded to buy for her, giving a last sad glance at the familiar houses on Millikin Place.

⚜

The Decatur Herald published the following article in the newspaper the next morning:

WEDNESDAY, MAY 18, 1921

CHARLES NEWLON AND MRS. W. J. GRADY PAY FINE AND DISAPPEAR

Charles T. Newlon, an automobile salesman, and Mrs. W. J. Grady, of Millikin place, were arrested in a room in 258 North Main street about 9:30 o'clock last evening. Arraigned before Justice Noble on disorderly conduct charges on both state and city warrants, they pleaded guilty, paid fines totaling $14.80 and were released.

Mr. Grady, who was in Chicago, was apprised of the arrest by a telephone message from the police. He requested that publicity be not spared and that nobody be allowed to enter his home before his return. Two police were stationed at the residence all night. He left Chicago last evening and was due to arrive this morning.

"Sarah Gray of Maroa."

The arrest was made by a squad of five policemen, headed by Captain Cline who gained entrance to Newlon's room at the southeast corner of Main and William streets. The couple were in scant attire when found.

They were taken at once to the police station and questioned. Mrs. Grady was suffused in tears, but finally was able to recover her self-possession. She gave the name of Sarah Gray of Maroa, age 44. Newlon gave his own name, and his age as 38.

Drive Away in Car.

After paying the fines the couple left, and disappeared toward the north in Mrs. Grady's car. It is understood that their movements had been under investigation for three months. The raid followed a tip that Newlon had been seen to enter Mrs. Grady's car and drive to his room last evening. Mrs. Grady is thought to have been in the room practically all the afternoon.

Mrs. Grady has been prominent in welfare work and society in Decatur. Mr. Grady is sales manager for the Faries Mfg. Co. Newlon is said to have been employed by the Charles Bradley Motor Co. He was formerly a waiter in a Decatur restaurant.

Reports of an improper relationship between the prominent society woman and the automobile salesman had been a subject of gossip for several weeks. Apparently they did not reach the ears of friends of Mrs. Grady, but they were common knowledge among associates of Newlon.

Two weeks later, Ed sat alone at a dining table in the Hot Springs Resort that meant the world to Sarah and him. This was where they met. It was here that they danced, walked in the gardens, and played golf. It was here that they fell in love. At every glance around the room he found a memory of his beloved Sarah.

He had been here for three days hoping against hope that Sarah might show up. Out of his pocket he pulled a letter and a newspaper clipping dated May 18th, that he had received at his office in New York, he read it again for the tenth time.

> *Mr. Rockafellow,*
>
> *I dislike writing to you but I am hoping you still have some feelings for Sarah and might be concerned about her welfare. My concern is that she has left town without a word to anyone, including her lawyer.*
>
> *For almost twenty years I have been part of her life and I cannot believe she would have disappeared without telling me where she was going.*
>
> *I have tried to refrain from being an alarmist, but I worry that our friend may have come to some harm.*
>
> *Please inform me if you have any news of her. If you have not heard from her, can you help me locate her? I'm concerned for her safety.*
>
> *Thank you in advance for your help.*
>
> *June Ewing Johns*

Ed refolded the parchment once again and reread the newspaper article. June was right to be concerned. The oddly-phrased account deftly encouraged both their uncertainties. With each passing day, Sarah's absence reverberated a growing hollowness within Ed's chest.

As he sat, Ed imagined his love, her eyes sparkling, arms open to the wind, as she had been on that final afternoon when they were last truly together. As he gazed at her within his memories, her ethereal image solidified forever as the last of Sarah Grady, the last of his Sallie. He rose from the table and prepared to go home.

Truth Be Known

Decatur, Illinois 2016

JUNE EWING JOHNS, Sarah's best friend, remained prominent in Decatur society until she died in 1984 at the age of 92. Throughout the years she explored many leads trying to find Sarah, but was never successful. Once she went to Chicago sure that she had located her living in a rooming house, but it was not Sarah.

Charles Newlon's records cease after May 18, 1921.

Charles Elwood's wife Clara sued him for separation, in 1925. In court proceedings Clara said, "I want to save him from himself. The man I married is dead because he was kind and sweet and wouldn't have hurt me for anything. This man is only his shadow. I want to take care of him to shield him from others. That is why is want a separation not a divorce." On the witness stand Clara continued, "After an unusually happy married life, he now is in love with Mrs. Caroline Anderson, a brass molder's wife and a grandmother." According to a newspaper article, Clara was eventually granted a divorce and given a share of Elwood's estate valued at $97,000.

Ed Rockafellow used all the resources at his disposal to locate Sarah, but to no avail.

Ed remained with his wife for the rest of his life. He retained his job with Western Electric for only three years after he and Sarah parted, never able to excel as he did when they were together. In 1924, he left Western Electric and took a lesser job with Piedmont Company as their New York representative. Ed died in 1946 leaving Florence, two married children, and four grandchildren.

William J. Grady was awarded his divorce by the court in July of 1921. Sarah's plea of "not guilty" did not impress the judge despite all the character witnesses her attorney produced. Neither William nor Sarah was present for the final decree. At that time William claimed no knowledge of Sarah's whereabouts and declared he had no intention of ever seeing her again.

In May, during the court proceedings, the attorneys for Sarah and William presented their financial agreement to the court and the judge allowed it. The agreement provided that Sarah be paid thirty-six thousand dollars either in a lump sum or spread out over a period of ten years; she received nothing else. However, since William was instructed to pay the money to her through her attorney and Sarah never claimed it, William eventually got his money back after a period of seven years.

William was seen the morning after Sarah's arrest, disposing of Sarah's things in a huge pile in the back yard, directing James to get rid of all "the garbage". In his rage, William determined that there was still one thing in the city of Decatur to remind him of Sarah and that was the monument they had erected to honor Sam's grave. It was on the Grady plot in Fairlawn Cemetery where William had initially expected that he, Sarah and Sam would be buried. Determined the monument had to go, in anger or grief, he saw to it that the rather large monument that denoted Sam's gravesite was removed on the second day of Sarah's disappearance.

Today Sam's whole existence is reduced to a piece of paper in the cemetery office that says Samuel W. Elwood is buried in the Grady plot; but visitors at the cemetery can see nothing marking his grave, only the stone of William and his second wife Esther.

After the divorce, William became a recluse. He did not go out in public for nearly two and a half years. James took care of him and no one else was allowed into the house nor would he speak to anyone on the phone, except occasionally to give an order to an employee at Faries Manufacturing. Finally in 1924, he decided to take a trip abroad and booked passage on a ship to France. While on the cruise, he met a woman named Esther Bonney who was able to bring him out of his seclusion. She was attractive in a proper sort of way, not beautiful, but was smart and wealthy. She owned and operated a large cosmetic company in Chicago and was sole owner of several large tracts of farmland. They were married in 1926 and by 1928 William had the money to purchase Faries Manufacturing Company and become president, fulfilling his dream.

William and his new wife entertained occasionally, mostly at Esther's farm and the invited guests included few people that had attended Sarah's parties. The country club set treated the new Mrs. Grady with a certain amount of aloofness as Sarah had been so well thought of. William remained active in several of his organizations, but did not participate on the level he did when married to Sarah. Her name was never spoken in front of him and over time his friends seemed to forget that she had existed.

Esther Grady passed away in 1961 and William in 1968 at the age of 92, willing his home to Millikin University.

In 1969, my husband and I purchased 3 Millikin Place from Millikin University. When we moved into the house, we were the first family to live there since Mr. Grady, which is why we were able to find the box of letters that had not seen the light of day since Sarah carefully tucked it away sometime in early 1920. Mr. Grady never found that box or he would have discovered that his wife had a lengthy affair with one of his good friends.

For decades, husband and I kept the box of letters and gathered information about Sarah Grady's life in Decatur and finally in 2014, I began compiling the story of Sarah's existence. Curious as to Sarah's fate following her arrest and divorce from William, I continued with my research as June Ewing and Ed Rockafellow had done, scouring every source I could think of to try and find what happened to Sarah, but--nothing. Finally, in an effort to subdue my mounting suspicions, I began to explore the Grady burial plot in Fairlawn Cemetery in the spring of 2016.

In my final exploration of the Grady plot, my husband and I recruited our friend Adam, a former Cemetery Superintendent, to join us. Through his work, Adam developed a unique gift of "grave witching"; much in the way some people "witch" for underground water, Adam is able to determine the placement and gender of bodies buried within the ground. On many occasions we have seen the unbelievable and accurate results of his efforts-- in our association with him, he has never once been wrong.

I waited impatiently while Adam brought out his equipment, which consisted of a metal wire encased in a hollow plastic tube, and walked around the Grady's plot surveying the land. Then he stood at the edge of the site by the large stone denoting William and Esther's burial. He took his wire in hand and said, "I don't understand why or how this works, but it always does."

As he began to slowly walk forward the wire inside the plastic tube soon shuddered a bit, then dipped to the left.

"Here is a male body," he announced as he passed the place where William should have been buried.

Moving on, he held the tube in his hands as the wire dipped to the right.

"Now we have a woman," he declared in front of Esther's spot, jokingly adding, "Women are always right."

At this point I held my breath. What would he find in the last space? Sam's unmarked space. He stepped forward again and the wire dipped to the right. "A woman was buried here."

I got chills. Were my suspicions validated?

"But where is Sam? He is supposed to be buried here. You should have found a male body," I said.

At this point we related to Adam the fact that Sam is recorded as being buried in this spot with a large monument denoting his grave. To prove that we were in the correct spot, he thrust his wire into the ground and found the base of the monument that had been there at one time.

"Well Mary, perhaps Sam's body is underneath a woman's remains? My procedure would only pick the body closest to the top."

I stared at the ground before us, settled by the near-century since William tore away Sam's monument in the days following Sarah's disappearance, undoubtedly exposing fresh, loose soil in the demolition process.

"Sarah," I whispered with a nod, "I know."

A Note on the Research Process from Author, Mary Lynn

WHAT AN EXCITING journey I have experienced putting together the story of Sarah Grady.

When my husband found old love letters in our attic in 1970, we determined they should be burned. How grateful I am that we decided to keep them. With my background as a Historian, I began to read the documents a primary source, trying to put the parts together, but they would not readily fit. It was like a large jigsaw puzzle with tiny pieces. But I could feel an interesting story bound up in that box wrapped in a 1919 newspaper. I wanted to make a whole picture out of those small pieces.

My first task was to find out who wrote the letters. Significant portions of the documents were written in Morse code so I had to make a cheat sheet to interpret the dots and dashes. In addition there were other signs and symbols throughout the text and even the date at the top of the paper was expressed in signs. Beautiful handwriting embellished the typical eight stationary pages of each letter, but the 1915 script was difficult to read. Besides the name "Ed", the only clue to the origination of the document was the logo printed on the stationary from many different swanky clubs all over the United States. The envelopes had been destroyed. Although I am a speed reader, each of the 450 letters took me several hours to decipher.

As I read I found hints that revealed the meaning of the signs and symbols in the texts, such as the author referring to the Missouri Compromise with symbols following. Since the slogan for the compromise was "fifty-four forty or fight", I had a five, four, and a zero to begin to decode the characters. Little clues, like the writer stating that Valentine's Day would be on Tuesday this year, prompted me to consult old calendars to date the letters. Finally, due to one act of carelessness on Sarah Grady's part, I found a newspaper clipping showing a picture of four business men tucked into one of the documents. One of the men was identified as Ed Rockafellow. I now had the name of the lover.

Each letter I studied provided another small clue to the lives of Sarah Grady and Ed Rockafellow. I discovered the letters were written between 1915 and early 1920 during one of the most interesting periods in American history, the World War I Era.

In 1970, when I started questioning the neighbors on our street, I realized none of them knew anything about Sarah Grady though many were longtime residents of Millikin Place.

One person suggested I call Mrs. Whitley who was the wife of Sarah Grady's attorney. "If anyone knows about Sarah, it would be her," she said. And I followed her advice.

Mrs. Whitley was elderly but still very knowledgeable. She told me Sarah's disappearance was mysterious. No one could find her. The money that William was to give her from the divorce settlement went unclaimed and it was returned to him after a period of seven years. I gained many facts from her, but as I found out later, only a little of the real story.

In 2015, when I retired, I knew the time had come to discover the whole story of Sarah Grady.

The logical place to begin the rest of my journey was the archives of the Decatur Herald and Review newspaper. The older newspapers covered all the details of the stories and people they wrote about, providing minutiae not found in today's news articles. Pulling up the name of Sarah Grady in the archives, I found only twenty-four references to her. This seemed strange since I knew she had a very prominent place in Decatur society. Remembering I was looking at stories written in 1915-1920, I realized I had the wrong name. At that time women were addressed by their husband's name. I typed into the computer: "Mrs. William J. Grady" and found thousands of articles mentioning her.

Between the newspaper archives, Mrs. Whitley, and the love letters, I had much of Sarah's story, but there were still many pieces missing. I found Sarah had been married before she became Mrs. Grady and had a son named Sam Elwood. Again I turned to the newspapers and learned Sam had died during the flu epidemic of 1918. From his obituary I learned his birthplace was Elkton, South Dakota. He was in the navy so from military records came more information, basically his father's name. With that detail I was able to go to census records which told me where Charles Elwood and Sarah lived. I found their divorce. Then I looked in Illinois marriage records and discovered when Sarah and William married. The story was beginning to come together, but I wanted to know where Sarah came from.

I could not find her maiden name. From census records I determined she was born in 1878 and had immigrated to the United States from Norway in 1883. Ed's letters told me the basics of her family make-up. She had three sisters and a younger brother who was killed during the war, but nowhere could I find her last name. After studying the manifests of the ships that came from England in 1883, I found a family that perfectly matched what I knew of Sarah's. Their name was Petersen, so my character in the book has that name.

I went on with my research knowing that I had the wrong family name, but I couldn't find anything else. One clue appeared in the box of letters. It was a postcard sent to "Sadie" from her mother wishing her a Merry Christmas. No last name appeared but the postmark on the card was Verdi, Minnesota. Since Elkton, South Dakota was near the border of Minnesota, I looked in both states for information. From Ed's letters I knew Sarah had attended a business college in St. Paul, so I checked their records. Can you imagine how many "Sarah's" there were in the late 1800's?

As I came to the end of my story and hunted for her actions in 1921, I went to my local courthouse and got a copy of Sarah's divorce from William, or I should say William's divorce from Sarah. This document dated May 18, 1921, gave much insight into Sarah's activities over the previous year. Nothing was hidden in the court proceedings.

Early on May 19, 1921, in the hours after her trial with Charles Newlon, Sarah disappeared. I searched vigorously every record and document I could obtain. In the census report of 1930 from Chicago, Illinois, I found a Sarah Grady who lived in a rooming house. Upon investigation some of the details of this woman corresponded with my Sarah, but many of the facts were not a match. I determined it was not her.

Already having my suspicions as to Sarah's demise, I decided to call on a friend who is a "grave witcher" (or "grave dowser") and asked him to tell me the gender of the bodies buried on William Grady's grave site in Fairlawn Cemetery. My friend knew nothing of my reason for wanting to know who was buried on this plot, but took his plastic tube with a wire inserted and began his process. When he went to the third site and announced "There is a woman here," I experienced chills. My suspicions were being supported. He also offered the fact it would be easy to dig up a grave that had not been in the ground for five years because it takes that long for the dirt to settle. Sam was buried in late 1918, so the ground would have remained soft until 1923, two years after Sarah disappeared. And I recalled that William removed the monument only a few days after Sarah's disappearance, undoubtedly disturbing the grass. No displacement of dirt would have been noticed.

Following one of my library presentations earlier this year, an individual from the audience came to me after my speech and presented me with a document. It was the last will and testament of Sarah Grady, leaving her entire estate to William. The woman from the audience had read my book and discovered the will while searching through some old papers for a book she was writing. The will, dated in 1924, had been sent to Macon County in 1949 because it was found in an abandoned safe deposit box in Chicago and concerned a Macon County resident. It was a strange piece of paper, detailing that Sarah should be buried with Sam. The signature on the will did not match the ones I knew were Sarah's. The interested lady was of the opinion it was a fake and upon examination I had to agree with her.

My novel was published before I knew Sarah's real background because I was unable to find her given name. Seeing my frustration, my husband suggested we take a road trip. Colo, Iowa was our first stop. At least I knew Elwood was the name of the grandmother. Colo is a small town, friendly but small. No one there knew any Elwoods. If the town had any pertinent records, they were not available. We stopped at the only cemetery in town and walked the paths until we found a marker for Grandmother Elwood and one of her children. Outside of feeling closer to my story, I gained little from the visit.

We drove west across the entire state of Iowa, then turning north we finally arrived in Elkton, South Dakota. Sarah and Sam would have simply jumped on a train in the nearby Brookings to get to grandmother's in Iowa. I felt that would have been easier.

Arriving in Elkton we saw a building identified as the community center. We felt this would be a logical place to start. It was a spacious new structure, pleasant, clean, and unlocked, but there was no one in it. After touring the whole space, we started to leave.

Just then a woman breathlessly came down the hallway. "Hello. Sorry I was gone. Mrs. Grant's son is ill and I had to take them lunch," (You can't make these things up.) "How can I help you?"

I explained our purpose was to find information on a lady living in their town in 1898 whose name I did not know…but I knew her husband's name. After some discussion, the kind woman took us down the hall to a room that was designated as the library. Gathering old books containing the weekly newspapers in our time frame, she left us with the stack of dusty volumes. It was noon so she had to go home and fix lunch for her husband. She would be back in an hour.

After plowing through most of the newspapers, we found several articles about Sarah's first husband and Sam, but no mention of her. Every bit of information added to my story, but we still had no clue what Sarah's maiden name was. We quizzed several other people in Elkton without success.

Our next stop was Brookings, South Dakota. As the county seat, I assumed if any records were to be found they would be at the court house in Brookings. Having had no luck with our search so far, I confess I might have been getting a little testy by this time. Still I smiled at the two young women behind the counter in the recorder's office.

"Can I help you?" said one of the girls.

"I hope so," I replied, "I need to find a birth certificate and a marriage license."

"That would be $15.00 for each," said the second girl.

"Fine," I said.

"Do you have a card?"

"For what?"

"A genealogical card for the birth certificate."

"No, I don't. Why would I need that?"

"We can't give you a record of birth unless you have a card showing you are part of the family," said the first girl.

"Okay, how about the marriage certificate?" I said.

"If we have it, it would cost you fifteen dollars," replied the first young lady.

"Yes, you have made me aware of that. I don't mind paying you," I said beginning to show some impatience.

"What year are you looking for?" chimed in the second girl.

"Oh, around 1896 or 1897. Look under the name of Charles Elwood."

"That's awfully old. I don't think we have any records that old. But if I go look it will cost you fifteen dollars," chirped the first girl.

At that point I reached into my purse, pulled fifteen dollars out, and placed it on the counter. "Please go look," I pleaded.

The second young girl went into the back room. She returned in less than two minutes. "I found it," she said beaming. "Your fifteen dollars will cover it if I make you a copy."

My frustration seeped away as I looked at the marriage license and saw that Sarah's given name was Sadie Knudesen. I guess when she climbed the social ladder she felt that Sarah was a more sophisticated name than

Sadie. I also had her father's name which was John Knudesen. Thus ended my two year search for Sarah's maiden name. Even though my book had already been published calling her Petersen, I felt satisfaction in knowing the truth.

We went to Verdi, Minnesota and could rouse only one man walking along the street in that town of approximately 50 people. He knew nothing about any Knudesens or if the town had a library. We drove around town twice and then went back to Elkton. There we found a very helpful librarian. She helped us search for Knudesens in the area. There were none and she could find no records of any sort that would give us information.

We headed for home and I was elated to finally have found Sarah's family even though they seemed to have disappeared from present day society. My guesses about her brother, sisters, and parents were very accurate.

I will not give up attempting to research Sarah Grady. I believe there are still things to be learned, but what a fascinating story so far. I hope you truly enjoyed one of the scandals of Decatur's past.

Mary Lynn
July 5, 2017

Questions for Discussion

1. Would you have been a friend of Sarah's?

2. Did you feel Sarah was a moral person?

3. What do you think was important to the ladies in upper society at this time?

4. Was Sarah typical of her generation? Does she reflect an under-represented number of feminists of the era?

5. What would Decatur, Illinois have been like for Sarah in 1915-1919?

6. How did World War I affect the characters?

7. Which letter is most thought provoking?

8. Do you believe Ed sincere in his relationship with Sarah?

9. Who was better suited for Sarah, William or Ed?

10. What do you think happened to Sarah Grady?

Love Sarah's story and want to know more? To schedule your own private or public speaking engagement or book signing, order signed copies, or communicate with the author directly, find us at:

Website: theforgottenlifeofsarahgrady.com

Email: theforgottenlifeofsarahgrady@gmail.com

Like The Forgotten Life of Sarah Grady page on Facebook

81522841R00205

Made in the USA
Columbia, SC
02 December 2017